Patient Zero

Todd Harra

Also by Todd Harra

<u>Non-Fiction</u>

Mortuary Confidential: Undertakers Spill the Dirt

Over Our Dead Bodies: Undertakers Lift the Lid

<u>Fiction</u>

Grave Matters

For Brooke, who always wanted me to write her a book.

"Preserve us from the dangers of the sea, and from the violence of the enemy; that we may be a safeguard unto the United States of America..."

- Morning and Evening Service on U.S. Naval ships while at sea, excerpted from the *1789 U.S. Book of Common Prayer*

The 1925 Geneva Protocol, and later the 1972 Biological and Toxin Weapons Convention (ratified in 1975 by 85 nations), forbade member nations from developing, manufacturing, and stockpiling biological weapons. It is well documented that the Soviet Union pursued a top-secret offensive biological weapons program code named *Ferment* until its dissolution in 1991, and possibly after. One of the subprograms under *Ferment*, code named *Factor,* was tasked with creating the type of weapon described in this book.

All Soviet documents relating to the program remain classified, as do many U.S. intelligence documents. Those released through the FOIA are heavily redacted. It is largely unknown what happened to much of the stockpiled matériel after the fall of the Iron Curtain.

The science is real. The technology is real. However, the weapon detailed in this book is not a known, type-classified weapon system. What I'm trying to say is that this is a work of fiction, as is the theoretical weapon. Names, businesses, places, and events are either products of my imagination or used in a fictitious manner. The characters are completely fictitious. Any resemblance to actual persons, living or dead, is purely coincidental.

Chapter 1

A sharp bang—the molar-rattling kind—jolted me conscious and made the situation starkly apparent. Dire would be an understatement. In short, I was completely and utterly fucked.

The smell of brine, the pitching motion, the suffocating blackness quickly added up to only one possible explanation: *I'm about to be buried at sea!*

One of the sailors cursed when the bottom molding of the casket collided with the launch ramp's steel frame. It was a quick utterance, a sound made by a man hurrying through an unpleasant task as quickly, and with as much dignity, as possible. My temporal lobe collected and processed the information, but I didn't really hear it. The rest of my brain had switched to survival mode. I was locked in a casket about to be tossed off the side of a ship.

The sailors collectively grunted and the casket slammed onto well-greased two-inch conveyor rollers yielding a sudden weightlessness sensation.

In seconds it would be too late.

I screamed for all I was worth. The sailors' ears were a distance of about eight inches horizontal and 30 inches vertical—a direct line of 31 inches, roughly the length of a baseball bat. Thirty-one unobstructed inches thanks to the 20 poker chip–size holes drilled into my metal tomb—per navy regs—to help it sink faster. It should've been as easy as screaming through a chain link fence. *Should've*. It didn't quite work out.

Two-hundred pounds of dead weight pressed down filling my mouth with petroleum-tasting vinyl body bag. My scream came out as a garbled sonic note, more akin to a sickly whale call, which was further knocked down by the thickness of the casket's lining—crepe fabric and polyester batting. The sailors may have heard me, had this happened in the relative quiet of the hold, but my scream couldn't conquer the ambient noise pollution. The howling wind and turbid surf, underscored by the thrum of the four General Electric turbines propelling the ship through the ocean with over a hundred-thousand horsepower, knocked my scream down to a nothing whisper by the time it traveled the thirty-one inches.

"Ready?" a voice shouted. His voice was muffled by the respirator I knew they were wearing.

The casket rolled back fractionally, like they were going to launch it, which was unnecessary since the ramp was steeply angled.

I screamed, and screamed, trying to flail my arms, do *anything* but was effectively immobilized by the amorphous form pinning me.

"Ho!" a sailor shouted.

The ship pitched sharply, tossing my companion and I violently. Fortunately, it was enough to shift the corpse, so I could free my right arm in a desperate attempt to pound the sides, anything to attract the sailor's attention. If the twenty-foot drop off the deck didn't scramble my brains, I'd drown within sixty seconds.

One minute. My life expectancy.

The casket would completely submerge in under ten seconds, rapidly filling with 68-degree water, through the conveniently drilled holes. Not that I'd die of exposure. It'd be much quicker. Out of reflex, I'd hold my breath. As the casket passed five fathoms there'd be another atmosphere of pressure—another 15 pounds per square inch—pressing on the air spaces in my body. A few seconds later, as it passed ten fathoms, there would be yet another. So, if I didn't give into my primal brain screaming for me to take a breath and fill my lungs with seawater, I'd literally be crushed to death by atmospheric pressure. By the time my tiny tomb came to rest on the sea floor I'd be buried under a crushing 120 fathoms of water.

I frantically landed a solid blow on the puffing of the lid just as a sailor shouted, "Now!"

The casket rapidly gathered speed on the ten-foot ramp span and went weightless as it took off into space. The air whistled through the casket scouring the plasticky smell, replacing it with the alkali scent of the ocean. I've done numerous jumps, mostly in training exercises, and it seemed intuitive that freefalling through the atmosphere would be noisy as hell. It's the opposite. Complete silence.

The roiling waves waited patiently below, the watery maw of the Atlantic ready to gobble me up.

A strange sense of calm enveloped me. It was like God himself reached out from the heavens to calm my soul before impact—before death. And to think, the whole mess started when a couple of cowboys decided to shoot it out at the Goose Creek Reservoir, and I got sucked into assisting with their autopsies.

Chapter 2

Maggie reached her delicate hand between the ilium and pubis bones, past the muscles of the pelvic floor, inverted the scrotum and pulled the testes out through the abdominal cavity. They glistened like bloody eggs on the purple nitrile glove.

"The deputy where I did my residency liked to scare the hell out of new lab assistants when we got to this point. He'd reach in and squeeze the bladder," she said, selecting a pair of pointed surgical scissors from an instrument array and snipping the spermatic cords. It looked like she was cutting Ramen noodles. "Most of those poor assistants had no prior lab experience, and all of the sudden they're exposed to all this." She made a twirling motion with the scissors over the filleted corpse. "And to top it all off the case is suddenly urinating." Still studying the testes, she added almost as an afterthought, "And he'd squeeze the bladder hard. Real hard. Maybe get a three-foot arc."

"That's an impressive stream." I eased an apple from my pocket and polished it on my jeans, continuing to watch Maggie finish up her first case of the afternoon.

By morgue standards the pathology lab at MUSC—the Medical University of South Carolina—was typical. Institutional. Cold. Four stainless steel tables dominated the generous room. Cabinetry lined parts of the room with Draconian-looking gadgets and instruments displayed on linoleum countertops. Where there wasn't cabinetry the walls were clad with white subway tile. The smell was typical too, putrefaction barely masked with cheaply perfumed industrial cleaners.

Maggie brought the testes up close to her face shield and examined each testicle under the intense beam of her headlamp. The headlamp, perched on her mane of rust-colored hair swept into a neat bun, was a gift from me, an impulse buy from the plumbing section at Home Depot. Satisfied, they looked okay in the macro sense, she cut a slice off of each one on a composite cutting board and placed the tissue samples in a stock jar that could've passed for a quart of takeout Wonton Soup from Happy Garden. Maggie stepped on a foot pedal on the floor that turned on the microphone suspended above the autopsy table.

"Testes appear normal," she said, in a slow precise way like she was speaking to someone with a hearing problem.

Then she slipped the testes back, reverting the scrotum.

"This one poor guy, named Ramone, actually fainted his first day," she continued. "The case was an indigent found behind the dumpster of a Vons—"

"Vons?"

"Huh?" she said, momentarily confused. "Oh, it's a grocery store chain out West. Anyway, this guy wasn't found for several days because he mounded newspapers and cardboard over himself at night to keep warm. It wasn't until the staff figured out it wasn't the dumpster producing the odor that this guy was unearthed. His appearance alone was enough to make Ramone green around the gills, but when he unexpectedly shot a stream a racehorse would envy, poor Ramone's eyes rolled back in his head and he hit the floor. Well, his head hit the table before the rest of him hit the floor."

"Sounds like I'd get along fine with that deputy," I said and bit into the flesh of the apple.

Maggie looked up from her grisly work. A horrified look crossed her face. "You know you can't eat in here!"

"Who's going to know?" I said, crunching.

The lab was deserted. It was a Sunday afternoon.

"I am. It's gross. I know what goes on in here."

"I do too," I reminded her. "This isn't my first rodeo. And it's not like I was rolling it around on the floor."

Maggie couldn't help herself but glance at the epoxied floor. Like most morgue floors, it sloped imperceptibly to drains set every eight feet. They made for easy clean up.

I took another bite and continued talking with my mouth full, "Besides, I never do the nasty on an empty stomach. It's an old undertaker rule."

Maggie arched her eyebrows. "The nasty?"

I crunched and swallowed. "Get your mind out of the gutter. I'm referring to anything that might upset the stomach. You want me to be your assistant today, I'm not going to shovel his organs back in and stitch him up without some insurance."

Being that it was a Sunday, Maggie hadn't been able to find an autopsy technician, and having nothing better to do, I tagged along to help with the prosections. It was better than sitting home alone waiting for someone to kick the bucket or painting the living room. I was exhausted from all the home-improvement projects, and she had only officially moved in two days ago.

Our relationship had been a whirlwind, one I certainly hadn't seen myself in when she swept into town five months prior. My shrink said it was healthy for me to make commitments; "progress" is what she called it when I announced Maggie was moving into the apartment over the funeral home with me. We're still in that phase of the relationship where we do everything together, even autopsies.

The dual autopsies today were a rush job, ordered by the Berkeley Coroner. Two John Does. An early morning fisherman found them near the Bettis Boat put in at Goose Creek Reservoir. They weren't fresh. Based on the marbling of the skin I'd guess time of death to be 48 hours prior. Needless to say, the smell left something to be desired. Hence the apple. I took another bite.

The John Does must've had something akin to an old-fashioned shootout à la the O.K. Corral. John Doe 1, the case currently on the autopsy table had been the worse shot. He had inflicted several non-life-threatening shots on John Doe 2, mostly in the extremities, but John Doe 2 bled out before he could escape. He had been found in the underbrush about half a football field away. The responding patrolman simply had to follow the trail of blood to find John Doe 2. A gruesome Hansel and Gretel, the reason I nicknamed him Hansel.

Hansel's marksmanship was on display by the fact that the back of John Doe 1's head was missing, hence the nickname Skully. The pieces of his skull located at the scene were together in a clear plastic evidence bag with a little orange biohazard label on it. Skully was blocked up on several body bridges on the table to allow the fluids to flow freely underneath his body where they filtered through a steel colander in the table drain to catch any evidence. A stork light illuminated his vacated thoracic and abdominal cavity—harsh light reflecting off the inner workings of a human—his organs and breastplate glistening on a side table. At this point in the autopsy, Maggie had already cut his scalp and pulled it down over his face, so she could cut off the calvaria and take a gander at his brain—or what was left of it. The point of entry for the kill shot had been Skully's left eye. A clean shot. If the body was ever identified and claimed the family could certainly have an open casket viewing. Easy restoration job for the lucky undertaker who got the call.

Maggie labeled the stock jar, screwed the cap on and pushed the stork light up. "Well, cause is pretty straightforward, high ballistic projectile injury to brain. Otherwise, I'd say this guy was a ticking time bomb." His liver, sitting on a side table was greasy and dimpled—signs of drug or alcohol abuse, or both, something Maggie had noted into her hanging microphone several minutes prior when she popped it out. "Based on his oral health, and general malnutrition, coupled with the substance-abuse signs, I'd say this guy lived on the street."

"Nice clothes for a bum," I said motioning with my head to the drying area where Skully's bloody clothes were drying on hangers, so they could be placed in paper evidence bags. "What bum wears Lucky Brand jeans and an Armani sweatshirt that collectively cost more than my suits?"

"I'm only paid to answer the questions the bodies tell me." Maggie held Skully's arm up. "Look at this hand."

I could see it clearly from my perch.

"His nails are cracked, and the cuticles are filthy, and," she pointed to his thumb and index finger, "these calluses are indicative of drug use. Old burns from a pipe."

"I believe you," I said. "I'm merely commenting on the fact he's wearing a three-hundred-dollar outfit."

Maggie placed Skully's arm back on the table and snapped off her gloves, dyed black with dried blood, dropped them into the biohazard bin and pulled on a fresh pair. "You about done? I'm ready to start number two."

I hopped off the countertop. "Where can I toss this?" I asked, flashing the core. "I imagine you don't want this getting mixed up in the evidence."

Her eyes narrowed. "Toss it in the locker room. I don't want the director finding food in here. She'll have a fit."

I saluted with the core. "Yes ma'am." I reappeared a few minutes later wearing a Tyvek gown over my street clothes along with a face shield, booties, and surgical gloves over cut-proof mesh gloves. Ribs can be unbelievably sharp.

Maggie was already busy with the visual inspection of Hansel.

"Gowned and ready."

She put down her clipboard where she was charting all external physical characteristics, natural and not. "Roll number one so I can get eyes on his posterior and then I'll be done with him and you can start sewing him up."

Before I could take a step, the morgue door flung open and a man burst in. He was wearing an odd combination of a suit with surgical mask and latex gloves. At first, I thought him to be one of my competitors, come prematurely to collect one of the John Does. The cheap suit was a tell. That notion was dispelled quickly when he held up his hands and commanded, "Stop what you're doing and step away!"

Chapter 3

Another man, shorter, but thick like an Abrams tank and wearing a matching suit crowded in behind him.

"Guys, seriously? I'm in the middle of something right now," Maggie said, her big-city Chicago attitude on full display. "You need to follow protocol and call security if you've come to collect a body."

"We've come for those two," the man said and pointed at the two John Does. As if to prove his point two men in NBC suits— nuclear, biological, chemical protective suits—jockeyed cots in. A stack of folded red biohazard bags sat on each cot.

Maggie laughed. "Fat chance. I'm not even close to done. Wait," she pointed her clipboard at the ringleader, "who are you and how'd you get in here?"

"Miss, you need to move away from the table," he ordered, stepping forward. His tone brokered no discussion.

Maggie had moxie, but she was new to this type of situation. She was used to academic debate, medical jargon, and the mysteries cadavers offered, not physical confrontation. Speechless, her eyes got wide and she shrank back.

Not me. I don't relish confrontation, but I'm no stranger to it. Between raising myself among a desperate crowd in a grubby trailer court and getting screamed at by drill sergeants during my army career, it didn't make for a shrinking violet. Some officious asshole in a polyester suit ranks behind puppies and babies on the list of things that scare me.

"Look pal," I said, taking a step in the opposite direction his finger pointed, "First off, it's doctor, not miss. Second, you're not supposed to be in here. So, do as the good doctor says and get lost."

The man hadn't anticipated resistance and was momentarily caught off guard. He recovered and fished in his jacket pocket, a more difficult process than normal with latex gloves on, digging out a badge case. "Agent Bailey. Homeland Security. Stand down son."

The goons in the protective equipment suddenly made sense. Only the government in their infinite fiduciary responsibility would send people in expensive hazmat suits to collect a couple of ballistic-related homicides. Dummies. I tossed my face shield, taking a step closer in the process so Bailey and I were face-to-face. He continued holding the badge up like I cared.

"Clip don't—" Maggie called. There was panic in her voice.

"Best listen to the *doctor*." His eyes belied a smirk.

"*Sir,*" I said, "you're interrupting a coroner's investigation. A state matter in case you need to go back and review your federal playbook." I pointed to the door. "Kindly leave." Bailey continued to stare, so I added, "Now."

The stout one crowded closer, but I didn't break eye contact with Bailey. They were alert eyes without alarm. This wasn't a federal officer, or even regular police. I recognized his eyes, the gaze of someone not unfamiliar with tense situations. I had met men like this overseas. Men that worked alone; men that did necessary things. Bailey was an operator.

Not good.

"I'm not leaving without those bodies," Bailey said evenly.

I wasn't feeling so good about this anymore. In fact, something cold was crawling up my spine—my intuition warning me. My shrink was going to flip. She loves to harp on situational avoidance. I'm pretty sure this qualified.

"Okay, I'll play," I said, offering a little smile. "Let me see the warrant."

Bailey blinked once. "It's a brave new world. I don't need one."

"Then why don't we call the coroner and let you sort this out with him?" I suggested. "He says it's okay, that's good enough for me."

"Don't touch the phone," Bailey said, unbuttoning his jacket.

I caught a glimpse of his shoulder rig. "What, you're going to shoot me over a couple of corpses?" Bailey's eyes gave the answer— yes. My heart felt like it was about to explode out my chest. *Stay calm,* I told myself. *Don't do anything rash.*

"I'll tell you one more time. Step aside." Bailey's voice was quiet. Firm.

I had done my duty by resisting. I could say I tried to stop them. But I was too charged up and the words tumbled out of my mouth before my brain could catch up. "You aren't the only one walking heavy, pal."

Bailey's eyes narrowed ever so slightly, trying to detect a bluff.

It was no bluff. There was a pistol holstered in the small of my back, although I had no idea how the hell I was going to get to it through the protective gown.

"Who do you think is going to be left holding the bag if I let you take these bodies?"

"Clip—" Maggie shrieked.

I held up a hand without breaking eye contract.

Bailey shrugged. "Not you. You're coming too."

"Like hell."

The sturdy one chimed in for the first time. Though his haircut screamed military, there was no way he could sustain the rigors of military life. He was sweating profusely, like the walk to the path lab had been a workout. "You decide if it's in cuffs or not."

That did it. My granny always warned me about taking candy from strangers, and I wasn't about to start with a couple poorly suited badge jockeys. "Mags," I said, without taking my eyes off the Homeland Security yahoos, "call security, and tell them to call the cops."

"Doctor, do not—" Bailey said raising his hand.

She must've lifted that receiver because something clicked in his eyes. Action.

Taking all four was out of the question, but I sure as hell could slow them down until security arrived. I launched into Bailey like a linebacker, driving him into his partner hoping to take both men down. The move merely sent his partner spinning off and crashing into an empty autopsy table. There was a satisfying grunt of pain as Bailey's back collided with the concrete. I rabbit punched him in the solar plexus, nothing that would do any lasting damage. But I miscalculated. It was one punch too many. The chubby agent was faster than he looked. And stronger. A meaty arm wrapped around my windpipe. I felt a hand on the back of my head as he dragged me off my feet.

I tried to hook his leg with mine and knock him off his feet, an old wrestling move, but he was skilled in hand-to-hand and shifted his weight tightening the pressure. I flopped and fought like a landed fish, raining increasingly weak blows on his head and sides. Tubby merely tucked his head down like a turtle.

My strength slackened and vision tunneled into darkness.

Maggie screamed in the background.

The last thing I heard before blacking out was Tubby mutter, "You just had to do it the hard way."

* * *

I came to handcuffed to a hard-plastic chair. My mouth was dry and my brain felt fuzzy, like a spiderweb was laying on it. Bailey drugged me. The room I was in appeared to be some sort of safe house. Unfinished cement board, spray foam, and moving blankets covered the walls and ceiling. No windows. The only door wasn't one of the standard flimsy contractor-grade luan doors. Reinforced steel mounted in a grouted jamb would be my guess.

"Hey!" I shouted. Clearing the gravel from my throat, I shouted louder, "Hey! Hey!"

Silence. There wasn't a clock on the wall, but my body told me several hours passed before the lock clicked and Bailey plunked a sweaty can of Diet Coke in front of me. His jacket was off and shirtsleeves were rolled up to the elbow, though the AC was turned down to an uncomfortable wintriness. He didn't look like what I'd pictured without the surgical mask. His features were thin, and his chin so weak as to be almost non-existent. It was as if his lower lip dissolved right into his neck.

"Want me to remove those cuffs?"

I glared at him. "Where's Maggie?"

"Here," Bailey said. "Cooperating." He leaned over and quickly snipped the plastic cuffs.

I didn't give him the pleasure of massaging my wrists. "I want to see her."

He folded his arms. Calm. Completely in control. "In good time."

"Where are we?"

"An undisclosed location Mr. Clipper."

We stared at each other for a long moment. Bailey pulled out the chair opposite me, "Okay—"

"I want a lawyer." I hadn't been Mirandized which was a good sign. I wasn't under arrest. Yet.

Bailey chuckled. "It's not like that. We're just having a friendly chat."

I wanted this on tape. There was no doubt in my mind this conversation was being recorded. "For the record," I said loudly, "I have asked for a lawyer and been denied. Furthermore, I protest that my fourth amendment rights, along with another private citizen's, Dr. Margaret Stryker, are being violated."

Bailey plunked down in the chair opposite me. "Sounds like you don't need a lawyer. You're doing just fine. But if you want a reason," he spread his hands, "you assaulted a federal officer."

"To set the record straight, you informed me I was going to be your unlawful prisoner *prior* to me attempting to do my civic duty and stop you from another fourth amendment violation, your unlawful seizure from the pathology lab." I popped the top to the soda and took a long draft and slammed it on the table with a *bang*.

Bailey sighed. It was so imperceptible only the flaring of his nostrils gave it away. "You know how this works Sergeant, you were a special ops medic."

I sat back and folded my arms. "Sergeant?" I scoffed. "Hardly. But it looks like you've been busy doing your homework."

"Jebediah Wesley Clipper III, named for your maternal grandfather. One May 1983 listed as your official birthday. Real birthday unknown. Should I continue?"

I shrugged. "You're doing fine."

"Biological mother, Mary Clipper, died a ward of the state of Georgia when you were 5. Your maternal grandmother raised you until age 14 when you entered the foster system after she was institutionalized. Seven homes in four years. Joined the army at 18. Served with the 75th Ranger Regiment. Two tours as a platoon medic in Iraq, one as a special operations combat medic in Afghanistan. No living relatives. Current occupation, funeral director, and you're the owner of Granville & Sons Funeral Home. Am I close?"

I nodded slowly, impressed. I knew, in broad strokes, what was going on. Maggie and I had unwittingly gotten caught in the middle of some sort of operation. "Sorry, what's your name again?"

"James."

A lie, no doubt. "Jim, right. You're correct. I met your type overseas and I'm familiar with what it is you do."

The corners of Bailey's mouth tugged up when I said, "your type."

I continued, "What I'm curious about is what my girlfriend and I got swept up in. As far as I can tell, our only crime is being in the wrong place at the wrong time."

"Who said anything about a crime Mr. Clipper?

"Clip is fine."

"Right, Clip. We just need to have a conversation and you and Dr. Stryker can be on your way."

I sighed. Rex was a bluetick coonhound that lived in the trailer next to my granny's. When he got to romancing on your leg it was better to let him finish than fight it. "Fine Jim, let's get down to brass tacks so I can get the hell out of here." He nodded, I held up my hand, "First, turn off the air and get me something else to drink. Coffee would be fine."

Chapter 4

The doors of the van opened and Maggie and I clambered onto the sidewalk and stood blinking in the harsh afternoon sunlight, as our cell phones and my pistol were tossed next to us on the concrete. Our pupils barely adjusted before the van roared away.

A septuagenarian with a hat that looked like the fluffy white dog she was walking stopped to stare.

"Are you all right?" I asked yet again. I couldn't seem to stop asking the question.

"What just happened?" Maggie asked, turning her head side to side to stretch her neck. She was still in scrubs, but Bailey and crew had confiscated the lab coat.

"Dammit!" I shouted, looking at the spider webbed screen of my phone. The dog started barking, and the woman quickly jerked at its collar and hustled along pretending not to notice I was tucking a pistol into my waistband.

"To keep us for over a day and have some doctor poking and prodding us like we're in some clinical trial is ridiculous," Maggie muttered.

A middle-aged physician, who was probably more comfortable on the golf course, collected vitals and a blood sample during the interrogation, and repeated the process before we were loaded into the van to come home.

"Try criminal." The doctor had trouble locating a vein with all the ink on my arms. It took him five tries; I felt like a pincushion and let him know it. "Come on, let's get something to eat and go to bed," I said, taking her elbow and ushering her up the steps of the funeral home. I could tell she was exhausted from being up for the past day and a half, and I wanted to get off the street before the old woman with the dog had time to call the cops. I was legal with the gun, but I didn't want another run-in with a Boy Scout with a badge.

Nikki Adcock and Isabella Granville rushed into the foyer when they heard the door chime.

"Where have you been?" Nikki, my apprentice, asked. Tall, blonde, and perky, she's the antithesis of the dour undertaker stereotype.

"The police were here looking for you," Isabella said, in her usual restrained way. "Hanahan *and* Charleston," she added. Isabella is old school. Not only does her fashion reflect the Kennedy era, she doesn't think its good form to have male and female decedents lay in repose in the same room. So, I could only imagine how indecorous she thought it was for the owner of a notable funeral home to have the police inquiring about his whereabouts.

I could understand why they were upset. We had been out of pocket for almost 30 hours. In this business we stay glued to our phones. To go that length of time in radio silence is unheard of. I stood for a moment with my mouth open, trying to figure out how to frame our experience, and settled on the abbreviated truth. "We were taken in by Homeland Security for, uh, questioning."

Nikki screwed her face up. "The Ten Thousand Leagues thing again?" she asked, referring to a drug smuggling brouhaha we got sucked into by my former girlfriend when Nikki started her apprenticeship over a year ago. "What's Homeland Security doing messing in that? Isn't it the DEA's thing?"

"No, something else entirely different—"

Maggie cut in. "There was a double homicide at the reservoir. Two male UIDs, that's unidentified decedent," she clarified to answer Isabella's puzzled look, "shot each other near the boat put in." Nikki and Isabella listened with rapt attention as Maggie told them about the rush autopsies, the arrival of the cavalry in the pathology lab, our abduction, and subsequent questioning.

When Maggie finished, Isabella leveled her piercing gaze at me. "You engaged in a brawl with a federal agent?"

I raised my hands. "Hey, I don't go looking for trouble. I always seem to be in the wrong place at the wrong time."

"I'll say," she replied crisply. "We were quite concerned."

That's about as close to warm and fuzzy as Isabella gets. Her late husband, my mentor, was the great-grandson of the home's founder. When he died, she sold me the business, and agreed to stay on. Part secretary, bookkeeper, office manager, and oracle of knowledge, all rolled into one, she's been a fixture at the home since Christ's dog was a pup. "Since the excitement's over, I have work to attend to." Isabella marched off leaving us standing in the lobby.

"Why you?" Nikki asked.

"I've asked myself that a thousand times," Maggie replied. Her voice sounded fragile; she had to be close to exhaustion.

"You okay here?" I asked Nikki, who nodded in response. "Good. We need to get some sleep. It's been an...ordeal."

"Yeah," Maggie agreed. "I feel like I could sleep for days, but I don't know if I'll be able to."

"I'll give you an Ambien."

Maggie hugged herself. "No, it's not that. I just can't believe those people...that they do that to people. It's not right."

"Go, go get some rest. It'll make you feel better." Nikki waved her hands in a shooing gesture. "Nobody is getting by Isabella."

Maggie and I climbed the grand staircase to our apartment. The staircase is lined with oil portraits of the Granville lineage, including the one at the bottom commissioned posthumously, Lauren and Isabella's only son who was killed in Vietnam.

When I opened the door to our private quarters a voice screamed, "Who's there?"

Instinctively, I reached for my pistol, a millisecond later feeling foolish and dropping my hand.

"That bird's lucky," I muttered, heart racing. "He almost got his ass shot."

"Clip," Maggie scolded, going to his cage in the corner of the piazza, "he's just worried his mommy wasn't coming home. Weren't you Matey?" she cooed through the bars.

"Polly wanna cracker?" the parrot shrieked in response.

"So talkative today," Maggie said in a baby voice, unlatching the cage and lifting the scarlet macaw from his cage. "Poor baby's been locked up all this time."

Matey fluffed his feathers in a big show of plumage and shuffled back and forth on Maggie's forearm. She offered him a handful of peanuts. The tension drained from her face as she watched the bird dig in with gusto.

"Want anything?" I asked.

"I need a drink. There's an open bottle of white in the refrigerator."

I poured the wine, and grabbed a coconut water for myself, though my hand lingered on the beer for a second—my shrink wanted me to cut back.

"Here," I said, placing a wineglass on the table.

Matey eyed me while making a mess of peanut shells on the floor.

"Here, feed him." She thrust out a handful of peanuts.

I took a long drink of water. "No thanks. He's mean." Matey had bitten me. Twice. Lesson learned. I honestly couldn't believe I had agreed to let this *thing* come live in my house. I could see a little cockatiel or something, but Matey's the size of a bald eagle—and a hell of a lot nosier. The guy at the pet store when Maggie was a first-year med student said he wouldn't grow bigger than a parakeet. The pet store guy was either stupid or a liar.

"You'll make a new friend," Maggie said scratching his head with her finger. "They're his favorite."

I took a step back. "Thanks, but no. I've made enough friends in the past day."

There was knock at the door.

"Come in," I shouted. "We're out here."

Nikki came in, picking her way over the paint cans just inside the door, part of Maggie's grand designs to spruce the place up. Not that it didn't need it. The Granvilles used to live in the apartment, and the décor was '60s-sitcom set—about the era they abandoned it. I never bothered because I didn't care. It beat military housing.

"Sorry to bother you—" Nikki stepped onto the piazza and stopped in her tracks, eyes wide.

Matey, unsettled by the new addition, flapped his wings and screamed, "Who's there?"

Nikki's head snapped back.

"It's time for you to go play," Maggie said, pushing the bird off her arm. He took flight and disappeared over the funeral home.

"That's Matey. Maggie's pet," I said.

"Uh huh." Her eyes still wide but displaying typical southern manners.

Avian gone, Maggie picked up her wine and put down a healthy slug. "Oh, that tastes great." I could almost see the alcohol lubricating her brain cells and smoothing the jagged edges of the past 24 hours.

Nikki recovered her composure. "Isabella was so flustered by your return, she neglected to tell you Moonie came by twice. And called no less than 20 times."

Maggie slapped her forehead. "That reminds me. I need to call Doc Marc! She must be having a fit." Dr. Terri Marcislin, director of pathology, was Maggie's boss.

"Thanks Nikki," I said. As a deputy coroner, it was his bodies we lost. "Mags, I'm going down to my office to make the call. Be back in a few."

"Will you join me?" I heard Maggie ask Nikki as I pulled the apartment door shut.

Maggie knows about my prior relationship with my apprentice. No secrets. I wanted to do things right with Dr. Stryker. Nikki and I were an item for a very short time after the Ten Thousand Leagues fiasco. It was more of a comfort thing than actual romance. Once we realized it we split. Thankfully, it hadn't made our working relationship weird. What Maggie didn't know wasn't my secret to tell. Though Nikki was the daughter of a local real-estate magnate, she had anything but a storied past. Her father banished her to Florida after high school when he found out she was going to bear a bastard child. A scuba diving accident got her addicted to prescription drugs that quickly turned into street drugs. She began stripping in Miami to support her habit, even sinking low enough to turn tricks, before hitting bottom. She found Jesus, got clean and returned home to start a new career and life. I give her credit. Nikki's tough; she's a survivor.

I powered up my broken phone. It was kind of like solving a puzzle on the screen; I could make out I had numerous missed calls, most of them from Moonie and the funeral home's number. Moonie picked up on the first ring. "Yeah?" he snapped. In addition to being the deputy coroner for Berkeley County, Moonie was a part-time employee at the funeral home, and a full-time annoyance to me.

"It's Clip."

His tone changed. "Clip, what the hell is going on?" He plowed on before I could respond. "The constables at the hospital," I heard pages turning, "told us these guys in hazmat gear came and took my cases." He let it hang, like it was a question.

"That's true," I said, propping my feet on the burled walnut campaign desk that had been Lauren's great-grandfather's. The desktop contains a monitor, business card holder, and penholder. Never anything else. The rest of the office is equally as spartan, just a bookcase with some memorabilia, a small club sofa, and two matching chairs. "It was Homeland Security. They claimed to be taking the bodies as part of a federal investigation—"

"They certainly didn't give the locals a courtesy call!" he said, interrupting. "I've been going crazy the past day. Hanahan PD is crawling up my ass, and Larry is none too happy either."

"I bet," I mused. His boss, Coroner Larry Koziner, was something of a political animal with his eye on the governor's mansion. He wouldn't be happy if the papers caught wind of this. "I guess Hanahan hasn't had any requests from Homeland Security for investigative reports?"

"They're just as much in the dark as the rest of us. Typical feds." He snorted. "How'd you get dragged into it?"

I eased a wad of dip into my mouth. It had been so long, it gave me a little rush. "I was there giving Mags a hand since it was Sunday and she wouldn't have a diener. Anyhow, this guy who called himself James Bailey burst in with a crew and told us they were commandeering the bodies and us too."

"How exactly does their investigation cross with a couple homicides in the creek?"

"Truth be told I don't know," I admitted. "It's not what it appears. They took us to some sort of safe house—it certainly wasn't a federal facility. I haven't compared notes with Mags yet, but Bailey kept asking me all these questions about the dead guys, and crime scenes. He couldn't seem to get it through his thick skull I'm just the boyfriend of the pathologist." I could hear scribbling on Moonie's end. "And a doctor took my vitals. Twice."

"Weird."

"Agreed. Listen Moonie; I'm going to try to unwind. It's been one hell of a day, and it's definitely unnerved Maggie. I need to spend some time with her. Sorry I don't have anything more concrete for you."

We said goodbye. After I hung up I glanced out the floor-to-ceiling plantation shutters. There, perched in the pastel blooms of a crape myrtle in a neighbor's yard, sat Matey staring at my office window. "Have a nice night out," I said, and snapped the shutters shut.

Maggie's wineglass was in the sink, and her scrubs were on the bedroom floor, and she was asleep by the time I returned upstairs. The bottle of Ambien was sitting on her nightstand. I picked up the bedside phone and punched in a series of numbers to forward the business line to the apartment and then peeled off my jeans and T-shirt and climbed into bed. Maggie turned over and barnacled on.

Chapter 5

I was awake, staring at the ceiling, when the phone rang shortly after five. Maggie groaned and rolled over. I tossed off the sheet and padded into the kitchen in the buff—Maggie woke me to tend to her needs during the night. After a swig of yesterday's coconut water to clear my throat I picked up the handset and said, "Granville & Sons funeral home."

"Hi! This is Kim with Carriage Hospice in West Ashley," a chipper southern voice said. "We have a patient who's expired."

Good news.

"Hold on," I told Kim, frantically scrabbling for paper and pen. I settled for a junk mail envelope and expo marker from the whiteboard on the refrigerator. Once Kim finished, I said, "I'll be there in about an hour."

Exactly 58 minutes later I wheeled my cot in through the front doors of the still sleeping facility. A plump nurse with a pleasant face greeted me with a smile. "You must be Clip." She pronounced it "Cleep."

"I am." We exchanged pleasantries, and Kim escorted me to Marshall Kyle's room.

"Things got a little messy toward the end," she said, stopping me at the door. "I cleaned him up, but there's a bit of an odor."

"Not a problem," I assured her with a smile. Death isn't clean—it's a messy process, one that I'm used to.

She led me into the dim room. A muted television provided flickering light. The still form of Marshall Kyle lay in a neatly made hospital bed. Kim had obviously tried to mask the odor, but it only succeeded in making the room smell like someone defecated in a strawberry field. I'd give her an A for effort.

I did the paperwork and was out of the hospice in less than eight minutes. Three hours later, before Maggie was up, or Nikki arrived for work, Mr. Kyle was embalmed, and I was churning down the city streets in my workout gear.

I was only slightly out of breath by the time I arrived at the transparent edifice called Muscle Bound. A score of people laboring on complicated machinery stared at me through the windows as I approached the front door. I hate my gym for a number of reasons, including the juice bar, the tanning beds, and the blaring techno music. But most of all I hate it because of the assholes it attracts, hordes of cackling housewives in their designer gear who never break a sweat, overweight businessmen who come too sporadically for any real benefits, and of course the 'roid heads who preen in the mirrors and barter drugs in the locker room. But it's exactly a mile from the funeral home, a good distance to warm up and cool down.

"He in?" I asked the cute and very well-endowed young lady at the reception counter.

She looked up from a magazine and smacked her gum. "Uh, yeah," she said, like she wasn't really sure.

I tapped on the first door in the hallway. "It's open!" a voice boomed.

I let myself in and found Risden Brooks sitting at his computer terminal. His chair squeaked in protest when he swiveled around, and with good reason. Risden is the biggest person I've ever met. It seems cliché for a gym owner to be a monster, but Risden exceeds even the clichés. He isn't chiseled like a competitive weightlifter, but he could easily pull an 18-wheeler a city block.

"Got a minute?" I shut the door.

"Close the blinds," he said, jerking his head. It was a spastic motion. His head sat directly on his shoulders.

I spun the little stick and separated us from the action on the gym floor, as Risden reached behind him and turned up techno music on his computer's speakers. I pulled a chair around the desk so we could hear each other over the music.

He was annoyed. "You know I don't like doing this in the office."

"It's kind of an emergency, otherwise I would've gone through the proper channels," I said. "I had the strangest adventure beginning Sunday and ending yesterday and I'm hoping you can shed light on things."

"Define adventure."

"As in, I got taken in by the feds."

"Taken in?"

"It sounds ridiculous but kidnapping would be the best description. I was taken against my will and held there, although I wasn't under arrest, and was denied the counsel of an attorney."

"Why?"

"I don't know."

Risden sat forward in his chair, muscles rippling, the whole of his attention focused now, and his previous annoyance completely gone. He was all business. "Tell me more," he said.

Not only is Risden the father of Nikki's child—yes, Charleston is a very small town—he's also an undercover DEA agent. The federal government, as part of a joint task force with some local police departments, set up the gym for him ten years ago when the heroin epidemic began to surge. It's the worst kept secret in the city that if you want to score performance enhancing drugs you come to Muscle Bound. Risden gets to know the little fish and cultivates relationships right up the food chain. The dealers can't figure out who's dropping the dime on them.

I found out his identity when I blundered into the cartel smuggling drugs in through the harbor in a narco submarine, what the media dubbed the "Ten Thousand Leagues Bust." Risden saved my life from a sicario—a cartel asset—and was my debriefing agent during the subsequent investigation.

I told him the whole story, leaving nothing out. He sat listening intently to every word. When I finished he plucked a clear cup looking like it contained marsh water off his desk and took a sip. "Interesting."

"What do you think?"

"I think you may be right, that this guy Bailey is in fact a spook. If so, I may not get anywhere. This day and age they can pluck you like that right off the street and hold you indefinitely without violating your fourth amendment rights in the name of counter terrorism."

"Are you kidding me? Terrorism?"

He held up his toilet-seat sized hands. "I'm just saying there's room to bend the rules post 9/11."

"I'd get it, *if* something nefarious was afoot. But they saw fit to violate my civil rights over a run-of-the-mill double homicide."

"Are you sure?"

"The evidence doesn't point to anyone else being at the scene...as far as I know."

Risden shook his head. "Tell me this," he said, leaning forward, "what's the significance of the victims?"

"I don't know. Two unidentified males got into an altercation and blew each other away. As far as I can tell they're both perp and victim. It's a nice neat little tidy investigation. All's that's left to do is identify, notify, and bury."

"You told me one was homeless, correct?"

"Mags thought he was from the street. There were physical indicators, but he wasn't wearing clothes you see those bums over at the on-ramp wearing."

"How many homeless people carry?"

I shrugged. "I hadn't really thought about it, but I guess you're right. They might carry a knife or something for protection, but I'd imagine a gun might be an expensive luxury."

Risden nodded. "I'm going to do some digging and see if I can find anything, but the answer seems to lie with those two victims." He pulled out a piece of paper. "The only one's name you got was Bailey?" I nodded. "Where was the safe house?"

"I'd guess it was a three-hour drive. It felt like we were going highway speeds. Say 150 miles."

"That's no help. You could've been in Georgia, or North Carolina, or hell, Tennessee."

Risden looked at his meager notes. "Okay. I'll see what I can do, but this screams need-to-know." He shrugged, "But I'll try." He waggled his cup of marsh water at me. "Want one? I'll get Kelly to make you one of these on the way out."

"What is it?" I really didn't want to know because I had no intention of drinking it.

"Kale dandelion with blueberries."

"Thanks, but I'll pass."

"Sure? It's not on the menu. Kelly makes it special for me, adds wheatgrass to give it that little something extra."

Sounded about as scrumptious as drinking lawn clippings. I held up a hand. "Maybe on the way out. I don't want to lift on a full stomach."

"Suit yourself. Say," he said, stopping me, "what do you normally wear when you go get a body?"

"A suit."

"Even if it has something infectious like hepatitis or HIV?"

"Yes. I'll gown up during the embalming, but the risk can be managed properly during the removal."

"What do you make of the space suits?"

"Hell if I know. The two shot each other in the woods. It's not like they had Ebola. Gloves would've been sufficient."

"Don't forget to hit up Kelly on your way out." Risden tapped the lid of his cup. "It's on the house. It'll make you feel like a new man."

"Appreciate it." Not a chance in hell.

He squeaked around in his chair. I was dismissed.

Chapter 6

After returning from Muscle Bound I stretched on the piazza. It was late enough in the morning that the crew had arrived for work. Isabella was in her office terrorizing someone on the phone. I found Nikki and Moonie in the viewing parlor.

The parlor reminds me of an aging beauty queen, a once grand space that's a victim of time. I was slowly restoring it, along with a lot of the rest of the building that had fallen into benign neglect. The millwork and trim needed painting, the worn carpeting, faded draperies, and wallpaper needed replacing, the plaster needed patching, not to mention the décor needed modernizing by at least a century.

Moonie was settled into a Victorian settee bothering Nikki as she labored over a casket. Her makeup grip sat on a foldable tray, a small black briefcase filled with creams, powders, and brushes.

"Want to go to Sarah's with me?" I asked, startling Moonie out of his monologue.

He swiveled his gaze from Nikki's behind, guilty look painted on his face, and said, "We need to talk."

Nikki turned holding a stipple brush and mouthed, "Thank you."

"C'mon," I motioned with my arm, "We'll talk while we eat. I'm buying."

Moonie brightened. If there's one thing Moonie loves as much as guns, it's a free meal. Unfolding his rangy frame off the ancient velvet upholstery, he drained his mug, plopped his ten-gallon hat on his head and said, "Let's go."

Moonie looks more like a Texas sheriff than a coroner. I think he watched one too many spaghetti westerns as a baby redneck. He wears cowboy boots—he calls Tony Lamas—and takes advantage of the statute that allows coroners to carry—a six-shooter, of course. Next to his giant belt buckle sat his deputy badge, a gold seven-point star.

"Nikki, I took a call this morning. Gentleman by the name of Marshall Kyle. We're meeting with the family," I consulted my watch, "in about an hour and a half."

She nodded.

"When are they coming in to view?" I asked, referring to the woman in the casket.

"One-thirty. First public visitation starts at two."

I went over to the casket, a cherry wood. In it were the remains of Ida Nailor—the wife of a prominent banker, who Lauren Granville buried eons ago. Ida had a facial cancer that ate away part of her mandible. Nikki was learning restorative work as well as one can. It's the type of work you have to do to get proficient. "Get a little lacquer thinner on a duo fibre brush and it will smooth that wax out," I advised pointing to the rebuilt jaw that still had brush marks in it and looked like a hen had pecked at it, "and then use a painter's sponge to reconstitute pores. It'll give her a more natural look than the technique from the textbook."

She looked relieved. "Yeah, the toothpick wasn't cutting it."

When Moonie and I hit the streets, he slapped on a pair of aviator shades that hid the crescent shaped scar where the bridge of his nose meets his right eyebrow. His real name is Durward Wise, but he earned the nickname Moonie when the recoil from the scope of a .50 caliber Barrett left a lasting reminder of that particular shooting outing.

It's only a few blocks walk to the brick and glass establishment that is Sarah's Lowcountry Café, and by the time we arrived I filled Moonie in everything I hadn't covered on the phone the night before. Typically, I sit at the counter, but since Moonie and I had delicate business to discuss we slid into the back booth.

"Whadilitbe?" Clara, one of the regular waitresses, asked. Typical, she was harried and sweaty.

I didn't bother to look at the menu. "The usual."

Put on the spot, Moonie's scar turned scarlet. He fumbled with the menu. Clara tapped her pencil against the pad like a metronome until he said, "Biscuits and sausage gravy. I'll have a double order of hash with two eggs, over hard, on the side."

"And two coffees," I called after her retreating form. "Can't get a kale dandelion smoothie here," I muttered.

"What?" Moonie asked.

"Nothing."

"The bottom line is," Moonie said without preamble, "word has gotten out and pressure is building. Fast." He twisted a paper napkin. "The governor's office has gotten wind of it and are starting to put pressure on Koziner to sort things out before any journalists start sniffing around. If the papers start reporting on this they're going to need a scapegoat."

He was right. They would need a sacrificial lamb, and Moonie would be the one to get slaughtered on the altar of the press Gods. Koziner and the governor were already looking toward the next election cycle. It would be easy enough to toss Moonie under the bus. He already had a black mark on his record for insubordination while helping me during the Ten Thousand Leagues bust.

"Don't worry," I said, pausing as Clara landed two steaming mugs in front of us.

"Creamer?" It came out almost as a monosyllable grunt.

Moonie nodded to which Clara spilled a handful of single-serving creamers out of her apron and disappeared.

"It's not your fault," I said. "I'm going to tell Larry exactly what happened."

"Oh, you'll be hearing from him. Soon. Right now he's over at MUSC meeting with your girlfriend, the directors, and the chairman."

Covering his ass, I thought. Larry was nothing, if not shrewd. I imagined there would be a lot of smart people in that meeting wringing their hands.

"I should've been there," Moonie moaned, "but there was a fatal on I-26 that tied me up." That would be how they got him—although not law that a deputy be present at a prosection, it's standard procedure, especially for unusual deaths. A double homicide would certainly fall into the category of unusual.

"It wouldn't have made a difference. You would've just been scooped up just like Mags and I."

"At least I could say I went down swinging," he lamented. "I've got an open investigation but no bodies. And I'm on the hook for losing them! How am I supposed to certify manner of death and confirm identities?" Moonie stirred two creamers into his coffee and threw his spoon down in disgust.

I took a sip. It was scalding and tasted like lead. "Risden is going to try to run down this Bailey character. If we can get in touch with him, what would you need? Some sort of federal warrant transferring Berkeley's custodial rights? And then let it be their headache."

"I've never heard of anything like that before." Moonie picked up his coffee and stared at it, contemplating. "And what, the federal government is going to issue a death certificate?"

"Not unheard of. Department of State does for civilian defense contractors, and the military does for soldiers."

"I know that, but this is clearly a state matter." He pointed at the table. "A *local* matter. Not some defense contractor killed in Sandland. I've never heard of the feds stepping in and issuing a death certificate. Even if someone dies in international waters or airspace the feds don't get involved. The death gets reported to the local authority where the body docks or lands."

"True. I don't know what to tell you."

At that moment Clara landed several heavy, steaming plates in front of us. "Dig in," she said. It was her way of saying bon appétit. "Want a reheat on those?" she asked pointing to the mugs.

"Please," I said.

Clara scurried away in search of the carafe.

I checked my watch. "Eat up. I have to get back and get showered before this family comes in."

Moonie didn't need prodding. He lowered his head to an inch or two from the plate's surface and commenced shoveling.

***

I sat with the Kyle family and tried to feign interest, but I was bored. At this point in Nikki's apprenticeship she was able to navigate making funeral arrangements without my help. I was merely window dressing. An unexpected knock startled me out of a daze.

Isabella poked her head in and cleared her throat. "Uh, Mr. Clipper?"

"Excuse me," I said to Mrs. Kyle and the two daughters. Deep in conversation with Nikki about the wording of the death notice, they hardly acknowledged my departure.

"Coroner Koziner is here to see you," Isabella whispered urgently. "He said it is of the utmost importance." I knew it must be; Isabella wouldn't interrupt a funeral conference to tell me the Titanic sank, or twin towers fell. "The police are accompanying him," she added, lowering her half glasses down her nose.

"Where are they?" I replied, like I received this type of company every day.

"I put them in your office."

I glanced at the closed door. "Interrupt me if Nikki comes looking for me."

"Very good sir."

I entered my office. It still smells a touch sweet from Lauren's cigars. The smell had intercalated into the bones of the mansion. "Please, stay seated." I waved the assembled crowd down with my hands.

With Larry Koziner was Moonie, who sat in the corner wearing a hangdog expression, and a woman wearing a shield who must be "the police."

Wearing a perfectly tailored Savile Row suit, and sporting a hundred-dollar haircut, Koziner ignored my invitation and stood offering me a death-grip and whiff of expensive cologne. "Clip, how are you?" His expression was grim. This clearly wasn't a social call.

In addition to bearing the title of Berkeley County Coroner, Koziner runs a successful car dealership empire. When his father died, Koziner inherited two car dealerships. His dealerships now number over 50 in the greater South Carolina area. His success isn't luck. Koziner is fanatical about business, health, and God—in that order. He gets up every morning at four, works out, reads a chapter in the Bible, and is at his desk no later than six o'clock. Six days a week. On Sunday, his day of rest, he's one of the lay pastors at his church.

His job as coroner falls under business so I knew he was taking these missing bodies as seriously as a couple of rednecks having a NASCAR debate.

"Been better," I admitted.

"Detective Hotapp," the woman said, also standing and offering a firm handshake.

Early middle-aged, Hotapp appeared to have earned her gold shield young. The early signs of riding a detective's desk and too much cop cuisine—coffee and doughnuts—were starting to show around her jaw line and chin. Her hair wasn't what I'd imagine a female cop's to be. It was long and pulled into a loose ponytail at the base of her neck.

She sat looking like a coiled spring. Hanahan PD doesn't get too much action. Their detective squad consists of three. A double homicide followed by a body snatching was going to be the biggest case of Hanahan's year—and probably Hotapp's career.

"Let's get right to the heart of it," Koziner said, clearly leading the meeting. The custody of the bodies fell to the coroner, so this was his show. "We," he motioned with his head to Hotapp sitting next to him, "just met with the concerned parties at MUSC, including your, uh, Dr. Stryker. Everyone involved has been interviewed. We need to take a statement from you."

This was Hotapp's cue. She pulled a digital recorder, set it on my desk and recited the necessary preamble before letting me re-tell the story for the third time that day.

"Dr. Stryker gave us a similar account," Hotapp confirmed, once I sat back and steepled my fingers. "Any idea why the victims were taken?"

I hadn't editorialized like I had for Risden. "None," I said honestly.

"Do you think you and Dr. Stryker were taken because of your physical altercation with the agents?"

My face reddened slightly. I had glossed over what she nicely called "the altercation." Obviously, Maggie had told them about my ass whipping. "No, as I stated earlier Agent Bailey told me—us—upfront we would be accompanying him. The altercation," I used air quotes, "was a result of me trying to stop them from what I thought was an illegal act."

"You may be correct Mr. Clipper—"

"Clip."

"Excuse me?"

"Call me Clip."

"Right. No paperwork has been forthcoming from the Homeland Security, and my calls have been thus far ignored. So, where we stand a crime has been committed until DHS straightens this out." Consulting a small notebook, she said, "And you never had contact with Carmen Dean, correct?"

"Who?"

"The agent who interrogated Dr. Stryker."

My face flushed again. I hadn't debriefed with Maggie about her interrogation. It no doubt had been traumatic. I made a mental note to do so later; talking about it would help. "No, no, I didn't. I assume you're talking about the big guy, built like a linebacker?"

Hotapp nodded. The way she was firing information back, I knew there was a reason she had caught the double homicide in the first place. She was sharp, probably the department's A-list detective. "Care to speculate why your vitals were taken at two different times along with blood samples?"

"Honestly detective, that's all I can do, speculate." She nodded encouragingly, so I continued, "I've got to believe it has something to do with the John Does. They came to collect them wearing hazmat suits. Why?" I spread my hands on my desk. "They shot each other to death. Nothing unusual about that, as far as a method of killing goes. So, I've got to believe DHS knows or suspects something."

"Suspects what?" Hotapp prodded.

"The way they were dressed they were concerned about exposure. Of what?" I shrugged. "Something infectious. My guess is if they confirmed their suspicions they never would've allowed Mags and I to leave. They were evidently testing us, and the tests were negative."

Hotapp nodded, like I was confirming a working theory she had.

"What now?" I asked the assembled crowd.

Koziner cleared this throat. "To go along with what Detective Hotapp said, since we have no official documentation from the government saying otherwise we need to proceed accordingly."

Hotapp chimed in, "I have reason to believe the homicides and the illegal removal of the corpses are somehow connected, so I'll be treating it as one investigation."

Koziner leaned forward, as if to reassure me. "And even though we no longer have physical possession we're still going to work to establish the identities of the two John Does, and issue provisional death certificates. Dr. Stryker is going to use scene photos and whatever she can recall from the autopsy to issue my office some sort of opinion, and I'll make a ruling from there. As you know, they took everything from the lab, even downloading the server and wiping it."

"MUSC isn't happy about that," Hotapp muttered. I could imagine.

"They didn't get everything," Moonie interjected, speaking for the first time.

Hotapp and Koziner swiveled to stare at him. Based on their faces, this was news to them.

"They didn't get everything," Moonie repeated. His eyes shifted back and forth. "John Doe 1 was wearing a backpack."

"Skully," I said, almost to myself as to keep the John Does straight.

"What's that?" Koziner asked.

"Nothing." I motioned for Moonie to continue.

"I removed the backpack before signing the remains over to the pathology lab." A backpack would be a personal effect, and therefore under the control of the coroner's office, not the police.

"I remember that," Hotapp said. "There wasn't anything in there was there?"

Moonie nodded. "Nothing of interest. A long sleeve T-shirt and water bottle."

"I'll want to print the water bottle."

Moonie nodded. "I'll bring it by the station later today."

Koziner turned back, disappointed; the addition of a backpack certainly didn't change anything. "So, as I was saying, they got *almost* everything. All we have is the footage of the entourage entering and leaving the facility."

I suspected it had been reviewed ad nauseam during the little hospital powwow. "License plates?" I asked, knowing the hospital has more cameras than a prison. "Surely you have some footage of the vans."

Hotapp shook her head. "Not GSA plates. Vans are registered to an LLC that is subsidiary of a corporation headquartered in Belgium. My people are working on tracking that down."

Good luck. If it was a government owned vehicle, like one DHS would drive, it would have a GSA, or General Service Administration, license plate. They might as well just advertise to be spook vans.

"Back up a second," I said to Koziner, "How are you going to establish identities of the John Does *in absentia*, especially when DHS took all the physical evidence?"

"Not everything," Hotapp said, matter-of-factly. "I have the scene evidence, and AFIS has already hit on one set of prints." She allowed herself a smug smile and consulted the notebook again. I noticed the hand gripping it was devoid of a ring. "Samuel Badgers. Age 29. Last known address is his parents place in Riverland Terrace."

"Which one is he?"

"John Doe 1," Moonie said.

Skully, the one shot through the eye. "That's encouraging," I said.

Hotapp shrugged. "Good and bad. The parents haven't seen him in close to two years. He's in the system for a petty burglary charge he caught three years ago."

"Drugs?"

"What else do these kids steal for?"

Kids. Badgers was only a few years younger than me. But Maggie's observations had been right; it sounded like he lived on the street.

"Having a name will give us a leg up," Koziner said, "though Durward has his work cut out for him." Behind him Moonie flinched. "We're going to do this the old-fashioned way, before they had DNA and dental records to track down John Doe 2." He rapped his knuckles on the campaign desk. Meeting adjourned.

"Thank you for your time," Hotapp said, standing. We exchanged business cards and I showed them out. I packed a wad of tobacco into my lip watching Hotapp head to her motor pool vehicle, an American-made sedan. Not Koziner. His car du jour was some Maserati model I didn't recognize. Fancy.

Moonie lingered on the steps and lifted his hand as Koziner roared off. "Things haven't been good today," he said, dropping his hand, and seeming to deflate. "On top of this mess with the stolen bodies the office was burglarized last night."

"What?" I said, nearly choking on a wad of tobacco. The coroner's office shares the building with the county detention center and the Department of Probation Parole. The place is crawling with cops at all hours of the day and night. "Who in their right mind would rob you?"

Moonie took off his hat and fanned himself, shaking his head. "Dope fiends. People sometimes come in with small amounts of narcotics on their persons that we store until we turn over to the sheriff's office for destruction. The burglars went through all the personal property lockers. Cut the padlocks off each and every one."

I whistled. No wonder Koziner had been so abrupt. It hadn't been a couple of good days for his office. He was in triage mode trying to salvage his political career. "They get anything?"

"A little dope. Not much: keys, wallets, some jewelry. Stuff like that. Koziner is going to have hell to pay when he notifies the families. Not that it was his fault. The thieves were able to beat the keycard locks."

"It wasn't a stolen badge?"

Moonie shook his head. "The computer tracks entries and exits, and the entry made during the robbery wasn't by anyone's badge. It was a completely new identity that the burglars were able to get the system to validate. They're over there installing a whole new system today that will require a thumb print and six-digit pin number."

"Sounds sophisticated for dope fiends," I said releasing a slug of tobacco juice into a rose bush. People bring valuables into the funeral home for their loved ones to be buried with on an almost daily basis. My security system is comprised of a couple of ancient cylinder locks, a key hidden under a rock for the casket deliveryman out back, and a loudmouth bird. Perhaps it was time for me to consider tightening things up.

"Just 'cause they're junkies don't mean they ain't smart. All right, I've got to git."

I offered a mock salute and watched him trudge to his van. I headed back inside to see what kind of progress Nikki had made with the Kyle family.

Chapter 7

After wrapping up for the day at the funeral home, Nikki announced she was heading to a meeting. I decided to tag along. Like most church cellars, Calvary UAME smelled musty and hadn't been seen any updates since Roosevelt proposed the New Deal.

It was my first time with this group. All these groups are the same; they just arrange the chairs differently. The group at Calvary UAME was seated in a circle of metal folding chairs. Folks were sharing.

"I woke up naked in my car parked under an overpass," a gentleman who had identified himself as Toby intoned. "In the passenger seat next to me was a prostitute with a needle in her arm. Problem was," he paused and blinked, "an uncircumcised penis protruded from under the mini-skirt." Toby added unnecessarily, "It was really a man. When I became upset, she, I mean he woke. I told him to get out of my car, and he asked why. When I told him it was because he was really a man, he got mad. Real mad." Toby paused and cast his eyes downward. "He beat me and robbed me. That didn't stop me from using. No, I didn't hit bottom until seven months after when a blood screen tested positive for HIV after giving blood at my son's school's blood drive." Toby scanned the group, taking a moment to look at each person seated in the circle. A couple of people squirmed under his gaze. "I lost everything. My family, my home, my health, and emptied my retirement account, all because of painkillers...that led to dope. I was on track to making partner at the law firm I work at, but have screwed things up so badly while high, I'll be stuck doing doc review for the rest of my career. The rest of my life," he added as an afterthought. "But today is a good day." Toby smiled. It was the joyless smile of man with nothing left to lose. "Today I'm 18 months sober." He sat.

"Thank you for sharing Toby," the leader, Martin, said. The group clapped.

I scrutinized Toby. He was thin in a healthy way, good looking, and dressed nicely. The only thing that gave him away was his disconsolate affect.

"Anyone else like to share?" Martin asked.

My attention was quickly drawn to an African-American woman in scrubs who stood. "Hi my name is Kendra."

"Hi Kendra," the group intoned.

She twisted her hands. "I've been sober seven days—" The group clapped and she continued.

When Kendra was done, and nobody else wanted to share, Martin distributed sobriety keychains and led the ending prayer, "God grant me the serenity—"

There was a selection of donuts and two ancient coffee urns sitting on a banquet table. Someone had gussied the affair up with a vinyl tablecloth that had daisies and watering cans on it. I eased a Styrofoam cup off the tower and was helping myself to the urn marked "regular" on masking tape when I felt a presence next to me.

"You didn't share," Martin said, and plucked a bottle of water out of a slushy tub.

"I came with a friend," I said, jerking my head toward the circle of chairs where Nikki chatted with some of the lingering members. I wasn't sure NA's exact rules on non-narcotics users attending. It wasn't an exercise of voyeurism. I had joined Nikki at an "open" meeting one time, and ever since started tagging along irregularly, especially when I needed to even out. The meetings seemed to help quiet the noise in my head, as I told my shrink, "I think it helps being around other people that are struggling too and knowing I'm not alone." And I definitely needed to even out after my run in with Bailey and his gang.

"First time?"

"No, well, yes, first time here." I usually went to the meetings that were walking distance from the funeral home. Calvary, on the Eastside, was the only place that offered an early evening meeting on Tuesdays.

Martin allowed a grin to peek from under his substantial mustache and nodded like a souvenir bobblehead from the ballpark. He was a bit nerdy in his pressed slacks and Argyle sweater vest over a button down that 't hide his muscular physique. "Well we're glad you're here, and hope you come again—" He let it hang so I'd add my name.

I did and added a handshake. "Clip."

"Clip. Interesting name." His coffee colored eyes danced. "What do you do Clip?"

"I own a funeral home here in town."

Martin's eyes flicked down to my arms and back up. "Really?" My shirt sleeves were rolled up exposing all the ink.

"Yup."

"Stressful job." The implication was clear.

I took a sip of the coffee. It was surprisingly good. Actually amazing. Flavorful. Just the right temperature and pungent. "So, I've heard." I took another gulp.

"I wouldn't know. I'm in IT."

"Computers stress me out."

"Well said." He held out his hand again. "My name's Artin. I hope to see you again. Maybe next time you can share."

"Artin?" I was glad I allowed him to introduce himself to me. I could've sworn he said his name was *Martin* at the beginning of the meeting. "Unusual name."

"It's a family name. Persian." Artin's hand danced over the donut display before landing on a bear claw, shiny with glaze. "I shouldn't; I'm trying to watch my weight." He patted his flat midsection. "But I'll treat myself. I kayaked this morning." He took a big bite.

"Where do you kayak?"

"All over. One of the reasons I settled here. I've always loved the water, and there are so many waterways surrounding this town. It distracts me from doing things I shouldn't. You look like you're no stranger to some physical activity."

"I've been known to hit the gym."

"Where do you work out?"

I didn't like how Artin was settling into this conversation. There was no end in sight. "Muscle Bound." Nikki was engrossed in conversation with another recovering addict. "Looks like my ride is ready to go. Happy paddling Artin." I refilled my cup and darted over to collect Nikki before someone else could befriend me.

Artin, mouth full, waved the bear claw at me.

Chapter 8

Moonie braked where the municipal road turned abruptly into a field and killed the engine. The morning was unseasonably chilly causing a fog bank to sit on the nearby Cooper River, its tendrils hugging the field.

"This the place?" I asked. The field was the old Holston Landfill. Capped and graded, you'd hardly know it contained a secret. There were a few cars parked in the lot of the adjacent recycling center, separated from us by a rusty cyclone fence. Across from the recycling center are acres of marshy woods. It's a lonely industrial part of the city, grimy, desolate and undesirable. Perfect for the fringes of society.

"A friend at CPD said there's a small encampment in the woods near One80 Place, but this one, Bushville, is much bigger. Homeless central."

"Bushville?"

Moonie shrugged. "It cropped up around the time of the market crash in '08. Obviously, they blamed the president."

"Makes sense."

"The ramps of the Ravenel," about a 15-minute walk, "are popular places to panhandle. According to the last PIT count there are over 5,000 homeless in the city, so it's going to be like finding a needle in a haystack, but my guy seems to think he probably would've passed through here at some point. This is our best bet."

"Let's get to it." I hopped out. There was the faintest whiff of campfire smoke even over the competing scents of the river and recycling plant. "Might want to lose the hat."

"Why?"

"And the shades," I added. "Makes you look like a cop. I'm going to go out a limb and say most of these folks have had some negative experiences with law enforcement."

Moonie had swapped his Tony Lamas for work boots and wore a loose camouflage windbreaker over his embroidered coroner shirt that also fit over his gun and badge.

"If you say so," he said, stowing the items in the van making sure it was locked before wading into the thick underbrush. I tried to keep up as best as I could. Moonie moves with the agility of the Catawba in the woods. He was raised in a rural area near Huger. Hunting, fishing, tracking, and other redneck pursuits are encoded in his genes.

Sapling branches slapped at my face. The ground, covered in leaves, was slightly spongy, and hard to navigate with kudzu and ground ivy entangling my legs. Twice, I walked into spider webs that left me spitting and picking at my face. I caught up with Moonie stopped on a faint trail. It could've been mistaken for a deer trail if not for the trash scattered along it.

"Dammit," I muttered, pulling thistles out of my pants.

Moonie seemed completely unfazed. Actually, he seemed relaxed, not his usual jittery self. "This way." He jerked his thumb in the direction of the river.

We turned right. The camp was another three-minute walk down the trail, far enough away that it was well off the beaten path, but not far enough that the inhabitants had to lug supplies too far. Bushville proper was a loose assemblage of shelters set in a muddy quagmire. The shelters ran the gambit from pup and large cabin tents to tarps draped over skids to cardboard lean-tos. Several fires smoldered, casting thin wisps of smoke into the treetops. It smelled like piss and sulfur. We picked our way past several peripheral tents, coming upon a man sitting on a camping stool in front of an ember heap, rocking.

"Excuse me sir," Moonie said.

The rocking stopping, and the man gazed in Moonie's general direction. His face was haggard and bearded, his eyes vacant.

"Do you recognize this man?" Moonie asked, producing a photograph of Samuel Badgers. It was a ten-year old photo obtained from the DMV, blown up and printed on glossy photo paper.

The man closed his eyes, lowered his head and resumed rocking.

Moonie didn't quite know what to do. He stood awkwardly for a moment before stuffing the photo back into his windbreaker, saying, "Thank you for your time."

We moved on, my shoes making sucking sounds as I pulled them out of the mud. A woman poked her head out of a pup tent, and startled by our appearance, quickly withdrew inside and zipped the flap.

"Ma'am? Ma'am?" Moonie asked the zippered flap. "May we have a word?" Silence form the tent. "We're trying to identify someone and hoping you can help us. It'll just take a second." He paused. Still nothing from the filthy little red tent. Looking at me, Moonie held up his hands as if to say, *what should I say*? He pantomimed knocking.

I should've let him try knocking on a tent; instead I shook my head and jerked it sideways. We moved on to another small fire. A man and woman squatted by it, not in a social way. Each engrossed in their milieu. The man wore a camouflage jacket, the old-fashioned woodland pattern. He was young, early thirties with the bulldog neck of someone ex-military.

I squatted next to him and put my hands out to the fire to warm them. "Where'd you serve?"

His head swiveled up and the military programming overrode his initial suspicion. "Iraq," came out of his mouth before he even knew he had said it.

"Tripp Clipper," I said holding a hand sideways. "Formerly of the 75th Ranger."

The man took it automatically. It was gritty, the grip iron.

"Wesley Harris. Two, seven Marines," he said, meaning 2nd Battalion, 7th Marines.

One eye didn't quite track correctly. It took me a second to realize it was glass. "You all were some of the first in country."

He cracked a small grin, perfect white teeth against his dark, almost ebony, skin. "Yeah brother, I was early."

"That was a long time ago."

"Yeah. I was just a kid that had been playing football the year before in high school."

Based on his build I guessed he had been a tackle or guard on the offensive line. "I won't hold it against you that you're a Jarhead," I said. Wesley laughed and I got the feeling it was an unusual experience for him. "Listen Wesley," I continued, "we need your help with something," I glanced at Moonie, his signal.

Wesley immediately stopped chuckling. "You cops?"

"No," I said nodding in Moonie's direction. "That's a deputy coroner and I'm a civilian."

"Civilian?"

"Undertaker to be exact."

"Serious?"

I nodded.

Wesley found that funny and smiled again. "Man!"

"We need some help in identifying a couple guys, who are dead," I added, so he wouldn't think he was diming on anyone, "and we have reason to believe one or both passed this way."

The older woman, wearing a filthy cloak of rags, had been enraptured by our exchange, and when I glanced in her direction she didn't look away, her eyes endless pools of brown humour, as if to say, *if he'll help you so will I.*

Moonie whipped out the photos, showing first the ten-year-old DMV photo of Samuel and then the photo of Hansel. The photo of Hansel had been provided by Detective Hotapp. Since Agent Bailey had taken everything from the pathology lab, the only existing photos of Hansel were in situ. Moonie had cropped all the blood out, but it was still a gruesome shot with his lifeless eyes and open mouth. There was nothing Moonie could do about that. If he inserted black bars to modulate the violence, Hansel would be unidentifiable. Also included in the photo array was a close up shot of a star tattoo peeking out from the left sleeve of Hansel's T-shirt, what Moonie would call an "identifying characteristic."

Moonie passed them to Wesley, who studied them. Shaking his head, he said, "Nah, never seen that dude. I just rolled into town a few weeks ago." He handed them back. Moonie made to hand them to the woman and Wesley shook his head. In response to Moonie's look, he said, "Won't do you any good. She's gone."

It was as if the woman knew that was her cue. She began making a noise more akin to a cackle than a laugh, continuing to stare at the fire. Wesley raised his eyebrows as if to say *told you so*.

"Anyone else around here that would be helpful?"

"Afraid not. Everyone has either gone to their job or is out begging. Morning rush and all."

"Appreciate your time." I pressed a twenty into Wesley's hand.

We poked around for a few more minutes, but Wesley was right. Besides a few slumbering forms, the camp was mostly deserted. As we left the camp, the red tent was still zippered shut and the man on the stool was still rocking.

"Where do we turn off?" I asked.

"It was a ways back. I want to see where this comes out on the road."

The forest thinned. We crossed disused train tracks, and a two by ten board over a small gully filled with stagnant water, emerging onto the shoulder of North Romney Street. It was as derelict and sad as everything else in this area of town. A bleached ribbon of asphalt stretched in either direction, strewn with trash and choked with weeds.

A young woman, head down, lost in a pair of headphones, nearly plowed into us.

"Sorry," she muttered, embarrassed.

I wouldn't guess her to be a year out of high school, if that. Her complexion was clean and unblemished and topped by a pixie haircut with a purple streak. She was wearing a pair of fashionable tight pants with lace up boots and a jean jacket. Although it was clear she headed for Bushville, she certainly didn't fit the stereotype in my head.

"Excuse me Miss," I said, holding out my arm, "could we trouble you for a minute of your time?"

The twenty-dollar bill folded between two fingers caught her attention. Pulling an earbud out, she said, "What?" Casual suspicion was painted on her face.

I smiled guilelessly. "Would you be willing to answer a question for us?"

She scrunched up her face, assessing the situation. I could almost see the gears turning. Strangers, who clearly didn't belong to the population of Bushville, were offering money in exchange for information. Finally, she asked, "Twenty bucks and all I have to do is answer one question?" Her voice contained the distrust of someone who had seen every hustle and con known to man.

I nodded, jerking the bill in her direction.

"What's the question?"

"Hoping you could look at a photograph and give us a name."

She wadded her hands in her pockets and made like she was going to step around us.

"Wait, wait," I said, "You aren't going to be getting anyone in trouble or ratting on them. We're from the coroner's office. We're simply trying to identify some guys so we can let their families know."

Moonie couldn't resist the opportunity to raise his windbreaker to reveal the hardware.

"They're dead?"

"They're dead," I affirmed.

The girl studied us for a second later, and then snatched the bill from my hand. It disappeared like a magic trick.

I pushed the photographs into her hands. "Do you recognize these guys?"

The girl recoiled at the postmortem shot of John Doe 2 and quickly shuffled to Samuel Badgers's photo. She looked at it for a long moment. "This is Sam," she said tapping the photograph, and then bringing her hand to her mouth. The fingernails covering her mouth were bitten to the quick and painted with chipped purple polish.

I was silent, wanting to give the situation a moment to breathe. When you're around grieving people enough you get a sense of when to say things and when to remain silent.

Not Moonie. He has the subtlety of a turd in a punch bowl. "How about the other fella? You know him?"

"Sam," she said, hand still covering her mouth. "He's dead?"

I put a hand in front of Moonie. "Were you friends?"

She nodded. Her face suddenly looked a lot older. "I knew him. He was already here when I first came."

"When was the last time you saw him?"

"Maybe six months ago. He got a job at the mall and a place." She shrugged. "And then I didn't see him around here anymore." She smiled ruefully. There were tiny freckles dusted over what I previously thought was a clear complexion. "That's what happens when you get a promotion."

"Promotion?" Moonie asked. I was glad he asked; I thought I had heard her wrong.

"Yeah, you know, like you get a promotion at work?" We nodded "Here, you get promoted off the streets." She expelled a breath. "Those that want to leave the street. But once you get promoted you don't have reason to come around anymore."

"You've never seen this guy?" Moonie persisted, shuffling the photos in her hands for her and pointing to John Doe 2's lifeless face.

The girl smoothed her short hair back, purposely not looking down at the photo. "Not that I can remember. People come and go all the time. It's hard keeping track of everyone, and sometimes I'll find a place I can crash for a few weeks." She smiled shyly, "You know, like a temporary promotion."

"We just came from the camp. Nobody would cop to recognizing him."

"Maybe he was Sam's roommate?" she offered.

"He had a roommate?" Moonie asked.

I wanted to remind Moonie the two in the photos killed each other in a gun battle. I seriously doubted they were roomies.

"I don't know," the girl said, shrugging. "I was only there once."

Moonie's eyes went wide. "Can you tell us where it is?"

The girl looked at Moonie and then me and then back at Moonie.

"Can you?" Moonie asked.

I took out my billfold. "Do you remember?" I asked, slowly counting out bills.

"Not the address but I know the general vicinity," she said. "I was pretty high the day I was at his place, but I think I can figure it out."

I offered her four tens. "Half now and half when you show us the right place."

Chapter 9

We started at the Citadel Mall in West Ashley. That's where the girl, whose name was Cam, found Badgers working at a cell-phone kiosk. According to Cam, she hung out until he was done and then they walked back to his place. It was cold out, she remembered, maybe seven or eight months ago. Maybe a ten-minute walk.

Badgers's place turned out to be fairly easy to find. The mall is hemmed in on one side by 526, and they certainly didn't walk to his place via the interstate, that left the main drag, Orleans Road. I rode in the back of the van, an experience I didn't relish. I hate confined spaces, but they don't cause the panic they once did. For the longest time I couldn't even ride elevators. When I'd go to a hospital or convalescent home where I needed to put the cot on an elevator, I'd push the button, take the stairs and meet it. Getting my head shrunk at the VA on a regular schedule along with taking up meditation at Maggie's urging had really helped take the edge off—the NA meetings didn't hurt either. Now instead of complete panic, riding in the back simply caused mild uneasiness.

The alternative was stuffing Cam in the back of the van or riding three across on the front bench. Cam never would've agreed to get into the back of a darkened van with two strangers, nor did I particularly want to cozy up to a girl who was looking for a "place to crash." That left only one option: me in the back.

Moonie's meat wagon was similar to the van Maggie and I were abducted in. White panel, same make and model. The only difference being that this one had a blue stripe down the side and the words CORONER emblazoned on the back, and of course the smell. The kidnapping van had smelled like any old van—axle grease and aluminum. Not the meat wagon. The hundreds upon hundreds of drownings, stabbings, shootings, decomps loaded in the cargo area left a residual odor that wasn't simply unpleasant, it was slightly nauseating. I read somewhere the average smell weighs 600 nanograms. Yes, smells have mass and weight. The damp air clarified the coppery smell of blood and putrefaction into a miasma so vivid I could taste the 600 nanograms resting on my tongue.

Cam directed us down a wrong street off Orleans, but quickly realized the error when it turned out to be nothing but commercial businesses. We got back on the main drag.

"Try this one," Cam said, pointing down the next cross street. "This is it, I think," she said after Moonie turned. "It looks familiar."

It was residential, the homes small affairs. Mostly ranches with tidy lawns and several cars—not new but not too old either—parked in the driveways. A short way down the road, Cam pointed at a sign that said COUGAR POINTE APARTMENTS. "There, there! I'm almost certain that's the place, Cougar Pointe." She rolled the name around like she was saying it for the first time.

From behind the tiny mesh window separating me from them, I could see Cougar Pointe was a collection of three buildings plopped around a large parking lot. The buildings were utilitarian. Brick affairs that looked like college dormitories from the '70s, before they started adding amenities. There were only a handful of older model cars in the weedy lot.

"Which unit?" I asked through the mesh.

Cam scrunched her eyes. "I want to say that one," she said, pointing to the back unit, "but like I said, we were partying. I don't really recall."

Moonie wheeled into a spot near the rear building, hopped out and let me out. Someone had conveniently bungee corded the security door open to unit B and we breezed in. Unfortunately, this wasn't the type of place with names on the faux-brass mailboxes in the entrance hall. I counted 32 boxes. Sixteen apartments upstairs. Sixteen down.

"Up or down?" I asked.

"It was definitely the first floor," Cam said, leading us left into a dank hallway smelling vaguely of urine. At door B7 she stopped. The casing was painted with glossy rust colored enamel chipping in several places to reveal a previous color.

No police yellow tape over the door. Nothing. Detective Hotapp hadn't gotten this far in her investigation.

"This might be it," Cam said, staring at it. Then, nodding her head, "Yes, this is definitely it."

"You want to call Hotapp?" I asked Moonie.

"We will once we take a look around," he said, studying the door.

I figured her investigation would have priority over Moonie's ID quest, but the bureaucrats could battle it out after the fact. "What now?" I asked. "You going to kick the door in?" Kidding.

"Why would I do that?" Moonie asked, producing a key from his jeans pocket. It was a substantial key, larger than its residential counterpart, the color of oil rubbed bronze with a big square bow. Definitely a commercial key, the kind apartment buildings give out.

"How the hell did you get that?"

"It was in a zippered pocket in his backpack," Moonie said, placing the tip of the key against the lock.

"Detective Hotapp know about it?"

"I just found it after dropping that water bottle off at her office."

I shook my head, hoping the lie would sound more convincing when Koziner found out.

"What?" Moonie's voice was shrill, defensive.

"Nothing. You may want to knock first."

"Why?"

"What if he has a roommate?"

"Good idea," Moonie said, wagging the key at me.

He pounded on the door like he was about to do a SWAT breech. "Coroner's Office!" A half-minute passed, and Moonie was about to key the lock when the door swung open.

A man the size of a bear filled the doorway. "Yeah?" he said scowling.

"Uh, I think we have the wrong apartment," Moonie said, having to almost look vertical.

The man scowled harder and began to shut the door muttering something about having to get off his couch.

I hissed to Moonie, "The roommate."

"Wait," Moonie said placing his forearm in the jamb. He grunted as over a hundred pounds of commercially graded steel core door slammed into his flesh.

The man jerked the door open and let out a little puff, now really annoyed. "What?"

"Do you know this man?" Moonie asked, fumbling in his windbreaker pouch. The question hung in the air for a moment, before he used his non-injured arm and whipped the photo of Badgers out and displayed it.

"You all cops?"

It must be the haircuts.

"No," Moonie said, puffing up slightly as he raised his windbreaker yet again, "coroner's office."

"Coroner?" He looked baffled.

"Official investigation," Moonie said with more relish than necessary.

The man made a face. "Nah. Never seen him."

"The other one too," I said.

Moonie shuffled the photos, displaying John Doe 2's lifeless face. "How about this one?"

"You serious? Man, get the fuck outta here with that." The door slammed in Moonie's face.

Unfazed, Cam moved down the hallway. "It could've been this one."

"Wait," Moonie said grabbing her by the arm, "I thought you said that was the one."

"Don't touch me!" Cam jerked out of his grip.

I stepped between them. "Cool it," I said to Moonie. The scar over his eye was red.

"Do you know which one is his or are you guessing?" he asked around me.

"Look man," Cam hugged herself, "I got high in the bathroom at the mall the day I found Sam. I wasn't really paying attention to apartment numbers!"

"Were you paying attention to where you were?"

"This is the right place!" she insisted. Her voice was small.

"It's fine," I said to her, trying to calm her. Noting the slight glassiness in her eyes, I wondered if she was high now. Pointing to B5, I said, "You think it could be this one?"

She nodded, purple streak bobbing.

It wasn't.

No answer. The key didn't fit.

We repeated the process six more times on that wing of the building. Three apartments answered. None of the residents had ever seen Samuel Badgers or John Doe 2 before in their life. Three went unanswered, and the key didn't fit.

"Must be this side," Cam offered.

We tried the other eight apartments on the opposite wing. No luck. The key didn't fit or nobody who answered could recall ever having seen either dead man.

"You're sure it was here?" I asked Cam, checking my watch. Thirty minutes had passed. I did a little mental math. It would take the better part of three hours.

"This is the place," she said, nodding. "I'm sure of it."

"Let's keep looking," Moonie said.

"Why don't we try the rental office?" I suggested.

"Let's keep looking." Moonie repeated.

We tried the first floors of the other two buildings. No luck. Standing near the mailboxes in Building C, I said, "What now?"

"We'll try the second-floor apartments."

"I don't remember stairs," Cam said. "It's definitely not on the second floor."

Moonie's face was an open book. She had been wrong this far and he didn't believe her. "We're going to give it a shot," he said, and trudged up the stairs.

Cam's face fell and she followed him, the lure of easily earning the second half of her bounty long gone. We canvassed the second floor of all three buildings. It took well over an hour. Nothing.

"This *is* the place," Cam insisted, as we hustled to across the parking lot for the Hail Mary play. We had canvassed the complex, tried every door. This couldn't be the place. Cam was lying or had been too messed up that night. The early morning fog had burned off and it was turning out to be a blistering day. I was already hot and sweaty from marching up and down humid, smelly hallways, and wasn't in the mood so I didn't justify her with a response.

The rental office was a little single story, single apartment add-on, an office and living-quarters combination. There was a mail slot in the plain steel door for after-hours rent payments. The door stuck in the jamb and it took a good pull to get it open. The inside was nothing more than a little room with worn linoleum on the floor, tired silk tree in the corner, and a wood laminate chair and table combination that had seen better days.

"Help you?" an Asian woman asked without bothering to look up. Her accent was thick and she cleaved off each syllable.

Moonie almost rolled his shoulders in anticipation of flexing his official muscle, a slight grin spread across his lips.

"Yes, Miss, you certainly can," he said loudly, slapping his identification wallet against the sliding glass partition. "Deputy Wise. Berkeley County Coroner's Office."

The woman looked up. She couldn't be more unimpressed.

I got the feeling she was no stranger to uniforms or badges showing up at Cougar Pointe.

"We're here on an official investigation," Moonie said.

The phone rang. The woman snatched up the receiver and held up a finger to the glass as she yammered into the receiver in her native tongue.

The three of us passed the time looking at literature about the amenities and "luxury living" Cougar Pointe offered. From what I'd seen so far there was nothing remotely luxurious about the units and using the word "amenities" was blatant false advertising. I hadn't spied a single amenity.

Hanging up, the woman said, "Okay. What you want?"

"Do you know this man?" Moonie pulled out the printout of Badgers. At this point in the day it looked a little creased and battered.

"Of course. That Sam. A7." She jerked a thumb over her shoulder to indicate the building attached to the office.

"I told you!" Cam said. She held out her hand. "Pay up."

Wordlessly, I peeled some bills off my billfold, still startled by our turn of fortune.

"How about this guy?" Moonie asked, swapping John Doe 2's photo for Sam's.

The woman's eyes flicked up from her desk momentarily. "No." There was no hesitation. No uncertainty. If nothing else, it was safe to say John Doe 2 wasn't a resident of Cougar Pointe. Which made sense, if John Doe 2 lived here, or even worked at Citadel Mall, they would've more than likely would've settled their gentleman's quarrel—duel—closer to home than a boat landing.

"We'll be needing access to Sam's place," Moonie asserted.

I braced for a fight and was surprised when the woman rooted in a little locked cabinet for a moment, pulling out a key, sliding the glass partition open and passing it to Moonie. "Other people already been. Bring back when you're done."

"What other people?" Moonie asked.

"Who you think? Cops," the woman said. "They come. They show badge. Tell me Sam dead."

Moonie turned. "Hotapp?"

I shrugged. "Got to be. Can you describe them?" I asked the woman.

The woman fixed a stare on me, hooked a finger on her purple glasses and pulled them to the tip of her nose. "No. You all look alike."

"What's that supposed to mean?"

"Cops. You all the same."

Moonie started to open his mouth. I cut him off, "C'mon." I said opening the door. "No need to remind her we're not cops," I muttered.

A7 was in the exact same location as Cam's original guess, one building off. Same smelly hallway. Same moldy carpet. Same chipped enamel paint on the door casing. Only difference was the A instead of B on the door. In retrospect, I wasn't shocked the neighbors didn't recognize Badgers. An elderly gentleman who seemed to think we were Meals on Wheels in A1 was more interested in inquiring in what was on the menu than looking at Badgers's photo. The very pregnant woman that answered the door of A4 had at least six kids clamoring in the background. She hardly glanced at the photo. And the guy that answered A10 was none too happy to have clean-cut guys knocking on his door. The way he fidgeted, I'd bet the farm he was running drugs out of his place.

Moonie held up the key from the backpack against the loaner key. Not even similar. The loaner was a small, silver number that looked like it came with a cheap lockset from a big box store. Moonie shrugged, pocketed Badgers' key, and used the loaner key to open the door. A wave of cool air washed out into the hall. The entrance hall was small and dark and contained the doorway to the galley kitchen. The kitchen was spotless and smelled faintly of saffron. There was nothing on the countertops; only a kettle and pan sat on the stovetop. Evidence of the forensic team in the form of black smudges were on all the hard surfaces.

"Not much here," I said, opening the cabinets and inspecting the contents. They were mostly barren except for a couple of cheap plastic place settings, and a few non-perishables.

"Same here," Moonie replied when I joined him in the living room. He had opened the vertical blinds, revealing shabby carpeting and dingy walls. The room was a lot like the kitchen, neat and sparse. There was a sofa facing a flat-screen TV on a stand. The one-by-twelve planks resting on cinder blocks serving as a coffee table contained only a remote. The only other furniture was a card table with four folding chairs pushed in neatly, and a tiny oriental rug about the size of a bathroom step-out mat. There were no personal touches, no wall hangings, no photographs, no mail sitting around. One bedroom was completely empty. I checked the closet. Empty too. The other bedroom only had a mattress sitting on the floor and a small desk that looked like it was rescued from the trash.

"Look," I said, pointing under the desk. A bundle of wires from the monitor, mouse, keyboard and modem terminated at nothing.

"Looks like Hotapp took the tower."

"That's why there's nothing here. She's taken everything of interest."

"What's this?" Moonie moved the mouse and picked up a white booklet serving as the mouse pad. "Narcotics Anonymous," he said, reading the purple type on the cover. He rifled through the slim booklet. "Listen to this," he said. I was in the closet. The clothes would fit into a small duffel bag. "'Many times in our recovery, the old bugaboos will haunt us. Life may again become meaningless, monotonous, and boring.' Ain't that something?" I stepped out of the closet as he tossed the booklet onto the keyboard.

The bathroom contained a few toiletries and more black smudges, but nothing interesting.

"Don't this just get my tail in a knot." Moonie joined Cam and I in the living room. "There's nothing that proves Badgers even lives here."

"What's the big deal? You don't need to prove he lives here." I was cranky. The weight of a wasted day pushed down on me.

"I know, but I was hoping for *something* on JD2." His emotional barometer, the scar, was white with despondency.

"Is this how you remember the place?" I asked Cam, strictly out of curiosity. There was nothing to be gleaned from the place. Moonie was going to have to grovel to Hotapp to drop any crumbs from her initial search. Not my problem. Badgers apartment certainly wasn't what I was expecting. A man living on the streets, supporting a drug and alcohol habit, would lead me to expect a sty. His place was almost spartan.

"I remember this couch," Cam said, trying to be helpful. "Like I said, we were partying...I remember we were watching QVC or something on TV and talking about the stuff we'd buy if we won the lottery."

The TV. It was obviously new and large and expensive and incongruous with everything else that seemed modest and castoff. "How does a guy like Badgers, who obviously has substance problems, afford a place?"

Outside, car doors slammed.

Cam shrugged. "He was a bright guy. Graduated from Purdue with an engineering degree. Maybe he just got his shit together."

"Yeah, there's that NA booklet," Moonie said. "Maybe he got sober and pulled himself together."

Something wasn't adding up. "I don't see someone working a menial job at the mall affording a place, even a dump like this."

"I'm so screwed," Moonie moaned, shaking his head. "Koziner is going to make me the sacrificial lamb if this goes south—when this goes south."

"You have as positive ID based on his prints, you can support that with his parents' ID of the scene photo, and you can always get Cam here and the woman at the desk, if you need supporting ID."

"That still leaves John Doe 2."

"Fifty percent isn't bad for a case like this."

"Think that's going to cut it when this hits the papers?"

"I'm sure he won't be the first unidentified in the county's history."

"The first that's been lost."

"You didn't lose them—" I was interrupted by the apartment door flying open. Four guys poured in. They wore black ski masks and tactical vests over street clothes. In their hands were submachine guns. "Get down! Get down now!"

Cam screamed.

I raised my hands, sank to my knees, put my hands on the floor in front of me like I was worshipping, and kissed the carpet. My arms were pulled roughly behind my back and I heard the ripping sound of zip cuffs, and everything went dark as a hood was pulled over my face

Chapter 10

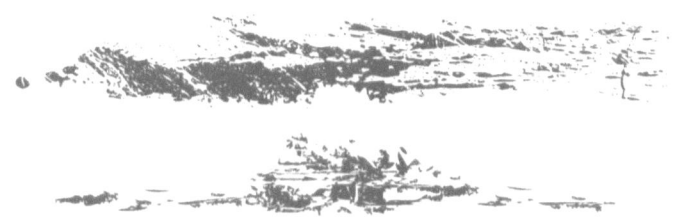

The chair felt familiar. Hard, molded plastic, much like the ones at the DMV. Cheap and durable. Nobody had the decency to cut the cuffs off, and I didn't give them the satisfaction of asking them to. The stillness in the room told me I was physically alone, but I figured there was an eye in the sky watching.

By my count it was about two hours before the lock snicked back, and hinges squeaked. The cuffs were snipped and hood was ripped off, and I was vindicated. Same unfinished cement board for walls. Same spray foam, and moving blankets tacked the walls and ceiling for acoustic benefits. I was back in the safe house and face-to-face with James Bailey, again. And he didn't look too happy. His weak chin quivered as if he wanted to say something but he remained silent. Next to him was the middle-aged physician who used me as a pincushion my previous visit. He was wearing a surgical mask and latex gloves.

"Arm out," he commanded.

I flopped my numb arm on the table and made a fist to get the vein to jump up. "We going to get it on the first try?"

The doctor didn't answer, sighed, and pulled out a rubber tourniquet from his lab coat. He wrapped it above my bicep and palpated the antecubital fossa searching for the vein.

Success on the first try. Doc gave me a few commands as he collected my vitals, "Breathe in. Exhale. Look up. Say Ah—" before looking at Bailey and nodding his head. He exited wordlessly.

The seconds ticked by. I stared at Bailey. He perched on the edge of the table. "You could be in a federal supermax by the end of the day. I warned you."

"Stop with your bullshit." I rubbed my wrists trying to restore feeling, noticing a trickle of blood inside my elbow. Dr. Feelgood hadn't bothered with a bandage. "I haven't done anything."

"Interfering with a government agency could be construed as domestic terrorism under the PATRIOT Act."

I unfolded my arms, a real prickle of fear running up my spine. "You're serious? Domestic terrorism?"

"What were you doing in that apartment?" Bailey asked flatly.

"Deputy Wise was tasked by his boss, the Berkeley County Coroner, to identify the two John Does from the double homicide scene. You remember, the bodies you illegally took while in my presence?" Bailey's face registered nothing, I continued, "He asked for my help in a perfectly legal, state sanctioned investigation."

"You nearly got yourself killed."

"Why have you abducted me yet again?"

Bailey ignored my question. "I'm curious. How did you locate Badgers's apartment? The lease isn't in his name."

I thought about stonewalling, but then my mind flashed to Moonie and Cam, who I knew were singing like birds wherever Bailey had them caged and decided against it. There was nothing to be gained. A pissed off Bailey might just hold me longer out of spite.

I sighed. "How about you get me something to drink and turn the AC up and I'll tell you what you want to know."

Bailey disappeared not bothering to lock the door and reappeared a minute later with a generic brand of bottled water. He slapped it on the table and pulled out a chair and sat down. Interested and concerned. My best bud.

I slugged the entire bottle. "The girl, Cam," I said wiping my mouth with the back of my hand, "we found her at a homeless encampment, and she said she knew Badgers and had been to his apartment." Bailey absorbed every word, not moving, as I spoke, every word being processed and analyzed. "News to us, that Badgers had a place. The last known address the police have for Badgers is his parents' address. We had the girl take us to Badgers's apartment and, a few minutes later, you assholes show up."

"Homeless encampment?"

"Yeah, this place out near the old dump."

"How'd you know he was homeless?"

"The pathologist said it looked like he lived on the street. Durward knows a guy in CPD who said to look out there."

Bailey studied me for a full two seconds. "Interesting story. How can a guy who has an apartment look like he lives on the street?"

"My guess is Badgers was crashing at someone else's place. His name isn't on the lease, right? A couple nights couch surfing doesn't erase years on the street."

"Couch surfing?"

"Like you said, his name isn't on the lease." I tapped the empty bottle on the edge of the table. "I can only tell you what I know, and that isn't much."

Bailey stood and wordlessly left the room. I stretched and paced for a spell. When Bailey returned I was back in my chair.

"Lucky for you, your phone backs up your story." He pulled it out of his pocket and waved it. "As we speak Coroner Lawrence Koziner is being put on notice the John Does are no longer his concern. Got it?"

"By who?"

"What?"

Was this asshole hard of hearing too? "Who is putting him on notice?"

Bailey sighed. He wasn't used to being questioned. "The Attorney General's Office. And just so we're crystal clear, because obviously last time I wasn't, stay out of this. If you continue to insert yourself federal prison *will* be in your future. You're above your pay grade soldier, capisce?"

I offered a little salute of acknowledgement. "Fine."

Bailey paused for a moment, searching my face for any signs of disingenuity before pushing off the table. "Sit tight," he said.

His hand was on the knob when I said, "Bailey?"

He turned.

"At least make me feel good about this. Who are you working for?"

"Homeland Security."

"Who's the leaseholder on Badgers's apartment?"

His jaw clenched. "Sit tight."

I sat tight for several hours, even managing a little nap, before Bailey came for me. This time there was no hood. It was dark out, and probably had been for some time. The night was cool and the dew had set. Cam had been crying. A lot. Her face was pinched and red. Moonie looked like a whipped dog. Bailey herded us into the back of the van. "Remember what I said. Don't find yourself up the river," were his parting words as he slammed the doors.

The van got underway. "Cam," I said, "are you okay?"

She made a noise of affirmation.

"I thought you would've escaped," Moonie whispered, "and gone for help."

"What?" I said.

"You were special forces. Didn't they teach you that sort of stuff?"

"I was a fucking medic, not Jason Bourne. This is serious," I hissed. Moonie was partially right. Though I wasn't with the Special Forces, I had been a special operations combat medic, meaning I had done some work the military would call "Special Operations," but that certainly didn't qualify me as some kind of super spy.

"I know this is serious," Moonie replied, offended.

"Good then shut up. They're listening right now." Bailey's words *you could be in a federal supermax by the end of the day* flashed in my mind.

"Oh," he said, and thankfully fell silent.

The van paused, turned and accelerated onto smooth asphalt.

The ride was relatively short, maybe a half hour, before the van stopped and shifted into park.

"Why are we stopping?" Moonie whispered. "Think we're home already?"

"Gas? I don't know," I replied, annoyed partly because I had just gotten kind of comfortable to the point where I could nod off. Another thought crossed my mind. Bailey might not have been bullshitting about federal prison. There were several federal facilities in South Carolina and more in the neighboring states. I strained, listening for the rumble of a prison gate opening, but there was nothing but the sounds of night insects.

The driver flung open the doors. The air that flooded the back of the van wasn't Charleston air—people and cars mixed with the tang of the harbor. It was the sweet smell of cut grass. "Everyone out," he ordered.

"Are we here?" Moonie asked.

"You're here. Get out." The driver wasn't big or stocky, but the way he stood holding the door, like a crouching tiger, he wasn't a man to be messed with. He had the look of a man who knew trouble was going to happen before it happened.

"Go ahead," I prodded the other two who seemed hesitant. "Get going."

We crabbed out into a gravel parking lot, trying to get our bearings. One thing was immediately clear: we weren't in Charleston. Nor did we appear to be in Kansas. It didn't even appear to be civilization, merely the dusty parking lot of a country convenience store. The store was dark except for a neon sign advertising a domestic beer in the window.

"What the hell?" Moonie asked, after completing a quick exploratory three-sixty.

He was met with the sound of the van door slamming and the crunch of tires on gravel.

"Hey!" I yelled after the accelerating van. "Our stuff!" My words died in the night air as the taillights receded and then altogether disappeared. With the taillights went our phones, wallets, and guns. "Dammit!" I shouted, kicking the gravel.

"Where do you suppose we are?" Moonie asked.

I almost strangled him. Again, with the stupid questions. Instead, I walked to the road. The asphalt disappeared in either direction, quickly swallowed up in the blackness. The lines were faded and cracked; it was a road without much traffic or budgetary consideration. Bailey, the bastard, had dropped us nowhere.

"You ever hitched?"

The words startled me. I turned to find Cam standing behind me. She was hidden by the darkness, but her words were calm and measured, the first words I had heard from her since Badgers's apartment.

"Sure," I replied. "Trouble is, we don't know which way we're going."

"Next guy passing by will be able to tell us," she said, matter-of-factly.

I took a deep breath and let it out. "Might be a long wait."

"Might be. Don't suppose you want to knock on a door?" In the distance, maybe a half-mile, was the glow of a house.

"If it was a respectable hour, sure. I don't think it would be a good idea now."

"Agreed," Cam said, plopping on one of the big boulders that formed a perimeter around the parking lot. "Folks tend to get jumpy in the middle of the night."

"They all right to you?"

She looked at me and nodded once before speaking. "Who are they?" For the first time she sounded small.

"My best guess is CIA. Honestly though, I haven't a clue."

"The CIA?"

"Sorry to involve you, but I had no idea this was going to happen."

"What happened?"

"I was doing a favor for my girlfriend and things went sideways." I didn't want to give Cam too much of the limited information I had. It was better for her sake if she was in the dark.

She chewed on that for a moment before saying, "Fine. They asked me about Sam. They asked me about you too. They also asked me some stuff I didn't know what they were talking about—"

"Like what?" I asked interrupting.

She shook her head, "If Sam had taken me places, or I heard him talking about places."

"Like what?"

"Out of state places he may have talked about, if he ever mentioned being in an airport, where he liked to go in Charleston. Stuff like that." She shrugged. "I told them all I know." She paused for a beat swinging her legs like a little kid. "Did they take your blood too?"

"Yup."

"Why?"

"Dunno," I replied, half lying. I honestly didn't know the exact reason, but suspected Samuel Badgers had gotten himself involved in something bad enough that they were threatening to toss civilians into federal prison. We lapsed into silence and listened to the crickets until Moonie joined us and commenced with his blather.

There was no way to tell how much time elapsed, but it felt like two hours elapsed before we saw headlights. Cam, unbidden, hopped up and stuck her thumb out.

***

"Park here," I directed Chester, and he pulled his wheezing 1971 Buick Skylark in front of the funeral home and killed the engine. Matey spied us from his perch on the neighbor's roof ridge. He let out a screech before retreating to the piazza like he was going to announce my presence to Maggie.

"Nice house man," Chester commented, taking in the funeral home.

The look on Cam's face mirrored Chester's. The mansion is grand, even by tony Charleston standards. Erected on the site of Lauren's great-granddaddy's city home that burned during the war, it was built in the classic single house style. Whereas most homes are one room wide, and have the narrow portion facing the street, the Granville mansion stands apart because of its sheer size. It sprawls across three lots with its expansive piazza—Charlstonese for porch—facing Broad Street and wrapping onto Logan. The old carriage house and shop—where freedmen joined caskets and coffins—were torn down in the middle part of the century, and the house was expanded even further and garage bays were added along with a hydraulic lift system to transport the dead to the cellar.

I ushered the group inside and Isabella appeared in the foyer, having heard the bell chime. The look on her face said it all. I had been completely off the grid for 24 hours and showed up with a young girl in lace-up boots and purple hair and a man who looked like a member of the Grateful Dead.

"Welcome back Mr. Clipper."

"Isabella," I said, genuinely grinning at her unease, "could you please get me," I looked at Chester, "What did we agree on? A hundred?"

He nodded eagerly.

"A hundred and fifty from petty cash?"

Isabella didn't bat an eye. "And how would you like me to mark it down?"

"How about executive transportation?" I winked at Chester. He was too busy spending the buck and a half in his head to notice.

"Very well," she said, marching off.

"Do you need a ride?" I asked Cam.

She pulled her gaze from the Granville portraits on the wall. "To where?"

"Where you stay," I said, choosing my words carefully.

"I'm good."

Isabella reappeared, and I gave the money to Chester, who offered his profuse thanks and disappeared before I could reconsider the extra 50.

"Come with me," I said to Cam, and headed back to my office.

I pulled my check register from the desk drawer while Cam carefully studied the items on my bookcase—mostly awards and memorabilia from my military career. I have few family photos to show. There are only three. An old snapshot of myself and Granny when I was about 3 in a little plastic pool in front of her trailer. It's one of only about a dozen photos I have of her. The other is Lauren Granville and I mugging on the golf course, and the most recent addition was a gift from Maggie, a memory from a weekend excursion at a resort on Kiawah.

"I feel bad dragging you into this," I said, scribbling my signature and tearing out the check. It was a big business-sized check. "Two hundred okay?"

She flickered her eyes to the piece of bonded paper in her hand and then back at me. "I don't have a bank account. I'll take less if you have cash."

"I'll have Moonie take you back," I said, feeling foolish. Of course, she didn't have a bank account. "Endorse it on the back and he'll cash it for you. Sorry, but the guy that kidnapped us has my wallet, and Chester cleaned out the petty cash."

"How do you do that?"

I took it, flipped it over and tapped the line. "Sign here," I said, handing her a pen.

She scrawled her name, folded it twice and jammed it in her pocket. As if remembering her manners, she said, "Thanks. Who's that," she asked, pointing to the vacation shot.

"My girlfriend Mags," I said slipping the register back in the drawer. "She's been kidnapped by those people too. I was with her. This was my second time."

"Seriously?" Her expression said she thought I was pulling her leg.

I nodded. "Seriously. It's becoming a regular thing."

She laughed, exposing perfect orthodontistry. "I'm sorry, it's just—" She waved a hand.

"No, you're good." My face flushed.

We found Moonie helping himself to coffee in the break room.

"How old is that?" I asked.

Moonie took a sip and rolled it around like a sommelier. "Maybe a day?"

I thought of the pot I made before meeting Moonie the morning before. "Pour me a cup please," I said. "Also, can you take Cam back to Bushville?"

"What about my van?"

"It's the other direction. I'll take you to get it after you take her."

His scar turned white; that wasn't the answer he wanted to hear, but he poured me a cup of coffee and followed me to the garage without protest. The van was gone; Nikki must be off on a removal. "You'll have to take the hearse," I said, putting the door up.

"Seriously?" Cam said, staring at the brand new gleaming S&S Victoria coach. She seemed to be partial to asking "seriously."

"There's nobody in there," I assured her, liberating the mug out of Moonie's hand. I didn't want him spilling coffee all over the interior. "And for Christ's sake," I told him, "don't pull into the bank parking lot in that."

"What bank?"

"You're going to cash a check for Cam."

Moonie saluted.

Cam settled stiffly into the plush interior, and I waved as Moonie backed down the driveway.

I was at my desk about halfway through the cold cup of coffee when Nikki poked her head in.

"Where have you been?"

"I ran into my buddy Jimmy Bailey again."

"No!"

"Seriously."

"Is this going to become a standing appointment?"

"If he wants to start paying for the privilege, sure. Otherwise, I hope it's the last time a hood gets thrown over my head and I get tossed into a van."

Nikki fixed me with a faux serious stare. "Sounds kinda kinky. I might want to join in." She motioned her head toward the hallway. "C'mon. You can tell me about it while we embalm."

"Perfect," I said, swilling the remainder of the coffee, grateful for an excuse to be finished with the financial report. "I'll be right with you. I have to make a call."

"Hotapp," the detective said, answering on the first ring.

"Tripp Clipper," I said.

"Yeah?" she said, sounding distracted.

"I was scooped up by the same guy."

"Really?" Her voice shifted in the receiver. I had her full attention.

I recounted the story to her. Hotapp stopped me when I got to the part about locating Badgers's apartment. "Wait, you entered the victim's residence?" She didn't sound happy.

"The landlord said the police had already been there. We assumed it was you."

She snorted. "It wasn't." Clearly, she was displeased Moonie and I had out-detected her.

I finished the story and gave Hotapp the address of Badgers's apartment and cautioned her, "They're watching the building."

"I hope so," she said. From the tone of her voice, it sounded like she was going to round up a posse and try to pick a fight.

"And another thing," I said.

"Yeah?" she said, now trying to get me off the phone.

"They're definitely worried about something that has to do with Badgers and the other guy. They did the vitals and blood work thing again."

She paused. "Interesting. And I think your Bailey friend knows who J.D. 2 is."

"Yeah?"

"His prints are in AFIS, but they're blocked. You need clearance to access the record. I have the captain filing a request." There was a noise in the background. "Gotta go." The line went dead.

Chapter 11

"What happened to him?" I asked, unzipping the light duty pouch provided by MUSC. A young man stared up at me; his eyes hazed over and opaque like marbles. He looked about my age, plus or minus a few years, fit and healthy—or had been until recently—and prosperous. Expensive haircut and his fingernails were well trimmed and clean. "Drugs?" A reasonable guess. Drug-related deaths had gone up every single year since I started in this profession, and there seemed to be no signs of slowing down, even if CPD was now equipped with Narcan.

"I don't believe so. Maggie did the case. I saw her there—"

"I need to call her!" I exclaimed. I had completely forgotten to let her know I was back.

"Call her," Nikki said, waving her hand toward the phone. "I'm sure she's worried sick."

I dialed the prep room phone as Nikki went to the antique wooden hutch where the embalming fluid is stored and selected a half dozen different bottles with assorted colored liquids in them. After several rings Maggie's cheerful sounding cover clicked on. "Hey, it's me," I said, watching Nikki dump a bottle into the glass tank of the embalming machine. "I'm back. Sorry. I'm sure you were worried, but our buddy Bailey and his band of merry men," I purposely left out the merry men were brandishing automatic weapons, "picked me up again. This time he wasn't kind enough to drop me off. I had to hitchhike home. Call me." I hung up. Nikki turned the selector on the machine to MIX.

Taking an aneurysm hook and scissors from the instrument tray, I began pulling out the temporary stitching put in by the pathology assistant. "You were saying?"

"Oh yeah," Nikki said. She had a hook and scissors and began snipping the bridge sutures in his scalp. "Maggie said this case is idiopathic until the tox comes back. But she doesn't think its drugs. There are no signs of drug abuse. This guy is 29, a chiropractor in West Ashley. Been practicing about a year. A very active person. Played lacrosse for Clemson and ran marathons for fun in his free time."

I made a face. "Marathons? I can't think of anything less fun. Several miles are good to stay trim, but 26? Barbaric."

Nikki ignored me. "His girlfriend brought him in Monday." She stopped and looked up like she was trying to remember the details. "He was complaining of cramping, diarrhea, nausea and...vomiting. They did a workup and it was shigellosis."

"And?" I said, finishing pulling the stitching out, removing his breastplate and the bag of organs, slick with blood and fluid.

"They started him on something. Prince something or other—"

"Principen?"

Nikki retracted his scalp by pulling it down over his face until it rested on his chin and removed the calvarium. The skullcap was notched like a puzzle piece. "Yeah, that sounds right. Anyhow, whatever they put him on seemed to work. He started to get better and then he started to get much worse. They couldn't figure out what was wrong. The *Shigella* infection was under control, or so they thought."

"Interesting," I said, stepping back so Nikki could access the blood vessels in the thoracic cavity. At this point in her internship she was doing most of the work and I was there to offer guidance.

The intercom buzzed. "Mr. Clipper?"

"Yeah?" I always felt like I had to shout to get my voice around the mask.

"A package just arrived for you from FedEx."

I looked at my bloody gloves; I wasn't ungowning. "Can you open it?"

There was a long silence before Isabella came back on. "It's your and Deputy Wise's wallets, some phones, two guns, and a few other items."

Bailey! I stabbed the button. "What's the return address?"

"Wingo's Market in Smoaks."

The darkened sign above the neon beer sign flashed in my mind. The gas station Bailey's henchman dropped us. Hilarious.

"Thank you, Isabella. When Moonie gets back please give him his stuff."

"Very good sir."

Chapter 12

Isabella flagged me down as I climbed the stairs to my apartment, "Can you pin Mr. Kyle's death certificate and I'll get Ms. Adcock to pick them up?"

I nodded and wearily lumbered down the stairs. Isabella refuses to accept my pin credentials, insisting I do every death certificate. It's a stupid four-digit passcode, much like an ATM login, that puts my name on an electronic death certificate, not the nuclear football. But Isabella is a stickler for the rules.

She already had the screen pulled up on her monitor to the spot I needed to be, but I tabbed over to see cause of death. Cachexia. That's fancy medical jargon for wasting syndrome. Due to osteosarcoma. Duration: Twenty-nine months. Contributory cause: Dysentery. Duration: 1 day.

He put up a good fight. Two and a half years. The cancer wasted him away to nothing, and the diarrhea sped things along at the end. I tabbed back, pecked in my pin, and submitted.

"Thank you," Isabella said.

I grunted and skedaddled before she could saddle me with any paperwork.

"Who's there?" Matey screeched as I opened the door to the apartment.

I found Maggie crouching on a drop cloth carefully cutting in with a paintbrush. "I was so worried!" she said, springing up and bear hugging me. "I got your message." She pulled away and stood tiptoe for a kiss.

"I know. I'm sorry. He took my phone again."

"Is he serious?" There was a rare look of fury on her face. There was a fleck of gray paint on her glasses. "What was it this time? Did you jaywalk?"

I almost cringed. Maggie may be the smartest person I know, but her humor is a little dry. "Moonie and I were in Badgers's apartment—which he was surveilling—and his henchmen swooped in mad as hell."

"What?" she said waving the brush. "I thought you told me last night Badgers was an indigent?"

"We stopped at Bushville and ran into this homeless girl—"

"Bushville?"

"A homeless encampment near the Ravenel Bridge. Anyhow, this girl said Badgers was working at the mall, and had a place."

"Couldn't the police run that down? I mean, if he had a place?"

"That's the odd thing. The lease isn't in his name, but Bailey was able to run the place down all the same *and* have it staked out."

"What were you doing there in the first place?" Her voice had an edge. "I thought Bailey told you to lay off."

"Yeah, no shit," I said, thinking about the federal prison threat.

"No shit! No shit!" Matey shrieked.

I gave the bird the bird.

"Clip!" Maggie scolded. "That's not nice."

"Sorry." I lowered the finger. "Koziner ordered Moonie to establish identities for both the John Does, so he can prove to Columbia he's doing his due diligence and trying to clean this mess up. Apparently, you're issuing some sort of provisional death certificate?" She nodded. "So, Moonie thought we could find someone who could finger John Doe 2, a mutual friend, acquaintance, or something. Moonie wanted backup going to Bushville, and I felt like I owed him after losing his bodies."

"Poor thing," Maggie said, running her hand over my day's stubble.

"I'll live."

"No shit! No shit!" Matey squawked.

I kissed Maggie again, glared at the bird then ducked into the kitchen. My hand lingered on the coconut water before grabbing a Palmetto Lager. My nerves were shot. Snatching an extra drop cloth, I tossed it over the peanut gallery's cage, popped the beer, and sank onto the covered couch. "Why'd you even bother? Don't you want to get rid of this thing?"

"We can't put it out on the curb covered in paint," she answered, back on the floor, concentrating on not getting paint on the baseboard. The tip of her tongue stuck out the side of her mouth. Thankfully, her cutoff sweatpants were cut too short and her paint-splattered halter-top was too revealing. I could watch this show all day. "It drives me crazy that that jerk can just basically abduct people with impunity," she commented.

I decided to let the paint-covered-couch comment pass. Some things were above my pay grade. "You can thank bin Laden and all his cronies. National security has gotten a little Gestapo-*esque* thanks to those assholes." I took a sip of icy beer. It tasted good. "Tell me something. How many people die of dysentery each year?"

"In the U.S. or worldwide?"

"Here, in the U.S.

"Maybe 1,500, why?"

"Just wondering. I saw it on this guy's death certificate and can't remember ever recalling seeing it before as a cause of death. It sounds so Civil War."

"It still happens, but it's rare. When it does happen it's usually with immunocompromised folks or the elderly."

"Makes sense. This guy was both. But tell me about the chiropractor, Mark Owens. Nikki told me when he was admitted he was diagnosed with shigellosis." I was a little rusty with some things from my medic days, but I did recall the *Shigella* bacterium is one of the causes of dysentery.

"Yeah, but that was treated with Principen and cleared up. I'm fairly confident he died from something else." She turned from her painting. "What are you getting at? Do you think they're related?"

"I'm just saying."

"Did the death certificate say what caused the dysentery? It could've been viral, bacterial, amoebic, or parasitic."

"No."

Maggie laughed, a low chuckle like she had heard a joke. "They're not related. I can promise you that. There are over a half a million cases of shigellosis—that are *reported*, probably many more—each year in the U.S. alone, and only a handful progress to the point of patient death. I seriously doubt we're on the brink of a dysentery outbreak in Charleston."

I held up my hands. "I know." Dysentery is common in third-world countries where food and water sources easily get contaminated with feces. "But the thought crossed my mind. Seemed coincidental."

"I don't know what that causative agent for your death certificate was, but a culture revealed Dr. Owens to be infected with *Shigella dysenteriae*. He competed in a triathlon on James Island on Saturday," she recited, like she was reading from the chart, still methodically painting. Maggie has an almost eidetic memory, so in her mind she was reading from the chart. "The water he was swimming in is fed by the Stono River, the suspected point of infection. He began complaining Sunday midday, and by suppertime the pain had become so bad his girlfriend brought him in. He was treated with 500 milligrams q.i.d. of Principen. Symptoms were much better the following day, Tuesday. Wednesday morning his fever spiked accompanied by severe headache. Labs revealed leukopenia. Dr. Owens was treated with steroids."

"Leukopenia? Odd." It's a condition when the bones don't produce enough white-blood cells.

She nodded. "Which is why I don't think it's directly related to the shigellosis. I believe Dr. Owens had an undiagnosed autoimmune disease that may have been exacerbated by catching a nasty bacterium during his triathlon."

Draining the Palmetto, I said, "Excellent theory Dr. Stryker." I stood up to get another beer and my phone dinged with a text. It was Nikki. "Gotta head downstairs for a minute."

"Wait," she said, unfolding herself off the floor. "I have a surprise for you."

"Do you?" I was very interested.

"I'm taking you out to dinner tonight." I was still getting used to some Yankee parlances like calling 'supper' 'dinner'.

"Are you?"

"For our six-month anniversary. Poogan's Porch." The location of our first date.

"That's thoughtful."

"I made the reservation early, 6:30, because I need to be in early tomorrow." She made a pouty face. "Tonight's a school night. So," she slapped my ass, "you need to be showered and ready to leave by quarter of."

"Yes ma'am," I replied, helping myself to another beer and heading downstairs.

There's a small porch on the back of the funeral home, next to the garage, and adjacent to a set of stairs leading up to the apartment. That's where I found Nikki, her son Jackson, and Jackson's father Risden.

"Hey pal," I said high-fiving the 11-year old. Blond haired, Jackson boasts delicate features, clearly inherited from his mother's side.

"Clip!" Jackson said.

"What are you doing out of school?"

He shrugged.

"In service day," Nikki said. The look on her face said she was thrilled for there to be no school after a whole summer of juggling her and Risden's work schedules to watch him. "Do you mind?"

"Not at all." I love having the boy around the funeral home, though Nikki thinks I'm just being tolerant. If it's a slow day, I'll battle Jackson in *Call of Duty* on PlayStation or if there's body work to be done, I'll give him a couple bucks to do chores. He's saving up for a pair of shoes and jumps at the chance to earn money. "Here," I said, fishing in my pocket and retrieving a five spot. "Can you go pull the weeds out of the front flower beds for me?"

His eyes got big at the sight of the money, and he looked at his mother who nodded. The money disappeared into his fist.

"You know where the lawn bags are in the garage."

Jackson nodded and darted into the garage, emerging moments later and disappearing, bag in hand.

"I've got some stuff to finish up," Nikki said, letting herself into the funeral home.

Risden looked around like someone might be listening. He'd been undercover too long. "I heard you were gone last night."

"Yeah," I said, and pulled out a tin of Copenhagen.

Risden involuntarily flexed. "Bailey?"

I was busy stuffing a wad into my mouth and merely nodded.

"I had to kick it upstairs to my boss. I don't have the clearances to make those sort of inquiries. There's nobody in Homeland Security by the name of James Bailey. To be thorough, he also ran the name against DIA, DOJ, and our personnel at the DEA. There's a financial fraud specialist with OIG who is a Charles James Bailey if your guy is a 57-year-old African American."

The Office of Inspector General is the arm of the Department of Justice that employs investigative agents. Charles James Bailey didn't seem to fit the bill. I shook my head, and Risden continued, "I didn't think so. So, bottom line. Your guy, Bailey doesn't exist, which adds credence to your theory that he's a spook."

"So much for not being able to operate on American soil."

He snorted. "Could be DOD. They can be just as sneaky as the spooks. What did he want this time?"

"Same as last time. Drove me to the same location. Issued the same threats. Got poked by a guy in a lab coat."

"Did he scoop you off the street?"

"I was helping Moonie run down some information for Koziner. Bailey had one of the John Does—a guy named Badgers— apartment staked out. Actually," I said, "do you want his fingerprints?" The comment about Badgers had jarred my memory.

"Whose? John Doe's?"

"No. Bailey's."

"How did you get the guy's fingerprints?"

I smiled and held up a finger, disappearing inside. I reappeared wearing a latex glove and holding my phone. "The screen looks like a spider web, but I bet you can pull some prints off the case."

"If there's a print on it my tech will be able to pull it off," he assured me. "It really pisses me off that this guy is playing on my field and not even bothering with a courtesy call."

"You think its drugs?"

Risden made a face. "It's always *drugs,*" he replied, reminding me of the parable about asking a barber if you need a haircut. With Risden it's *always* drugs. "Come on, two guys don't just shoot it out over nothing. The only thing that's going to get two guys that hot is money. And the only thing generating that kind of money are narcotics."

I inverted the glove so it covered the phone and handed it to him.

"I'll have someone drop it by later tonight or first thing in the morning. I know how much you rely on these things," he said, pocketing the phone.

I grinned and slapped his shoulder. It was like slapping a marble statue. "You're a good egg."

***

"Here," Maggie said pulling a small blue box tied up with a thick red ribbon from her clutch and sliding it across the white linen tablecloth.

"What's this?" I asked, fingering the box—heavy, bonded cardboard. The restaurant's courtyard was dim, the sun an orange melting pat of butter on the horizon throwing long shadows. Maggie's expression, partially obscured by her hair, brushed out and expertly curled, was unreadable.

She picked up her wineglass and took a sip. "It made me think of you."

I untied the substantial ribbon and lifted a thin velvet box out, a little larger than a deck of cards. The box snapped open like a clamshell. Nestled inside the white satin interior were two small silver shovel cufflinks.

"Turn them over."

I undid the strap and turned a shovel over, squinting in the low light. There, etched to the underside of the shovel's blade was CLIP.

Maggie giggled. "I told the woman those were your initials. That you had two middle names. I figured you'd want that rather than your real initials. Do you like them?"

I felt the same sensation I did the day my captain called me into his office in Iraq to tell me Granny—the only family I had in the world—died. It felt like I was trying to swallow my fist. Sure, Lauren Granville had treated me like a son, but nobody had ever given me a gift with such sentiment. Really, aside from some military memorabilia I didn't have any personal effects.

I nodded, swallowed the lump, and managed to croak, "They're perfect Mags."

There was a flash of white, a knowing smile, and she tipped the glass back.

"What's the occasion?"

"A girl doesn't need to have an occasion, but if you need one it's because I'm happy with our current situation."

It hadn't been a week cohabitation yet, but I was quick to add, "Me too."

"Really?"

"Of course."

Maggie opened her mouth, only to close it when the server bustled up to the table. "Made some decisions?" she asked.

We ordered, and after the server departed, I said, "You were saying?"

"Oh, nothing," Maggie said, waving her hand.

What remained unsaid was the fact Maggie was halfway through her fellowship. If there wasn't a reason to stay in Charleston she'd return to her family and friends in Chicago.

***

"Who's this?" Maggie asked, tracing her finger along the new ink on my forearm, a Byzantine-looking portrait of Jesus being carried to his tomb.

It was much later than was reasonable for a work night. After supper, we walked Waterfront Park eating ice cream like tourists, and watching boat lights winking in the harbor. "You have some ice cream on your lip," Maggie had said, as we sat on a park bench in the dark, her tongue darting out lizard-like, eyes smoky. Things unraveled quickly. We groped and fumbled like a couple of kids on prom night, and barely made it back to the funeral home. Our clothes still lay in a pile in the foyer downstairs. The first round was frenzied and quick. We migrated upstairs and the second round was slow and methodical, until the chill of the evening set in and drove us inside where we currently lay tangled in post-coital bliss.

"Joseph of Arimathea. The patron saint of undertakers." I rolled over, grabbed a tin of tobacco from the nightstand.

"Clip," she said.

I sighed and released the tin.

"Are you religious?"

I laughed. "Outside of work, not particularly. As far as I can recall, Granny didn't have me baptized."

"And these?" she asked, tracing a line of stars along the underside of my forearm.

"The guys—" The room started to shrink. I closed my eyes and took a deep breath. "The guys that were able to make it home because of—" Heart hammering, I sat up and swung my legs off the bed, rising unsteadily. Nobody, not even my shrink, knew about the stars. It was something I kept for me.

Maggie propped herself up on an elbow, the sheet falling. "Where are you going?"

My heart was hammering so hard I thought it would explode out of my chest. I was sweating. Not the hot, sweaty sex sweat, but a sheen of clammy moisture. My brain screamed for me to get out of the room before the walls collapsed inward. "Just need a...drink," I managed, trying to hide my panic.

Maggie reached out and took my hand and firmly pulled me down, wrapping both arms around me and hugging me. "It's okay," she said softly, one hand brushing the stars lightly. When she felt me stop trembling her lips brushed my ear. "I love you."

I've only ever said that to two people. One actually wasn't a person, rather a mangy mutt named Rebel that lived two trailers down from Granny. More accurately, Rebel lived under the trailer. She was an ugly thing that took a shine to me and followed me to elementary school every day and waited in the woods until the last bell and followed me home. Out of the blue one day I told Rebel I loved her. I meant it. The day she was killed on 158 I wept bitterly and couldn't eat for days. The other person was my granny.

I'm sure someone old fashioned like Isabella whispers with her bridge club, or whatever rich old ladies do, about Maggie and I living in sin. She'd be horrified to know Maggie and I started playing house without even exchanging "I love you's." But it works for us. This relationship hasn't had a roadmap with waypoints mapped out ahead of time.

Turning, I brushed a strand of hair out of her face. The attack had left a pit in my gut, but I felt calm. At ease. Smiling, I added a third person to the list.

The normally present insomnia wasn't a problem. We fell into a fitful sleep in each other's arms.

Chapter 13

The day started off great with back-to-back death calls. I fielded them from my kitchen table, drinking coconut water mixed with a scoop of whey protein and reading the stocks—what I call the obituary page.

The first call was a woman. She sounded young. She was calling on behalf of her sister, whose husband was dead. I took the information, set an appointment, and as soon as I hung up the phone rang again. "Granville and Sons," I said, thinking it was the previous caller with a forgotten question. No. It was a different woman. More distraught than the first.

"My—" she said, pausing, taking a breath and starting again. "My sister's dead."

I switched gears from brisk and businesslike to compassionate and launched into the tricky business of navigating this woman's grief. After gathering the information, and setting an appointment, I finished my coconut water, texted Nikki, and went to find something funereal to wear.

I found Nikki in the driveway sitting in the hearse. Tapping the glass, she buzzed the window down, her eyes hidden by immense Jackie O sunglasses. "Put her away." Nikki cocked her head, so I added, "We have a twofer pickup. We'll need the van." Both cots can't fit inside the hearse, but there's plenty of room inside the van.

She made the swap and moments later we were on our way to Roper Hospital. We stopped at the front door and Nikki disappeared inside to sign us out. I hopped into the driver's seat and drove around back. I parked between skids of stock and piles of old medical equipment and loitered near the dumpsters until Nikki emerged with our hospital escort, a member of the security team. So engrossed in conversation, they didn't acknowledge me, merely swung the door open. The escort was the reason I brought Nikki. Middle-aged, red faced and imperious, the bastard makes me wait forever when I come alone. Not Nikki. There could be a gunman on the loose in the hospital but this guy will drop everything for her.

I trailed them through the rabbit warren of hallways, the escort prattling on, "...So I say to him, I ain't going to throw you that towline until you throw me a cold one."

Nikki laughed and put her hand on his shoulder, "Oh Chuck, you are too much!"

Oh yes Chuckie, you are.

I wasn't quite sure it had even been a joke but Chuck laughed and added, "You'll have to come out on my boat sometime. It's a blast."

You know you're close by the smell. The morgue is near the kitchen. It's about as palatable as the stinking dumpsters out back. Chuck stopped short and jangled his jailer's key ring. "After you," he said, selecting a substantial key, not dissimilar from the one found on Samuel Badgers, and holding the door for Nikki. He didn't bother to hide his ogling as she breezed in.

I played hide and seek amongst the white sheeted gurneys in the reefer, checking tags affixed to the pouch zippers until I found Frances Tidwell. Chuck continued to regale Nikki and ignore me while I unzipped the pouch to check the armband, the Holy Grail of identification. Escorts can mix up bag tags, but the bracelet is issued at the time the patient checks in. Frances Tidwell looked to be in her mid-50s and other than being dead, looked, dare I say healthy. There were no signs of recent surgery or trauma. Aside from the IV line, there weren't any other visible medical devices. Roper had obviously been treating her for something or there would've been an autopsy to determine cause of death.

I zipped the pouch, transferred the remains to the cot, and signed myself out.

"Ready?" I asked, rudely interrupting Chuck in the middle of another knee-slapping yarn.

Chuck shot me a dirty look, but I didn't care.

"Sure," Nikki said.

Chuck gallantly led the way. Outside, I loaded the cot, and got into the driver's seat, waiting for Chuck to detach.

Nikki climbed in the van and pulled her shades down off the top of her head. "What a sad man."

"I think it's rude, him hitting on you in front of me. We could be together for all he knows."

She smiled. "I think it'd crush him."

"Good point. You want to stay in good graces with your morgue angel."

She hooked her fingers in her shades and pulled them down an inch so she could peer over them. "Morgue angel? You're fucked up, you know that?" I nodded, and she held out a piece of paper. "My *morgue angel* gave me his digits. Want them?"

I shifted the van into gear and pulled away. "Maybe. He's quite the catch. I understand he has a yacht." I pointed. "Wave bye-bye to Chuckie."

Nikki raised her hand. Chuckie stood at the loading dock waving like a simpleton. Poor guy was going to jump every time his phone rang for the next few days.

It's about a minute-and-a-half drive from Roper to MUSC. I left Nikki in the van with Ms. Tidwell to, as the Irish say, observe the proprieties.

I signed out in Health Information Services, and returned to the pathology lab where I was buzzed in. The smell of burnt carbon smacked me in the face as soon as I stepped in the lab. Maggie was busy weighing some organs on a scale that looks comparable to the produce scale at the grocery store. Her boss, Dr. Terri Marcislin, paused from her work at the next table where she was busy snapping a ribcage with a bypass lopper—basically, a branch pruner—and waved. Maggie murmured something to her assistant, and broke away from the table, herding me toward a corner of the lab like a sheepdog.

"Who are you here for?" she asked. Blood flecks dotted her face shield.

"Grey Balling."

I didn't like the look on her face.

"Something's going on," she whispered.

"With what?"

"There's a buzz going around the hospital. Almost 30 people have been admitted in the past two days complaining of bowel-related symptoms."

"As in dysentery?"

"I don't know firsthand. Some of the labs are still being processed, but yes, it sounds like shigellosis."

I took a step back. "Are you serious? *All* of them are bacterial dysentery?"

Maggie stood with her hands held in front of her gown like she was worried about a sterile field. She nodded gravely. "It would appear so. This afternoon my department is going to have a roundtable and discuss Mark Owens. It seems I may have been a little presumptive with the conclusions I shared with you last night." She craned her head in Dr. Marcislin's direction, almost as if to double check she wasn't trying to eavesdrop. Dr. Marcislin probably wouldn't be too happy with her fellow sharing patient information.

"This guy, Grey's sister-in-law called. She sounded young. Is he?"

Maggie nodded. "Forty-one. He's one of them who was admitted with shigellosis. Doc Marc did the prosection. Nothing unusual except some encephalitis which would explain the seizures."

"Did he have a history?"

She shook her head. "No, not of seizures, and no documented trauma to his head that would cause the swelling."

"Viral?" Most encephalitis, if not caused by physical trauma, is viral. And it usually isn't fatal.

She shook her head again. "Doc Marc sent a sample to the lab for a rush immunoassay. Came back negative."

"That's odd."

"No kidding. He was treated for dysentery, seemed to get better, and all of a sudden started having violent seizures. I don't know if Doc Marc found anything else. I haven't read her notes. The only reason I know about the swelling is she called me over to show it to me."

I pursed my lips. This sounded like the beginnings of an outbreak. I had seen an epidemic firsthand, and it wasn't pretty. While physically devastating to the population, it's the psychological effects that are scarier. It leaves everyone immobilized, thinking: *who's next?*

I was stationed in Mosul and ordered out to a collection of huts near Ayn al-Jahesh to assist with a typhoid outbreak. I'm sure the village had a name, but to us it was just coordinates on a map. Five villagers were already dead and scores more lay ill.

While my escort lounged around the Humvees chugging water to stay ahead of the heat, listening to the radio chatter, I checked on several villagers and gave the elders antibiotics to treat the worst cases. Through my interpreter, Malid, they declined my offer of vaccination, suspicious of taking injections from Westerners.

There's a vaccine for typhoid in pill form, but it's a four-pill regimen that must be taken in a proscribed manner, one that I wasn't confident they would take according to my directions. The injection is one and done. They wouldn't hear of it. There were so many ill, old men and boys carried the *kafan*-shrouded bodies through the streets to graves scratched out in the rocky soil.

I didn't want to say outbreak. Instead I said, "How serious is the administration taking this?"

"We've alerted DHEC and the CDC." She looked over her shoulder. Dr. Marcislin had finished clipping and was busy pulling glistening organs out. "The CDC is on their way now."

"Dysentery case?"

"Dr. Marc is working one. I'm working on a coroner's case. Guy decided to continue golfing during a lightning storm."

Suddenly, the smell made sense. I couldn't help it. I smiled. "Ever see *Caddy Shack?*"

Maggie rolled her eyes. "Stephanie will help you sign out the body," she said waving her arm at her assistant. "I need to get back to my case."

"Hold her off. I'll be back in a minute."

I couldn't stop thinking *outbreak* walking through the hospital's bowels to retrieve a surgical mask, gown, and extra pair of gloves from the van.

Back at the funeral home we placed the cots on the ancient elevator and sent them down to the cellar. "Why don't you knock off for chow," I suggested.

"I'll be down in minute. I just have yogurt and crackers."

"Isabella never came in today. Why don't you answer the phone and work on paperwork when you're done your lunch?"

"It's okay. I'll give you a hand."

She wasn't getting the hint, so I laid down the hammer. "Please answer the phone. I'm going to do this alone."

Nikki waved her hand. "There are two cases. Don't be ridiculous. It won't take long if we both tackle them."

"Mags thinks there may be something going around. They've been catching a lot of dysentery cases recently. It could be infectious."

"That's what Universal Precautions are for."

"Nik, you have a son at home. Just let me do these, okay?"

Her face, usually softness and charm, hardened, "I've done infectious cases before."

True, Nikki had done a couple of AIDS and Hepatitis C cases, but this was different. I placed my hands on her shoulders. "We know how to deal with those diseases." She started to open her mouth and I cut her off, "More importantly we know *what* we're dealing with. Until the CDC figures out what's going on, I don't want to expose both of us unnecessarily. I understand your dedication, and I appreciate it, but you have a child who depends on you. I can't have something like that on my conscience."

She worked her jaw slowly, tensing for a fight, and then all at once I felt her shoulders go slack. "Thank you." She locked eyes with me. "Be careful."

"I will," with more bravado than I felt. "I'm sure it's nothing." The two people lying on the elevator were proof it was more than nothing.

I started with the Roper case first, Frances Tidwell. Placing an absorbent pad on the embalming table, I pulled the hospital pouch onto the table. The pad is not unlike the ones used by auto mechanics to absorb oil, and typically used by embalmers in cases of skin donation. The pad would catch any stray fluids not caught by the drain line running into the sink.

After stoppering the drain of the slop sink, I sprayed the outside of the pouch with a professional grade disinfectant that's like Lysol on steroids before even opening the pouch. I repeated with the spray disinfectant after opening the pouch, and then used cotton soaked in a phenol solution to plug up any orifices before even moving her remains. The mystery bug could be residing in her respiratory tract, and my moving the remains could cause it to be expelled from her airway. After discarding the pouch, I washed the remains with a commercial grade germicidal soap and commenced the embalming process.

A typical embalming solution is 2% formaldehyde. Playing it safe, I more than doubled that when I mixed up the fluids in the machine's tank to ensure thorough disinfection of tissues. At the conclusion of the process, I poured a gallon of bleach into the stoppered sink and let it mix with the blood while I carefully, stitched everything up.

I had to pee but didn't want to run the risk of tracking any contaminants out of the prep room, so put my discomfort aside, and began to repeat the process again on Grey Balling.

When he was complete, I immersed all the instruments in a cold chemical sterile tray, wiped all surfaces down with bleach, and backed out of the room spraying the disinfectant. At the door, I sprayed the outside of my suit, then removed my Tyvek coverall, mask, booties, apron, and outer gloves, sealed them in a Biohazard box and sprayed the box. Only when I was in the little locker room did I remove the respirator and second pair of gloves. After swapping out the filter, I scrubbed out at the utility sink with a pink industrial soap that contains exfoliators until my hands and forearms were raw.

"Everything okay?" Nikki asked, meeting me at the top of the stairs.

"Fine, you should shove off for the day." I didn't feel fine. In fact, I felt a little queasy.

"I can stay. Risden has Jackson for the evening."

"Go. Enjoy yourself."

"Another call came in while you were downstairs." Nikki paused and brushed a strand of hair out of her face. "Another from Roper."

I had changed into shorts and a sleeveless undershirt, and rubbed my hand absentmindedly over my bicep "Oh?"

"They aren't releasing the body."

"Until when?"

"The exact words the woman in Medical Records used were, 'a temporary and indefinite hold.'"

I squeezed my bicep until it hurt. "Jesus Christ."

Nikki nodded. "I know. What's going on?" Her eyes flicked behind me to the cellar. There was something in them that very well may have been fear.

I sighed. "Nothing's going to be accomplished by wringing our hands here. So why don't you head on home. Tomorrow's a new day."

I drained my bladder and re-hydrated with two coconut waters. Sitting on the piazza, I was able to catch a few breaths of fresh air and the nauseous feeling abated, replaced with dread. The words "indefinite hold" kept repeating in my mind. The CDC had arrived and was starting to lock things down.

Chapter 14

Ethel, Isabella's housekeeper, called just as I was returning from my morning run. It seems ridiculous that a secretary has a full-time housekeeper, but Isabella needs to work like I need another tattoo. Her late husband was old Charleston money. Isabella started as his actual secretary—apparently their marriage scandalized Charleston society—and returned to work after their only son was killed in Vietnam. She continues to work out of habit, and I suspect to keep an eye on her husband's legacy.

"Mrs. Granville asked me to phone and let you know she won't be in. She isn't feeling well."

It took me a moment to interpret Ethel's Gullah—a Lowcountry dialect that almost sounds Caribbean. When I did, a bloom of fear materialized in my gut. "What's wrong?" I asked, trying to sound as casual as possible.

There was a pause, and I imagined Ethel checking to make sure she was out of Isabella's earshot. "She's got the skitters."

I gripped the phone and tried to remain as calm and rational sounding as possible. "Ethel, listen to me carefully. You need to get Isabella to a hospital as quickly as possible."

"Why? She's got a little sumpthin', that's it. Mrs. Granville will be fine in a day or two." Ethel had raised six children. There wasn't much that alarmed her, especially not a little fever and diarrhea.

"She won't be. Trust me on this one Ethel. I'm calling an ambulance."

There was a long pause on the other end of the line. Finally, Ethel said, "Mrs. Granville isn't going to like this. Not one bit."

"Call me when you know what hospital they're taking her to. Tell Isabella I'll explain everything to her in the hospital." I hung up before she could argue any more about the ambulance.

My heart racing, I dialed the non-emergency line and had an ambulance dispatched to her house in Old Village. I sat at my kitchen table, heart racing, and not from the jog. *It could be she caught a little something like Ethel said. I'm overreacting,* I told myself, as I helped myself to a coconut water from the refrigerator. I prayed I was overreacting, but knew I wasn't. Another death call had come in during the night. The decedent was at the Veterans Medical Center. Release was pending. I was quite sure what pending meant and had asked the details clerk who snapped at me, "Pending means until we say it's released."

Appreciate the clarification ma'am, I thought, and mustered a polite response. Fear was beginning to spread. The administration had received some scary and confusing orders from the CDC, and the blowback was trickling down the ranks in the form of irritability and anger.

I showered and was waiting in the foyer for Grey Balling's family to arrive when a blocked number appeared on my spider-webbed screen. "Yeah?"

"It's me," Risden said. He didn't waste time with pleasantries. "Got some news. It isn't good." I waited for him to continue. "We ran the set of prints pulled off your phone. The system hit on them, but they're classified. No real surprise there. A lot of government guys have files you need special access to see the file. A dead end. The interesting thing was within 15 minutes of hitting on this file, my boss received a call from DOD. He kicked the call down to me, and I had to explain the situation to someone in Washington who told me to lose the prints and forget all about them."

"You think its spooks?"

"I don't know," Risden admitted. "I've never dealt with the CIA."

I spied a gaggle of people mounting the piazza stairs. "Gotta go," I said. "My appointment is here." I jammed the phone into my pocket just as the doorbell rang.

"Welcome," I said, effusive and sympathetic. "The Balling family?"

A middle-aged woman with her arm around a young woman, both with puffy eyes and tear stained cheeks said, "This is my daughter, Grey's widow."

I took the widow's hands and ushered her in. A dumpy man, who wasn't introduced, and didn't introduce himself, trailed the women in. I assumed him to be the widow's father. By the look on his face he'd rather be anywhere else in the world right now, maybe even dead himself.

"Would you like to spend some time with your husband before we take care of business?" I asked Mrs. Balling. It is a normal course of business for me to have the decedent laid out in our slumber room—essentially a small viewing room—for the family to view prior to making the funeral arrangements. It takes the emotional edge off the experience once they see their loved one laid out peacefully and calms everyone down.

Mrs. Balling nodded and squeezed her eyes shut. Silent tears fell.

"Follow me," I said motioning down a hallway.

"I'll wait here," the man announced plopping on a sofa and picking up an informational brochure.

Mother held her daughter under her armpit like she needed help walking to the slumber room. Grey was waiting on a dressing table with a blanket draped from his neck down. I left mother and her wailing daughter in the room with several glasses of water and plenty of tissues. When I returned to the lobby a man with big glasses and John Lennon hair, from his Bed-In era, had joined the dumpy one.

"May I help you sir?"

The man with Lennon hair glanced at the man on the sofa. "You Jebediah Clipper?"

"That's me."

"I'm Josh Gorman with DHEC. Epidemiology," he said fumbling to get a laminate out from under his fleece vest. When I didn't bother with his laminate, Gorman stowed it and glanced at the man sitting on the sofa rifling through a cremation brochure acting like he wasn't eavesdropping. "Is there somewhere we can talk?"

I ushered him into Isabella's office for the sole reason it was closer, and I didn't have a lot of time, something I told Gorman as I shut the door.

"Then I'll keep it quick," he said, consulting a tablet balanced on a notebook. "I'm a communicable disease investigator with the state. I've been tasked by the CDC to look into a," he almost couched it. I could see it in his eyes. But at the last moment said, *"outbreak."* He cleared his throat and blinked. Gorman looked like he spent more time in the lab than the field. His skin was alabaster. "Your name continues to surface. It appears that you're in the eye of the storm Mr. Clipper."

"Outbreak of what?"

Gorman shook his head. "That's what we're trying to determine."

"If you know I'd appreciate a heads up. I've been working with *it* as you say at the eye of the storm."

His face was guileless. "There's no need for secrecy here Mr. Clipper. As soon as we know what exactly we're dealing with it will be broadcast from the hills so health-care workers can take the proper precautions. I'm in the business of keeping people out of places like this." He saw the look on my face and said, "Look, Mr. Clipper, the investigation right now hinges on a diagnosis. Initial tests are inconclusive, and a literature search isn't giving us any matches. We have something acute. Establishing the parameters of who is infected and when and where they were infected will lead us to the source. The sooner we find the source, the sooner we can turn the tap off and keep everyone healthy."

I sighed and glanced at my watch. I figured Mrs. Balling would be good for at least a ten-minute cry. Seven minutes to go. "It started Sunday with the discovery of a double homicide at the Goose Creek Reservoir."

Gorman was completely unprepared for that. "Excuse me?" he said squinting owlishly.

"These two guys, one homeless," I paused and thought about Badgers's apartment, but didn't amend my statement, "and another, a John Doe, killed each other in a shootout. My girlfriend, who is a pathology fellow over at MUSC, was doing a rush cut for Larry Koziner on a Sunday."

"They died by shooting each other?" Gorman asked. His look said it all: *what's this have to do with my investigation?*

I was immediately disappointed, then annoyed. This guy was supposed to be an investigator, and he wasn't even aware of the two snatched bodies. "Yes, but Homeland Security came skating into the hospital and took possession of the remains in the middle of the prosection, as well as Mags and I."

"So, Homeland Security questioned you about some murders. How does this figure in?"

"They didn't just *question* us. They illegally took possession of two corpses who were part of a state investigation. They illegally abducted and detained us *and* took biological samples without a warrant or consent. Twice. That sound like routine questioning?" I didn't give him time to answer. "*And* I have a friend who works for the DOJ. He checked. The guys weren't Homeland Security."

Gorman squeezed his eyes shut and pinched the bridge of his nose. "Jesus." After a moment he opened his eyes and produced a miniature recorder. "Mind if I record?"

I held out an open palm. Gorman hit a button, the recorder blipped, and I started from the beginning and told him everything I knew and had heard, even Maggie's theory about the chiropractor, Owens, getting sick from the Stono River, ending with the call that the woman's whose office we were standing in was being rushed to the hospital at this moment. That comment caused Gorman to go a little green around the gills. His eyes darted around trying to remember if he had touched anything. Deciding he hadn't he almost drew in on himself like a turtle.

It took me ten minutes to recount all the details, and after Gorman clicked off the recorder I said, "Listen, this may be nothing, but I got this guy, an older guy, by the name of Marshall Kyle out of Carriage Hospice on Tuesday morning. Dysentery is listed as a contributing cause, though duration of symptoms is listed as only a day."

Gorman produced a pen and added Kyle's name to all the others I had already given him. "Thank you," he said producing his card. "This information will be helpful as we construct a contact tree."

"A what?"

"A method of working backwards using the infected cases to discover the index case, or patient zero. If we can identify the index case it goes a long way in understanding how everything started."

I took the doorknob. "Keep me informed."

"Is that one of the families in the lobby?"

I met his gaze. "You can set up your own interviews. They're here to grieve."

"We're on the same side Mr. Clipper," Gorman said with an unexpected harshness.

"I rely on repeat business."

Gorman wasn't sure how to take that, so said, "Call me if you have any new information." He pursed his lips. "Frankly, the preliminary models aren't good; we need to move fast."

"How can you know? You don't even know what it is."

"We know how many new cases are being reported."

I twisted the knob. "I'm not sure of how much further help I can be, but I'll be in touch if I know something."

Gorman put his head down and let himself out. He didn't have long to wait for my call. Ninety-three minutes to be exact. At that point I had bigger problems on my hands. Maggie had a headache.

Chapter 15

The Citadel Mall looks like every other shopping Mecca Americans pilgrimage to. Bright and airy, it's shaped like a star with anchor stores at each of the five points. Gorman was waiting at the end of the boulevard in a white pickup with the seal of the state on the door. I waved to him as we entered and he followed me to a parking space near the northeast entrance.

"This is Steve," Gorman said, unlocking the bed cap.

Moonie and I introduced ourselves. I couldn't tell if Steve wasn't thrilled to be at a mall that was maybe the epicenter of something nasty, or he had the natural disposition of most state employees.

Gorman handed Steve a surgical mask that looked like a swine flu mask and offered them in our direction. I declined as did Moonie. "We don't like to alarm the public, but in this case we don't know if the disease is airborne, so we need to err on the side of caution," he explained, pulling on a pair of latex gloves, and then a second pair of extended cuff gloves over them.

He pulled out a suitcase-like item for Steve and an oversize tackle box for himself and we headed in the food court entrance.

"Is the store at this end?"

"I don't know. Moonie wants pizza."

Gorman looked at Moonie, eyes wide behind his thick glasses. "Seriously? You're going to eat something here?"

Moonie winked at me and spat. "Eaten worse places partner."

Gorman shook his head. I couldn't be sure but I thought I heard him mutter, "Dear God."

Inside, a couple of shoppers shot us curious looks, but that was the extent of it. It's America. Two guys in masks and gloves accompanied by a guy in a suit and a guy who looks like a Texas sheriff aren't cause to stop shopping. I located the mall map and ran my finger down the indexed store names. Locating the cell phone store, I tapped on a little colored store with a matching code to the index. "Here. This is where Grey Balling worked." I looked at the index again and realized I didn't know the name of the business Samuel Badgers worked for. Cam had implied it was near the food court—the star that said "You are Here"—so I started cross referencing the closest kiosks to the food court on the index. When I located a business cleverly called CELL PHONE ACCESSORIES AND REPAIR my heart sank. It was located almost directly across from the cell phone store. I moved my finger infinitesimally from the cell phone store to Badgers's kiosk and tapped. "This is where one of the homicide victims worked."

This was ground zero. It had to be. Too coincidental that Balling and Badgers worked mere feet from each other. I looked around; mothers shepherded laughing children, teens ate mall fare and stared at their devices, and elderly folks in comfy shoes walked laps.

"Let's go," Gorman said, a slight rise in his voice.

He and Steve moved off, Steve already on his phone. I started to follow, and Moonie called after me. "Aren't you hungry?"

"No," I replied, incredulous. "You're not actually going to eat here, are you?"

"Hell, yeah I am."

"I'll wait for you."

Gorman and Steve were already swallowed up in the weekend crush of humanity.

By the time I got to the cell phone store Gorman was having a conversation with a lady who I assumed to be the newly minted manager. Steve was nowhere to be found. Based on Gorman's hand motions it appeared he was asking to clear the store of customers. The total customers were an Asian man browsing flip phones, three adolescents playing with tablets and a young woman at the payment kiosk. I saw the manager shake her head and make a *help yourself* motion. Gorman shrugged and plunked his tackle box on one of the glass display cases and began unloading it, spilling petri dishes, sterile swabs, empty vials, and reagent bottles onto the counter. The woman at the payment kiosk glanced at Gorman's traveling circus, finished up, and left with her head down. The kids continued playing on the tablets. Flip Phone Man stared with unabashed curiosity but made no move to leave.

The man from the cell phone accessory kiosk got off his stool and joined me. "What's going on?" He seemed to be the only person in the mall worried about a man wearing a mask and gloves.

"The manager died. They're just ruling some things out," I said, choosing my words carefully.

"Yeah, I heard Grey died. Tough break. He was a nice guy. Always sent people out to see me. I sell a lot of the same stuff but for a lot cheaper." He shrugged and smiled. It reminded me of Mr. Ed, he had horse-sized teeth.

"Name's Clip." I extended my hand. "You knew Grey?"

"Bob Darwish," he said, extending a slender but ferocious hand out. "I knew Grey as much as I know the other people that work here. We were friendly, you know? Maybe chat a little if it was a slow day." He shrugged. "But I wouldn't say I *knew* Grey."

Darwish looked young—maybe late 20s, or early 30s. His swarthy complexion was flawless, framed by a meticulously barbered pompadour hairdo, and Bambi eyes behind a fashionable set of eyeglasses.

"Why you ask? You with them?" He pointed through the plate glass window at Gorman busily swabbing a touch screen.

As if on cue, Moonie strolled up still chewing and wiping the corners of his mouth with a paper napkin. Darwish sized him up and seemed to answer his own question. To clarify, I said, "Moonie, this is Bob. He works at the kiosk here."

"Deputy Wise," Moonie said, still chewing. He grabbed the badge on his belt. I strongly suspected Moonie liked people to believe he was law enforcement. He swallowed. "You own this here stand?"

"My uncle does," Darwish said, turning from the window. "He owns many, so I manage this one and the one at Northwoods." The pride in his voice was obvious.

"We understand you employed a man named Samuel Badgers."

The smile on Darwish's face twisted. "Yeah," he said, "I gave him work from time to time. Just casual labor type-stuff. I knew the guy needed money. He disappeared though. I haven't seen him in awhile."

The weird look on his face suggested he had been using Badgers for more than "casual labor." To put him at ease, I added, "Look, we don't care about that. Deputy Wise is with the coroner's office."

Moonie used the opportunity to jump in and say, "Badgers is dead."

There was no shock or surprise in Darwish's big eyes. He slowly nodded his head. "No surprise there."

"What makes you say that?" Moonie asked.

"We met at Narc Anon," Darwish said. "Like I said, I knew the guy was down on his luck, and I tried to help him out as much as I could. "When he was clean, he was great. Very good with the customers and could fix any of the phones." Darwish shook his head. "But he was clean so infrequently I couldn't put him on the payroll. He just wasn't dependable. Sad, but with Sam it was just a matter of time."

I felt a stab of pity for Darwish and could almost see it written across his face that his charity simply hadn't been enough to save Badgers. I didn't bother telling him it hadn't been the drugs that had brought his friend down.

"There was a man who died with Sam that we're trying to identify. Would you look at his photo and see if you recognize him, maybe from Narc Anon?" Moonie asked.

Darwish nodded. "If I can."

"Christ," Moonie said, feeling his back pocket. "I left it in the truck."

"No worries," I said, whipping my phone out. "I have it here." I brought up John Doe 2's photo and handed the phone to Darwish. "Pardon the cracks."

He studied it carefully for a moment. "Nope," he said. "Never seen him before." He continued to hold my phone. "Want me to fix this for you? No charge," he added, holding up the spider-webbed screen.

"You can?" I asked, surprised. "I thought I was going to have to get a new phone."

"Nah. It'll just take me a few minutes. Fix it up good as new."

I shrugged. "Sure." There was nothing I hated more than going into a store like the one Gorman was swabbing and going through the hassle of getting a new phone. I always feel like I've lost a fight afterwards.

Darwish retreated to his stand that looked almost like a wooden wagon with a wall sprouting in the middle displaying all sorts of accessories, gadgets, and novelty phone cases. He opened a small drawer and retrieved a small foam mat and some tools. I turned my attention and plopped onto the lacquered bench. Gorman was busy swabbing the keypad of the kiosk, capping the swab when he was done and carefully writing on the label of the cap the details of the collection. Watching Gorman, I decided I didn't need to be here; just thinking of it made my flesh itch. As soon as Darwish was done with my phone we were double timing it out of the hot zone.

"Can I borrow your phone?" I asked Moonie.

When Maggie picked up, I asked without preamble, "Have you been to Citadel Mall recently?"

"I don't think ever," she replied, confused. "Why?"

"Nothing." I realized I was holding the phone with a death grip and relaxed. "How's your head?"

"Worse. I'm headed home."

"Take something and lay down. I'll be home shortly."

I hung up, satisfied her headache was just that: a headache. Maggie had never been to the epicenter. She was fine.

Steve reappeared with a security guard. Gorman came to the entrance of the store. "He's getting maintenance out here," Steve said, jerking his thumb in the direction of the uneasy looking guard, "so I can get to the HVAC system and get some cuts of the filters."

The addition of another masked and gloved man was too much for Flip Phone Man. He abandoned his quest for a phone relic and fled. The teenagers continued fooling around on the tablets, oblivious to Gorman.

Steve dropped the case and unsnapped it. He removed a cylindrical machine from the foam. It looked like a car's air conditioner compressor, but bigger. Steve opened it up, slipped a blue cartridge in and plugged it into the wall. Checking several gauges, he appeared satisfied and turned his attention back to the case. Steve pulled out a plastic disc which quickly popped into a bucket, similar to a collapsible camping cup. He unfurled a mini trash bag, carefully lined the collapsible bucket, and pulled out a reagent bottle. I watched him take the bucket and bottle into the middle of the store, stop and study the ceiling, and set the bucket down. He unscrewed the cap and dumped the bottle into the bucket.

"What the hell is he doing?" I murmured.

Moonie, to my amazement, answered, "It's called grab sampling."

"What?" I turned to see if he was joking.

A grin spread across his face, and his scar turned pink. "They evacuate a bottle of DI water so they know all the air replacing the water is the source air they're trying to sample. Then they'll take it back to the lab and run it through their fancy machines to see what's in the air."

"How do you know this?"

"I've observed," he spread the word out like it was two separate words, *ob-served,* "enough arson investigations to pick up a trick or two. That thing over there," he pointed to the machine Steve plugged into the wall, "is a high-volume air sampler. It'll sit there for a spell running air through it. And then they look at the filter to see what's been caught."

I was sure it was a little more involved than Moonie's explanation as I watched Steve place the jar back in the case, retrieve another and shuffle around the atrium staring upward looking for the perfect spot. He reminded me of a dog sniffing around for a place to shit.

"Reminds me of this case I caught back when I was with Charleston. This guy Carey Peterson burned to death in his parent's home shortly after his parents died. Gruesome." Moonie smirked.

He liked gruesome. No, he *loved* gruesome. "I had to use a putty knife to scrape him off the dining room floor."

He made a scraping motion, still grinning like a fool. There was a fleck of oregano on his front tooth.

I listened, because, frankly I was trapped until Bob finished. I desperately wanted to pack a lip but didn't want to run the risk of putting my fingers in my mouth. I couldn't remember touching any surfaces here but didn't want to risk it.

"House was old," Moonie continued. "Had that old-fashioned knob and tube wiring. Place was like a hoarders lair, newspapers and all sorts of flammable stuff. So, I figure he was over cleaning out their junk and this terrible accident happens. Seems open and shut, but Gary from the Fire Marshall's office takes a look and using one of those bottles," he motions to Steve, "finds accelerant in the air. Know what the idiot did?"

I shook my head, sure Moonie was going to fill me in.

"He had a spray bottle filled with gasoline. He knew if the house burned the Fire Marshall would check to see if it was torched. So, he sprays some in the air thinking it would burn off and tosses a match toward an outlet in the kitchen. It worked. Room ignited like a fireball, especially with all the newspapers and such. Problem was, he had to run through the dining room. All those coats of lacquer on the dining room furniture are like dried gasoline. Soon as that fireball touched the dining room, it went up in flames. Poof!" Moonie flicked his fingers open mimicking explosions. "And there's dumbass Carey standing there with a bottle of gasoline.

"Apparently, he owed some people money and thought it'd be easier to collect the insurance money rather than clean the house out and sell it. That boy melted right into the floorboards. My supper tasted smoky for two days after that."

"Fascinating," I replied, feeling a bit queasy.

"I ever tell you about the Klansman who torched himself when he was lighting a cross?"

Fortunately, Bob interrupted. "Clip?" he called, waving my phone.

I scrambled up, glad to escape the gore monger. "This looks good as new," I marveled, accepting the phone. "Sure I can't pay you?"

Bob shook his head. "You're helping my good buddy Sam, may he rest in peace, so count this as my contribution."

We shook, and I turned, but stopped. "Bob, any idea where Sam lived?"

Bob shrugged. "He said he had a place near here, but I was never invited. It must've been close, because I don't believe he owned a car."

I thanked him, and we beat a hasty retreat until the food court where Moonie stopped to grab a cinnamon roll for the ride back. I waited for him in my truck dousing my hands and forearms in hand sanitizer

Chapter 16

Roper Hospital is a stone and glass edifice with clean, modern lines. It's the first structure people see coming over the bridge from James Island. I parked behind a WCIV van. A dapper newsman was set up near some landscaping so the camera captured the harbor and could pan dramatically to the hospital. I left Moonie waiting in the drop-off area eating his cinnamon bun and hoping security would come hassle him about the illegal park job so he could flex his credentials.

The lobby, which normally only contained the errant physician playing on their phone and sneaking a caffeine fix, seemed abnormally hectic. The crowd reminded me of a cattle pen about to be stunned and brained; the cattle aren't quite sure why they're nervous. I pushed my way through the milling mass of humanity. The pleasant volunteer at the front desk tapped the information into her computer, stared at the screen and frowned.

"Uh, sorry sir," she said. "It appears Mrs. Granville can't accept visitors." She smiled and dropped her voice to a whisper. "Isolation procedures."

"Even for immediate family?"

The smile never left her face as she shook her head and apologized again.

"Can you at least tell me where her room is?"

"I'm afraid that wouldn't do any good sir."

"Is that what this is about?" I asked jerking my head to the crush of people.

She continued smiling. It was all the answer I needed.

"No problem," I said, rapping my knuckles on the counter, and cutting around the welcome desk.

"Sir," she called after me, "where are you going?"

"Get a coffee," I lied.

The volunteer turned her attention to another guest and didn't notice as I breezed by the coffee bar and continued walking into the bowels of the hospital where the patient transport elevators are located. If the woman at the front desk was turning visitors away, I was sure security would be posted at the visitor elevators to enforce the isolation procedures. I made a couple of turns and found the elevator bank. After a few seconds of waiting the doors dinged open and a cute doctor who was young enough that I guessed her to be a resident asked, "What floor?"

The seventh floor was surgical ICU. I figured the hospital wouldn't want to jeopardize the post-op patients. Same with the fifth floor, the critical heart patients. Roper didn't have any proper isolation units. I knew from my days as a military health-care provider only a handful of hospitals nationally do. As in four. Roper was just making do to get by. "Two please," I said. Critical ICU seemed the most logical.

The woman looked at me for a long minute, and, probably noting the suit, decided not to say anything. For the second time in five minutes, a non-answer gave me all the confirmation I needed.

When the elevator doors dinged open at the second floor I stepped off and picked a pod at random. Left or right. I went right. As soon as I stepped in to the area dominated by a circular nurse's station, a fireplug of a woman in blue scrubs hurried out to intercept me with both hands up.

"Going to need to see some ID," she said, planting herself in my path. The nurse was wearing a surgical mask, as were all the other nurses and orderlies, that obscured most of her face. The badge clipped to her pocket told me her name was Jackie. The photo on her badge revealed a very pleasant face. The voice didn't match. I assumed by Jackie's officious air I had located the charge nurse.

"I'm here to see Isabella Granville."

"How'd you get up here?" Jackie asked.

I couldn't help myself. "The elevator."

"I'm not going to confirm someone by that name is even here. But this is an isolation ward. You aren't going to see *any* of the patients here. You need to get back on that elevator because I'm calling security. All non-essential personnel aren't allowed up here, *especially* visitors." Jackie made a shooing motion with her hands.

It was my turn to be officious. "Jackie, my name is Tripp Clipper and I'm working in conjunction with DHEC as a special investigator. It's imperative I see Isabella Granville." I made the part up about "special investigator" but wanted to sell it. "Call Josh Gorman, the DHEC liaison with the CDC, if you want," I offered, holding out Gorman's business card.

Jackie snatched it and studied it. "Wait here," she said, and stomped over to her command center. She picked up the phone and made a call. I noted the isolation signs taped up to all the glass doors of all the patient rooms: STOP. MEDICAL ISOLATION. There was a little graphic of a man's face wearing a mask, presumably for those that couldn't read. The pod was dim. The rooms were dim. Isabella could be any of the blanketed figures behind the glass doors. The phone went down, and Jackie picked it up again, and spoke in to it while glaring at me.

My phone buzzed. The number that popped up on the screen was a county issued number. I could tell because it was similar to Moonie's number. "You're a special investigator now?" Gorman asked when I answered. Based on the background noise he was still at the phone store.

"Something like that," I said, not dropping Jackie's stare. "Isabella is family."

Gorman sighed. It was the sound of a man at the end of his rope. "Doesn't seem like a good idea."

"You said so yourself. I'm at the eye of this thing. Whatever it is I must be immune or I'd have caught it by now." Gorman started to protest but I cut him off. "I've been working with their bodily fluids for Christ's sake. Besides, you owe me. You got the mall because of me."

"I doubt you're immune. You're lucky, or well trained," he snapped. "But I already told that guard dog over there you're cleared to visit whoever the hell you want."

I grinned. So, Jackie had been rough with Gorman too. I watched her make a few more calls before marching back over to me and handing me Gorman's card. "You're good," Rough Jackie said curtly. "She's on the seventh floor. Security is on the way up to escort you." She pointed to a makeshift station. "You'll need to gown up prior to entering an isolation room."

With that, Rough Jackie spun, returned to her command center and I was forgotten about. I meandered over to the station that was nothing more than a compartmentalized cart with a sign printed on a piece of computer paper that said ISOLATION ROOM PPE and selected an XL surgical gown, cap, booties, and surgical mask. I waited an eternity before Chuck came ambling into the pod. His mask obscured his red face.

"Hey Chuck."

He squinted at me, trying to place me.

"Nikki told me if I saw you to say hi."

Chuck brightened and stood an inch straighter. "Really?"

I nodded and fell into step with him. The mention of Nikki gave him his swagger back. "Why aren't they wearing masks downstairs? They seem a little hysterical about all this."

Chuck cast a glance over his shoulder to make sure Jackie was out of earshot. "From what I hear the administration doesn't want to create panic."

I lowered my voice into a conspiratorial tone. "How bad is it?"

Chuck stabbed the call button. "It's bad. Real bad."

"How bad?"

"This isn't the only floor. They're using the surgical ICU for overflow." He chuckled. There was no humor in the sound; it was the sound a man makes when he knows not what sound to make. "They've cancelled all scheduled surgeries until further notice. Don't want to get anyone healthy sick."

The elevator dinged open and we stepped in. Chuck badged the console and selected the seventh floor. "Last I heard there are 30 piled up in the morgue."

"Thirty!"

Chuck nodded. "Yeah. 'Bout 15 or so just last night."

"Is anyone getting better?"

He shrugged. "There are people who seem to be lasting longer than others. Maybe they get better. Maybe they don't."

"Are you worried?"

"Sure," he said. "But what can I do? They aren't letting any of us go home until the higher-ups figure out what it is. Don't want us to spread it around town. We're all sleeping on cots in the service areas that have been shut down."

He looked up. I could tell by his eyes, he was grinning. "Good news is I'm making some serious overtime. Probably be able to finally buy this 19-foot Bayliner I've had my eye on."

"There you go," I said, validating his bullshit. Here was a man riding the wave of fear and uncertainty that looked like it was going to break over our fair city. I had to give him credit; Chuck had a stiff upper lip.

Chuck shook his head. "And you walk into it?"

The elevator doors opened. The smell of antiseptic was stronger than normal. It still couldn't cover the underlying scent of feces. Hematochezia is what doctors would call it. Shitting blood is what we'd call it in the army. "I've been in it for the better part of a week."

"That way." Chuck pointed. "A week?" he shook his head and fell silent. No sense burdening himself with problems above his pay grade.

With surgical services all but shut down except for emergencies, the floor was quiet, but still brightly lit. It was eerie without the normal hustle and bustle of hospital activity. The only person we passed as Chuck led me down several hallways was a masked and gloved guy from environmental services mopping the floor.

Chuck stopped at the edge of the pod, like there was an invisible fence keeping him out. "I'll wait for you."

Rough Jackie had briefed the charge nurse, a giant of a man with a neatly trimmed beard and dainty glasses that looked almost feminine. "This way," he said. "In there," he indicated, stopping at one of the rooms. Isabella was watching TV inside. "When you come out discard your PPE here," he indicated to a biohazard can with a lid sitting outside the door, "and get new stuff over there."

I nodded and the giant disappeared. I slid the door open, and Isabella managed a weak smile. Her skin was the color of parchment, her eyes red and sunken.

"You came. The nurse said they weren't allowing visitors."

"He was being dramatic. How are you feeling?" I dragged a chair next to the bed and sat. The intensive care room was equipped with all sorts of fancy equipment: pulse oximeter, a-line monitor, ventilator, intracranial pressure monitor, EEG, infusion pump. The only one hooked up was the cardiac monitor that issued a continuous *beep, beep, beep* like a metronome. On the rolling tray sat two bottles labeled ORS. Oral Rehydration Salts. Orange and Berry flavored. The fancy flavorings don't come close to covering up how bad they taste.

"I don't feel bad now. Just weak. They're rehydrating me," she freed her right hand from under the blanket and pointed to the IV line that snaked under the sheets, "and have me on some medicine to clear up whatever was wrong with me."

"Did they tell you what's wrong?"

"The doctor did, but I can't remember. I was in a lot of pain."

I wandered to the door. Nobody from the nurse's station was looking this way. I eased the door open and looked at the chart bin. Empty. *They've migrated to electronic records.*

I was about to ask Isabella to use her call button to summon the nurse, so I could look at her chart when my phone vibrated. I pulled it out and my blood froze. It was from Maggie: CALL ME ASAP

"I'll come back to visit tomorrow," I said, trying not to show alarm, "when I can stay for a bit longer." I held the straw in the orange flavored ORS to her lips. She drank and made a face. "I know it tastes bad. Try to drink as much as you can. It'll help. Is there anything I can bring you?"

She smiled and for the first time I could remember she looked every year her age. "No son, I'm fine."

Son? Isabella had never once called me anything other than Mr. Clipper. I started to speak but my voice caught. I cleared my throat and started again. "I'll bring some of your magazines and see if I can get Ethel to make some of her lemon cookies, how about that?"

Isabella held up her hand at the wrist, the skin on her hand so thin the blood flow patterns were obvious and throbbing. I took it and she squeezed. It felt papery and cold through the nitrile glove. "Goodbye," she whispered.

"Goodnight."

As I stripped off the infectious gear, it was if Isabella was making a point to stare at the muted TV, and not glance in my direction. She looked small and frail in the vast Hill-Rom bed—the irony not lost on me that they supply our caskets too.

Though I was in a hurry I stopped at the desk and asked Giant, "Diagnosis for Mrs. Granville?"

Having been briefed by Rough Jackie, he didn't even argue HIPAA laws. "Same as all the others," he said, glancing up from a tablet. "Acute shigellosis. She's been treated with a loading dose of 750 milligrams Amoxil, maintenance of 500 migs every six hours." I nodded, remembering from my medic days that Amoxil is the brand name of an antibiotic called Ampicillin typically used to treat this type of infection.

"What are you doing for the encephalitis?"

Giant looked a little startled, but only momentarily as if remembering Rough Jackie had briefed him I was a "special agent." "Uh," he glanced at his tablet, "She isn't showing signs of encephalitis."

"Yet. Aren't the others?"

Giant cleared his throat. "We gave Mrs. Granville an EEG about an hour ago, normal. All blood work is coming back clean for anything other than *Shigella*."

"Right, but you're seeing that in the other patients, no viral or bacterial titers until they've developed encephalitis. And then what?"

Giant cleared this throat again. He liked clearing it. "And then we're seeing nothing. We have no clue what's causing the encephalitis, or even if it's related to the dysentery."

"It has to be," I snapped. "With this many people," I splayed my arm out to the glassed rooms with their little signs and dedicated biohazard bins outside, "it's a pattern."

Giant's eyes never left mine. They were clear but there was the slightest flutter of fear lurking in them. He was a man holding it together, but close to the edge. "I don't know what to tell you man. Everyone seems to get better, and then some of them..." He let it hang and shrugged.

"I'd like you to get a spinal tap ordered for Mrs. Granville and continue to do periodic EEGs."

Giant cocked his head slightly. He wasn't used to taking orders. He looked like the type who gave orders to everyone, even doctors. Especially doctors. I could really get into my new fictitious role. "I'd need the patient's consent," he said.

"Done."

I went over and rapped on Isabella's glass wall. When she looked I pantomimed signing motion on a clipboard and pointed at Giant. She nodded.

"There," I said and handed him a business card. "Call me with updates."

Chuckie was lurking in the hallway watching one of the muted TV's in the vacant SICU waiting room. He was anxious to escort me—and himself—away from the hot zone. "I'll have to escort you out, or they'll never let you leave," he said, and keyed the walkie-talkie on his shoulder and issued a stream of commands.

Moonie was restless in the truck. "Let's go," he said. Gone was his normal guileless expression. He looked downright grim. "Command just radioed up. Chatter on the scanner is they snared the critter that's causing the swamp sickness."

Chapter 17

Traffic was a nightmare. I called Maggie, dodging and weaving, trying to escape Charleston proper on a Saturday evening, a near impossible feat.

"Jeez, that's ASAP?" she said.

"I was in an isolation unit visiting Isabella. What's wrong? Are you okay?"

"I'm fine," she said. "They're backed up here at work so I came in. It's all hands on deck. Like an assembly line." She dropped her voice. "Twenty-two died in the last 24 hours."

"Twenty-two?" I wasn't sure if I heard correctly.

"It's bad."

"Your headache?"

"It went away," she said dismissively. "I took a few aspirin and started feeling fine. I texted you because the cops just caught this guy pumping his septic truck into Foster Creek."

"I heard," I said, nearly rear-ending a VW Beetle. I cranked the wheel and laid on the horn.

"This might be the cause."

"Yeah. Moonie and I are on our way out to the scene."

"Oh," she said, sounding a little deflated. "See you at home. Don't wait up. I'll probably be late." There was a commotion in the background. "Gotta go," she said, I didn't even get to squeeze in a "bye" before the line went dead.

I heard honking and looked over as the man in the Beetle pulled abreast. His face was red and his window was down. I rolled mine down to catch the tail end of a string of obscenities. I was about to respond with a less than gentlemanly gesture when Moonie wordlessly pulled his badge off his belt and handed it to me. I flashed it out the window, and for the first time all day, nearly cracked a smile as the guy's face melted into an expression of shock and he slammed on his brakes in an attempt to get away.

"I mean, come on, he's driving a Beetle," I said handing the badge back.

Moonie's mustache twitched. "He have one of them fancy daisies in the cup holder?"

It took 45 minutes to fight our way out of the city, through Hanahan, and over to Goose Creek. Moonie spoke when we passed the Nuclear Power Training Command. "Turn here."

It was unnecessary. There was a sheriff's cruiser stationed on the shoulder. A deputy heaved himself out when he saw the truck turning and flagged us down.

"Where you headin'?" he asked, peering in the window.

"Coroner's Office," Moonie said, unclipping his badge and flashing it.

"Coroner?" the cop asked, puzzled. "You sure you're in the right place son? There ain't no bodies back there."

"This ties into several open investigations."

"Illegal dumping?"

I wasn't sure if the deputy was going for a double entendre or not, but I chimed in, eager to use my new, fictitious credentials, "Look Deputy, I'm a special investigator working a task force with DHEC and the Coroner's Office and we need access to this scene. Call your boss if you need to."

The deputy stepped back and keyed the mic and spoke into his shoulder a few times, before reaching into his cruiser to retrieve a clipboard. "What're your names?" he asked, scrawling our answers. "Go-head," he said, waving us forward with a flick of the wrist.

We wound through the forest on the twisty road for several miles until the asphalt ended abruptly and we bumped along the last mile on a sand and dirt road. At the creek the road opened up into a weedy roundabout where several marked cruisers sat along with a vintage Bronco that had a pair of Sea-Doos trailered to it. A small tanker truck was backed up near the boat put-in, W's SANITATION SERVICE stenciled on the side. Uniforms milled about talking in small groups. A guy in a trucker cap, and sleeveless shirt with the name Roy embroidered on a name patch was the center of attention of one such group who had notebooks out and were pointing and writing.

I backed my truck up against some scrub brush so it wouldn't be in the way, and not a moment too soon. A forensic van pulling a mobile light tower rumbled into the clearing and parked behind the sanitation truck.

Moonie met me at the bumper and hitched up his belt and spit into the grass. "Smells like the Carolina Country Music Festival." I had never been to that particular event but knew what 50 portable toilets baking in the sun smelled like.

"Clip. Deputy," a voice called.

We turned to see Detective Hotapp climbing out of an unmarked Chevy Caprice. She was dressed smartly in gray slacks and a blue blouse that was billowy around the neck in a way that seemed to be fashionable.

"What are you doing out here?" she asked, intercepting us before we could get to the group of crime-scene techs in blue windbreakers piling out of the van.

"Ma'am," Moonie said touching the brim of his hat. "This could be tied to several open investigations." Moonie won the prize for understatement of the year if he called scores of people dying from a mysterious illness "several open investigations."

She nodded. "I guess your office would be interested in the root cause." A generator roared to life and the sanitation truck was suddenly bathed in brilliant light. She put a hand on her hip, next to her gun. "Are you tagging along for fun?"

"Not really. I'm consulting with DHEC."

A smirk played over Hotapp's lips. "You're the special investigator scene control radioed about?"

I nodded. Behind Hotapp the techs were gowning up in protective gear. "Dysentery—which is how this is presenting—is still a common illness in third-world countries. As such, I'm familiar with it from my health-care specialty training in the army. Plus, as the liaison with the CDC said, 'I'm at the eye of the storm.'"

"I don't dispute that. You seem to pop up a lot," Hotapp said.

I couldn't tell by her tone if she was implying I was a suspect or just making a casual observation. "Believe me, this is the last thing I want to get involved in, but now Isabella Granville, the closest thing I have to kin, is sick so I decided to lend a hand." I made a twirling motion with my hand around the clearing. "How'd this come about?"

Hotapp pointed to a couple in their late 40s sitting on a felled branch at the perimeter of the action. They wore cutoff jeans, the woman in a bikini top and the man a muscle T-shirt. "The Carvers came down here to take a quick ride on their water toys before it got dark." Based on their sunburns it looked like the Carvers spent a lot of time on the water. Hotapp continued, "They interrupted Roy emptying his truck into the creek. They called it in. Though it's the sheriff's jurisdiction, one of my guys was the first responder."

"You put it together, that Roy might be causing the outbreak?" I asked, admiringly. It was quick thinking. Most cops wouldn't think further than illegal dumping. Normally, it would take hours or days before someone in DHEC made the kind of reasoning leap Hotapp made.

"It's scary what's happening. Honestly, it was my first thought."

"You're not kidding it's scary," I said. "Twenty-two have died at MUSC in the past 24 hours."

Her eyes darkened, "This scumbag better hope to God he's not the cause of this. I'll make it my personal mission to see that every single death is hung around his neck."

"Was he trying to save a buck?"

Hotapp's normally pleasant face twisted into a scowl. "Isn't that what they all do it for? Money? Roy's a real gem. His wife left him because he was shacking up with another woman. Who, by the way, has called in several domestics when Roy starts drinking and beating on her. Anyway, the wife got the house and alimony and thus began ole' Roy's money troubles right into our taps."

"How long's he been at it?" Moonie asked.

"Haven't established that for certain yet."

"I'm guessing this ain't his first rodeo."

Hotapp nodded grimly. "Timeline fits. He cops to starting about a week ago. Shortly thereafter people started getting sick. Claims this is his third dump. Scumbags like this lie. I'd bet he's been at it longer."

I cringed thinking about that volume of raw sewage going directly into the watershed. Something Hotapp said previously caused me to pause. "Wait, did you say taps? As in Roy's sewage could be getting into our drinking water?"

Hotapp nodded vigorously, her cop ponytail bouncing. "This creek feeds one of the reservoirs—Bushy Park—for the Hanahan Water Treatment Plant."

I took a step back. "Jesus," I muttered. On the ride over I supposed people were being exposed to the *Shigella* by swimming like Dr. Owens, the chiropractor, who fell ill shortly after competing in a triathlon, or other water activities like the Carvers and their Sea-Doos, or Isabella reading on her dock like she spent many evenings. Detective Hotapp had just presented a completely different idea: the disease was being pumped right into everyone's home.

"It fits to reason," Hotapp said. The handheld clipped to her belt squawked and she turned the volume down. "Would explain why it's so widespread."

I'm not an expert in epidemiology, but I knew there could be many other explanations for the speed the disease was spreading, although her theory seemed plausible.

A familiar white pickup rumbled into the clearing with the state seal on the door. Josh Gorman and Steve hopped out.

"That's the local, Gorman, I was telling you is the CDC liaison," I said to Hotapp as Gorman and Steve opened the back cap and began gowning up.

"Mr. Gorman, Detective Jennifer Hotapp," she said, striding over and sticking out her hand.

Gorman looked up in surprise, blinking owlishly, first looking at me and then Hotapp before taking her hand. Introductions were made and Hotapp got down to business, "This is all new to me Mr. Gorman. Where do we go from here?"

"Well," Gorman said, pulling on a second set of gloves and taping them at the wrist, "Steve and I are going to collect samples from the suspected source, and then we'll take samples from the water at various points from shore and at various depths."

Steve dug out a pair of waders and began tugging them over his protective gear.

Gorman continued, "After that we'll take samples from various places upstream and downstream, and I've dispatched units to collect from other locations along the Back River and Cooper River and the harbor. This way we'll be able to determine how far the contamination has spread." He looked at me, and said, "Busy day, huh, Mr. Clipper? Fancy meeting you here."

I wasn't sure if he was implying anything. Thankfully, Moonie blundered into the conversation with his usual grace. "How you aim to tell how far it's spread? Hell, the turds could be at Sumter by now, bobbin' on out to sea."

Gorman cleared his throat, thrilled someone had asked. I could almost envision Professor Gorman in front of a lecture hall. "Based on the number of samples that contributed to that waste tank, I'm going to go out on a limb and say with a fairly high confidence interval that there will be the presence of *Salmonella* and or *Shigella*. Both genera are similar: gram negative facultative anaerobes."

I watched Moonie's mustache droop. He was sorry he asked.

"The thing about portable toilets is they used to contain formaldehyde, which kills just about everything, but the states have cracked down on them because the wastewater treatment plants couldn't safely process that volume. Formaldehyde is a known carcinogen." For some reason Gorman looked right at me when he said it. "Instead, they now contain three main ingredients: dye, deodorizer, and biocides which are basically enzymes that inhibit the growth of the gram-positive bacteria that cause the odors, and do nothing about the gram-negative bacteria—"

Hotapp cut him off, "How are you going to tie the two together?" Her detective mind was working to connect the dots.

Gorman blinked, opened his mouth and shut it. Making up his mind, he said, "Simple answer: we'll spin down the DNA and use PFGE to compare the isolates—"

"Can you clarify?"

I was glad Hotapp asked. I was lost too.

"Oh, sorry. Pulsed-field gel electrophoresis produces a DNA fingerprint." Gorman used air quotes around *fingerprint*. "The governor has made this priority number one so we should have answers a few hours after sampling."

I was still kind of lost. Based on their expressions so were Hotapp and Moonie. Hotapp pressed Gorman, "The takeaway as I understand is you're going to compare the DNA fingerprints from the bacteria to see if they match?"

"In a nutshell."

Hotapp nodded and Moonie's mustache perked up.

"If you'll excuse me, I need to get to work." Gorman tied a surgical mask around his face, adjusted his glasses, and pulled up his hood.

We hung around until Roy was hauled away in a sheriff's cruiser and his sanitation truck was hooked to the back of a wrecker.

"You want to get something to eat?" Moonie asked, climbing into the cab.

The dashboard clock said it was after suppertime. With the smell of excrement in the air my stomach ruled to skip supper. "Thanks, but no. Nikki texted me while we were fooling around at the scene. There's work waiting for me back at the shop."

Moonie screwed up his face. "They're releasing bodies in Charleston County? Ain't they worried about the swamp sickness?"

"Apparently some old lady on hospice. Cancer."

Chapter 18

Cancer has a distinct smell. Acrid and vegetative, it's easily identifiable to the point where I can walk into a house and know if someone has it. I propped the little cellar casement windows open to rid the prep room of the cancery miasma. It was almost midnight, and I was just beginning to embalm Mrs. Holland.

Despite what I told Moonie, my stomach got the better of me after we returned from Foster Creek. After sending him on his way, I headed down the street to Sarah's for some chow. On the walk, it seemed automobile and pedestrian traffic was much lighter than normal. I wasn't sure if it was my imagination, but school was back in session and the streets are usually crowded with tourists and college students Saturday nights. Was the public starting to get spooked? DHEC's press releases were cautioning the public about an extra virulent strain of stomach flu. It was their effort to spin the narrative until they had a handle on things. I was sure the media was busy digging for the truth. Things weren't adding up; they could smell blood in the water. It wouldn't be long before some reporter uncovered the truth and all hell broke loose. For the moment, however, it seemed to be business as usual for those hardy souls who dared brave the stomach flu on the streets of Charleston.

Back at the funeral home I plugged into my sound dock before gowning up. It was a Whiskey Myers kind of night. The cancer ate her to the bone. No doubt I'd been introduced to her at one of the Granville's yearly Fourth of July bashes, but that had probably been a hundred pounds ago. Mrs. Holland and her husband were friends of the Granville's. Mr. Holland owned a textile factory, and they were part of the set the Granville's ran with. Old Charleston money.

The curtains at the cellar windows fluttered as the pressure in the house changed as the backdoor opened and shut. The floorboards above squeaked ever so slightly as someone—probably Nikki—padded down the back hall.

I let the water run into the glass tank of the embalming machine as I selected fluid from the hutch. The antique walnut hutch looks out of place amongst the tiled sterility of the prep room but made for better organization. When I started, Lauren kept all the fluids in their cardboard shipping boxes stacked haphazardly on the floor.

Selecting a couple of bottles, I measured out the proper amounts, turned off the tap, and set the machine to MIX.

Tossing the empties, I heard the van doors in the garage opening and closing.

"Nikki?" I shouted up the elevator.

The elevator is ancient, at least 50 years old. Lauren put it in when he added the garage bay and expanded the funeral home's footprint. The building used to be a house. Lauren turned it into a functional place of business that happens to look like a house. The elevator is used to bring bodies and caskets from the garage down to the prep room, and casketed bodies ready for viewing upstairs. The thing is as temperamental as an angry badger, and, perhaps, the most unsafe piece of equipment in greater Charleston. It sinks like a stone and rises like a rocket—and there are no safety rails to keep things in place like the newer elevators. I learned early on to have the cot or casket positioned perfectly or there was going to be a tragedy. If ever there was an OSHA inspection I'd have some business when the inspector stroked out after testing it.

The noise in the garage stopped.

I pressed the button and buzzed the elevator up a little so it cracked the steel trapdoor in the garage. "Nikki?"

Nothing.

I doubted it was Moonie. He'd be downstairs bending my ear, and Maggie wouldn't have any reason to be in the garage.

"Fred? Harry?" I called the names of the part-timers.

No response.

I put the elevator back down and checked the clock. Zero 15, or quarter after midnight. I couldn't fathom what Nikki would be doing at the funeral home at this time of night. There were no new calls in to my knowledge. Returning my attention to Mrs. Holland, I flipped the switch from MIX to INJECT and opened the drain tube. A life of clean, healthy living made for a quick injection. Twenty minutes later I was using a piece of dental floss to sew up the incision. Ten minutes after that, once the final washing was complete, I was de-gowned and washed up at the utility sink. Wiping my hands on a paper towel, I went to pull out my phone see if Maggie texted while I was embalming. It wasn't there.

"Ah." I slapped the counter, remembering I set it down next to the register at Sarah's. Leafing through the phone book, I used the prep room phone to place a call.

Clara picked up after six or seven rings. "We're closed."

"It's Clip. Did I leave my phone?"

"Sure did honey," she said, brightening. "I'm locking up now. You can get it when the morning crew opens." That was six a.m. I could live without my phone for six hours.

"Can you check if I got any calls or messages?"

Clara set the phone down and a moment later returned. "Nothing."

"Thanks," I said, hanging up, and making a mental note to give her an extra tip next time. Picking up the handset, I punched a series of numbers forwarding the business line to my apartment. Flicking off the lights, I climbed the stairs and grabbed the doorknob. The knob turned and I plowed into the door.

"What the hell?" I muttered, pounding with my forearm and closed fist. The door didn't give an inch.

"Nikki? Nikki?" I called. "Can you give me a hand here? The door's stuck."

There was only silence on the other side.

I debated going down to the prep room and calling her but decided against it in case she was home asleep.

I jiggled the knob and pushed. Nothing. Backing down a couple of steps, I sprinted up and rammed my shoulder into the door like a linebacker. Not so much as a shimmy. It was stuck fast. The doors in the building are solid inch-and-three-eighths thick long leaf pine doors from before the turn of the 19th century. Not the Masonite or hollow core crap found in new construction. A wrecking ball was the only thing bringing this door down.

"Dammit," I muttered, rubbing my shoulder, wondering what on earth could've happened. Maybe one of the area rugs got wedged under the door.

I flicked on the lights in the prep room and climbed onto the elevator. Punching the green button, the hydraulics whirled to life and it shot up and deposited me in the garage with a loud *clang*. The only noise were the overhead fluorescents buzzing gently illuminating the tidy space where the van and hearse sat, polished and ready for the next funeral.

I let myself into the back hall. The funeral home was mostly dark except for the dim cast of a few table lamps I keep on so the place doesn't look eerie to passerby on the street. "Who's there?" Matey screeched flapping down the hall.

"Jesus!" I ducked, narrowly missing the storm of feathers. "How'd you get down here?"

Matey flapped frantically at the end of the hallway, having nowhere to land, he sailed back my direction. I stepped aside, giving the winged rat plenty of berth but he had other plans, landing heavily on my shoulder. "Clip! Clip!" he shouted.

"Did you say my name?" I asked, my annoyance momentarily forgotten.

"Clip!"

The surprise was quickly replaced by a funny feeling in my gut. Something wasn't right. Maggie would never let him loose in the funeral home, and Nikki wouldn't have a reason to be in the apartment. I headed down the hall, Matey digging his claws into my shoulder for traction, stopping short at the cellar door. Coins were wedged around the door's reveal, effectively jamming it shut. Someone had deliberately trapped me downstairs. A chill ran up my spine. Why would someone go to the trouble to lock me in the cellar unless they needed time alone?

Easing the pistol from the small of my back, I didn't even check if it was hot. There's always a round in the chamber. Tiptoeing around the corner, I pushed my office door open. It swung silently on lubricated hinges. Ambient light from the street lamps spilled through the plantation shutters. The room was empty. Padding across the Oriental rug, I yanked open my desk drawer and grabbed Hotapp's card off the top of the neat little stack. Lifting the handset, I punched in her number.

She picked up on the second ring. "Hotapp."

"It's Tripp Clipper," I whispered. Even at the fewest decibels I could muster and be heard, my voice still sounded loud. I wished I had closed the door behind me.

"Yeah?" It sounded like she was eating, and a little annoyed to be disturbed at such a late hour. A TV blared in the background.

"I'm at the funeral home. Someone broke in and trapped me in the cellar."

"Trapped you—"

"I rode the elevator up and found the cellar door purposely wedged shut. I'm in my office now. The intruder may still be here."

"Get out!" she ordered. "I'll be there shortly. In the meantime, I'll get CPD rolling."

I didn't need further urging. Hanging up, I listened to the silence of the funeral home. There was nothing unusual; the ticking of the grandfather clock in the foyer and the dense stillness of a big old house—the pervasive quietness you can cut with a knife. Carefully, walking the perimeter of the hallway to avoid squeaking boards, I eased down the hall toward the backdoor.

When I drew close Matey let out a little squawk. I reached up to silence him and he bit my finger. Hard.

"Fuck!" I screamed in the quietest whisper. I could feel blood running down my finger.

The air whooshed faintly as the kitchenette door moved. I didn't hear it, and when I felt the breeze hit my face it was too late. Something hard connected with my back and propelled me face-first into the backdoor. My nose connected with the casing and crunched. I dropped the pistol.

Matey screeched and took flight. Flailing and curses sounded behind me, and I clung to the wall and tried to drag a breath in. There wasn't time to scrabble around for the gun. Matey had momentarily distracted the attacker, but not for long. I turned just in time to see the outline of the guy coming at me, bat raised. Lashing out with my leg, I caught him mid-thigh. He let out a grunt of surprise and his well-aimed blow glanced off my shoulder sending an explosion of pain up across my chest. Ignoring the pain, I jabbed in the direction of his face and caught a piece of something. It wasn't a big enough piece. He recovered and poked me in the solar plexus. Intense pain mushroomed from my gut. I doubled over, blood running freely from my nose. The guy used the opportunity to punch downward. It was vicious. Stars exploded in my eyes, and it was all I could do not to fall to my knees. If I went down I was dead.

I counter jabbed. It was weak. My assailant easily swatted my arm down, spun me, and pressed my face against the wall.

"Where is it?" he hissed.

"What?" I gasped.

"You know. It was at the scene."

"What scene?" I asked, my mind flashing to Roy and his sanitation truck. "I didn't take anything from the scene. I swear!"

"Somebody's got it." The guy jammed the bat in my kidneys and I cried out involuntarily. "Tell me and you live."

CPD wasn't going to make it in time. They were going to find a corpse. I took a breath to steady myself. Time slowed to a crawl. When at Ranger School one of my instructors liked to quote Yogi Berra, saying, "Gentleman, baseball is 90% mental, the other half is physical." Like shrugging into a pair of well-worn jeans, I was able to instantly focus. The plan of action was clear.

"It's..." I muttered something unintelligible under my breath.

He took the bait and leaned in. "What'd you say?"

I rocketed my head back with as much force as possible, driving the thick, parietal bones of my skull into his fragile facial bones, simultaneously pushing off the wall with all fours, like a leaping frog. There was a wet crunch and the man screamed, crashing backward into the kitchenette.

I didn't wait to hear the sound of the smashing furniture. Ripping open the garage door I sprinted toward the elevator. Footsteps pounded behind me as I dove onto the platform and smashed the red button. The elevator dropped like a stone. I turned in time to watch the steel trapdoor nearly taking off a piece of the intruder's arm. The platform slammed onto the prep room floor. I hit the kill switch.

The wail of sirens came through the open casement windows. I limped over and stood on tiptoe to peer out. A hooded figure hurried out the backdoor and headed up the little garden path that lets out onto Broad where he'd blend in as one more nighttime reveler in the Holy City.

Chapter 19

"**Y**ou never got a look at the perp?" Detective Wallingford asked. He snapped a piece of gum, pen poised over his notebook. Over his shoulder flashes emanated from inside the funeral home as the evidence team documented the scene. A detective with Charleston Police Department, he seemed competent and thorough but with his slicked-back hair and jerky movements he reminded me of a ferret. I was getting annoyed. Wallingford had asked me the same question at least five times, though phrased differently.

I managed "uh-uh" as the EMT holding splints in my nose said, "You're going to feel a little pressure."

It was more than a little pressure. I almost screamed as she cranked my nose back into position.

"Hold still Mr. Clipper," she said, withdrawing the sticks and packing gauze up my nostrils.

It hurt like hell. I gripped the edges of the stretcher willing myself to stay still so she could do her job.

Placing a piece of tape over the bottom of my nostrils, she said, "Go see your doctor tomorrow and he'll instruct you about changing the packing. You'll probably also want to get an X-ray of those ribs," she said, handing me back my shirt.

I winced as I eased the shirt back on. I agreed with the EMT's assessment: they were cracked or bruised; not broken. I'd be short of breath if there were any breaks. An X-ray wouldn't do any good other than to confirm I didn't have a broken rib. There's nothing to be done either way. "Thanks Doc," I said, hopping off the rig.

The EMT looked at me funny. Any medic in the army was called Doc. It wasn't personal. "Sign here." She shoved a clipboard into my hands. It was a release form stating I denied treatment at a hospital. I scribbled my name and handed it back.

The EMT slammed the doors to the rig and climbed in the passenger side. The ambulance continued to sit in front of the garage bay idling, the running flashers casting eerie strobes off the building as the two wrote out their reports.

"Come on up." I started up the outsides staircase to my apartment.

Hotapp, who had been loitering in the shadows drinking in the details of the scene, set aside a broken spade handle and fell in behind Wallingford. The spade had been broken while working in the yard several months previously, and I had leaned the piece up against the garage wall as a reminder to buy a replacement handle. Little did I realize it would be used to beat the shit out of me.

"Care for anything to drink?" I asked the two detectives, moving some drop cloths and painting supplies, and motioning for them to sit.

"Water would be great," Wallingford said, perching on the edge of a sofa.

"Same," Hotapp said, sitting opposite Wallingford in a club chair.

I returned with two coconut waters and excused myself. The reflection greeting me in the bathroom mirror was a scary sight. My nose was three sizes larger than normal and a large bruise was spreading across my cheekbones. *Great, double black eyes,* I thought, opening the medicine cabinet and shaking out a half dozen aspirin. Nothing instills confidence in the bereaved like an undertaker who looks like a street fighter. I gulped the pills down dry and heard shouts and a crash in the living room. Dropping the aspirin bottle, I raced down the hall.

Hotapp and Wallingford were standing with their backs against the far wall. The chair Hotapp had been sitting in was overturned.

"What is that?" Wallingford pointed to Matey, perched on top of his cage. He was busy itching under a raised wing. When he noticed me, he ripped off, "Clip!"

"He just flew in," Hotapp said, a bit more collected than the CPD detective, but just as unsure.

I breathed a sigh of relief as my heart rate returned to normal. "That's my girlfriend's pet," I said, striding over and holding out my forearm.

"I thought a bald eagle, was attacking," Wallingford muttered, sweeping imaginary lint off his blazer and smoothing his gelled hair to appear calm.

The bird hopped on my arm. I carried him to the door and shooed him out. "This must've been left open by the burglar," I commented, shutting the slider. "That's what cued me that someone had been in my apartment—this is before I saw the cellar door—I found Matey flying around downstairs. Mags probably let him out before she went to work and the intruder left the slider open."

"Let him out?" Wallingford looked confused.

"Yeah. Mags lets him fly around town."

"And it comes back?" Wallingford was having trouble wrapping his head around the idea of a pet bird. I liked him.

"Sadly."

Hotapp righted the chair and sat. Though this was clearly CPD's scene, Hotapp asked, "So the perp asked, 'Where is it?'"

I nodded.

"Any idea what it is?"

"His exact words were, 'It was at the scene.'" I shrugged. "I didn't take anything from the scene."

Hotapp pursed her lips and cut her eyes to the ceiling.

"Hair color? Skin color?" Wallingford asked.

I shook my head. Mistake. My head exploded in pain. The backwards head butt had hurt me as much as my assailant.

"Are you sure it was the scene today?" Hotapp asked suddenly, effectively cutting Wallingford off.

"What other scene would he be talking about?"

Hotapp cracked the bottle of coconut water, took a sip, made a face, looked at the label, and shrugged. "Where else were you today?"

Wallingford popped his gum noisily and scribbled in his notebook.

"Before I came out to the creek I was at Roper, and before that I was at the mall. And before that," I paused. It seemed like eons ago I had made funeral arrangements with the Balling and Tidwell families, "I was here. Working."

"The mall," Hotapp said, seizing on that. "What did you do there?"

"Basically, watched the guys from DHEC work." I leaned forward in the chair and spread my hands. "I mean, I literally sat on one of those benches and watched them swab and sample." I didn't think it relevant, but I said, "Moonie ate at the—"

"Who?" Hotapp asked, cutting me off.

"Oh, sorry." I pointed to my eyebrow, the place where Moonie's crescent shaped scar is located. "It's what we call Deputy Wise."

"Right," Hotapp said, nodding, "he thinks this is somehow tied to the John Does."

Wallingford cocked his head at her and she did a little head jerk thing that I assumed to be some sort of detective shorthand for *I'll fill you in later.*

I rolled my eyes. "Moonie has a lot to say about everything. But, as I was saying, Moonie ate at the food court." I snapped my fingers. "He did take a cinnamon bun, coffee roll, whatever you want to call it to go." Hotapp and Wallingford nodded in unison as I continued, "In fact, he ate it waiting in the truck while I went into Roper."

"I'm going to need his number," Wallingford said, pen poised. He snapped his gum excitedly at the prospect of a lead.

I felt my pocket, remembering. "Sorry. I left my phone at a restaurant tonight. I don't know his number offhand. Call the Berkeley Coroner's Office and get them to patch you through."

Wallingford nodded, snapped his notebook shut and stood. "I'm going to want to print up here, if you think the perp was up here."

I shook my head. I didn't want Wallingford and his posse splashing fingerprint dust around and photographing my underwear drawer. "I'd rather you not. See what you can do downstairs."

"Mr. Clipper, don't you want us to catch who did this to you?"

"I do, but I realize it's a long shot."

"You're tying my hands here," Wallingford said, and I thought I caught a glimmer of relief in his eye. This way, the blame could be put on me when the perpetrator wasn't caught. "I want to get this guy for you."

Something tweaked my guts; I had the feeling the guy would find me first. "I appreciate your time detectives." I stood and offered my hand.

They shook it and ambled out.

"I guess I owe you," I said, opening the slider after the detectives departed.

Matey shuffled back and forth on his perch and shrieked, "Who's there?" There was no doubt this bird had saved me—intentionally or not—from a much worse fate than a broken nose and two black eyes.

"We've got to expand your vocabulary," I said, returning from the kitchen with a handful of peanuts and offering them to the bird. He cawed with delight and dug in.

When the crime techs left an hour later the horizon was pink. I was exhausted but still jacked up. I considered heading down to Sarah's to retrieve my phone but knew that would just mean I'd be up for the day. I desperately needed sleep.

Lighting a candle in the bedroom, I sat cross-legged on the floor and did my best attempt to focus on the flame. Meditation is something my shrink encouraged me to try when I refused the heavy-duty scripts. Initially, I wasn't open to Eastern-philosophy feel-good horseshit and just paid lip service to my shrink about meditating, but Maggie caught wind of it and started meditating with me. She's done Kundalini yoga for years. It's not that fake sweat-your-ass-off variety at the gym, rather it's as much spiritual as it is physical and incorporates meditation. With Maggie's guidance, I've gotten quite comfortable meditating. So much so, my shrink is starting to wean me off the sleeping pills, not that they help much.

My mind clear, I tumbled into bed and instantly fell asleep.

I awoke with a start from a deep sleep when a form thumped into the mattress.

"Go back to sleep," Maggie murmured, draping an arm over me.

I closed my eyes and plunged back into blackness.

Chapter 20

The urgency of the phone woke me. My hand groped past the pistol and snatched up the receiver. Clearing my throat, I said in the best funereal voice I could muster with a broken nose, "Granville and Sons. How may I help you?"

"Why aren't you answering your cellphone?" the female on the other end of the line demanded.

"Pardon, who's this?" I asked, opening my eyes and wishing I hadn't. My face throbbed like it had its own heartbeat. The nightstand clock read 7:30. Two hours of sleep. I almost groaned out loud.

"Jen Hotapp." Her voice was gravelly from lack of sleep.

My mind went into overdrive, and I instantly shook the cobwebs from my brain. "Why are you calling? Did you locate the guy?"

"No. I'm calling about something else. Want to go for a ride?"

"Uh, sure." I was a little thrown by the unexpected invitation.

"Can you be ready in ten minutes?"

"Where are we going?"

"Meeting with an exec from public works."

My brain ran down several scenarios, none of which I could draw reasonable conclusions, so instead of pressing her, I said, "Fifteen minutes," and recited the address where to pick me up.

"See you there." The line went dead.

I swung my legs over the edge of the bed. The pain shifted and intensified as I moved from horizontal to vertical. I sat for a moment to collect myself. I considered leaning over and giving the head that poked from under the blankets a kiss, but the pressure in my sinuses reminded me it was too risky. Instead, I patted her hip, sucked in a deep breath and stood. In the bathroom I gulped down six aspirin and glanced in the mirror. "Jesus," I muttered. Staring back was the vestige of a raccoon, deep purple, puffy bruising around both eyes, and a nose the size and color of a turnip.

I shrugged on a suit to at least look official for the meeting and staggered downstairs. The cellar door was still jammed shut with the coins and covered in black fingerprint dust, so I rode the elevator down and gritted my teeth while dabbing opaque mortuary cosmetics over the bruising. The elevator deposited me back in the garage and I let myself out and cut down the alley onto Broad Street. Five minutes later I was at Sarah's Lowcountry Café. The fresh air cleared the cobwebs but did little for the pain.

The place was mostly deserted. A few regulars slumped over the counter acknowledged me with a mixture of grunts and raised mugs.

"You tussle with a bear?" Sarah asked, lumbering to my end of the counter, Bunn carafe clutched in her hand. So much for the makeup job.

"Unhappy customer." Not wanting to give Sarah grist for the gossip mill, I plowed on, "Where is everyone?" The place would usually be hopping on a Sunday with the church crowds.

"The stomach flu has everyone all bothered. Business has been slow for a few days now."

"I left my phone here last night. Clara set it aside. And," I pointed at the carafe, "I need two large coffees to go."

"Sure hun. You look like you need them." She slipped two large Styrofoam cups off a stack behind the counter, her eyes bouncing over every feature of my face memorizing the wounds, so she could recount them with accuracy throughout the day. "I needed an extra cup myself this morning. Someone broke in here last night."

"Folks these days." I shook my head slowly. Very slowly.

Sarah poured from an unrealistic height creating a waterfall of coffee. "If a bum needs a meal I'm happy to feed him. There's no need to jimmy the back door and all that nonsense. Made quite the mess. Cut the safe right off the wall." She cackled. "He'll be disappointed. I only keep a few hundred bucks here anyhow." Pushing two lids on the steaming cups, she moved to the register, reached under it and came up with my phone.

"Can I interest you in something to eat?" she asked, as I pushed a ten-dollar bill across the counter.

The offer of chow, coupled with the smells of comfort food, made my belly rumble, but there wasn't time. "Not this morning." I jammed my phone in my pocket. I saw Hotapp's cruiser sitting at the sidewalk. It was easy to spot—even unmarked—a dark Caprice with a commercial bumper and black rims screamed cop. Balancing the coffees, I opened the door and felt Sarah's eyes on my back as I climbed into the sparse interior. Hotapp quickly closed the laptop mounted on the center console. The air conditioning was running. It felt like a walk-in reefer.

"To what do I owe the pleasure?" I asked, handing her one of the cups.

"Do you all sleep in your suits?" she asked, accepting the cup.

I assumed by "you all" she meant undertakers in general. And come to think of it, every time we had met I was wearing a coat and tie. "Makes things easier for night calls," I quipped. By the look of her eyes, she hadn't slept at all. But she was freshly scrubbed and wearing a different outfit than she had several hours prior.

"Cream and sugar?"

"No, it's black." She made a move to get out and I put my hand on her arm. "I'll get it." I didn't want a badge and gun walking into Sarah's.

She looked down at my hand and I withdrew it quickly. One of my part-timers, an ex-cop named Fred Pinne, told me cops hate being touched. "Thanks." She offered a crooked smile.

I regretted my offer as soon as the throbbing intensified to an unbearable level from the strain of pulling myself out of the car. I stifled a groan.

"That a cop car?" Sarah asked, as I bellied up to the counter again.

"Yup. Cream and sugar?"

Sarah reached under the counter. "Charleston?"

"Hanahan," I replied as she handed me a fistful of sugar packets and creamers. "Thanks." I beat a hasty retreat before she could pump me for more information. The game would be afoot all day at the café as Sherlock behind the counter tried to puzzle things out.

"Thanks," Hotapp said, dropping a few of each into the cup, checking the mirror and easing away from the curb.

"What are we doing?" I lifted the mouth flap on the lid and took a sip. It was scalding.

"There's a meeting with the water company. CID from the sheriff's department and DHEC will be there."

"Why me?"

"When I was with the detective bureau in Philly, my partner hammered into my head 'never ignore the clues in front of you.'" Hotapp took her eyes off the road to glance at me. "And you keep surfacing."

"Philly? How'd you get from the big city to here?"

"I have a sister who lives in Hilton Head."

"To go from real police work to Hanahan. Quite a jump."

"I saw something I shouldn't have."

I looked sideways at her. "Cops?"

Hotapp nodded and switched gears. "More died last night. It's only a matter of hours before the mayor implements ERP."

"Earp?"

"Emergency response program. There's panic behind the scenes."

I could imagine. It explained the sleep lines under her eyes. The lack of people on the streets seemed to be almost a symptom of a city on the verge of panic.

It was a quick eight or nine blocks to Charleston Water System headquarters—or CPW as the locals call it. Commissioners of Public Works is etched intaglio in the faux brick wall. Hotapp parked illegally on St. Philip Street across the street from the building. Public Works is a monolithic concrete and glass structure that runs the length of the block. Hotapp left her coffee balanced on the dash; I brought mine and tagged along as we jaywalked.

We were the last to join the party. Judging by Gorman's raised eyebrows when we walked into the lobby, I hadn't been extended an invitation. Introductions were made. I was introduced around as, "Tripp Clipper." No title.

I recognized the investigator from the Berkeley Sheriff's Office from yesterday at the dump site, a guy by the name of Peligrad. New faces were Charles Quaid, the COO of the water company. A squatty white man, Chuck looked like a toad in a double-breasted suit. Harlan Preacher, in-house counsel for CPW, was Chuck's exact physical opposite.

"Ladies and gentlemen, this way," Quaid said with a wave of his hand once it was established everyone was present and led us across the lobby—which was deserted since it was Sunday. We piled into an elevator.

Quaid ushered us into a nicely appointed conference room overlooking St. Philip Street. The empty coffee service on the side table meant Quaid wanted this to be brief. Joke's on him. I'd brought my own.

Quaid seated himself at the head of the table, Preacher to his right. The detectives and DHEC scientist clustered near Quaid, but I left a few empty chairs and sat opposite Quaid. Maybe he's a naturally nervous person or isn't used to staring at someone who looks like a drag queen that lost a back-alley brawl. Quaid pulled out a linen hanky from his pocket and dragged it across his head. "Anyone want a bottle of water before we begin?"

That would be like me pulling up Costco's website and offering a grieving family to pick the casket from there, and not my showroom. The man *makes* tap water. My confidence in Quaid was already zero.

Five sets of eyes stared at him. He coughed awkwardly. "Detective Peligrad, what exactly is this all about?"

Gorman held up a hand. "Detective, may I?" he asked before the sheriff's deputy could open his mouth.

Peligrad nodded.

"Dr. Quaid, I'm an epidemiologist with DHEC, and I'm currently liaising with the CDC on the, uh, situation here in Charleston."

When Gorman said "situation" Quaid tugged at his shirt collar but didn't ask him to expand.

"As you may have been made aware prior to our meeting, an individual was caught dumping raw sewage into Foster Creek. Aside from the obvious environmental concerns, there is the current, more pressing, situation happening here in Charleston. Which, in light of the sewage-dumping incident, may be causing the situation. This brings us to our meeting. The first step is to find out CPW's role, if any."

That caught Preacher's attention. "What do you mean by 'role' Mr. Gorman?"

Gorman pushed his glasses up his nose. "I'm not suggesting anything nefarious, but the fact of the matter is there's been an outbreak of *Shigella dysenteriae*. *Shigella* is a water-borne bacteria, and raw sewage was pumped into a creek that is a tributary for Bushy Park, the main reservoir for CPW—" Preacher tried to interject, but Gorman held up his hand again and plowed on, "and we're recording infections as far southwest as Meggett and southeast as Johns Island—places you retail water to."

Preacher was about to retort, but Quaid held up both his hands in a "stop" gesture. "I understand where you're coming from Mr. Gorman. Everyone including me is upset," he raised a finger, "*and* concerned, about what's happening, but frankly I don't care for the implication." Gorman opened his mouth, but Quaid didn't give him an opportunity, he plowed on. "And in a moment here you're going to see why it's impossible for the *Shigella* outbreak to have originated from CPW. In fact, in light of the recent outbreak, our crew has doubled their monitoring efforts to ensure CPW isn't involved." I could almost see visions of mass tort litigation dancing in his head. Quaid mopped his brow, and added, almost as a rejoinder, "And we don't retail water to Johns Island."

"Dr. Quaid," Gorman replied, "I'm not implying anything. I'm stating facts. And you're right, you don't retail water to Johns Island, but it is *your* water, albeit wholesale."

Quaid dropped the folded handkerchief onto the conference table and glared at Gorman. Gorman continued, "After these folks," he jerked his head to Peligrad and Hotapp, "caught the illegal dumping, my colleague and I took cultures of the truck's contents and samples from several points downstream from the dump site in Foster Creek as well as Back River. Of course, for comparison we took samples upstream. We found *Shigella* as would be expected when dealing with human excrement; the puzzling thing is we found no significant quantities of the serotype causing the outbreak."

Quaid did his famous "stop" gesture again. I was glad Quaid was being the conversation police. Gorman was starting to lose me. "Okay, Mr. Gorman, you can stop right there." His face had been getting redder and redder during Gorman's dissertation. Quaid nodded to Preacher, who opened the leather folder squared neatly before him and slid out several packets.

"This is our Water Quality Report, gentlemen, and lady," he added hastily. "Turn to the second to last page." Quaid sat silently, giving everyone a moment to orient themselves with the chart. As the members of the meeting busily turned papers I eased a tin out of my back pocket and pinched off a wad. Quaid watched with a slightly horrified look but couldn't bring himself to inform me of CPW's tobacco policy. He tore his gaze away and cleared his throat. "As you can see at the bottom are *total coliform bacteria*. Those are the types of nasty organisms Mr. Gorman is referring to," he clarified for us laymen. "There is a maximum level allowed by the EPA. Five percent. Our goal, which is 0%, and the actual number that topped out at 1.1%."

There was a printed notation: ALL REPEAT SAMPLES WERE SATISFACTORY. It made me feel good that CPW was trying to beat the federally mandated minimum, and was doing so by, at worse, 3.9%.

Peligrad was all over him. "So, what your report is saying is your water is contaminated."

"Detective," Quaid said with the tiniest note of exasperation in his voice, "we test our water over 50 times a day for the various substances listed in the report to ensure quality. What that means is that the absolute highest yield of coliform bacteria in a single test was 1.1%."

While Quaid was speaking, Preacher pulled out a tablet and tapped on it a few times, before handing it to Peligrad. "Here detective, this is the result of that single test."

Quaid cut back in, "And coliforms aren't necessarily disease-causing organisms; they are simply indicators that nastier bugs *could* be present. We call them indicator organisms."

"This test," Preacher said, "occurred in March in Ladson."

"As it turns out," Quaid said, "one of the pumps had been repaired at the pumping station, and the contamination occurred during the repair. We flushed the line and took the pump offline to sanitize it." He shrugged. "Problem fixed. We're not perfect, though we try to be." He laughed and looked around the table. When nobody joined in, he continued, "CPW distributes water to nearly a half a million people through 1,700 miles of pipeline. There are a lot of moving parts, so to speak."

I finished my coffee and released a slug of tobacco juice back into the cup, all in one motion.

Peligrad handed the tablet back to Quaid's guard dog. "So, what are you saying Dr. Quaid? There's no way this guy dumping sewage into the creek, and has admitted to doing it in the past," he added quickly, "could be causing the sickness?"

Quaid shook his head. His jowls jiggled. "Absolutely not Detective. For three reasons." He held up three fingers like a European: middle, ring, and pinky. "First," he ticked off his middle finger, "the water piped in from our reservoirs is collected into sedimentation basins. We add alum that causes the particles to clump together into floc. The floc falls to the bottom of the sedimentation basins."

Peligrad looked like he was sorry he asked, but Hotapp had produced a notebook and was busy scribbling.

Quaid ticked off his ring finger. He had settled in and was enjoying the comfortable territory. "Next the water is siphoned off and filtered. We use micro filtration in which the feedwater passes through a membrane that filters between 0.1 and 5 microns. Essentially, it can remove stuff as small as the tiniest bacteria—including *Shigella*—and stuff like paint pigments and tobacco smoke.

"Finally," he was left wagging his pinky at us. I wished he had ticked off his fingers in the opposite direction, so he ended up giving us the middle finger. It felt that way anyway. "We have the disinfection step, or chlorination. That kills any remaining viruses and protozoa. Then we adjust the fluoride and voilà, safe tap water." Quaid dropped the pinky and shrugged like it was almost too easy.

Gorman had been nodding along, "You'll have to excuse me Dr. Quaid, but I don't know too much about your processes. Is there any way that the clean water could become contaminated after the fact? I'm attempting to wrap my head around the fact that the public is being infected with *Shigella*, and water is a common infection vector. And someone is dumping sewage into your water source."

"The short answer is no. Aside from some equipment malfunction, or someone deliberately tampering," Preacher winced as Quaid said that but remained quiet and allowed him to continue. "With the product water then no, there's no chance of a bacterial contamination."

"What do you mean tamper?" I asked. All the faces at the table swiveled to look in my direction. "Aren't the lines all underground?"

Quaid looked startled. "Yes, the piping is almost exclusively underground. However, there are pumping stations and water tanks which are aboveground. But they're locked, and you'd need special tools and knowledge of the equipment. It's highly unlikely."

I spit. "How secure are these facilities?"

Preacher smoothly cut in. "Mr. Clipper, I assure you they're secure by industry standards, and as Dr. Quaid stated if on the off chance there was tampering we would catch it immediately with the battery of *daily* tests."

Hotapp underlined something twice in her notebook.

I dug in my pocket and pulled out my phone and scrolled through my photos for a moment.

Quaid looked around. Satisfied, he put his palms on the table. "Well, if you all don't have any further—"

"This key look familiar?" I asked, cutting him off and sliding my phone down the conference table like a hockey puck.

"What?" Quaid asked, confused before even looking at my phone.

Hotapp focused a laser stare on me. I could read her mind: *tell me what you know.*

"Does that key look like it could access your equipment?" I clarified.

Quaid picked up the phone and held it between him and Preacher. They both squinted at the screen.

Preacher looked up. "What exactly is this? Where did you get this?"

I cut my eyes in Hotapp's direction as if to say: *Your turn. I've overstepped my official authority.* She was all over it. "Are you still using keyed locks Mr. Preacher?"

Preacher didn't have a clue. I could see it in his eyes. He was just the mouthpiece. Quaid did. "We are," he stammered, "offsite.

Headquarters and the treatment plant have been converted to electronic locks. However, from a photo I can't identify this as belonging to CPW." He snorted. "I don't know if I'd be able to identify one of our keys if it was sitting in front of me. They're keys!" There was a long pause. "Why are you asking?" There was a note of apprehension in his voice.

"That's not your concern Dr. Quaid," Hotapp said briskly, turning some pages in her notebook like she was looking for something, "it's part of an ongoing investigation and therefore I can't comment on it."

***

"Tell me about the key," Hotapp said as soon as we stepped onto the street.

"Moonie found it in a zippered pocket in Sam Badgers' backpack."

She didn't look happy about just finding out about the key, but plowed on, "Where's the key now?"

"Gone," I said, waiting for her to get in and unlock the doors from the inside. Cop cars don't have fancy key fobs with buttons. "When that fed scooped me for the second time at Badgers's apartment they confiscated the key. At the time we thought the key was to Badgers's place."

Hotapp cranked the ignition and executed an illegal U-turn.

"To be completely honest with you I kind of forgot about the key until now, but it was heavy-duty. Definitely commercial. Like to a lock on a pumping station or treatment plant or water tower."

Hotapp steered with her knee and peeled the tab back on the lid of her coffee cup. "Interesting." She took a sip. "Especially given where they were found, the boat landing at the reservoir near the treatment plant."

"Quaid said the locks at the plant are electronic."

"I know. Something is connected here, but I can't seem to bridge the gap."

"I agree. There's too much overlap. In Islam they don't believe in coincidence. Everything is 'God's will,' meaning there's always an underlying reason that might only be visible to God."

"God's will," Hotapp repeated, testing the words out.

God's will. The words transported me from Charleston to a hardscrabble village in Takhar Province in the foothills of the Hindu Kush. The cold was bracing, but it was sunny and clear. We'd come to the village to meet with the tribal elders and broker a deal to oppose the recent resurgence of Hezb-e-Islami Gulbuddin. I was leaning against a Humvee in the village square offering candy to the children, while the officers met the elders in the hall, when all hell broke loose.

The first RPG warhead exploded 20 meters from my position, its blast knocking me to the ground, followed by the distinct *tat-tat-tat* sound of AK-47s.

"Contact. Four insurgents on the ridgeline," my radio crackled. We took cover and returned fire.

Close air support rolled in 12 minutes later doing multiple gun runs across the hillside, ending the attack.

We rolled out with the A-10s providing aerial coverage. Through the window of the Humvee, I spied an Afghan woman running into the square. She dropped to her knees and hugged the mangled form of a boy, one of the children I had given candy to 15 minutes ago. Dark arterial spray covered a wall. She gathered him in her lap—shiny, wet blood reflecting off her dark dress in the harsh sunlight—and rocked him. Her screams still visit me at night. A man rushed to her side and hugged her crying, "Insha'Alla! Insha'Allah!"

I tapped the translator. "What's he saying?"

"Who?"

"The man."

I couldn't see the translator's eyes behind his wraparounds. He continued staring straight ahead, and said, "God's will."

"I don't believe in coincidence either," Hotapp said, snapping me back. "No cop does. There's too much reoccurring around the theme of water, and I'm convinced it's tied up somehow."

"How do you reconcile their constant monitoring? If someone did attempt to contaminate the water supply CPW would detect it immediately, at least according to Dr. Quack."

Hotapp pulled in front of the funeral home. Sitting on the steps was a familiar figure with a pixie cut and purple streak. I groaned inwardly. Giving her that money had been akin to giving a stray cat milk.

The detective drummed her fingers on the steering wheel. "Like I said, there are certain logic gaps I can't jump right now." She shrugged and sipped the coffee.

"How sure are you?" I pointed to her cup. "I bet that was brewed with city water."

Hotapp made a face, rolled down the window and pitched out the contents of the cup. For a minute I thought she was going to spit out the mouthful she had, but she swallowed it with the relish of castor oil. "Can you text me the photo of the key?" I nodded, and she recited her phone number.

Despite my best intentions, I winced climbing out of the car, shut the door and waved. Hotapp didn't notice. Her laptop was open and she was busy typing.

"What happened to your face?" Cam asked. She was wearing the same jean jacket and lace up boots as last time along with a skirt that matched the jacket over tights with rips in them that I couldn't figure out if they were on purpose or from living on the street.

"Fight."

"Seriously?" Cam stood. On the steps she was taller than me.

"What do you want?" There was a jar of white lightning under the kitchen sink. All I wanted was a sip from the jar and to lie on the couch with a bag of frozen peas on my face.

"I was in the neighborhood."

I pulled a couple of twenties out of my wallet. "Here."

She looked at the bills, scorn tugging the corners of her mouth. "I didn't come for a handout."

"What did you come for?" My face was throbbing. I wasn't in the mood for a social call. I started to withdraw the money but she snatched it and marched down the steps and past me muttering, "Fuck you dude. I thought you were cooler than that."

"You're welcome," I called after her.

Without bothering to turn around she raised her arm and extended the middle finger. I started laughing, but quickly stopped as pain blossomed behind my eyes.

Chapter 21

As soon as I opened the apartment door I knew something was wrong. The smell was overwhelming.

"Who's there?" Matey screamed.

I ignored the bird perched on a dining room chair and rushed back to the bedroom. "Mags? Mags?" I called, trying to remain as calm as possible. The room was empty. I found Maggie curled in the fetal position between the tub and toilet.

"How long have you been like this?" I asked, kneeling and placing my hand on her forehead. It was burning up.

She let out a groan and opened her eyes. They were bloodshot and unfocused. "The cramps started a few hours ago. Diarrhea, I don't know..." She seemed confused.

"Is it bad?"

"Hematochezia."

My heart sank. Blood in her stools. The swamp sickness. "You should've called me!"

"I was hoping it wasn't this. When I started," she paused and sucked in a ragged breath, "started vomiting I knew."

"We've got to get you out of here." I scooped her up like a baby, ignoring the fireworks going off in my sinuses. Downstairs, I held her with one arm and yanked open the pickup's door and laid her sideways on the seat. After an awkward moment with the seat belt I decided to forgo it.

Roaring up Broad Street, I dialed the operator at MUSC and demanded to be connected to Terri Marcislin. The operator connected me and it rang five times before Dr. Marcislin's cheerful cover message played. I hung up before the message could finish and dialed the operator again.

"Medical University of—"

"Connect me to the pathology laboratory."

"Pathology Department?"

"No. The laboratory."

There was typing while the operator brought the connection up on her screen. "Hold please." There was a click and a pause and the line rang once, twice, and continued ringing. After the twelfth ring, I was about to hang up when harried voice answered. "Yeah?"

"Put Terri Marcislin on. Tell her it's regarding Maggie Stryker. And it's an emergency."

The handset was placed on the counter and I heard the voice calling, "Terri, phone for you. It's an emergency."

"It's Tripp Clipper," I said when she picked up, "I'm three minutes out from the hospital with Maggie. She's contracted the illness." I continued out of pure reflex, the medic in me ticking off her vitals, "Pulse is 110. Blood pressure is 91/54. She's feverish and presenting with cramps and hematochezia."

This was a woman not used to trauma. In her specialty everyone was already dead, so there was a note of alarm in her voice. "Bring her around the ER entrance," she said as I made a right onto Ashley Avenue and gunned it by the lake. "I'll make sure there's a bed waiting for her." There were no goodbye salutations. The line went dead.

Health care is no different than other professions; they look after their own. I clicked off and suddenly had to stand on the brakes for a pedestrian in the walkway. Maggie flew off the seat and into the wheel well with a groan. "Hang in there," I said, stomping on the gas, "we're almost there."

Screeching to a halt under the emergency portico, I hopped out and collected Maggie out of the wheel well. Cradling her in my arms, I rushed into the waiting room. It was packed. There were patients doubled over on the uncomfortable waiting room chairs. The ones that couldn't get seats huddled on the floor clutching their guts. The unmistakable odor of feces hung in the air.

Dr. Marcislin charged through the glass doors followed by an escort pushing a bed. They were wearing gowns, masks, and gloves. I gently laid Maggie on the bed, and Dr. Marcislin led us back to an open bay where a nurse and physician were waiting. Both were male and looked to be in their late 20s but exuding an air of calm and competence. Based on their calculating stares, they probably thought we both were being brought in for treatment. I was sweating from exertion, and the makeup was running down my face, fully revealing the bruising on my face. But Dr. Marcislin quickly set them straight.

If you counted her permanent hairdo to her height Dr. Marcislin might clear the five-foot mark, but according to Maggie she compensated with ferocity, which was on full display as she pointed to nurse and doctor, both with at least a foot on her. "This is one of my doctors, which means she's one of your colleagues. You will work her up immediately, have the lab work expedited, and have answers for me before noon."

The nurse checked his big digital watch. "Ma'am, that's in about two hours."

"Exactly. Get it done. You can reach me in the path lab," she said. Changing tones, she took Maggie's hand. "You're in good hands, hun. If you need anything let me know."

Maggie blinked and offered a weak smile. Dr. Marcislin spun and marched out.

The nurse and doctor exchanged a look as if to say *okay*. The nurse got busy collecting vitals while the doctor began taking a history. I plopped down in the vinyl chair wedged in the corner and tried not to get in the way.

***

Maggie's condition worsened by the time they got the test results. My heart jumped into my throat when the young doctor, who seemed very competent, came back into the ER bay and shook his head. "She has dysentery." Maggie writhed and pawed at her abdomen on the bed next to me, the sheets soaked with sweat. "She's lucky," the doctor continued, "we managed to get her an isolation room. Everyone else is having to make do with whatever we can come up with." He shrugged. "Escort will be down shortly."

Once in her room, Maggie got a new team of doctors. Two women and a man, people I suspected Dr. Marcislin handpicked. Because of her penicillin allergy the doctors decided not to chance it with Amoxil, the standard course of treatment. The team decided on Ciprofloxacin as the course of treatment. I kept my mouth shut and let them do their work but was well aware many *Shigella* strains are resistant to that drug. They gave her an antidiarrheal in her IV as well as something for the pain that kind of knocked her out. I held her clammy hand as she lay writhing in the twilight zone occasionally moaning.

My phone vibrated sometime mid-afternoon. I pushed the extendable arm TV away from my spot next to the bed. The news was covering the closing of Charleston. It was a never-ending loop of the mayor's Emergency Response Plan. First it was the highway patrol sealing off Charleston at all major arteries, I-26 and 78 near the airport, I-526 north and south of the city and 17 to the east, their cruisers dramatically blocking the roads. Interspersed was footage of the National Guard mobilizing, convoys of Humvees and troop transport trucks speeding toward Charleston. The official line—at least on the airwaves—was, "a highly infectious strain of *Shigella* is causing a deadly outbreak of dysentery." History was being made. The city had never been under quarantine before, even during the 1918 flu pandemic. The local media was having a field day. The national media was descending.

I had to answer the phone in the corner of the room because I wasn't allowed to leave. I too was in isolation for refusing the protective equipment. The health professionals didn't know what I was now almost positive of, the disease was coming from our water supply—nothing a mask and polypropylene gown would do a damn thing for.

It was Maggie's mother. She was frenzied.

"Clip, what's happening? I talked to Margaret yesterday and she said everything was fine." The words tumbled out quickly.

"Don't worry Liz," I said, switching to my soothing funeral director tone. "Maggie is being cared for at her hospital by her colleagues. They're providing the best care possible."

"Don't worry? I saw on the news there's been some kind of outbreak in your city, and you leave me a voicemail that my daughter's in the hospital."

"Yes, there's been an outbreak of a virulent type of dysentery," I said, feeding her the media propaganda. "The doctors know what she has and are treating her for it." I added, "Aggressively."

Her voice edged toward hysteria. "The news here says people are dying!"

"You know the news. It's the elderly and children that are in the most danger. Maggie is a healthy adult. The doctors are very optimistic." I glanced at the sweating form on the hospital bed. The color of her face next to her red hair looked a little green.

"Max and I are getting on the next flight out of Midway—"

"Don't bother Liz," I said, harsher than I intended. "The city has been put under quarantine until they can get this under control. You'll never get in."

"We'll wait in a hotel until we can," she said stubbornly. "We need to be close."

Great, my girlfriend's parents waiting on the outskirts of the city to rush to the funeral home and hover over their daughter. Probably how the Romans felt when the Visigoths besieged them. "Why don't you wait until the travel restrictions have been lifted?" I offered. *And your daughter's better and will convince you not to come.*

"Are you with Margaret?"

"Yes. I'm sitting right here in her room," I hoped my proximity to her daughter would offer some solace.

"Let me talk to her, please." Her voice was pleading.

"She's sleeping now." I could detect panic in the silence, so I added, "I'll have her call you as soon as she—" The call ended abruptly.

"God," I muttered, looking at my dead phone, "not the smoothest way to end a conversation." There's so much metal and concrete in the hospitals that the phone has to burn a lot of power to get a decent signal. Six hours had sapped the battery. I called the answering service and asked the operator to page Nikki and have her call me, reading the number off of the clunky old-fashioned room phone.

"Clip?" Nikki said, when I answered on the first ring.

"Hey, Maggie has contracted the sickness. I'm at MUSC with her."

"Oh no! Is she all right? Are you sick too?"

"I'm fine," I said. "They tucked me in isolation too. I'll tell you about it once they cut me loose. I need you to do a couple of things for me. First, can you bring my phone charger by MUSC? Second, stop by Roper and check on Isabella. Your boyfriend Chuck is trapped there, so you'll be able to get an escort up there to see her. Go in the back way and give him a call. You still have his number don't you?"

"Uh, I think so." There was silence and I heard some rustling. "Here, got it." There was a long pause. "Is there a chance I could contract the sickness? I mean, I have Jackson to think about."

"Don't repeat this to anyone because I'm not one hundred percent and I don't want to add to the frenzy if I'm incorrect, but do not, I repeat, do not drink the water—that's the vector. I'd go insofar to say avoid all contact with tap water until this gets sorted out. You'll be fine going to Roper to check on Isabella. I wouldn't ask you to do anything that could get your boy sick."

Nikki started to breathe a sigh of relief. "Wait, you're saying I shouldn't shower?"

"If you're feeling adventurous my advice is to keep your mouth shut."

After hanging up, I pulled the TV back in front of me and continued to watch the news cycle feed on the drama unfolding outside the hospital walls.

***

The medicine had started working. Maggie was sleeping fitfully, no longer moaning. I was watching the kind of bad programming that only comes on after the rest of the world has gone to sleep. The remnants of an institutional supper: Salisbury steak with gravy, lumpy whipped potatoes, string beans, and vanilla pudding, sat uncollected on the rolling bed tray. The hospital staff had brought my phone charger, and Nikki called shortly after to brief me on Isabella. The hospital staff wouldn't give her any information on her status, but because of her connection with the security guard, Chuck, she had been allowed to view her through the glass.

"Mrs. Granville was sleeping when I saw her. She doesn't look good, waxen and frail."

I thanked Nikki for getting eyes on Isabella, it made me feel better, and after hanging up called Roper and battled my way through the phone tree until I finally landed at the nurse's station in the former surgical ICU.

"SICU," a harried female voice said. She added her name but it was so fast I couldn't tell if it was a first or last name.

"I'm calling about the status of a patient, Isabella Granville." I was standing at the window of the room, whispering into the vertical blinds in an effort not to disturb Maggie.

"Sir, you'll have to speak up." I repeated myself and heard keys tapping. "Are you a family member?"

"No. She has no family."

There was a sigh. "Sir, I can't give out information about our patients."

"Is the big nurse there?"

"Huh?" The question caught the nurse off guard.

"You know, the big nurse, the giant with the beard and glasses."

"You mean Jerry? I think he's in the break room." How quaint: Jerry the Nursing Giant. Sounds like the makings of a children's fable.

"Get him on the line, now," I said, adopting my faux-official persona. "Tell him Special Investigator Clipper is holding."

The line went quiet and I thought she had hung up on me and was about to start climbing the phone tree again, when the handset clattered. "This is Jerry."

I almost said Giant but caught myself. "Jerry, Special Investigator Clipper calling for a status update on Mrs. Granville."

He sighed. "She's developed encephalitis—"

"Symptoms?" I demanded, cutting him off. The bad hospital supper was rumbling around in my gut angrily.

"Uh," he replied, caught off guard. I heard tapping of keys. "Fever, some mild confusion, and photophobia."

"Shit," I muttered under my breath. "Any diagnostics or is this pure guesswork?"

"Lumbar puncture, the latest one done today was inconclusive. Her EEG is showing some sharp spiking in the left temporal lobe."

"CT?"

"There's no baseline for comparison."

I kicked myself for not making them give her a CT yesterday when I was there. "What course of treatment is she on?"

There was a pause. "Her attending has her on Dexamethasone, 10 mg IV and 800 mg Acyclovir." Dexamethasone is a corticosteroid used to treat cerebral edema and the other medicine is an antiviral.

"Is it viral?"

"No viral titers detected in the lumbar puncture. The Acyclovir is a precaution."

A hefty precaution, if I recalled correctly from my medic days. "What's the mortality rate?"

Jerry let out a deep, contemplative sigh. "I don't know, man. I really don't."

"Look Jerry, this is completely off the record. Isabella is a friend, colleague, and the one of the closest things to family I have. I just want to know what her prognosis is. What would you *guess* the mortality rate to be?" Silence. I imagined him mentally wrestling with himself, his training against the plea of humanity.

Finally, he said, "Probably about 25 percent. Maybe 30."

I placed my head against the vertical blinds and smashed them into the window, the glass cool. No wonder there was panic. One in four people were dying that contracted the undiagnosed brain disease. Encephalitis was rare, and normally was fatal in less than one percent of cases.

Jerry dropped his voice and continued, "Seems the numbers are skewed more toward the elderly and immunocompromised." Made sense. Disease is typically harder on those demographics.

I thanked Jerry and hung up. MUSC, like most modern health-care facilities, is tobacco-free, but nobody frisked me when they booked me, so I pulled out my tin and pinched off a wad. The tobacco eased my anxiety a bit, but I couldn't sit and watch more fear mongering on TV, so I began pacing and spitting into the little juice cup that came with my supper. The hospital staff wasn't too active at this time of the night, so I was a bit surprised when a gentleman, not in hospital scrubs, badged himself into the room.

Seeing the mess on my face gave him a moment's pause, but he professionally pushed past it and said, "You Jebediah Clipper III?"

I eyed him for a long second. Good things never followed when people started using my legal name. The man's clothes said he wasn't a health-care specialist. Under the polypropylene gown he was wearing heavy canvas cargo pants—the type paramedics usually wear—and an airman's jacket. And his eyes, behind wireless eyeglasses frames, said he wasn't military or law enforcement; there wasn't that sharp vigilance. I spit. "I am. Who's asking?"

He took two steps across the room and offered his hand. "Terry Bluechel. Deputy commander for DMORT." I stared at the blue nitrile for a moment—it represented death and pestilence on a grand scale. Disaster Mortuary Operation Response Team is a federal response team activated for mass fatalities. Things were worse than I thought. I took Bluechel's hand. His grip was fierce.

"What can I do for you Terry?" Bluechel glanced in the direction of Maggie, as if unsure we should talk in the room. "It's okay," I assured him. "They've given her a sedative."

"I was told you're the man I need to see."

"By whom?"

Bluechel shook his head. Gray hairs peeked out from under his cap, and the lines around his eyes told me he was pushing 60. "Not sure who on your end. Order came down from my boss."

"Okay then, for what?"

"We're setting up the incident morgue to process the fatalities. My boss prefers to have local talent overseeing things."

"My understanding of DMORT is because you're under Uncle Sam's umbrella your team's home state professional licenses are sufficient."

"No, no, you're correct." He waved his hands like a ref would call a missed touchdown. "But after the Katrina fiasco and the media spotlight that was shone on the disaster relief, the higher ups prefer to have someone local helping direct things. And technically," he added, "we work under the local authorities, your coroner, Earl Blood."

"No thanks." I'd been in a bureaucratic organization long enough to translate: *we need a scapegoat in case things go sideways.* There was a very good chance Moonie was going to get sacrificed for "losing" two bodies, but it was his livelihood. I didn't work for Uncle Sam anymore. I wasn't about to volunteer to be their whipping boy.

"My girlfriend is extremely sick, and because I refused the personal protection they're keeping me too."

I couldn't tell because of the mask, but I thought Bluechel smiled. "I can spring you."

I can spring myself, I thought. *Just walk out and threaten to cough in anyone's face that tries to stop me.* "No thanks. Even if you could spring me, I'd want to be here with her. I'll give you the names of some of my competitors that can help you if you need a local undertaker."

It was subtle, but Bluechel shifted his weight so he fairly loomed in front of me. "Look Jebediah, the commander was very specific. Apparently, you have the kind of background needed for an operation like this. Won't you answer the call to serve the greater good?"

I didn't like Bluechel's psychological play one bit. I drew myself up, set the spit cup down and crossed my arms. "Terry, I've served my time. I owe my country or my fellow citizens nothing. I'd consider it in other circumstances, but I have something more important happening now." I cut my eyes over Bluechel's shoulder. "Tell your boss to find someone else. Kindly leave."

Bluechel whirled, badged himself out of the room, and immediately got on his phone in the hallway. He's the type of guy who talks with his hands, and I could almost hear the conversation based on the gesticulations. By my count he was on the phone with three different people before he badged the door and it *whooshed* open. "Here," he said, thrusting the phone in my direction. "The governor."

"Ma'am?"

"Mr. Clipper," a no-nonsense voice crackled through the earpiece. I recognized the voice of Catherine Scotney from the news. "I have a favor to ask of you. I understand you're a little reluctant to help the emergency response effort because of a sick family member." Her voice softened a little. "I can certainly understand that. Would you consider joining the effort if I assigned a 24-hour, dedicated nurse to your loved one?" Without waiting for an answer, the governor continued, "Obviously, I can't make you do it, but I understand from Commander D'ambrosio you're the person best suited for the task at hand. So, Mr. Clipper, I'd count it as a personal favor if you'd help the State of South Carolina."

She was good. No wonder she was the state's youngest governor. I couldn't refuse, and she knew it. It was a forgone conclusion when I said, "Of course ma'am. It'd be my honor."

"Thank you, Mr. Clipper." The line disconnected.

I handed Bluechel his phone. There wasn't victory in his eyes, and suddenly I felt bad. "Be down at the yard at zero seven hundred. We'll begin processing the backlog."

I held up a finger. "One condition."

Bluechel raised his eyebrows to say *go on*.

"I get to bring my apprentice."

He shrugged. "Fine." Bluechel turned to leave.

I called after him, "How bad is it?"

Bluechel stood in the open doorway. "One hundred and sixty-four."

"Jesus." I closed my eyes and nodded. "Zero seven hundred."

Chapter 22

A barricade blocked the entrance to the Columbus Street Terminal, which ironically is nowhere near a street by that name. I pulled perpendicular to the roadblock, rolled my window down and waited. A corporal stepped from behind the stacked sandbags and approached with practiced movements, his hands resting easy on the slung M4.

"Sir, port's closed. You'll need to turn around." He twirled his finger in a circular motion.

Beside the fact he and all his colleagues were wearing surgical masks, I suddenly felt uneasy. The patches on his fatigues indicated he was with the 82nd Airborne Division out of Fort Bragg. Regular army, not national guard.

"We're with DMORT."

The soldier held out a gloved hand. Utility gloves, the kind with grips that laborers use. "I'll need to see some identification." I acquiesced and the corporal took a couple steps back and got on his comms. Satisfied, he returned my license and motioned for his colleagues to raise the barricade.

"Ever been here?" Nikki asked as I navigated a winding drive through the marsh.

"No." The drive opened into a concrete jungle, hundreds of cars sat lined up on acres of weedy asphalt, and rows of freight cars sat motionless behind a backdrop of stacked metal containers and warehouses. It was a ghost town.

"Know where we're going?"

"There." I lifted my finger off the steering wheel and pointed to the distinct logo of rolling hills conveniently painted on the side of one of the smaller buildings. It looked cheery and verdant and definitely out of place amongst the sun-bleached color palette.

"Terra? Don't they import produce?"

I shrugged and pulled into a parking spot. "That's where this Bluechel fella told us to report."

Nikki hunched her shoulders and clasped her hands. "Are you nervous?"

"A little." It was a lie to make her feel better. The army had programmed nervousness out of my head a long time ago; my brain was busy running down scenario analyses.

We rounded the building to the side that abutted the river, and the hanger doors were open revealing the warehouse crawling with activity. The workers looked like snowmen in their protective gear, white hooded Tyvek coveralls with black rubber boots taped off with yellow tape. A small device that looked like a compressor was belted to their waists, with a black hose snaking up under the hood.

We approached a moving truck that was backed up to the warehouse. A whimsical illustration of a couple canoeing was stenciled on the side of the truck. The fun stopped there. A group of snowmen unloaded shiny white body bags onto portable gurneys that another group pushed into the biggest walk-in-refrigerator I'd ever seen. It was easily the size of three basketball courts. "Hey," I said hailing a worker pushing a gurney. She reeked of chlorine. "We're looking for Bluechel." I spoke louder than necessary, not sure how well sound penetrated the hood.

The woman looked confused at first, probably due to our complete lack of protective gear, but said, "Try the office." Her mask fogged as she shouted loud enough for me to hear. The blank look on my face prompted her to point a blue glove into the bowels of the warehouse.

"Look at this," Nikki breathed as we walked into the warehouse where more snowmen were assembling temporary exam rooms that reminded me of cubicles. They were three sided and had a computer console, instrument array, and space for a gurney to be rolled in. Next to the exam area were rows upon rows of plastic banquet tables. People were stringing cables and setting up dozens of computer workstations on the tables. The activity reminded me of an anthill.

Terra's business office was nothing more than a single room bump-out in the rear. We entered and found Terry Bluechel hunched over a desk with a curly-haired woman and the Charleston coroner, Earl Blood. They looked annoyed to be interrupted, but Bluechel forced a smile when he saw who it was.

"Jebediah—"

"Clip, please."

Without missing a beat, he continued, "Clip, this is Dr. Cynthia D'ambrosio, and I believe you know Coroner Blood."

Earl Blood and I nodded at each other to feign cordiality, but it was for the benefit of the DMORT folks. He hates me because I made him look like a fool regarding the Chloe Maas murder last year, and I hate him because he's small-minded and petty.

"Tripp Clipper," I said, offering my hand to D'ambrosio. She reminded me of a young, hip college professor. Her blonde mane, gathered back in a sensible manner, framed a face that looked like it was sunny most days. Today was not one of them.

D'ambrosio was all business. "You come highly recommended. With your background you'll be a real asset to the team. Welcome aboard."

"It's an honor." Sucked in for a penny, I may as well throw in for a pound. "Your team did some fine work at Bush Field a year or so ago." Eagle Air, a regional carrier, hit a flock of geese climbing to altitude out of Augusta Regional. The flight hadn't been full, but close to 30 souls perished—including a golfer who played the Masters in the mid-'90s.

D'ambrosio shot Bluechel a look. "That wasn't us."

"Isn't that your region?" DMORT teams respond to incidents that fall into their geographic region. Region IV includes the Carolinas, Tennessee, Georgia, Florida, Alabama, Mississippi, and Kentucky.

"That's Four. We're All Hazard." My stomach did a little flip. Things were much worse than I thought.

"What's—" Nikki said.

Pretending not to hear her, I cut her off and introduced her around. D'ambrosio shook Nikki's hand and looked at Bluechel. "Terry, can you please bring these two up to speed." It was an order, not a question. "Coroner Blood and I have a call with Secretary Fouraker," she consulted her watch, "in two minutes."

We were dismissed.

"Here," Bluechel said, pointing to a box of surgical masks and several boxes of latex gloves sitting on a table. "Put these on before we go back out on the floor." He tugged the mask that was around his neck back up and snapped on a pair of gloves. Nikki and I helped ourselves.

"Fouraker is the secretary of HHS," Bluechel explained, as we followed him out of the office.

"Pardon?" Nikki asked. I was glad; I was in the dark too.

"Oh, HHS?" Bluechel said, distracted. "Department of Health and Human Services, it's what DMORT falls under. Here are the changing areas." He pointed to the curtained areas we passed on the way in. "Men's and women's." Bluechel pointed to the left and right, and his finger traveled to the decontamination stations that looked like a portable toilet sitting in a baby pool. My mind flashed quickly to the scene of Roy emptying his tanker full of chemical toilet waste into Foster Creek. "That's the pre-decontamination area," Bluechel continued, "to strip off your outer gloves, aprons, and booties. That's the first decon shower, a water flush. After that you dispose of all protective gear, the second decon shower is with an emulsifier." He looked at us and nodded. "A germicidal soap."

Nikki and I nodded along.

Walking again, Bluechel pointed to the partitioned areas, still being set up. "We're setting up identification areas. This is an unusual scene because many of the victims have already been autopsied by the pathology staff at the local institutions and have been identified. Typically, we're involved in situations where we're trying to identify victims or," he raised his eyebrows, "pieces."

When Bluechel said "pieces" Nikki closed her eyes and silently crossed herself.

"However," Bluechel continued, "the DPMU is en route from Frederick, Maryland in case we need it for further postmortem examination. Though I doubt it."

"Dip mu?" I felt like I was back in the military with the acronyms.

"Portable morgue," Bluechel said. We were at the opposite end of the warehouse where there wasn't as much activity. "But I doubt we'll be doing many autopsies, at least initially. Right now, we'll simply be affirming identities already made by the institutions and entering the data into VIP. Victim Identification Profile is a mass fatality software-tracking program that allows us to rapidly collect and collate data from a disaster area. We'll be photographing, taking radiological images, doing visual documentation, and blood draws to work up a file on each victim—a DVP, or disaster victim packet—prior to disposition. Of course, this location was chosen, along with other reasons, because of the availability of cold storage." Bluechel jerked his thumb at the massive cold area where the snowmen were busy jockeying gurneys into some sort of order. "The hospitals ran out of cold storage several days ago, and health officials are leery of leaning on mortuaries for fear of spreading the sickness further into the community. So, in some cases we're dealing with decomp too." *It gets better and better*, I thought as Bluechel continued, "If things get worse there's plenty of room. Basically, all the produce imported for South Carolina and the three neighboring states comes through this warehouse."

Nikki's face mirrored my thoughts. I was never eating anything healthy again.

Bluechel wove us around several staggered, opaque screens, and stopped at the warehouse door where an 18-wheeler trailer was backed. "Of course, we have a dentist to analyze dental records if needed to complete the identification, but in this situation, I suspect it won't be likely." Bluechel climbed onto the trailer and tugged at the door latch, swinging it open and hopping out of the way at the same time. The door slammed open with a *bang*. It was filled with shrink-wrapped caskets standing on end like soldiers at attention.

"This," Bluechel said, sweeping his arm like he was a game-show host presenting a lucrative prize, "is what you'll be doing. I need you to prepare the caskets prior to disposition."

"You want us to *unload* and *unwrap* caskets?" I hoped the derision in my voice was evident. This is the job that only I could do, a task so momentous a request had come directly from the governor? Commander D'ambrosio's words replayed briefly, "With your background you'll be a real asset to the team." Unbelievable. I was going back to the hospital to be with Maggie, and let some longshoreman—hell, anyone with a pulse and strong back—unload those caskets.

"Well yeah," Bluechel said. He directed our attention to a table full of industrial looking tools. "That'll be the first step, unload the caskets, before you prepare them for burial at sea. And then you'll—"

I shook my head and held up my hand in a *stop* gesture. "Wait, did you say burial at sea?"

Bluechel looked confused at being interrupted. "Uh, yeah."

I pointed to the far end of the warehouse where the snowmen were still busy offloading white pouches out of a different moving truck, this one with some evergreen trees decaled on the side. "We're burying *these* people at sea?"

Bluechel used a knuckle to push his glasses up the bridge of his nose and nod. "Yes."

"How did you get the families to agree to this?"

"We didn't. This is one of the emergency measures we're taking to contain the outbreak."

"On whose authority?" Despite my best efforts to remain calm, my blood pressure had spiked and with it the volume of my voice.

"Fouraker is acting under the National Health Security Strategy."

"Bullshit Terry! You can't just dump people's loved ones in the ocean without their consent. And, I won't be a part of this." My role became crystal clear. They needed a patsy for the lawsuits that would follow, and why not? I'm sure they were planning on putting my name on the death certificate. If that was the case it was probably Earl that offered up my name by whispering it in the Governor's ear. He may be an asshole, but he's a well-connected asshole. "Come on." I motioned to Nikki. "We're not going to be part of this madness."

Bluechel's voice stopped us. "It goes above Fouraker, you know. The President has quietly declared an emergency under Title 50."

I turned and slowly walked back to Bluechel. He hadn't moved a muscle. "That's for national emergencies and...war," I said. My gut said we wouldn't be dumping people off the side of a ship for a run-of-the-mill national emergency.

"It is."

I pulled out my phone. I needed to make a call to Risden. He had his finger on the pulse of the federal machine and would be able to confirm some things.

"It won't work here," Bluechel said. "Army's running a signal jammer. Clip," he said, pulling my attention away from my phone screen with no signal, "I need to know. Can we count on you?"

Can we count on you? That's something you say before a bar brawl, not asking someone to disappear hundreds of human beings "No. This is crazy."

There was a flicker in Bluechel's eyes, and all at once I understood. If I didn't play ball I'd be kept under lock and key until there was an endgame. There wouldn't be any whistle blowers. I continued shaking my head.

Bluechel drew himself up. He thought I'd be an easier sell. "I know it's crazy," he said. "But it's the only thing we know to do at this point. The CDC is completely baffled, but the thing sent up major red flags in the DOD."

"They know what it is?"

"I don't know for sure," he said, shaking his head, "but there's talk," he craned his head and looked around to make sure nobody could hear us which was ludicrous considering we were standing at the far end of a warehouse the size of several aircraft hangers and separated by several privacy screens, "it's weaponized."

I squinted at Bluechel like I was having trouble comprehending. There was a quarter-inch scratch on the left lens of his glasses I hadn't noticed before. It was crescent shaped. My senses came rushing back like being snapped out of hypnosis. All I could manage was, "Shit."

"Shit is right. That's why we have the regulars out front, and why it was decided this would be the best method of disposition. Burying could lead to ground water issues down the—"

"What about cremation?" Nikki asked.

"Two reasons." Bluechel held up two fingers. "There aren't enough crematoriums in the area to handle the demand in a reasonable amount of time, and since we're not completely sure what we're dealing with we're not sure cremation would kill it."

"Like what?"

"There's still debate if cremation completely denatures prions. The infectious protein particles that cause CJD—"

"Creutzfeldt-Jakob," I said for Nikki's benefit. She had been with me ten months and we hadn't had a CJD case, so I figured she needed the refresher from pathology class.

"Right," Bluechel said, "and other TSEs."

Nikki looked at me and I shrugged. The man loves his acronyms.

Catching the shrug, Bluechel didn't even pause. "Transmissible spongiform encephalopathies. *If* we are in fact dealing with something that's weaponized then it's been modified to be extremely infectious and resistant to degradation, like cremation. We can't take the chance. This has been deemed the only viable alternative."

"Oh," Nikki said. Her voice was small.

"What are the implications if it is," I paused, unwilling for a second to say it, "weaponized?"

"Chaos. Anarchy. A seismic shift in the bedrock of America—"

"No, I mean from a public-health perspective. How bad is it?"

"Until we get a handle on exactly what we're dealing with, it could mean fatalities on a pandemic scale."

I closed my eyes and shook my head slowly. Exhaling, I opened them, looked at the trailer full of caskets and to Bluechel and slowly nodded. "Okay. I'll do it. But so we're clear, my name doesn't go on any of these death certificates." He nodded. "I need to hear you say it."

"Fine, your name doesn't go on the death certificates."

I looked at Nikki, my witness. She nodded.

"And Clip? This is a need-to-know operation." He motioned at the screen. "The team will park the gurneys in the holding area created by the staggered screens and you'll be responsible for bringing the gurneys to your side and preparing them. The ship will arrive once all but essential personnel has gone for the day."

It just gets better and better.

"Okay," I said, clapping my hands. "Guess we better get to work."

"Great. A hundred is the maximum capacity of the ship. It'll dock at 2000 and load at 2100. You need to have them ready for loading by then."

I looked at my watch, it was a little before eight o'clock. That gave us 13 hours to prepare a hundred people for burial. It was going to be a long day.

"I'll walk you through the procedure." He stepped up onto the trailer. "Help me pull one of these off." I climbed up and we wrestled a casket out of the trailer. Bluechel spent the next 20 minutes walking us through the exact procedure he wanted us to follow. "Questions?"

Nikki and I shook our heads.

"I'll be back to check on you or you can radio me." He produced a radio out of one of his cargo pockets and squelched it to make sure it was functioning. "You best go suit up."

"One more thing Terry." I called after him.

He turned.

"Where's the MH?"

"The what?"

"Mess hall." It's not a real acronym, but I thought I'd plant the seed so he could add it to his repertoire.

"Oh," he said, brightening, "a food truck should be onsite within the hour." He turned and walked off and I could almost see his jaw working, practicing the new jargon.

"Guess we can start pulling some tin off the truck." Nikki gathered her hair in a ponytail and kicked off her heels. Reaching into her purse she produced a pair of flats. "Thank the Lord I thought to bring comfortable shoes."

Chapter 23

The *USS Roosevelt* docked in front of Terra at the appointed time of 2000 hours and made preparations to load. There's a deep-water dock—Union Pier—farther south down the river, at the end of the French Quarter near Liberty Square where the cruise ships depart. If the weather's nice, the scene reminds me of an old photograph: friends, family, well-wishers, and looky-loos all line up to wave adieu. The government wanted none of that fanfare which is why the *Roosevelt* docked at Columbus Street Terminal after dark. The destroyer's running lights were off, and power had been cut to all the sodium halides pole lamps around the terminal giving the fruit warehouse the feeling of a roach nest—things scuttling around in darkness.

"Lordy," Nikki said, slapping a barcode on the head end of the casket. Her voice sounded tinny over the comms in the respirator. "One more to go."

"You can make it," I said. Her eyes were glassy; if she felt like I did then I knew she was beyond exhausted. I took a scan gun and lasered the barcode. It gave me an affirmation *beep*. I leaned against a concrete bollard and checked my watch. "We have about 20 minutes before they start loading."

A group of sailors jockeyed a wheeled conveyor belt in to place. Wearing their dark blue coveralls, they were almost invisible, except for the occasional curse or shout. It reminded me of the type of thing used at airports to move luggage on and off planes.

"Let's get on with it then." Nikki picked up the industrial Hilti drill, grunting from the weight, and began drilling the lid of a new casket.

There was one final white pouch waiting on a gurney—this person had been inspected, entered into VIP and was ready for final disposition. I pulled a length of plastic off a roll and laid it on a worktable, before pulling the final victim of the day on top. It's a multi-layered plastic and metal foil military-grade product for creating leak-proof, custom sized pouches. A printed page of barcoded labels rested on top of the hospital pouch. I took the page, compared the name written on the pouch to that printed at the top of the page, before flipping the top flap of vinyl over the pouch. Using scissors, I trimmed the plastic to the proper size, and was about to crimp the sides, when the cacophony of metal on metal stopped and Nikki muttered, "Shit!"

"What's wrong?"

Nikki yanked the shank out of the drill. It glowed, but she was wearing heavy leather gloves, and tossed it. I heard it clatter onto the concrete floor. "Blew through another." She dodged the field of caskets to the worktable and picked up another drill bit, a two-inch spade cutter. A moment later the sound of drilling metal continued.

I took the heat crimper and quickly went around the vinyl sheeting creating an airtight body bag. After practicing all day, I had gotten quite speedy. Satisfied, it was sealed properly, I affixed a barcode label where the head would be.

"Ready?" I asked.

Nikki stopped drilling. "Four to go. I'm not as quick as you with the drill." I flashed her the okay sign. She resumed drilling. Navy regulations stipulate there be 20, two-inch holes drilled into a metal casket: eight in the bottom, eight in the lid, and two at each end. The requirement of a metal casket and 20 holes ensures the casket sinks.

I sprayed the gurney with a heavy-duty disinfectant to avoid cross contamination and wheeled it over just as Nikki set the drill down. Wordlessly, she grabbed the foot end and we lowered the body bag into the casket with as much dignity as possible. The caskets were cheap 20-gauge units supplied by the manufacturer who could pony up the most units in the shortest amount of time; therefore, they were a delightful assortment of colors and styles. This one was white with gold trim. White crosses were decaled on the corners. Hopefully the decedent wasn't Muslim or Jewish.

Nikki placed two cinder blocks at the foot end of the casket and then locked it. The cinder blocks, really, any weight, are another navy requirement to ensure rapid, feet-first sinking. We hoisted the casket up onto a wheeled apparatus called a church truck, and I draped four nylon bands around the casket. After placing a metal ferrule in a strapping tensioner, I fed the loose ends of the first band into the tensioner and clicked the handle back and forth until it was tight and squeezed the trigger to crimp the ferrule. The next three were secured quickly. The purpose of the banding is to keep the lid on. The caskets hit the water with such force that without the bands, the lid could potentially pop off. Nikki had a long band pre-cut to run from the head end to the foot end that she quickly secured once I was done.

Five straps. Done.

Three minutes to spare. I ripped off my gloves and pushed the respirator up onto the top of my head. Bluechel would have a fit if he caught me not decontaminating properly before doffing my suit, but I wasn't worried. Worst he could do would be to fire me, and that would be a dream come true. Taking a razor knife, I cut a slit in the gown so I could access the pocket of the itchy scrubs. I pinched off a monster load of tobacco and had just tamped it down with my tongue when Bluechel appeared. He stared at me hard but let the attire infractions slide. "Ready to load?"

One hundred caskets, looking more like Swiss cheese than caskets, sat ready for burial at sea. I spit and offered a two-finger salute. "Yessir."

Nikki slapped on the last barcode and scanned it. It gave her the affirmative *beep*. "Ready to go."

It was 2100.

Bluechel turned in the direction of the ship and whistled and held his arm in the air making a twirling motion with his finger.

***

I watched as the sailors, now gowned up in protective gear, loaded the last casket onto the ship. "Another load tomorrow?" I asked Bluechel.

"Yup." He paused. "But I need you to do something before then."

I spit. And waited.

He got the hint. "I need you to oversee the burial."

I spit again. "No need. Captain has jurisdiction at sea. Even under normal circumstances, the undertaker doesn't go out. His job stops at the pier the moment the navy men lay their hands on that casket."

"These aren't normal circumstances. I—er, the commander— want to make sure we're covering our bases."

Covering your asses, more likely.

"Of course, I'll compensate—"

"I'm not doing this for money." We stared at the dark ship; the sailors were wrestling the conveyor belt away from the ship amidst a lot of cursing. "Nobody ever got rich off working for Uncle Sam." Bluechel snorted. I spit. "I'll do it."

Nikki who had been standing by quietly piped in, "Me too."

Nikki would just as soon dig her heels in to prove a point than concede, so I choose my words carefully before speaking. "Why don't you go home and see Jackson? All I'm going to be doing is watching sailors push caskets into the ocean. There's really nothing to do, sounds like it's just a formality." I looked at Bluechel for affirmation. He nodded.

Nikki looked relieved to be given an out, especially since she could hardly keep her eyes open. "Same time tomorrow?"

"Zero seven hundred," Bluechel said. Directing his attention to me, he said, "Go decon, hit up the food truck in the parking lot, and then check in with the nurse. She'll fix you up. Boat leaves in 15." I didn't know what he meant about getting fixed up, but parking lot food sounded appetizing.

"Make it 20. I need to use the office phone and call the hospital to check on Maggie." If they really wanted me onboard that ship, he'd make it wait. Checking on Maggie was a top priority, something I hadn't had a chance to do all day because of the jammer the army was running. I had left a note with the nurse for when Maggie woke up, but still felt guilty this was the first chance I was getting to check in.

Bluechel nodded. "Done."

Chapter 24

The Command Master Chief, accompanied by the Officer of the Deck, greeted me at the top of the gangway wearing his khaki service uniform and a surgical mask. "Master Chief Wes Walls." I took the offered hand. Walls didn't look to be old enough to be shaving regularly but was in one of the top command posts for a two-billion-dollar warship. "We've been waiting for you sir."

I had exceeded the allotted 20 minutes. Ignoring Wall's accusatory tone, I said, "Can you direct me to the mess? I didn't get a chance to eat today."

My request wasn't what Walls was prepared for, and it showed, but he quickly recovered. "Certainly sir." Turning to the Officer of the Deck, he said, "Secure the brow."

The OOD spoke low and quickly into a handheld, something I couldn't catch, but it was obviously communication with the bridge the ship was ready for cast off because the rumbling under our feet increased in pitch.

"This way sir," Walls said, leading me toward the nearest door on the superstructure. I followed him through a maze of hallways and watertight doors until we came to one he opened and gestured inside. "Officer's mess. Make yourself comfortable. I'll get the cook."

"Send a corpsman too."

A look of alarm crossed Walls' face, understandable since we were transporting a load of infectious cargo, and I had been elbow deep in said cargo all day. In fact, Walls got a little green and touched his mask. I could almost see his thoughts: *did he breathe in my face?*

"My eye is bothering me." I pointed to the swelling. "I need something for the pain."

Walls relaxed and nodded smartly. "Of course, sir." He pivoted and disappeared.

The officer's mess was nothing special; a small, spartan room with a few tables. No sooner had I selected a seat then a kid younger than Walls appeared wiping his hands on his apron. He was wearing a mask. "What can I get you sir?"

"Did you escape junior high?" I asked. Kidding. I gave him my order and he disappeared. I was famished. I hadn't been able to get to the food truck because my phone call to the hospital was longer than planned. Maggie was doing great. The Ciprofloxacin was working. Her abdominal pain was completely gone and thus far there was no sign of encephalitis—there had been scans and spinal taps. Maggie's colleagues were keeping a close eye on her. I felt much better after the phone call, having felt guilty all day for leaving her, but Maggie assured me I was doing much more important work than sitting by her bedside keeping vigil. Even facing a possible death sentence, her physician ethos never wavered. Her exact words were, "Charleston needs strong people to make hard decisions. That's you babe."

Who are you, Winston Churchill motivating a nation? Instead, I informed her, "Your parents are in town, but outside of the cordon."

She groaned. "Oh, I know. My mother has been terrorizing the hospital from her hotel room. God love her, but I'm thankful for the quarantine so I can have some peace."

We both laughed and I hung up feeling great. My second phone call hadn't gone quite so well. Jerry the Giant at Roper informed me Isabella was dead.

"Sir?" I looked up to see a female corpsman standing at attention inside the doorway, wearing blue camouflage, a sailor's working uniform. It almost goes without saying, but she sported the obligatory mask. "Master Chief Walls said you needed to see me?"

I nodded. "Yes, I need Provigil."

"Sir?" The corpsman looked confused. "How is that going to help your face?" Walls had obviously preempted the reason for the visit.

"It's not. My face isn't bothering me," I lied. "I've been up for over a day and half, and I don't see any sleep in my future for the next day and a half." It was true. After we buried these caskets, we'd head back to port, and Bluechel would want Nikki and I to prepare another hundred caskets.

"I'm not sure I can get that," she said, uncertain. "If you'd like you can follow me back to sick bay and I can drop a line in your arm to hydrate you. That may help."

"Would you mind checking for me? Your chief may be able to get his hands on some," I said, as a way of letting her know to green light it with her superiors. Provigil is labeled to promote wakefulness for narcolepsy. Of course, the military had been tinkering off-label with it for years, specifically on helicopter pilots. I had always known where I could get my hands on the "go pill" if need be, and I damn well knew this corpsman knew where to dig up some.

She nodded. "I'll check."

The cook appeared balancing a heaping plate and mug. "Hot sauce is there." He pointed to a little caddy set in the middle of the table with a lip to keep the condiments from sliding all over the place in rough seas. "Can I get you anything else?"

I thanked him and dug in with gusto to the feast: six eggs, T-bone steak, and grits. The coffee tasted like bilge water, but it was hot. Someone had left a copy of the *Orlando Sentinel* on the table, so I leafed through it while I ate. Apparently, Charleston was making national headlines. The headline of the national section read: HOLY CITY UNDER QUARANTINE! I read it carefully, but the news outlets were scratching for information too. There was the obligatory color photo of armed National Guard soldiers blocking I-26, but the copy was sparse. The media was still reporting a virulent strain of *Shigella* as the culprit, but the journalist hinted at more sinister undertones. The rest of the article was fluff, background information on *Shigella*, as well as listing some cities that battled disease outbreaks and had quarantines: yellow fever in Philadelphia, typhus in New York, and the bubonic plague in San Francisco, and of course the flu pandemic of 1918 that swept the nation.

"You must know the right people," the corpsman said, reappearing with two white 100 mg pills in a paper cup and a small bottle of water. She extended her arm, exposing a bird tattooed inside her wrist.

"Today I do," I said, taking the cup and washing the pills down with the dregs of the coffee. "Any significance to the bird?" I jerked my chin in the direction of her exposed wrist.

The corpsman pulled her sleeve down and blushed, self-conscious. "It's a swallow. Sailors get them every five thousand miles they sail." She slipped two packets of Advil out of her uniform. "I also took the liberty of bringing you something for your face. And this." She slid a packet of Dramamine across the table.

I swept up the Advil. "Thanks, but I'll be fine. I don't get seasick."

"My advice, take it. Just in case." She had kind eyes. I'm sure the recruiter had reeled her in with the lure of 'helping people.'

"Thanks." I jammed the three packages in my pocket.

She slipped a surgical mask out of another pocket and held it out. "Captain's orders."

I took the mask, set it on the table and tapped the mask with my index finger. "Is everyone onboard wearing these?"

"Yes, until further notice."

Moving my finger, I tapped the newspaper. "I'm guessing you came up from Florida?"

She nodded. "Mayport. Anything else I can get you?"

"That's all. Thank you."

As if to read my mind, the cook reappeared and refilled my coffee and took my plate. I stared at the newspaper, not seeing it. I couldn't believe Isabella was actually dead. We'd had our differences in the past, but since her husband died, we had almost become close.

"Mr. Clipper?" Master Chief Walls said, interrupting my reverie. "We're about on location." He handed me a coat, he was wearing one too. "Here put this on. You'll need it."

I took the coat and shrugged it on. "What time is it?"

"Almost 2300."

"That was fast."

Walls allowed himself a tiny smile. "She's a bit faster than a cruise ship." He pointed to the table. "Please put your mask on."

Despite the boost from the pills, I was too weary to argue the fact we weren't dealing with an airborne disease, so I downed the last of the coffee, slid the straps around my ears and followed Walls through the maze of passageways. "To do a burial at sea we have to be a minimum of three miles from shore and 100 fathoms." If I remembered correctly a fathom is six feet. "Where we are now the bathymetry is a little tricky—"

"What?"

"Sorry," Walls said, without breaking stride. "The ocean floor topography. There's a shelf that runs the length of the coastline, so we need to get out a ways to hit the proper depth. There's something called the Charleston Bump, it's at the north end of the Blake Plateau. We're heading to a piece of the bump around 32° 14' North and 79° 12' West where it first starts dropping to our desired depth." I was lost until he added, "It's roughly 75 klicks off shore." I nodded. That I could understand.

Walls shouldered open a watertight door and we stepped into a cavernous space, for a ship. "This is the hangar. It normally houses two Sea Hawk helos."

The Sea Hawk is the navy's version of the Black Hawk. Instead of the helicopters, were 20 rows of five caskets with tie-down straps over each row to keep them from shifting.

Walls's radio squawked. He held up a finger and turned, speaking into it. Turning back to me, he said, "We've arrived at depth." No sooner did he say it then ten sailors hurried through the door. They were dressed head-to-toe in protective equipment. Unlike the white snowmen suits, the sailors wore blue NBC suits. The respirators made them look sinister.

"That's the mortuary team," Walls said unnecessarily.

The team didn't waste any time. As soon as the hangar door opened the ocean wind howled through the hanger. Walls didn't even seem to notice. Two sailors got to work removing the straps from the first row, and four retrieved a steel contraption tucked in the corner. It was a ramp, about ten feet long, angled at 15 degrees, with rollers spaced along the decline. Six sailors lifted it onto their shoulders and walked it out. Walls and I followed them onto the helipad. The wind intensified, causing the lapels of the jacket to flap madly. Ocean spray stung my face. This far from shore there's no light pollution; it's a kind of crushing darkness where light doesn't exist—almost like a black hole.

My stomach started doing somersaults. I wished I had heeded the corpsman's advice and taken the Dramamine. The ship plowed through the slight chop without a problem, but the boat rocked enough that I had trouble keeping my footing. Walls seemed completely unaffected. I fumbled in my pants pocket. In the dim light of the *Roosevelt's* running lights, I figured out the correct packet, opened it and swallowed the pills dry.

"Feel okay?" Walls asked.

"Fine," I croaked.

The sailors set the ramp at the edge of the fantail and dropped down onto the deck to secure it. Then two of the sailors popped out a section of the safety gate that encircled the fantail.

Walls spoke into his handheld, listened with it close to his ear to overcome the roar of the wind. We waited for several minutes on the helipad, Walls not offering any information, and me too preoccupied with finding the nearest place to puke to care, before a man strode out onto the helipad trailed by a staff member. The four gold bars and star on his shoulder gave away he was the captain before he introduced himself.

"Mr. Clipper, Captain Bathurst," he shouted. "Good of you to join us."

I shook his hand and nodded; afraid I'd vomit on his uniform if I tried to speak.

Captain Bathurst pulled a small book from his coat and, turned to a pre-marked page and without preamble started reading. "God is our refuge and strength—"

When he finished reading he nodded to Walls. Walls spoke into his handheld, and then turned to me. "This is it. Mission is a go."

Two sailors wheeled out the first casket on a truck. One of the six sailors at the ramp scanned the barcode with a handheld scanner. As soon as the six sailors lifted the casket onto the ramp, foot end first, the two wheeled the empty truck back to the hangar. The six sailors hardly hesitated. They let go and the casket disappeared over the side and into the blackness. Another set of sailors was already waiting with another casket.

Call it morbid curiosity, I had to see it. "Careful," Walls cautioned, as I staggered to the fencing near the ramp. I clung to the wet metal of the safety fencing and watched as the second casket soared by me, dropped about 20 feet and hit with a terrific splash. The two cinderblocks at the foot end made sure it hit foot-end first, and the 20 holes made sure it sank in under five seconds.

The boat pitched. My stomach flipped and I emptied the contents into the churning surf. Wiping the acid off my lips with the back of my hand, another casket zoomed by my head and careened into the sea.

The splash was silent, drowned by the howling wind. In seconds, the evidence was gone as the inky surface returned to normal. Grabbing the slick railing, I heaved bile over the side, until there was nothing left and I was consumed with great, wracking coughs.

With the two teams frog-hopping caskets to the ramp team it took about 45 minutes to bury all the victims. The *Roosevelt* didn't slow its speed once.

Chapter 25

"Go ahead," I told Nikki. She flicked the toggle switch on the embalming machine and it whirred to life. It was Wednesday morning. Outside thunder crashed. The lights flickered and then dimmed for a moment, but miraculously held. I waited a moment for the arterial pressure to build before opening the drain tube. A torrent of crimson blood poured down the gutter.

"I feel like a criminal," Nikki said, gazing down at the remains of Isabella on the embalming table.

"Don't." *But you are.* I was under no illusions as to what kind of holy hell would rain down upon me if Bluechel discovered I stole a body. Stole sounds criminal. Really, I re-appropriated her remains. It hadn't been too difficult. The tropical storm that swept up the coast made it possible.

***

Isabella's body was brought in to the incident morgue late Monday night while I was out burying the first round. By the time the *Roosevelt* arrived back at the dock and the safety officer made me decontaminate yet again, it was almost three o'clock. Instead of heading home, I tried to catch a few winks on one of the luxurious cots the federal government provided. All I ended up catching was a stiff neck.

It was raining, and a new tractor-trailer was parked in front of our prepping station when Nikki and I resumed work. "How was it?" she asked.

I was exhausted; my hands hurt from gripping the wire fence, and had to search for the proper words. "Powerful...and very sad." The experience would haunt me.

"I made a mistake not going. I'm going tonight." She put her hands on her hips and stuck out her lip, daring me to talk her out of it. I'm just not that stupid.

"Suit yourself. But don't say I didn't warn you. Both of us don't need PTSD."

Deflecting, Nikki picked up the drill and hefted it. "Good news. I didn't need to hit up the gym after handling this baby all day yesterday. Say, what did you want me to bring a disaster pouch for?"

I called her early in the morning from a landline and asked her pick up a pouch on her way in. On the phone I had been cryptic. You never know who's listening. Pushing the mask up, I motioned her to do the same just in case they were monitoring the comms line. "Isabella died yesterday."

Nikki put her hand in front of her face. "Dear Lord!"

Looking around, I wanted to make sure we weren't overheard. But we were safe, walled off at the far end of the warehouse, the wicked stepchildren in charge of packaging the dead. "Keep your voice down," I murmured, just to be safe and pointed to a white pouch on one of the gurneys in the waiting area. "That's her. They brought her here last night."

Nikki made a face. "That poor woman is going to get thrown into the ocean."

"Fuck no. Lauren hated the navy, and I'll be damned if I let them toss his wife off the side of the *S.S. Minnow*. So, we're going to take her—"

I stopped mid-sentence hearing footsteps on concrete. It was Bluechel.

"Everything okay with your gear?"

"Just wanted to dip a bit before starting." I spit on the floor.

Bluechel frowned and then looked at Nikki as if to say, *What's your excuse?* He opted to let it go and turned to me. "Captain Bathurst tells me everything went according to plan." I nodded. The *Roosevelt* relocated to the Navy Yard, farther up the river, after dropping me off. "We have another hundred cases to prepare today." Looking at Nikki, he asked, "Get some rest last night? Are you up to do it all over again?"

She nodded vigorously. How sexist. *I* was the one who had been up all night. Bluechel pointed to the open warehouse door. The drops were getting fatter. "This is supposed to get worse. Forecast is for a tropical storm to sweep up the coast. If that's the case, Bathurst tells me we may not be able to make another run tonight." The corners of his eyes crinkled above the mask. "We need to be ready in case we can make the run. I'll keep you posted."

I saluted. Bluechel disappeared.

Nikki and I settled into a rhythm, and by seven—1900 hours military time—only a handful of cases were left to process when Bluechel came over with the verdict. "There isn't going to be a run tonight." That wasn't news. It was teeming outside; the ocean conditions must be miserable. "Once you've finished up here, go ahead home." There were still a few stragglers wandering around the examination area, but the rest of the team had already hung it up for the day and headed back to the Patriot's Point Best Western. "I won't need you tomorrow morning since you already have the next wave ready," he said, motioning to the rows of holey caskets. "But Clip, I may need you tomorrow night for the ocean run."

"Nikki's coming for this one."

He shrugged. "Fine. I'll be in touch."

"Where's the pouch?" I asked as soon as he was out of earshot.

"In the truck like you said."

"Think you can pretend to take a break and go get it?" Nikki nodded. "Will you have room?"

"Honey, these things are like muumuus." She gathered all the extra material to illustrate. "Seriously, I don't know who they're making them for."

I grinned. "Aren't you ready to take a break?"

Nikki sauntered off. Using a razor knife, I slit the side of my suit open and peeled off both sets of gloves and retrieved my tin. Standing in the doorway of the makeshift morgue, I let the wind-whipped rain sting my face. It smelled clean. There was something comforting in the ferocity.

Nikki returned and made a big production of pulling the folded vinyl pouch from under her PPE. We unfolded the black pouch on an empty gurney and, after a quick look to make sure nobody was coming, dragged Isabella in—white body bag and all—and zipped it up. Grabbing the sturdy nylon handles, I said, "Follow me." The privacy screens shielded our activities from the rest of the warehouse. We carried Isabella to a side door I identified earlier. She weighed next to nothing. "Here." We tucked the pouch against the wall, and I piled some empty wooden fruit crates in front of it in case Bluechel came back. "After we finish I'll decon and bring the truck around and have you let me in. Then I'll wait for you."

Nikki nodded along, but her eyes were wide.

I finished processing the rest of the cases, making sure to throw eight cinderblocks into the casket earmarked for Isabella, before decontaminating under the watchful eye of the safety officer. Putting on my street clothes, I ran out to my truck. It was raining so hard it seemed like it was coming from the ground up. I drove around the outside of the warehouse until I spied the barcode I slapped on the door earlier in the day. I wasn't worried about prying eyes in this rain, so I backed the truck almost to the door, hopped out and knocked. Nikki cracked the door, and I dragged the body bag through. "Go, go," I said, motioning for her to shut the door. The door clanged shut. Isabella hadn't been a big woman in life, and I was able to lift her up into the bed of my truck with minimal effort. I did nothing to cover her. The black pouch blended in with the color of the bed liner. I doubted the soldiers were going to do more than wave us through in this weather. They were more worried about not letting unauthorized people in, not crazies snatching infectious bodies.

Thankfully, I was correct and we sailed back to the funeral home without incident.

At the funeral home, we placed Isabella in repose. "She's going to have to wait until tomorrow. I've been up for the past three days straight," I said to Nikki.

"I got to sleep last night. I can embalm her."

"Thanks, but this is something I need to do. I owe it to Lauren."

Nikki smiled a knowing smile "Let me help. What time tomorrow?"

Chapter 26

"Who's there?" Matey screeched when the prep room door slammed open and Moonie entered shaking rain droplets off his ten-gallon hat.

"Christ almighty!" Nikki placed her hand on her breast. "Do you ever get used to that?"

"Which one?" I said out of the side of my mouth. The other side had several screws protruding from it.

"The bird."

"They both grow on you." I plucked a screw from my lips and drove it into the Ziegler Case with a staccato burst from the impact driver. "Like a cancer."

The giant bird perched atop the antique hutch eyed the assembled trio.

"It's still raining pretty—" Moonie stopped. "Hey partner, who'd you lose a fight to?"

"A woman got upset when I told her how much it'd cost to bury her husband." I drove the final screw into the Ziegler Case. "There," I said, patting the lid. "Let's put this on the rack for now." Nikki went to grab the end handles but Moonie pushed her out of the way in a misguided chivalrous attempt—the redneck Lancelot.

He grunted and heaved the case up. "You serious?"

"I had to have Nikki intervene. Over there," I motioned with my head to the casket racks in the corner of the cellar.

His scar pulsed; it meant he was thinking. "He serious?" Nikki frowned and nodded. "What's in this anyway?" Moonie placed his end on the roller and I pushed the case into the niche.

"Isabella."

"Ain't all deaths being processed by DMORT?" The scar looked like it had its own heartbeat.

"Yup, they've processed it and released it to me." Not an outright lie, at least the part about being processed. I added for good measure, "As a personal favor."

"Ain't they worried about her spreading the swamp sickness?"

"I had to agree to seal her up." I tapped the end of the case. A Ziegler Case is a metal storage and transport case. The lid has a rubber gasket. Once screwed shut it forms a hermetic seal. The nice thing about the Ziegler Case is it can be placed directly into a casket, for a nicer looking burial, without having to unseal it. They're typically used for disasters or infectious cases, and sometimes international shipping. Even though Isabella was embalmed I wasn't sure how long she'd be hanging around the funeral home until things returned to normal and I could quietly bury her next to her husband in St. Michael's churchyard. It's not that I was worried about Moonie dropping a dime on me, but I didn't want him to wrestle with his conscience regarding his duties as a sworn deputy versus his loyalty to me if he knew I had pilfered a body.

Moonie winked at Nikki and turned to me. "I don't know how you do it. You certainly have a silver tongue."

Nikki made a face, disgusted.

It annoyed me to no end that Moonie liked to reference our previous relationship. "Did you bring it?" I snapped.

"Yeah," he said producing the bottle from his poncho, "But I told you Hotapp wasn't able to lift any prints off it." Moonie set the bottle on the edge of the utility sink. It was nothing special, a liter of Poland Spring water. PROUDLY FROM MAINE and EST. 1845 were emblazoned on the familiar label of water rushing by evergreens. Aside from the water level—several sips had been drunk out of it—there was nothing unusual about the bottle.

"Who do I look like, Columbo? I don't know how to dust for prints." I snapped on a pair of latex gloves and unscrewed the cap. I wafted the contents, a much safer technique than directly sniffing an unknown liquid. It smelled like nothing; it very well could be water. Carefully, I poured several ounces from the water bottle into a sterile specimen cup, screwed the caps on both bottles, and sprayed the countertop down with bleach.

"Am I missing something?" Moonie asked, as I used a disinfectant wipe to sanitize the outside of the bottle and cup.

"I hope it's just me being paranoid." I whipped off a note and put the specimen cup and note into a shopping bag with Granville & Sons embossed in gold foil on the side. It's what we send the post-funeral goodies home in, register book, acknowledgement cards, grief book, vigil candle, and some other crap I'd now have to make because Isabella certainly wouldn't. "You know where Risden's gym is?"

"Off Market Street, near the river."

"Take this to him. Call the gym when you get there and get him to meet you outside. I don't need you traipsing in there with your badge and gun."

A supercilious grin spread under the mustache. "That suits me just fine."

The front of the gym is glass, and the treadmills are always chock-full of toned millennial females in spandex bouncing and jiggling. The inference sailed over Nikki's head, thank God for Moonie or he'd be the proud owner of a new asshole. "Have some sense and be discreet."

"My middle name." Moonie wouldn't know discretion if it tackled him and bludgeoned him to death.

I placed the bottle into another shopping bag. "C'mon," I said to Nikki, "Jen is picking us up in a few." Matey hopped off the hutch and landed on my shoulder.

I was just as surprised as the look on Moonie and Nikki's face, but the bird seemed comfortable. Clearing his throat, Moonie said, "You going to fill me in on what's going on?"

"I think this water bottle," I held up the shopping bag, "is where the swamp sickness came from, or a bottle like this."

Moonie looked like I just told him the Easter Bunny isn't real. "You serious partner?"

"It makes sense." I flicked the light off in the prep room and headed up the cellar steps. "All the evidence points to this being vectored through food or water, and I'm leaning strongly toward water. Maybe not drinking water, *per se,* but in a contaminated body of water that people are coming in contact with. Despite what the water company says, my opinion is that it's somehow connected to potable water—"

"Look partner," Moonie said, cutting me off, "you mind losing the bird? It's giving me the eye."

I opened the front door and pushed Matey off my shoulder. "Go play." Matey took off with a protestation squawk and soared across the street, taking shelter from the pouring rain in the branches of a large magnolia growing next to the boutique. A familiar figure exited the shop and popped a big, black umbrella, obscuring a— purple streak? *Cam?* My mind flashed back to snatched twenties and a raised middle finger. *No. That's ridiculous. A homeless girl wouldn't be out shopping at a posh boutique in a tropical storm.*

"If it's the drinking water," Nikki persisted, tearing my attention away from the umbrella bobbing down Logan Street, "why isn't everyone getting sick? It doesn't make sense. Especially if it's weaponized."

"Weaponized?" Moonie asked.

"That's one theory." I glared at Nikki. Bluechel didn't want us announcing all we knew around Charleston.

"How on Earth do you weaponize water?"

"I haven't quite figured out why some people are contracting the illness, and others aren't," I said, trying to change the subject. "A lot of infectious diseases are more likely to affect certain groups like the young, elderly, and immunocompromised."

"I could see it in Mrs. Granville," Nikki said, "but what about Maggie, or that chiropractor who was a health nut?"

"Either that, or not everyone is being exposed to it."

"How would some people be exposed and others not if it's the drinking water?" Nikki asked.

"I limit my fluid intake to coffee, coconut water, and the occasional beer. I don't think I've ever drank the tap water." Both Moonie and Nikki looked with stricken expressions. Obviously, they imbibed.

"But what's *that* bottle have to do with it?" Moonie persisted. He adjusted his gun belt. "That ain't even tap water."

A familiar Caprice pulled up to the curb. "Why can't you get a hit on Hansel? John Doe 2?"

"I dunno, partner. Because he's never been in trouble?"

"Or because he doesn't exist." Moonie started to open his mouth, but I held up my hand. "I had Risden run the prints from my phone that Bailey handled. Within minutes DOD is on the phone telling him to lose the prints. I suspect we can't get an ID on Hansel because someone in DOD has his identity locked down, the same someone who came and snatched his body."

"Are you sure their interest wasn't on Badgers? The water bottle was in his backpack," Nikki said.

"I think their interest *was* Badgers."

Nikki shook her head. "Okay, I'm confused."

"The night before last, a corpsman brought me an Advil." I decided they didn't need to know about the anti-puking pills that didn't work. "And I saw a tattoo on her wrist, and I remembered something from the crime-scene photographs. Hansel had a star tattoo on his forearm." I outlined the star in the air with my fingers. "Yes, it's a normal five-pointed star, but that's also a nautical star. The kind superstitious sailors get so they can find their way home." Nikki and Moonie nodded along, lapping up my narrative. "Where do all those shadowy alphabet organizations attached to DOD pull their talent from?" Not waiting for answer, I plowed on, "The military. I'll bet Hansel was a squid before doing whatever it was that he was doing when Badgers shot him up like Swiss cheese."

Moonie and Nikki turned their attention to the bag in my hand. "You think the government suspected a plot to taint the water supply?" Nikki asked.

"They had a shoot-out near a reservoir where the water treatment plant sits. Several days later people start getting sick. I wasn't valedictorian at Coffee High, but things sure seem to be pointing that way. Wait, a second." I held a finger up. Moonie's comment about the "bird" made me think of Purdue. I wasn't interested in a chicken roaster. The university, yes. "When you were gathering vitals for the provisional death certificate for Badgers, you learn anything about what kind of engineering degree he received?"

"Don't need that for the certificate, partner."

"I was hoping maybe you'd gone above and beyond."

"Nope. Why?"

"Something occurred to me."

"Can't help you on that account." Moonie raised his souvenir Granville & Sons bag in front of his face as if the contents within were some sort of oracle. His scar pulsed with enthusiasm. "But you know you can count on me to take care of things."

"Don't get thirsty on the way," I said.

"Nah, I'm good. There's a Gatorade in my truck."

Nikki shook her head, and muttered, "Idiot."

"What?"

"Nothing, go play," Nicki said, and made the same motion I'd made pushing Matey off my shoulder. Moonie plopped the ten-gallon hat on his head, clutched the bag near his chest, and soared off.

I popped out the monogrammed golf umbrella we keep near the door for grieving folks. "Shall we?" Nikki ducked under and we hustled into the tempest.

Chapter 27

"We do all our testing on site," Charles Quaid said, badging an electronic lock. The light in the pad turned green and beeped and the door lock released with an audible click. The COO of the Charleston Water System tugged it open, holding it for Hotapp, Gorman, Nikki, and me. "It appears you haven't been in any back-alley brawls recently," he commented brightly.

Not funny. By the looks of merriment on Hotapp and Nikki's faces you'd think Quaid's the next Don Rickles.

"This way," he motioned, thrilled to have found an audience. "Several years ago, we brought all the testing in-house to ensure speed and," he held up a chubby bejeweled finger, "most importantly, quality. Here we are." He paused at a faux-wood laminate door with a slim inset of wired glass.

I was the first through the door. The room reminded me of high school biology class minus the desks. Glass fronted cabinetry lined most of the wall space. The counters were black epoxy resin. Computers and various sundry scientific gadgets crowded the counters. A lab bench dominated the center of the room—what some might call an island if it were in a kitchen. Sitting at the bench with an open laptop was a familiar face, the Tuesday evening meeting leader at Calvary UAME.

"Artin here runs our computer mainframe," Quaid said by way of introduction. He retrieved a hanky from his pocket and dabbed his face. The walk through the building had winded him.

Artin half stood.

"Nice to meet you," I said taking Artin's hand, doing the odd dance addicts do when we see other members out in public.

"Likewise."

The others took turns shaking Artin's hand.

"And this is Lannie, one of our quality-control technicians." He nodded to a slight girl wearing a lab coat standing in the corner. She looked only a year or two out of college. "She'll be handling the sample."

Lannie stepped forward, smiled, and held out a gloved hand. "Please."

"Bag stays here."

Lannie looked to Quaid who waved the hanky at the bag like a matador. "Fine, fine."

Lannie's smile vanished, and she disappeared through a door.

"I really appreciate you doing this for us Dr. Quaid," Hotapp said, after a moment of awkward silence. "Even if we expedited this through the state lab it would take until tomorrow to get the results, and this is something of utmost priority."

Quaid waved his hand as if to say *think nothing of it.* "Always glad to help. What did you say it was for again?" His mood was breezy—almost whimsical—because he and his company weren't in the hot seat, as evidenced by the absence of his attack dog, Harlan Preacher.

"We strongly believe it's connected to a double homicide."

"Really?" She had his attention. I smiled inwardly; Quaid had a morbid streak. I've found most people do though they try to hide it.

"That turned into a body snatching."

"Seriously?" He puffed his cheeks out and contemplated something like that happening in bucolic Charleston.

I couldn't help myself. "*Double* body snatching, *and* kidnapping." Quaid opened and closed his mouth like a landed fish. I was on a roll. "How do you think this happened?" I pointed at my face.

Quaid looked momentarily worried, no doubt remembering his earlier quip, but Lannie bustled back in with a pipetter and sample cup.

"What am I testing for?" she asked, carefully lifting the bottle out of the bag. She unscrewed the cap and placed the disposable tip in the bottle and pressed the plunger, and then squirted the sample into the cup.

"Definitely test for coliforms." Gorman handed Lannie several sheets of paper. "Here's the Southern Blot for the *Shigella* that's causing the sickness and the DNA profile."

"I thought you said this was related to a homicide?"

"It is," Hotapp answered, "but we're not ruling out they're not connected."

Quaid didn't like that. His expression was strangled. "Run it for everything," he ordered Lannie.

She nodded and disappeared into the inner lab. "She should have some preliminary results soon," Quaid said. "Our equipment is state-of-the-art. Everything is automated. While we wait, I called Artin down here to demonstrate our system capabilities."

Sounded exhilarating. While the others plastered phony smiles on their faces my fingers inched toward my back pocket.

Artin spun the laptop around. There was a little pictograph of a pipe system, not unlike a subway map. There were changing numbers at various locations on the map.

"This is our water system." He hovered a cursor over one of the numbers. "As you can see we can keep an eye on water usage in real time. We have a set schedule of testing—"

"I went into all that with them earlier in the week," Quaid said.

"They test the water over 50 times a day," I murmured into Nikki's ear. She nodded. Impressed.

"The test results are logged into the system, by the technician, and we're able to tell in real time if there's a problem." Artin hit a button and a spreadsheet replaced the map. "This is the most recent testing data. As you can see we're able to tell instantly if something is out of range and needs to be addressed." Indeed, the columns showed green. He turned the keyboard slightly and his fingers danced over it. The numbers on the screen started cascading. "We archive the data for the annual water quality report, but we can go much farther back than a year."

"Could anyone gain access to your network?" Nikki asked.

"Hardly," Artin said, not able to contain a smug grin. "I designed it myself. All the data transmitted from the field is sent through a VPN using the highest encryption, AES 256-bit with HMAC authentication."

"Pardon?"

"It means it's secure," Artin said. "The NSA couldn't break in if they wanted."

"I agree," Quaid said. "I'm a scientist, but my expertise is natural sciences. All this computer talk confuses me. But it's necessary to have robust cyber security in this day in age, especially when dealing with utilities. People usually think of banks when they think of cyber security, but utilities like power grids, telecom, and water suppliers need it just as much, if not more. CPW hired Artin because he's one of the best in the field."

Artin beamed while his fingers flew over the keyboard. "Here let me give you a little layman's tour of our network—"

I lost interest in the demonstration and faded into the background. Quaid's lab equipment wasn't as speedy as he had bragged it to be. As the minutes ticked by, I worried on a wad of tobacco while Quaid and Artin regaled the others in the group with tales of the fascinating world of water supply and network security.

After 50 minutes Lannie reappeared. If 50 minutes was Dr. Quack's idea of "soon" I was beginning to doubt his definition of clean water.

"Well?"

"Typical in the respect that VOCs and SOCs levels are within range. That's volatile organic compounds like benzene and formaldehyde and synthetic organic compounds like dioxins," Lannie said for our benefit. The group nodded along, though Gorman was the only one who nodded with confidence. "The inorganics were what'd you'd expect, some mineral concentrations, and there were no perchlorates, or bacterial coliforms detected." All this sounded normal like "normal water" in geek talk. "However," Lannie added, "it contained a fairly high concentration of enterobacteriaceae, specifically the one you're interested in: *Shigella dysenteriae*."

"What's the concentration?" Gorman asked

Lannie pitched her hand back and forth. "About 10^7."

I love a scientist who estimates.

"Odd," Gorman said, adjusting his glasses. "Ten million organisms. If you," he pointed to me, "drank this you'd be sick as a dog. You only need as few as ten organisms to get infected, but if you diluted this into a swimming pool or water tower the chances of getting sick are..." He shrugged.

"So, it's not enough to get a whole city sick?" Nikki asked.

"Doesn't seem so."

"It's the same DNA profile as the blot you gave me," Lannie added.

"The concentration just isn't there," Gorman said, almost to himself. "It must be a collection vessel."

"It's certainly not consumer drinking water," Quaid said, seizing the opportunity to jump in. "The bottled water people market the stuff like they plunge the bottle right into the source." He shook his head. "Their water undergoes almost the same purification process municipal water does. There's almost no difference between drinking tap water and bottled water, except for one thing." He paused for effect. "Tap water is better for you because we add fluoride." He smiled revealing crooked and yellowed teeth.

Nikki and Hotapp nodded along, thrilled with the little life hack. Gorman ignored him, lost in thought.

Mr. Biology wanted to retain his audience. He wiped his forehead with the now soaked hanky and launched into another boring dissertation. "There are over 12 serotypes of *S. dysenteriae*—"

I tuned out.

Back in Hotapp's cruiser, the water sheeted on the windows like we were in a carwash. "Badgers had a bottle of contaminated water," I said. "What does that mean?"

Hotapp combed her fingers through her hair, and then squeezed excess water out. Nikki's hair was perfect, as usual, thanks to the monogrammed umbrella. "It's got to be connected to the homicides."

"Because you don't believe in coincidence?" Hotapp nodded. I shifted in the uncomfortable molded plastic seat in the back. They make them like that so they can easily be hosed out. I tried not to think about what I was sitting in; the same avoidance technique I use when sitting on a hotel bedspread. "He was living in Bushville. Perhaps he was dumb enough to refill his water bottle from the creek."

"You're the one with the Islamic saying about God's will. They're connected. I just can't seem to figure out how."

"When you interviewed Badgers's parents, did you happen to find out what kind of engineering he studied at Purdue?"

Hotapp laid the hammer down; the car rocketed away from the curb causing me to slide across the smooth plastic. "No." She drew the word out and stared at me in the rearview. Her interest was piqued.

"Can you swing by MUSC and drop me there?" Hotapp nodded. "Maggie is supposedly being released this afternoon."

"Really?" Nikki asked.

"She's been asymptomatic for over 24 hours, and her blood panels are all clean."

Nikki turned. "Did you stock the fridge?" The look on my face answered her question. "Hon, I know you've been busy so I'll run over to the Harris Teeter and pick up a few things for you." She glanced at her watch. "I'll have plenty of time before my meeting." It was Sunday; her meeting was at the Catholic church up the street.

"Grab some Pedialyte, if they still have it." The news had been showing barren grocery store shelves. Folks were out panic shopping, and new supplies weren't being brought inside the cordon.

"What, still don't trust the city water?" Nikki quipped.

Her comment caused me to think back to Artin sitting at the lab bench, smiling, and waving goodbye. If only Quaid knew "best in the field" once woke up in a flophouse with a dead hooker and a gangrenous arm.

Chapter 28

My phone did the vibration dance on the adjustable bed tray. It was a restricted number. "Do you mind?" I asked Maggie, glad for a break. We had been sitting in her room waiting for hours for discharge orders. The small talk was spent: talk about her parents, who were still barricaded outside the city—her mother driving her father nuts cooped up in a hotel room, and how her beloved pet had taken to riding on my shoulder. We lapsed into a numb silence watching bad television.

Maggie shook her head. "Go for it." She was sitting on the bed in a pair of surgical scrubs. Aside from remembering to re-stock the fridge, I had also neglected to bring her a change of clothes to leave the hospital in. There's a learning curve to this domestic thing.

"Clip."

"Terry Bluechel." There were no pleasantries. "I just got off the phone with Captain Bathurst. The last band of the tropical storm is set to move through and be cleared out within the hour. Conditions will be stable enough to proceed. I'll see you at 2100 for loading."

"Okay," I said into a dead line.

Maggie turned her attention from the courtroom proceedings. "What's up?"

"DMORT. They need me tonight."

She shrugged and nodded. We had the type of jobs where it didn't make emotional sense to get upset at the unexpected. "Are you leaving now?"

My watch showed it was a little after four. "I have plenty of time. Five hours." I texted Nikki the update.

"Good. I want to have dinner and the tiniest glass of wine and sleep in my own bed." She looked around the room. "I never knew you couldn't sleep in these places. They poke and prod at all hours. It's barbaric." She swept her eyes my direction. "Hopefully, you'll have enough time to take care of other business too."

My cheeks flushed like it was prom night and we were in a musky limousine. Things had been so hectic carnality had been pushed into the recesses of my mind, but the urge came flooding back.

"You're up for it?"

She stuck her tongue in her cheek and grinned. "Ya."

My pulse quickened and hands grew sweaty. Waiting wasn't an option. The urge was unrelenting. "Now?"

Maggie hopped off the bed with more pep than someone who had been through her ordeal ought to have. She peeked out the door and motioned with her hand. "C'mon."

I once read about the correlation between babies born and a family member's funeral. Nine months was statistically significant. Close proximity to mortality causes humans to seek the closest connection—sex. That particular study was related to single deaths. I was about to witness a hundred caskets be pushed off the side of a ship, death on a grand scale. Connecting with Maggie was an absolute necessity.

Heart hammering, I took her outstretched hand. The nurses at the station hardly gave a second glance to another scrub-clad person. Maggie led me through a twisting maze of hallways and stairwells until we reached an elevator bank.

"Act like you're looking at that," she said, pointing to a bulletin board. "We need to wait for someone with a keycard." I studied up on the latest informational gems OSHA had to offer while Maggie went down the hallway trying doors until she found one that was unlocked. She came out pushing an instrument with a dustcover on a cart. It didn't take too much loitering before a guy in pink scrubs walked up and badged the elevator bank and hit the down button. Maggie followed him in with the cart as did I. Pink Scrubs stood and faced the closed doors not moving a muscle as elevator etiquette requires. When the chime sounded and doors opened, he strode right—a man on a mission. Maggie abandoned the cart in an alcove and took my hand, leading me in the opposite direction of Pink Scrubs through a confusing warren of passageways. We ended up in a dimly lit hallway jammed with beds, chairs, and other assorted furniture, pieces of computer paper taped to them with hand scrawled messages describing their ailment. The bone yard smelled vaguely of rotting food and antiseptic.

"Here?"

"Here." Her voice was breathy. "Nobody comes down here." Without another word she hooked her arms around my neck and locked her lips on mine. Her mouth was salty and orangey from the rehydration salts. No further encouragement was needed. I pushed her back against the wall and she wrapped her legs around my hips. It was animalistic. Her hands everywhere groping, prodding, kneading. Tearing her mouth away, she bit my earlobe and whispered, "I need you."

Peeling her legs off my waist, I fumbled with the drawstring on her scrubs. They fell away revealing nothing underneath. Her nimble fingers undid my belt and button in a few deft movements. Both of us were more than ready. Maggie gasped when she wrapped her legs around my waist, and whispered in my ear, "Go. Go!"

The encouragement was unnecessary. With everything happening inside and outside the hospital walls it felt like we were at the end of the world.

Her breathing came out in ragged gasps, squeezed out between the wall and I, and her arms felt like a vice around my neck. Sweat beaded and ran down my face. My vision grew fuzzy from the pressure on my neck, not an unpleasant experience.

"Don't stop, don't stop," she repeated faster and faster, louder and louder, until our bodies shuddered and convulsed together. A moan escaped her lips, and we collapsed, motionless against the wall like a statue. Maggie rested her head on my shoulder, silent.

Rubber-soled shoes squeaked down the hallway.

Maggie's head snapped up. "Get down!" She shimmied off and dragged me down behind an old bed. We landed in a pile of arms and legs.

"I thought you said nobody came here," I hissed.

"Shush!" She giggled, clamping her hand over my mouth.

The footsteps grew louder. Maggie eased a bare foot out between two beds and used a toe to pull our clothes out of the view.

"Your glasses," I whispered, my lips inches from her ear, and pointed. Her glasses were sitting on top of an old piece of equipment where she tossed them. They were in plain view. But there was nothing that could be done. The person was almost on top of us. If they stopped to inspect the glasses they'd surely see us. Maggie would have some explaining to do.

The footsteps passed and receded.

We waited a full minute, stifling hysterics like naughty children. "Who was that?" I asked, rising and pulling her up.

"Probably one of the food service people. There's a smoking area somewhere around here." That explained the vague rotten smell. The kitchen was nearby.

I picked up my pants. "Isn't this place tobacco free?"

Ignoring me, she pulled off her scrub shirt and climbed onto one of the damaged beds—SIDERAIL INTERFACE BROKEN the sign read. "You're going to have to do me one better than once."

"Serious?"

"You going to be gone all night?"

I nodded.

Maggie bit her bottom lip, held out her hands and motioned with her fingers. "Then yes."

"I don't know if I can manage."

"I wasn't asking."

Who is this? I thought, dropping my pants. But I am good at following orders. "Yes ma'am." I approached the bed into her waiting arms and legs.

***

"Sorry I can't stay babe." I planted a chaste kiss on Maggie's lips. She smiled up at me in post coital bliss. "But the refrigerator at home is full and there's a bottle of white in the door. I'll see you in the morning."

"Aw, you stocked the fridge?" She smiled that smile women do when they're touched.

I hadn't physically done it or even had the bright idea and decided not to lie. "I thought it'd be a nice idea." I did think it was a nice idea.

"That's so sweet." She pulled me down for another kiss. "You better be there when I wake up."

"Absolutely."

She pointed to my blue bag sitting on a visitor's chair. "Don't forget your bag."

I gathered up the bag containing Badgers's water bottle. "Stick to bottled water," I reminded her. "CPW claims it's not coming from the tap water, but I'm not sold."

"I've got something better." Maggie held up a bottle of rehydration salts and made a face as I headed out of the room and to the elevator bank. It was going on suppertime and I needed to get some chow at Sarah's and hit the showers before going into work at the field morgue. Maggie wasn't going anywhere anytime soon.

Dr. Marcislin had arrived in the room shortly after we returned from our field trip downstairs with bad news. There was a problem at the lab, and it would be several more hours before Maggie's final blood work would be complete.

"Can't you just release me?"

"Under normal circumstances, yes. But not with what's going on. You need to be *Shigella*-free, with no intracranial pressure for at least 24 hours before I'm authorized to release you."

"Can I leave and you discharge me out when the lab work comes back?"

Dr. Marcislin's look quickly wilted Maggie's hopeful one.

"What's another couple hours Mags?" I said, trying to bolster her spirits. "You spend enough time here as it is."

"If I'm stuck here can I at least go downstairs and work?"

"No, and even if you could there'd be nothing to do. DMORT has taken over all posts. They're doing them onsite." Dr. Marcislin looked at me and nodded as if to confirm. I returned the nod. That was that. Maggie was trapped for a few more hours.

As I waited for the elevator, I opened the Uber app and requested a ride. It looked like it'd be a 20-minute wait. There weren't nearly as many little cartoon cars cruising around the downtown map as there normally are. No tourists. No drivers to squire them about. Keynesian economics. Worst-case scenario I could walk, but I didn't want to get soaked unless absolutely necessary. At the security checkpoint I showed my new federal credentials and breezed through.

The sky was still ominous and it was drizzling steadily. Standing under the hospital's canopy with two National Guardsmen guarding the hospital's entrance, I pinched a wad of tobacco and placed it into my lip and made a mental note to have the Uber driver stop at a pharmacy so I could get some Dramamine. Nikki didn't need to see me hurling off the side of a ship; the aftermath of the storm wasn't going to be smooth sailing. My phone buzzed. It was a text from Hotapp: Followed up with Badgers's parents. Not a coincidence. Degree in hydrologic engineering.

Jesus. Badgers was a water engineer.

I slipped the phone back into my pocket as a two-toned Ford Explorer roared up. One of the tinted windows buzzed down. "You request the Uber?" the driver yelled from the dim interior.

I dashed through the rain and opened the back door, pleasantly surprised my wait time had only been a couple of minutes. The interior was cool and smelled like cherry air freshener.

"Can you stop at the Rite Aid first?"

"You got it." The truck accelerated away from the hospitals pick/drop-off area.

The driver looked familiar. It took me a second to process his face. The glasses were the giveaway. It was Bob. The phone accessory salesman from the mall. Despite a population of three-quarters of a million in the metro area, Charleston can be a small town. A fleeting thought crossed my mind that something was off.

Wasn't the driver that accepted my ride request a woman in a Prius? By the time I sensed someone behind me it was too late. The warning bell in my head went off the moment a hand clamped a rag over my nose and mouth.

Bracing my legs against the floor, I pushed back trying to ram my assailant in the face, but he was smart. He ducked behind the seat, using the headrest as a fulcrum to keep me pinned in place and himself protected. The chemical on the rag tore through my lungs like wildfire, choking and gagging. I tried walking my legs up the seat and backwards somersaulting out of the chokehold. But I was too big for the cramped confines, and my attacker too strong. Fuzziness crept into the edges of my vision. As a last-ditch resort, I flailed my arms behind. It was useless. Blackness closed in. My vision shrank to a pinpoint. Then nothing.

Chapter 29

Consciousness rebooted in steps. First was feeling. My body jerked and jostled violently. There was a whole body rumbling sensation like hitting rumble strips on the highway. Next was sound. Gulls cawed in the distance. In the foreground bangs and scrapes echoed, there was the rustling of plastic and the sharp sound of metal on metal—a zipper. Next was vision. I opened my eyes and blinked hard a few times. The guts of an industrial ceiling—rafters, wires, a fire-suppression system—slowly came into focus. *Where am I?* Though my body felt like sand, I could tell I was laid out on something rigid. Sweeping the nausea aside, I turned my head. It was a Herculean task. I only succeeded in moving it a few degrees. But it was enough. Horror spread through every fiber of my being.

A snowman used a pair of bolt cutters on the nylon strapping around a casket ready for sea burial. *Click, click.* The sound of the snapping bands echoed loudly in the big space. Finished, he leaned the bolt cutters against the casket and operated the locking mechanism, opening the head and foot panels. The snowman turned and I caught a glimpse of his face behind the convex face field. He looked vaguely familiar, but I couldn't place him.

Seeing me awake, the man smiled. "I figured you'd be coming around soon." I struggled to move, succeeding only in twitching. My body seemed unwilling to comply with my brain's neural commands. "You'll find your muscles aren't working as you'd like them to." He held a syringe in my field of vision. "I've given you something to put you in twilight."

I organized the words carefully in my mind and managed to get out, "Who are you?"

The man pulled the hood and respirator off revealing a shaved head and thick features. His nose was puffy from recent trauma. Half grinning, he said, "Recognize me now?" His voice bore the faintest trace of an accent.

My blood pressure spiked. I tried flexing my fingers into a fist. They wouldn't respond. His mangled nose looked like the perfect target. "Who are you?"

"It doesn't matter."

"Bob?"

"Who?"

"The guy driving."

Baldie chuckled. "Oh, yes, his American name. His role is separate." He reached down and held up the funeral home bag. "I've been looking for this. First at the coroner's office and then, as you know," he pointed to his nose, "at the mortuary."

I began running a system check, testing each extremity. The best I could get was an involuntary jerk, more akin of a spasm. Baldie noticed and placed a gloved hand on my shoulder. "Don't bother. You could have your fingernails pulled and not feel a thing."

I relaxed, letting my metabolism burn through the drug, and buying some time. "The bottle, what's in it?"

Baldie pulled the water bottle from the bag looked at the liquid through the clear plastic. "It's called Blackwater."

"What is it?"

"Can you believe we drove this right across the border from Canada? TSA won't let you bring more than three ounces onboard a plane," he frowned a little and swirled the liquid like a moonshiner proofing liquor, "but this sailed right across at Ogdensburg in the cup holder without so much as a second glance." He lifted his eyes toward mine. "Homeland Security is worried about suitcase nukes because of their size. Do you know how many people died in the Hiroshima blast?"

I jerked my head to approximate a "no."

"A hundred thousand men, women, and children." He said it slowly like he was savoring the idea. "And that's a conservative number. This bottle has the potential to do better if deployed in the correct water system."

My vision shrank to a pinpoint. I struggled to focus as my head swam with the information.

Baldie continued, "A weapon of such magnitude isn't inexpensive. So now you can see why we've been so anxious to retrieve it."

Everything clicked together. Badgers worked for Bob more than just at his cell phone kiosk. Hansel discovered what Badgers was up to and killed him while he was in the process of deploying the weapon in the water supply. "This is what's poisoned our water supply?"

Something spooked Baldie. He slapped a hand over my mouth and craned his head around searching for danger. Satisfied we were alone, he pulled his hand off my mouth and tapped the bottle. "This is it, right here."

"A bottle of untreated water?" Things weren't making sense. "But how?"

"The Soviets developed a weaponized version of *Shigella* in the '80s as part of their Biopreparat program."

I shook my head weakly. "How can that be? Biological and chemical weapons have been outlawed for almost a hundred years."

"What does outlawed even mean? Nothing. That treaty is just a piece of paper. Do you think signatures on a piece of paper stopped your government from making them? No, they had to maintain the upper hand. There's been a top-secret arms race going on for years. Imagine the power you'd have if you could wipe out an entire army before even stepping foot onto the battlefield." Baldie held the bottle aloft. I couldn't help but stare at it, sickened by its power. "Fortunately, with the chaos surrounding the fall of the Soviet Union, a lot of things got misplaced."

"Weaponized? How?" I couldn't wrap my head around the fact that a bacteria that could be treated with penicillin, was so deadly.

"There's a promoter in the bacteria's genetic code. When triggered, it morphs into a virulent strain of Venezuelan equine encephalitis virus. I'm not sure the exact mechanism for conversion, but it's a brilliant piece of biological engineering."

"Bacteria to virus? Is that even possible?"

"Look at your city. Apparently."

I bared my teeth. "You're a monster."

Baldie smiled benignly. "You were a pawn in the American war machine, no?" I started to answer but Baldie continued loudly, "But you were never a soldier, a *warrior*. You never fought for something you believed in your heart." He tapped his chest with two fingers. "No, you fought because the corporate war mongers and politicians told you to. You're mercenaries. Americans are such a mongrel breed. You stand for nothing and worship the almighty dollar."

While he was engaged in his diatribe I ran through my extremities again. My faculties were returning, but I was acutely aware time was running out.

Baldie waved the bottle in my face. "Where's the rest?"

The crux of the matter; the reason I was still alive. I had to keep him going. "Why Charleston?"

Baldie motioned around the warehouse. "For all your pride in heritage, and charm, and manner, really you're just a little backwater town full of oppressive bigots. We needed a test subject that would simulate dispersal in a big city, but without the risks. New York City," he looked at me in a conspiratorial way, "is on high alert at all times, and we just weren't sure it'd be worth the effort. It is 30-year-old technology, after all."

"Why? If you're a soldier you've got to realize you're killing civilians: men, women, children, and the elderly. Innocent people."

Baldie leaned down so his face was inches from mine. His eyes shone with rage. "What do you think your government engages in? The killing of innocent people with your indiscriminate drone strikes. You Americans are the animals. And then you're surprised when we bring the fight to your shore."

"I was there. I know—"

"Know what?"

"What's going on over there."

"Enough talk," he thundered. "You know nothing. Where's the rest of Blackwater?" Seeing my hesitation, he added, "Before you consider lying, know this: I'll behead your *aurat* if you don't tell me the truth. I know where you live. In fact, I tracked you with you this." He pulled my phone out of my pocket. "You recall the day you had this repaired at the shopping mall?"

Of course. That explained the burglary at Sarah's Café. My phone was there. Baldie went looking for the Blackwater at the café. "His name is James Bailey. He says he's with Homeland Security, but I don't think he is," I said, letting the words tumble out trying to convince Baldie I was scared. I needed to protect Risden's cover; there was no way Baldie would be able to track down a ghost like Bailey. "His people are the ones that killed Sam Badgers." My muscles were getting that tingly feeling like when your arm falls asleep and all the blood rushes back. I slowly, very slowly, flexed my fingers.

"How do you contact him?"

"I don't. I know his people are watching Badger's apartment. If I show up there, they come find me." I tried not to make a face as I clenched my hand into a fist and squeezed.

Baldie nodded slowly, mulling the information over. "So, your government has a sample of Blackwater. That changes nothing. They have no idea what the real target is, but this compresses the timeline. In the meantime, you will vanish," Baldie winked. "If your body turns up, Homeland Security will realize how close you were. But if you disappear?" He shrugged. "Maybe you fled the quarantine. Nobody will know. Problem is disappearing someone in a city under martial law. Thankfully, you appear to already have a system in place for disappearing citizens." Baldie pointed to the opened casket, grinned, and turned to the tool bench to put the water bottle down. I seized the opportunity to act.

Baldie turned around holding the syringe. I leaped off the gurney. Things didn't go as planned. I completely overestimated my strength and underestimated the strength of the drug. My muscles wouldn't respond to my brain's commands. The leap was more of a flop. The floor rushed up to meet me as I crumpled in a head. Baldie laughed and knelt next to me. *"Khodā hāfez."* I felt a pinch in my neck.

Everything went black.

Chapter 30

The impact of the casket against the launch ramp jolted me conscious. It took a moment to figure out what was going on. It was dark. Something big and heavy was crushing me. There was the sound of surf and smell of brine. Everything clicked. My predicament was grim. Beyond grim. I had seconds to live. Scant seconds. I fought for my life.

It was all for naught. The mortuary detail didn't hear my screams over the ambient roar of the wind and ship's engines. They didn't feel my pounding and thrashing with the pitching motion of the sea.

"Now!" a sailor called.

Their hands released the handles. The casket rolled down the ramp.

"No!" I screamed.

It gathered speed, sailed off the launch ramp and hung midair for a moment. Wind buffeted the holes, but otherwise everything was still and silent.

This is it. I'm dead.

The moment didn't last long. My stomach leaped into my throat as gravity took hold and the casket dropped like a stone. There wasn't enough vertical distance—only 30 feet—to attain terminal velocity, but it felt so. Imagine skydiving strapped to an engine block. The casket hit the water with a brain-scrambling crash more akin to colliding with concrete.

My head connected with metal. Everything went black.

Aspirating water is like getting hit with a cattle prod, painful and electric. My eyes snapped open. I was underwater. *The bubbles! Follow the bubbles!*—my brain screamed. Kicking, my legs, I followed the bubbles until my head broke the surface of the water. Spluttering and choking, I retched and vomited. My lungs felt like fire burned in them. Sucking a ragged breath, I wiped my eyes. There were stars. Stars? I should be trapped in a casket falling through the ocean depths. Stars meant I was alive.

A field of bubbles roiled around me. The casket's lid had popped off upon impact, throwing me out like so many of the unseatbelted auto-wreck victims I'd embalmed over the years.

I heard a splash, and saw the running lights of the *Roosevelt* receding, its powerful wake buffeting me. "Hey!" I waved my arms frantically. "Hey!" It was no use. Unless someone was leaning over the railing watching the caskets drop there was no way they'd see a floating speck in the night sea. There was another splash, this one farther away. "Help!" I shouted, for want of a better idea, a wave washing over me causing me to struggle back to the surface, retching more saltwater. I watched until all the ship's running lights melded into one, and then completely disappeared.

I was alone, bobbing 50 miles off the coast with no survival gear in abject darkness.

Things weren't looking good.

One of my survival instructors said the first day of class, "The first thing to do in a survival situation is not panic. Panic *will* kill you. There's a solution to every problem."

I pictured his face as panic clawed at my gut. He was a nasty, petty sonofabitch. I concentrated on his mean mouth, and pock-scarred face—rumored to be leech scars earned by spending days partially submerged in an Ethiopian swamp—focused on him until the panic receded to a manageable level.

"Set small goals," he said on day one before the screaming started.

I stopped treading momentarily to feel my face and head. Miraculously, everything seemed okay. There didn't appear to be anything broken, fractured or lacerated. There's a check mark in the positive category. A broken bone could spell disaster, likewise something as trivial as a bloody nose could attract sharks. Not that I felt great. The adrenaline was ebbing, and it felt like I put a phone book against my face and let someone swing a baseball bat at it. But I'd live for the moment.

Another thing I had going for me was the fact it was early September and I had gotten tossed into the Gulf Stream. It pulls warm water from the Caribbean up the coastline. It wasn't pleasant, but I certainly wouldn't immediately die from exposure. The positives were adding up.

I'd been treading water about ten minutes but was already exhausted. Reaching down, I untied my shoes and kicked them off. Next, I unbuckled my belt and shimmied my pants off. Tying the cuffs together, I dropped the knot behind my neck and slipped one pant leg under my left armpit. Cupping my right hand, I churned it in a circular motion from above the water into the waist of the pants so it forced air into the cavity and inflated the fabric. By keeping the waistline underwater, the fabric retained a goodly amount of the air, and I was able to float for several minutes before refilling. Now I had a floatation device. Another positive.

The swells weren't too bad considering the storm. I spent the remainder of the night riding the erratic swells and trying to keep from getting swamped. It was exhausting, vigilant work. The worst part was the mental fatigue: not knowing where the night sky ended and the ocean began, from what direction I'd be thrown next, or how big the crest would be. Worst of all was the thought of what lurks beneath. Every time that thought popped into my head I forced the image of the pock-marked face into my mind. "Panic *will* kill you."

It was a long night.

The sky turned gray then purple and the sun hoisted itself out of the ocean and started its ascent. The day was clear and calm as it often is after a storm; there was nothing to hide the relentless sun. In an effort to shield myself I tore strips from my shirt and laid them over my head like an old leather football helmet, occasionally ladling water onto the fabric to keep cool. It helped, but there was nothing to mitigate the growing thirst. The inside of my mouth felt like a salt mine from the aspirated water, coupled with the heat from the sun made me beyond parched. If I ran my tongue over my lips I could feel salt crystals the size of small diamonds. A childhood rhyme popped into my head and played over and over, *water, water everywhere, but not a drop to drink*. It had to have some kind of maritime origin. Sailors would be well acquainted with the bitter irony.

To get my mind off my thirst I tried naming Skynyrd's catalog. I got to 54 which seemed low to me, but then again a plane crash cut their career short. In fourth grade we had to memorize the preamble of the Constitution. For extra credit I had also memorized part of Article One. It only took a few pass throughs before 20 years disappeared and the words tumbled over my cracked lips with ease. The sun continued to burn relentlessly as I chipped away at the hours keeping my mind busy. Boredom was as much an enemy as the sun or thirst. I needed to keep my edge.

The occasional contrail of impossibly highflying aircraft was the only life in the sky but I wasn't alone. Sea life bumped my legs. It's a disquieting sensation, but so frequent I quickly lost a sense of alarm. As long as a dorsal fin didn't accompany the bump I'd be fine.

In Afghanistan I participated in a joint operation with the SEALs to do a personnel recovery from Pakistan. It was a Tier I priority. Orders came straight from D.C. The victim was the daughter of a representative on the House Committee on Armed Services. She had been taken hostage while doing Peace Corps work in western India and transported into the Haqqani stronghold in Waziristan. The fear was the girl would be used in a propaganda video. My role was to make sure she survived the ride back to civilization.

While we waited for the birds in a dusty hanger on the outskirts of Lashkar Gah the team prepped for the mission. Some of the guys meditated while others checked and rechecked their weapons. I was in the former category, sitting, staring, occasionally spitting. No sense wasting energy. After several hours, and no ride, the guy next to me flashed a deck of cards. "You want to play a few Bones?" Bones is a navy catchall term for medical people. Until now I had been largely ignored.

The guy across from me gave a half roll of his eyes. Apparently, I was the mark.

I spit, and considered my answer, not taking long enough that I'd be considered rude. "I don't know too many card games."

"Anything to pass the time." He was a little guy, wiry and slight in an ultra-marathoner sort of way. Aside from his bushy beard, the most distinguishable feature was a set of energetic eyes—like two hawks in flight. His body language was completely opposite.

"Go fish?" It was the only card game I knew the rules to.

He nodded, hands already busy dealing cards. "They call me Shark, by the way."

"Clip."

"How'd you get that moniker?"

"God given."

Shark blinked once, grinned, and placed the deck between us and swept up his cards. "Ever been fish food, Clip?"

"Just gators." The final phase of Ranger School is conducted in the Florida swamps. I nodded at the cards he was sorting. "Go ahead."

"Here's a tip. If you ever encounter a shark, stand your ground. You'll know when it's getting ready because it'll start circling. If it comes at you punch it in the eye."

"That how you get your name? You punch one in the eye?"

"Know what to do when you encounter a card shark?" His hawk eyes danced with merriment.

"I don't reckon I do."

"Run like hell." He laughed. It was more of a bray. "Got any queens?"

"Go fish."

I never saw Shark after that day. We rescued the girl. Another few days and she wouldn't have made it. Barely conscious, dehydrated and bruised and lacerated from multiple beatings, we located her chained to a stake in a storeroom like a dog. The chain was unnecessary. She had been raped so many times she couldn't walk. Shark and his team got their vengeance, six dead tangos, but where was the justice? The girl's life was over; she'd never be normal again. Every time I pictured her all I could conjure was the huddled mass on the chopper's litter.

That mission, the conversation, and card game remained largely buried in my mind until a fin popped out of the water. Everything was forgotten: the raging thirst, the unrelenting sun, the gnawing sense of hopelessness and my attention was laser focused on the gray fin cutting the surface a few dozen feet in front of me.

Panic almost won the day. I started kicking my legs and flailing my arms in some sort of primal attempt at escape. With iron will, I summoned my instructor's face. "Don't panic." I stopped moving. The fin cut a lazy arc about 30 feet away. *Maybe it doesn't even know I'm here,* I thought, feeling foolish for thrashing around. That kind of movement would certainly attract it. My hopes were dashed when the fin suddenly turned 90 degrees and headed directly for my location.

Balling my fists, I took a deep breath, ready to duck underwater to confront the beast. It wasn't in a hurry. It came closer and closer at a slow, steady pace. Ten feet. Five feet. My world shrank down to that triangular protrusion. Just as I was about to duck down and confront my aggressor, the shark executed a neat turn and disappeared. I caught a glimpse of it. It was maybe seven or eight feet long with a pointed snout, like a bullet, and eyes as dead as pennies.

After the beast disappeared I continued turning tight revolutions, trying to spy the fin, expecting the worse, an attack from the depths, something with no warning. As the seconds stretched into minutes and the minutes passed, my fear started to dissipate and I began to think the beast had decided to leave me alone. That hope was short lived. The fin popped up at my three o'clock and began to work a slow pattern like a plane on approach to an airport.

"Shit," I muttered, through cracked lips. It would be several hours before the sun set, but I wasn't looking forward to bobbing around like a cork in pitch-blackness with a man-eater stalking me. But there was nothing I could do about that. In frustration, I slapped the water. My arm hit something hard in my pants. Curious, I felt along the fabric and eased out my Copenhagen tin. Dropping the life vest momentarily, I treaded and cracked the tin. Miraculously it was dry. Using trembling fingers, I eased a hefty portion past cracked lips. The flood of saliva was an unbelievable welcome relief in my parched mouth, and the tobacco rush so intoxicating I swooned like an elementary schooler sneaking snuff out of his daddy's tin.

That's how the rest of the day went. I worried on the wad of tobacco, and my new best friend hovered a stone's throw away, occasionally venturing closer, but never close enough so I could see him. The sun dropped lower and lower in the sky. I waited to the inevitable, darkness. That's what my escort seemed to be waiting for too. Then the solution literally hit me in the chest.

I didn't see it because it's profile was flush with the water's surface, and my eyes were fatigued from the sun's rays. It slammed into my sternum; surprising me so much I thought the shark had launched a sneak attack. Momentarily flailing, my arms landed on something hard and flat. When I realized it was a piece of floating wood, I dug my nails into the wood fibers and clung to it gathering my strength. It was a substantial piece, not just a little piece of driftwood. Traversing the piece, I determined it was a door, probably a marine door because of the circular hole near one end where a porthole once sat. It was roughly six by three feet, little smaller than a door in a residential home, but probably enough surface area to keep me afloat.

Kicking my legs, I hauled myself up onto the door and promptly flipped off the other side. I popped to the surface and quickly scrabbled around, my hands coming in contact with the wood. This time I kicked one leg up onto the door and eased myself onto it sideways until my center of gravity was in the middle. Success. My 6'3" frame was longer than the door. By bending my knees, I could keep my feet out of the water. The door didn't exactly float, but rather achieved neutral buoyancy to where I was more or less above the water's surface.

Nightfall came. My head felt like it was on fire. The cool night air helped to alleviate the pain, but after an entire day of being exposed to the blistering sun my face throbbed with pain. I fell into a series of exhausted micro naps. I didn't want to allow myself to fall into a deep sleep and risk falling off the door. Something bumped the underside of the door on more than one occasion throughout the night.

"If you want me, you're going to have to breech," I growled after the first bump. Anticipating such a move by the shark, I had worked a large splinter off the corner of the door before the sun set. It was about the dimensions of a kitchen knife. I shivered, dozing occasionally, clutching the jagged piece of wood and waiting for sunrise.

Morning broke and with it came a bigger enemy. Thirst. It had been 36 hours since I last had a drink and my body screamed for fluid. My tobacco tin had one lip left. With shaking fingers, I packed it in my Mojave mouth, and skipped the empty tin out across the waves. It took several moments to work up any saliva. It was enough that the seawater stopped looking like a good idea. Though I knew drinking seawater would be the end of me, but my body was almost physically urging me to take a sip.

I didn't want to get any more sunburn than absolutely necessary to contribute to my already unbearable thirst. After the tobacco gave me a little burst of energy I shifted and sat up on the door. Carefully, I pulled apart my life vest and very slowly worked my legs back into the pants. My escort's fin sliced the water 20 feet away. After the pants were back on, I tore a section of the front of my shirt off for my head. I had lost the strips falling off the door the previous day. After placing the piece of cloth over the back of my head, I pulled my arms under me to minimize their sun exposure, and worried on the wad in my mouth until the tobacco molecules dissolved and there was nothing left but my thirst and misery and the relentless sun.

Chapter 31

The voices started as dreams—or were conflated as such. Exhausted, I slipped in and out consciousness. It was the day I first arrived at Granville & Sons. Isabella answered the door and was as excited and welcoming as one might be to a door-to-door vacuum salesman. Thomas, the other funeral director at the time, escorted me down to the prep room where Lauren was hunched over a post on the embalming table. The dead guy looked young, but it was hard to tell with his scalp pulled over his face. Big band music played softly.

Thomas cleared this throat. "Mr. Granville?"

Lauren turned. Distinguished looking with a full head of white hair, he wore two pieces of a three-piece black suit. A gold pocket watch chain was strung across his waistcoat, and gleaming wingtips completed his haberdashery. Despite the mess on the table, his crisp white sleeves rolled to the elbow appeared spotless.

"This is the applicant," Thomas said. The way he said it might as well have been, "Here's the mouse I caught."

"Hi sir," I said, stepping forward, about to offer my hand, but withdrawing it quickly, feeling foolish. "Tripp Clipper." This was not how I envisioned my interview.

"I understand you're an army man."

"I was. I'm out."

"I promise you son, soldiering stays in your blood. Who were you with?"

"The Seventy-fifth."

Lauren's flinty eyes flicked up and down and he motioned to the person on the table with a quick jerk of his head. "Ever seen this before?" He pointed to the inside of the abdominal-thoracic cavity. It was green.

I hadn't, but I recognized the smell. "Probably gangrene. I'm guessing necrotic enterocolitis."

Lauren gave me a peculiar look. I got the impression that wasn't the response he was expecting. "What leads you to that conclusion, soldier?" The tone was sharp, that of someone who was used to giving orders.

"I was a medic. You don't soon forget the smell."

"You don't," he agreed, "but why are we on a raft?"

"Lauren, lie down. You're going to tip us," I pleaded. Lauren was standing dangerously close to the edge of the door-cum-raft like a high diver on a diving board.

"What's Matey doing here?" he asked, ignoring me, and pointing up.

"You died before Mags moved in with Matey—" I shook my head and Lauren disappeared as did Matey, but not the cawing. It was a seagull. A seagull? A seagull! *I must be near land!*

Snapping myself out of delirium, I strained my eyes in every direction trying to see if I could spy land, but all I could see were clouds colliding with water.

"How far out to sea do gulls fly?" I asked the fin. It slipped beneath the surface, disappearing as it often did, sometimes for minutes at a time, but it always reappeared. Occasionally, the fin ventured close, but never close enough for me to jab it. I had spent the better part of the day picking shreds of wood fiber off until the end resembled an ice pick.

Something trickled down my chin, and my hand came away bloody. My lips were so dry, just moving my mouth was causing them to crack and bleed. I sucked my fingers, the blood tasting good, and tried tracking the seagull's flight path to figure out what direction land was. Not that it was going to do any good if I knew. I was far too weak to paddle for more than a couple of minutes. The gull flapped and rode the air currents for several minutes before disappearing leaving the fin and I alone once again.

I watched the direction he disappeared for hours, passing in and out of consciousness, but the sky remained devoid of life.

When the sun went down I lay curled on the plank in the fetal position shivering though my skin was engulfed in flames. I've heard people with shingles complain it's unbearable to simply move. It hurt simply to lay still. Seawater sloshed over the top of the raft constantly irritating the lesions, a combination of sun blisters and wet rot.

The night was cloudless and the waxing moon provided ample light. I noticed the shadow move near my raft right before I capsized. That was all the warning I needed. Pitching headfirst in the water, I wielded the splinter like a dagger. There was no fear; that had been systematically stripped. The Navy SEAL's words roared in my ears, "Who's the apex predator?" Coming up spluttering, I scrabbled for my raft. Spying it a few yards away in the moonlight, I swam wildly. Saltwater water stung my eyes, burned my nostrils and choked my throat, but I pressed on. I imagined the beast below me, ready to strike and dismantle me. Could I tourniquet a missing limb? My fingers smacked wood. Adrenaline alone allowed me to pull myself up on it. I lay retching seawater. The end was near. If the beast upended me again I wouldn't have the strength to swim or pull myself back up onto the raft. I knew it. The beast knew it.

Once I caught my breath I lay studying the surface of the water like I used to do when I was a kid hunting tadpoles at the creek. All was quiet. The moon shone on the black sea. The beast, normally cautious, was emboldened by its surprise attack, and it wasn't long before I saw something darker than the water surface. But the beast had done itself a disservice. The adrenaline flowing through my veins focused my attention and sharpened my reflexes. Shifting my weight, quick and careful, I stabbed into the water. Nothing.

*One, two, three...*I started counting. It was a trick I learned in the military to keep awake and alert. Like a metronome in my brain the seconds ticked by.

At 1,976 the shark made another attempt. This time it made the mistake of coming at the right side of the raft. I'm right handed, and hardly had to move. I sensed the water disturbance before I heard the splash, and simply adjusted the point toward the noise. The shark ran itself into the point. It jerked so quickly, and fiercely, it ripped the piece of wood out of my hand. The encore was a small burst of bubbles. The surface was calm once again.

Blood trickled from my hand. I could feel scores of splinters embedded under the skin. It hurt in a good way. The pain of victory. I sucked my hand for a moment, before starting to work another edge off the door. My hand bled freely into the water as I used my nails to claw a jagged hunk of wood out. If the beast returned I'd be prepared.

I was utterly exhausted. Bloody hand in my mouth, like a baby sucking its fingers, I lay back and was instantly out.

When the door capsized, I jolted awake. *My weapon! Where's my weapon?* I thought wildly flailing about, only to smash into a hard surface. My face dug into grit, like sandpaper rubbing across it. *Sand!* Gathering my legs under me, I stood in breaking surf. Stretched out before me was a dark beach. *Land,* I thought as my abdomen contracted violently and bile and brine filled my mouth.

Tears of joy filled my eyes as I slogged through the breakers and collapsed in the sand hugging terra firma. The urge to sleep was overwhelming. I was crazed with thirst, blistered, burned, soaking wet and cold, but I could've shut my eyes and slept for days. The pock-marked face loomed in my head, "Sleep will kill you. Stay alert soldier! No matter what *do not* succumb to sleep!" Come to think of it, he claimed everything would kill us. He was right. I had to stay awake. The water supply was killing the people in Charleston.

Groaning, I managed to push myself onto all fours and then upright. After a few days in the water, I was a little unsteady. The soft sand didn't help. Walking—staggering—in the general direction of the lights, I waded over a dune. Civilization was on the other side. A parking lot and pavilion, cheaply built that screamed government. *Restrooms!* I could care less about restrooms, which would be locked in the middle of the night. But restrooms meant pipes, and pipes at a public pavilion meant a water fountain. I lurched across the expanse of asphalt like a zombie. Sure enough, bolted to the wall was a pitted relic from the Civilian Conservation Corps days from which a feeble stream burbled. Though I tried to use some restraint, I drank greedily and promptly vomited. The violent spasms brought me to my knees. I passed out, and woke in the cold puddle of vomit, my brain screaming: *water, water!* Panting, I pulled myself back up to the oasis. This time I forced myself to take a few sips and then rest. It took all my will to count to 600 before drinking again.

After drinking my fill, I shuffled into the parking lot. Though reluctant to leave my water source, I needed to make my way toward the lights. Civilization. A phone. I noticed a dark smudge tucked up near a dune. As I got closer I could see it was a Jeep Wrangler with impossibly big tires. I couldn't be sure, my nostrils were fried by the salt, but thought I detected the odor of something. Marijuana?

"Hey," I called, or at least tried to. The word failed in my vocal cords and came out as a garbled sonic note. Clearing my throat, I tried again.

There was some muted cursing and scrabbling around. A blond head poked out of the rear cargo area where the rear seats would go.

"Your phone." I took a breath. "I need a phone."

The head rose up further, like a prairie dog coming up when it realizes there's no danger, revealing a shirtless teenager. The hair was thick and tangled like surfers prefer. "Dude, get lost." He was emboldened by the bum standing before him.

"Please." My voice cracked. "I need help. I fell overboard from a boat and washed ashore."

"I didn't hear any chatter about a Code Oscar." His voice had moved from hostility to suspicion. I wasn't sure what a Code Oscar was, but I bet it was marine lingo for man overboard. The Jeep did have a whip antenna meaning there was a CB that Blondie used to keep his finger on the pulse.

Looking around like it would give me a clue to my whereabouts I asked Blondie, "Where am I?"

"Atlantic Beach."

"Where's that?"

"North Carolina. East of Morehead City."

My knees went weak. It had to be at least 200 miles from Charleston. "Jesus," I muttered.

"Where'd you go over?"

"Charleston." The minute I said it, I realized the mistake.

Blondie got still. "Dude, isn't that city closed?" With that, a female popped up next to Blondie, covering her breasts with a tanned forearm. Her curiosity about a quarantine refugee outweighed her shame.

"Hi," I said, thinking it would be less awkward than not acknowledging the nude female. I was wrong.

She cocked her head.

"N—" I had to stop and clear my throat. "No. I mean, yes Charleston is closed. But I took a head boat out of Sunset Cay in Folly Beach. Nobody seems to know where Folly Beach is. Charleston is the closest landmark."

Blondie was right to be suspicious. There were stories of people escaping the quarantine by driving off in their pleasure craft and slipping through the Coast Guard cordon.

"No lifeboat?"

I shook my head and tossed out another lie. "It was rough when we were coming in, and I had been drinking all day. I went over and nobody noticed."

Blondie's jaw dropped a fraction of an inch. "How long were you in?"

"Best I can tell. Forty-eight hours."

"Dude!" He shed his slow surfer affect and scrambled to his feet. I wished he hadn't. Blondie wasn't wearing a stitch of clothing. "I'm going to hop on the box and get you some help. I'm a lifeguard," he added.

I motioned with my hands for him to sit and calm down. "No, really that's not necessary. I'm fine. Can I please just borrow your cellphone to get someone to come pick me up?"

Blondie scrambled between the front seats. "You're fucked up and don't even realize it. Relax man. I'll get you some help."

I stepped forward and placed my hand on his wrist before he had a chance to flick toggle switches. Blondie looked at me with big blue eyes that suddenly contained fear. "Look pal, I'm going to level with you. I'm a well-known lawyer in Atlanta. If you call your friends in there's going to be a paper trail, and possibly some press. I really want to avoid any fuss if you know what I mean." I withdrew my hand and forced a pleasant smile on my face.

He nodded dumbly. "Yeah, yeah, man. I get it. Totally. I get it."

"Can I borrow your phone, please?"

Blondie backed into the cargo area and rummaged around, producing a cellphone.

The girl draped a beach towel around her shoulders in a small show of modesty, produced a joint, lit it and took a puff. Holding it toward me, she said, "Here. It'll calm you."

I waved her off as the line connected. "Granville and Sons," an officious voice stated. "This is the answering service. How may I help you?"

"This is Clip," I croaked, "I need you to forward this call to Moonie." With everyone on speed dial, the only phone number I knew was the funeral home's. I didn't even know Maggie's.

"Right away sir," the operator said.

There was some muted tapping on a keyboard followed by a series of clicks. Moonie picked up after the sixth ring. "Hello?" He sounded like he had been roused from a deep sleep.

"It's Clip."

Moonie cleared the gravel from his throat. "Hey partner! Where have you—"

I cut him off. "I need you to come get me. I'm in Atlantic Beach in North Carolina—"

"How in the Lord's name did you get there?"

"I'll explain everything when you get here. Can you leave right now?"

"Uh, sure, sure." There was noise in the background. I imagined him stumbling around his bedroom.

"Where are we?" I asked Blondie.

Blondie was in the middle of hitting the joint. Leisurely exhaling, he replied, "Ft. Macon State Park. Tell your person to take 58 until they see the sign for the park. Make the first right."

"Did you hear that?" I said in the phone. "Take the 58 north until you see a sign for Fort Macon State Park. Make the first right and take it until you get to a parking lot. I'll meet you there."

"Turn the light off!" someone shouted on the other end of the line.

There was a click and the sound of Moonie apologizing and the sound of a door shutting. Moonie came back on the line, his voice hushed, "Sorry. Skeeter was a little upset I woke her."

"Stop off at the funeral home and get me some clothes and food and water and tell Maggie I'm okay."

"You can count on me."

I disconnected. "Thanks." I handed the phone back to Blondie. He took it and plucked a sweatshirt from the floor of his Jeep. It was red and emblazoned with *Lifeguard* in white block letters along with the requisite cross.

"Here."

I gingerly peeled off my damp, tattered shirt and dropped it in a heap, and tugged on the heavy-duty sweatshirt. Relief was instant. It felt so good to get the wet fabric off my sunburned and sore-covered torso.

Blondie rooted in the center console and tossed me a bottle of aloe. "Here dude, rub that on your skin. It'll help, but you should really consider getting looked at." He took another hit of the joint and passed it.

"Thanks. I really appreciate all your help." I held the aloe aloft as if to prove my point and started to walk away. "I need to get some more water." My brain was screaming for more water.

"If you change your mind man and want me to call for help let me know," Blondie called.

I nodded, offered my hand in a wave, and stumbled back to the pavilion. I did my drinking and resting rotations, with a two-minute rest period. After ten rotations I stopped, worried about vomiting, and then used the fresh water to get the worst of the salt off my skin and hair. With shaking fingers, I spread a thick layer of the aloe on my skin and pulled the sweatshirt back on.

Moonie would be awhile so I decided to rack out. It had been days since I'd had any proper sleep and I was at the point of delirium. Briefly, I considered hiding, but if I hid, then Moonie wouldn't be able to find me. So, I climbed onto one of the picnic tables. The wooden planks, stained and greasy from countless meals, felt as good as a plush mattress.

Across the lot the Jeep roared to life. Blondie flicked the KC lights on, bathing the immediate area in intense light and eased the rig forward and up the dune. The big tires easily navigated the soft sand. I pulled the hood up and the last thing I remembered were the Jeep's taillights disappearing over the dune.

Chapter 32

Something poked me in the ribs. Hard. I was too tired to care. Or move.

"—partner."

I struggled to part salt-encrusted eyes. "Wha?"

Moonie loomed into focus wearing his ten-gallon hat and aviator shades, toothpick dancing through his lips. "Fancy meetin' you here partner. I don't know what you got into, but your disappearance sure got folks stirred up." He dropped the shades down his nose and looked up and down. "And you look like the fox that got into a losin' brawl with a pack of hounds."

A groan escaped my lips as I sat up. My muscles had stiffened to the point they felt frozen, and my skin was on fire. It was just after daybreak. The coroner's van was the only vehicle in the parking lot. "You're going to have to help me." I held out my arm.

"What happened?" Moonie took me under the armpit, escorting me like an old lady.

"I'll tell you on the way. We need to get moving. You bring the stuff?"

Moonie flung open the door, revealing a stack of clothes, a case of coconut water and much of the contents of my pantry jammed into a shopping bag. I drank a water, peeled off my almost dry pants, and pulled on a new pair. "Let's go." I grabbed the overhead handle and carefully hoisted myself in.

Moonie climbed into the driver's seat and cranked the engine.

"Advil?"

"Check the glove compartment."

I pulled out a bottle of aspirin. "Koziner know you have the van this far off the reservation?" I cracked another water and drank greedily, popped a handful of pills in my mouth and washed them down.

"Nah, but I figured I'd need it to get through the cordon." He tossed me his phone. "Call your girlfriend. I damn near had to drag her out of the van. The only way I got her to listen to reason was when I told her she'd never get out of the cordon." Moonie smoothed his mustache with the tip of his pinky and turned onto 58. "She threatened my life if I didn't make you call her the minute I saw you."

Maggie picked up on the first ring. "Clip?" Her voice was hopeful, like she didn't want to believe.

"Hey Mags."

"Oh my God," she gushed, "Moonie told me where you are. Why didn't you call? I've been worried sick about you."

"It's a long story. I washed ashore here after falling off the navy ship."

Maggie sucked in a lungful of air. "How did—"

Cutting her off, I said, "Babe, I'll give you the whole story when I see you. The important thing is I'm on my way home, and I'm fine." I figured it'd be easier on her if I parsed the information out.

"Jesus," she muttered under her breath. "I finished painting the living room. I couldn't sleep."

"You should've been resting."

"I know, but I was so worried."

In an attempt at levity, I said, "Does it look good?"

Maggie paused and laughed. "Looks like a new place." She started crying.

"Don't cry. I'm fine," I lied.

"I was so worried!"

"I'm sorry to worry you babe, but this thing is almost over. I promise and then we can get back to normal. And enjoy that newly painted room."

"Normal." She paused, sniffing. "That'd be nice."

"That would."

Maggie breathed heavily into the phone for a moment before blurting out, "Let's get married."

Speechless, I recovered. It was my turn to say, "Jesus." Spluttering, because that wasn't the response Maggie was expecting, I said, "Absolutely, I mean, yes! Yes, of course I'll marry you."

Moonie elbowed me, and whisper-shouted, "Way to go partner! Sounds like yer gettin' hitched."

Normally, an outburst like that would've earned Moonie a dirty look. Not today. Grinning like a fool, I continued babbling, "Yes, yes, that's a fantastic idea. We'll make plans as soon as I get home. Right now, I need to sleep. I haven't slept in days—Wait, what's today?"

"Saturday."

"I haven't really slept since Tuesday, I think."

"Okay, hurry home to me." I could hear the smile in her voice.

"I will."

We exchanged "I love yous" and hung up.

Moonie squinted at a sign and put his blinker on. There was just the *tick-tock* of the signal. After making the turn he said, "So, you going to tell me about disappearing for three days and washing up five hours north." The normal officious tone was replaced with one of actual concern.

I sighed. "You have any dip?" Moonie retrieved a tin of Red Man from his hip pocket and passed it to me. After the nicotine rush, I told Moonie the whole story beginning with leaving the hospital and ending with the rendezvous in the Jeep. For the only time I can remember Moonie listened without interrupting.

When I finished, he said, "You're lucky to be alive."

The man is incapable of irony, so I simply said, "I know. Do you mind if I get some shut eye?"

He patted my knee. "No problem, partner. You rest up. I'll wake you when we get back to C-ton." He pronounced it *seton.*

I didn't need further urging. Closing my eyes, I was instantly asleep.

Moonie woke me by hitting me in the shoulder. The dash clock told me it was midday. We passed an electronic sign put up by SCDOT. *Road Closed Ahead. Last Turnoff Rt. 41*, it flashed. I stretched and groaned. The seats in the coroner van weren't exactly Posturepedic, and my muscles were still in knots from the fall off the navy ship and spending a good amount of time prone on a wooden door. A ways up the highway another electronic sign blocked the road flashing a big arrow to the right, funneling all cars to turn off onto 41. Moonie slowed, wove his way through the cones and continued on 17. The roadblock wasn't too much farther up the road. MRAPs and Humvees blocked all six lanes in both directions.

National Guardsmen lounged in various states of vigilance. On the shoulder of the opposite lanes of traffic sat three news trucks with their antennas raised. The crews fraternized under their little tent city. When we pulled up, one of the cameramen shouldered his rig and motioned an overly coiffed woman in a slinky dress into action. Another dramatic update.

Moonie stopped about 20 yards in front of the line and rolled down his window. A soldier wearing sergeant's stripes sauntered out to meet us. Based on the way he walked, and held his weapon, there were a lot of cars who ignored the signs and continued, hoping to talk their way into the city.

"Road's closed," the Guardsman said. The look in his eyes was one of utter boredom.

"I know. I left the quarantine on official business." Moonie handed his laminate to the soldier and jerked his thumb backwards to the lettering on the van.

The soldier's eyes sparked and jumped from the laminate to the side of the van. He pulled his surgical mask down to his chin revealing a salt-and-pepper broom mustache. "What kind of business?" He squinted at the laminate and then at Moonie.

"Coroner business. Can't comment on an ongoing investigation I'm afraid."

The sergeant peered at me. I stared back with an air of impatience. It worked. He didn't ask for ID, but said, "I'll have to check this out. You two hang tight." He tugged the mask back up—regulation, no doubt—and retreated to the command post, a couple banquet tables spread out under a canopy.

I offered Moonie a coconut water. "Nah, you know I don't do that health stuff."

"Suit yourself." I cracked it and drank the entire thing with several big gulps. "How'd you get them to let you out?" I wiped my mouth with the back of my hand. At the CP, several camo-clad soldiers clustered around the sergeant. There was pointing at the van, and nodding.

"Didn't. They got the area sealed off and ain't letting anyone in or out." He grinned. "They have big fancy blockades at the main roads like this, but at the back roads they just have a deputy or such. The stretch of road that crosses the Back River, near the naval base only had one car watching it, and Lester from my bowling league, was the one in the car watching the road. When I told him how important it was he waved me right through."

I shook my head. Unbelievable. The entire efforts of the government trying to control the spread of an idiopathic, fatal disease thwarted by two beer swilling pin kings. Back at the CP a consensus was reached and the sergeant came trotting back to the van trailing a woman sporting a lieutenant's bar.

"Sir," she said, handing Moonie his laminate, "I do apologize, but our orders are not to let *anyone* in or out of the perimeter. No exceptions."

"Ma'am, I realize—"

The officer cut him off. "No exceptions sir. I do apologize. Please turn your vehicle around." The sergeant gripped his rifle tighter, hoping for a bit of action.

I didn't want to do it, announce my presence. I had no idea how plugged in Bob, or his associates were, but there didn't seem to be any other way. "Ma'am," I said, raising my hand. "May I have a word?"

The lieutenant stepped crisply around the front of the van. Her patience was wearing thin. The sergeant's rifle inched downward. He spoke briefly into the comm line on his shoulder, readying his comrades for the ensuing fight.

"Lieutenant Hunter," I said, reading her nametape. "Would you please go back to the CP and radio Commander D'ambrosio from DMORT and tell her Special Investigator Tripp Clipper is at the perimeter. The deputy here," I jerked my thumb at Moonie, "and I are essential personnel."

'Special Investigator' peaked her interest and her eyes flicked up and down taking in my three day's growth and ratty lifeguard sweatshirt. Finally, she held out her hand. "Lemme see some ID."

"That's the thing—"

"No exceptions," she snapped. Making a turning motion with her hand she said, "Turn around."

"What a she-lion," Moonie said; executing a sloppy three-point turn.

"Let's go see your bowling buddy and see if we can sneak back in," I said, popping another coconut water. My tissues felt like they were made of sponge. I simply couldn't absorb enough water.

"Roger that partner."

Either they got smart, or they trotted out reinforcements, but when we got to the Back River crossing there was a National Guard barricade. I assumed Lieutenant She-Lion radioed ahead. They waved us off without even entertaining our tale of woe.

Moonie pulled off into in the deserted parking lot at Bushy Park Industrial. "Now what do we do?"

"I've got to make a call," I said exiting the van. I dialed my answering service and gave the operator a phone number to call and explicit instructions. And then paced, waiting for the phone to ring.

Chapter 33

Mosquitoes actively drew blood, but I didn't slap at them. Stillness was crucial. A patrol of Guardsmen trawled the river in an inflatable launch. Though they weren't exactly running a stealth beat, laughter and jokes floated over the noise of the outboard engine, I had to give the weekend warriors credit for at least deploying patrols. The underbrush provided ample camouflage, not that one person from the patrol glanced our way. They were more concerned with folks trying to sneak out of the quarantine cordon than nuts trying to get in.

Once the boat moved northward, I counted five minutes in my head and motioned to Moonie. He nodded and slithered down the muddy embankment.

There's a rail bridge that crosses upstream near the Cypress Gardens boat landing, but it's within view of the road bridge and the roadblock. In daylight we wouldn't stand a chance sneaking across unnoticed, and I wasn't so sure we'd fare much better at night. Some geardo would have NVG—night vision goggles. And I didn't want to waste a half-day waiting for darkness. The last thing in the world I wanted to do was get back in the water, *any* water. But this was the only option.

"Hey partner," Moonie hissed. "Ever heard of any gators this far inland?" He winked, and then grinned at the middle finger offered to him.

I submerged into the brown water, keeping only my head above. The wetness on the wet rot and sunburn blisters sent an involuntary jolt of electricity through my body, and I sucked in sharp breath. The river's current was quick from the recent rains. I stroked underwater to create as little disturbance as possible, charting a diagonal course. When we were about halfway Moonie's head snapped up. He shaded his eyes against the harsh sun.

"What?"

"Drone!" he whispered. At that moment I heard the distinct fan-like whirring.

"Has it seen us?"

"It's certainly coming this direction." There was no way it hadn't seen us, exposed in the middle of the river.

"Shit," I muttered. "Go, go!" I started stroking like an Olympian, stealth be damned.

"Don't look up!"

I kept my face in the water, only occasionally turning to gulp in a giant lungful of air. Reaching the opposite bank, I scrambled across a muddy delta and sprinted for the distant tree line a thousand yards away.

"Down! Down!" Moonie said, once we reached the trees.

I dove onto the ground and lay breathless. Turning, I peered back the way we came. The drone descended outside the tree line and hovered, trying to get eyes on us. "Dammit!" I muttered, seeing the markings on the little flying contraption. Of course, it wasn't some punk kid out stalking the Guardsmen with his toy. No, it was a black-and-white drone with the word POLICE emblazoned on it.

The drone started picking its way between the trees. There wasn't a cry of alarm yet, but there was no doubt in my mind, the platoon upstream would receive a radio call soon.

"Don't worry," Moonie said, dragging a liter soda bottle from the leaves. It was river trash, the plastic hazy and filled with dried silt. He lay on his back and pulled a plastic evidence bag from his pocket. He ripped it open, removed his Ruger. The sealing evidence bags had been his idea, to keep our stuff from getting ruined.

"What are you doing?" I whispered, eying the drone. The operator was nervous with the trees and the machine was retreating.

"Taking care of a problem."

"Are you crazy?"

Moonie pulled out a Swiss Army knife and notched the mouth of the soda bottle and slipped it onto the barrel of the gun. From another pocket he produced a roll of electrical tape. "They ain't seen our faces yet." He grunted and began wrapping the tape around the barrel like he was taping a baseball bat. "And this thing will track us like a bloodhound. It'll just go up to altitude and wait for us to make a move." Moonie stole a glance back. "Go on, lure that skeeter a little closer."

Keeping an arm in front of my face, I jumped up and darted to the nearest tree. It worked. The drone stopped retreating and started easing forward again. The drone pilot now had a lock on its target.

"Range?" Moonie whispered. His shirt was off, tied around his nose and mouth like an old-fashioned train robber. Smart. He didn't want the last second of video feed freeze-framed with his mug pointing a pistol at police property.

"About 20 meters."

"Tell me when it's 15."

I placed my hand in front of my face and peeked out. The drone had stopped and was hovering. *Come on you bastard*, I willed it. The seconds ticked by and it remained stationary. I darted to another tree, this one closer to the drone in an effort to coax it forward. It worked. "Now!" I hissed.

Moonie hopped up, sighted, and fired, all in a microsecond. The plastic bottle acted as a silencer and there was a loud *thunk*. The drone exploded as the .44 caliber round slammed into it. Little plastic pieces rained silently into the leafy carpeting.

Moonie pulled the bottle off his pistol, tossed it, and blew the smoke off the barrel.

I applauded quietly like a spectator at a golf tournament. "Yes, I know. Amazing shot. Truly a feat to behold." I'd have to offer up the praise sooner or later if I ever wanted to hear the end of his heroics. Best to just get it over with.

Moonie twirled the revolver and landed it back in his holster. "I once took out a turkey, mid-flight, with this—"

"This way," I said, pointing, refocusing his attention. The river carried sounds of a boat motor and shouts from the guardsmen. The drone had alerted them before it's accident. "You can tell me about the turkey while we walk."

"I was huntin' down in Hendersonville Thanksgiving before last—" Moonie began without missing a beat as we began a fast walk inland through the scrub. I wasn't worried about the soldiers catching up with us. They only had the last coordinates of the drone. They'd still have to scramble out of the launch, locate the pieces of the mangled drone, and then decide which way we'd gone before giving pursuit. But we'd be in trouble if the police or military had another drone in close proximity. There was no time to waste.

Moonie was finishing up the heroic tale of him taking down a flying turkey with a handgun when we came to a two-lane road.

"This way." I pointed left.

"You hear that?"

The sound of helicopter rotors beat faintly in the distance. Our pursuers were getting air support. I nodded and we took off at a trot. A few moments later, we came to a cluster of modern homes built around an old plantation. The road goose necked and waiting at the entrance of the mansion's formal gardens was Nikki's rumbling Escalade dripping water from the air conditioner onto the gravel shoulder.

"What is this?" Moonie asked.

"Medway."

Moonie swiveled his head around the little settlement in the middle of nowhere. "I never knew this place was back here." His tone was accusatory. Moonie being a dyed in the wool local was a bit hurt that a newcomer knew something about Charleston he didn't.

I pointed in the direction of some mature oaks, past the house. "There's a cemetery back there."

Moonie shook his head. "I should've known. You and the dead. You're like a coon sniffing out a trash bin."

"Get in." I grabbed the car handle. The helicopter sounded closer. Truth be told, I had never actually buried anyone in the little cemetery. The only reason I knew it existed was Lauren had driven me here one day after a burial. It was an odd detour, sitting in the hearse in front of the plantation with Lauren regaling me about the people planted under the loamy soil. In hindsight, when his dementia became evident, the trip made a bit more sense.

We startled Nikki who was staring at her phone. "Dear Lord!" She placed a hand on her breast. "Y'all look awful." Indeed, we must've looked quite the sight with our damp, muddy clothes, leaves and pine needles clinging to us, and me with my lobster-red face from sunburn. "And y'all stink." She switched the blower onto high.

"Apologies," I said, shutting the door and buzzing down the window. The truck's interior was freezing and reeked of perfume. "We didn't exactly come in the front door of Charleston. How about you get us out of here? The cavalry spied us crossing and it's only a matter of time before they zero in on our location."

I needed not say it twice. Nikki laid the hammer down. Gravel sprayed. The big truck leapt ahead.

"I shot down a drone," Moonie said from the backseat. "A police drone. Using a pistol."

Nikki shot me a look as if to say, *is he telling the truth?*

I shot one back that said, *unfortunately,* and then added, "How about you slow down a bit so as not to attract attention?"

Nikki eased off the gas a bit and jabbed me in the ribs. Hard. "Where the hell have you been? And why did you stand me up the other night? I've since been out with two more loads. Which by the way, Bluechel wasn't too happy me leaving—"

"I was in one of those caskets."

"Pardon," she said, swiveling her head.

"I was *inside* one of the caskets you watched get tossed into the sea."

Nikki studied me, waiting for the punch line or explanation, a look of horror creeping across her face. "No!"

I slowly nodded. "'Fraid so. I was adrift for over two days."

Nikki slammed on the brakes. The truck screeched to a stop in the middle of the road. "No!" she repeated. I nodded. "But, but, how?" A tear rolled down her cheek followed by several more.

"I'll tell you about it while we drive," I said gently, and placed a hand on her arm.

"It's a hell of a tale," Moonie piped up from the back.

I shot him a look. He shrugged, as if to say *what?* And added, "It is!"

274

I didn't even bother with a rejoinder. Shaking my head, I turned back to Nikki. "We need to get going. The cops are after us, and we need to tell some people exactly what's going on with this sickness. Do you need me to drive?"

She shook her head, mouth frozen in a frown, and punched the accelerator. Silent tears continued to stream down her face as I recounted my odyssey.

I was just at the point in the story when I encountered Romeo and Juliet in their jacked-up Jeep, smoking reefer and doing the nasty, when I pointed. "Turn here."

Nikki cranked the wheel and pulled into Cougar Pointe Apartments' lot.

"What's here?" she asked, surveying the sad collection of buildings.

"Hopefully the cavalry," I said, climbing out. "Did you bring the sign?"

Nikki hit a button on her fob and the back hatch opened revealing a rat's nest of shopping bags, papers, home décor, and kiddie sporting equipment. Perched on top was the big stand that said, "funeral parking."

"You got this in here by yourself?" I asked, grunting as I pulled the thing out. It was ancient, from back when they used to make things properly. A cast-iron base with an iron sleeve you could fit various signs into, it weighed every bit of a hundred pounds.

"I used the body lift."

"Grab that end," I said to Moonie.

A resident hustled by eyeing us suspiciously. Moonie tipped an imaginary hat and said, "Ma'am," before lifting the other half of the sign. The woman ducked into a Camry, belted it up and raced off. "Some people ain't friendly."

"I wouldn't say hello to some creep in a parking lot wearing a six shooter like he was Wyatt Earp," Nikki responded, bringing up the rear.

We humped the iron base into building A and dropped it in front of A7 with a thud. Things hadn't changed in the last two weeks, same pissy smell, same chipped paint, same spongy carpet. A baby screamed somewhere in the distance. "What now?" Moonie asked, wiping his brow.

I tested the doorknob. Locked. I figured as much, but one can always hope. "Pick up your end."

"For what?"

"We need to get inside this apartment."

Moonie looked at the sign stand. "You serious Clipper?"

"Go on, grab that end. The people that can put an end to this madness are on the other side of this door."

Moonie put his hands on his hips. "It's Badgers's place. Nobody lives here."

"For Christ sakes! It's a figure of speech," Nikki said. "Step aside."

As soon as she tried to grab the base, Moonie shooed her away and lifted the back end of the base. I positioned the top of the base, about two inches in diameter, right over the doorknob. "On the count of three."

At three, I drove forward with all my might. *Boom!* Wood cracked, but the door held. The vibration made my hands tingle.

"Again!"

We smashed the door again.

Two doors down a woman poked her head out.

"Ma'am, please get back inside. Official business," Nikki said, striding toward her. Wearing tight navy slacks with a loose white blouse that displayed her assets, and impossibly high wedge shoes, Nikki looked anything but police. Nonetheless the head disappeared and the door slammed.

"Again."

We hit the door again, and again, and again. My ears rang and hands had gone completely numb. "Are we making any progress?" Moonie asked. He was panting.

"We hit it until it breaks."

Down the hall, another door opened. "Nikki?" She was already charging down the hallway. "Go. Go!" I said. We hit it one time. Two times. Three times.

"I don't think I can hold on," Moonie said.

We were already mid-swing. "Hang on!" I pleaded. The stand connected solidly and sent vibrations up my arms that felt like lightning. Wood splintered and the door snapped open. Moonie plowed into me and we fell into a tangled heap inside the door.

"That was difficult," Moonie said, dusting himself off.

"What? Would you rather have shot the lock out?" Nikki asked, stepping past us, into the empty apartment.

I could tell by the look on his face that's exactly what he would've rather done, though he kept his mouth shut and mumbled, "Just sayin'."

Apartment A7 had been cleaned out. The smell of saffron still lingered. Nikki stood in the middle of the living room. "Now what?" she asked, turning in a slow circle. Gone were the couch and coffee table, and entertainment center made out of the cinder blocks and planks. Gone were the card table and chairs and tiny Oriental carpet. The only thing that remained were the indentations in the cheap commercial grade Berber carpeting.

"We wait," I said, walking into the galley kitchen.

"Wait for what?"

"The cavalry." I opened the refrigerator. Nothing. Not even a box of baking soda. "I don't know who they are, but they're some sort of government agency who I suspect are best equipped to handle this." The freezer was almost equally as barren. Two ice cube trays remained. One cube between them.

"How do you know they're coming?" Nikki asked.

"They're coming," Moonie said. He rubbed his neck, as if remembering getting roughed up by the men in black masks. "This place is under surveillance."

Nikki grunted and wandered into the bedroom. I opened a few cabinet doors and drawers. The cleanup crew had been thorough.

"Nothing in the bedroom or bathroom," Nikki announced, reappearing.

I joined the other two in the living room. We stood there awkwardly for a few moments, any minute expecting men with weapons to burst in. It was silent except for a cough coming from down the hall.

"Tell me again, why we broke into this place?" Nikki asked.

"The guy that was living here, John Doe 1, who was really a homeless man named Samuel Badgers, had a biological weapon in his backpack when he was killed."

Nikki screwed her face up. "Wait, he was homeless but had an apartment?"

"I need to sit," I said, sinking to the floor. My muscles were still weak. This was one of the things I had ample time to think about while adrift. "Badgers was an addict and petty criminal, essentially an outcast. I suspect it was easy to radicalize someone like that, especially if they groomed him by giving him stuff like this," I waved my hand around the room. "Pretty nice alternative compared to Bushville."

"You think he was radicalized?"

"There was a little Oriental rug here I'm guessing was a prayer mat."

Nikki frowned, thinking. "I imagine there are plenty of addicts who'd do something for a buck. Why go to the trouble with all this?"

"Ah, I forgot to mention this. Hotapp texted me right before those bastards scooped me up that Badgers had an engineering degree in hydrologics."

"Hydraulics?" Moonie asked.

"No. Hydrologics. Water."

Nikki put her hand in front of her mouth and closed her eyes. "Dear Lord."

I nodded. "Tell me about it. They were going to use him to maximize dispersion."

Nikki shook her head. Even Moonie was at a loss. We lapsed into silence, staring at each other, waiting.

Moonie's silence didn't last long. He had a captive audience. "Speaking of water, this reminds me of this time a couple years ago I got this case, a guy named Dwight Turner. Him and his old lady win this five-day cruise around a couple islands. Some kind of grocery store sweepstakes. All-expense paid, type-deal. Really classy." Moonie's idea of class and mine differed a bit and winning a room in steerage for a week on an overcrowded ferry didn't sound enticing to me. "Anyhow, ole' Dwight is feeling a tad ill when he gets home but doesn't have any insurance so he tries to tough it out. Next thing you know he's dead—"

After 20 minutes elapsed, Moonie's first story had segued into a second. Nikki looked like she would kill him if he uttered another word. It was time to call it. Sighing, I pushed up off the wall. "Time to move onto plan B." Obviously, Bailey's crew was no longer watching the apartment. Was it the quarantine keeping them out? I found it hard to believe a cordon of weekend warriors, that Moonie and I had been able to penetrate with relative ease, could keep out super spies.

"What's plan B?" Nikki asked, eyeing the splintered doorjamb.

Moonie simply continued his monologue. He's like a tornado in the sense that he won't quit until he's tossed the entire trailer park.

I paced for a moment, trying to think despite Moonie's droning. This scenario hadn't occurred to me. James Bailey gave the impression of omnipresence. Plan A was to dump all my information in Bailey's lap and allow him to do whatever it is he does and fix this disaster. I had visions of Bob and Baldie on a cigarette boat, giving the Coast Guard the finger and speeding up the coast, water bottle held in one hand, ready to slip it into New York or Chicago or Los Angeles' water supply. There wasn't another second to waste. "Can I have your phone?" Nikki handed me her phone, and I searched the internet for a moment, looking for the phone number.

The line connected after six rings. "Hotapp." She sounded annoyed.

"Jen, it's Clip."

There was a long pause. So long I wondered if the connection dropped. "Where have you been?"

Brushing aside her inquiries, I cut to the chase. "I know what's causing the sickness and who's doing it."

There was another long pause. She followed with, "Okay." One word that belied a detective's skepticism but said *tell me more.*

"Meet me at the Citadel Mall as quickly as you can. I'll explain there. And bring Gorman if you can find him."

"The mall?"

"Food court entrance." I hung up and motioned to my troops. "Let's go." I looked longingly at the faucet in the kitchen. My body was screaming for water, but I didn't dare chance it. The body count was too high. "Wait." I stopped in my tracks. "Nikki, do you have gloves in your truck?" She nodded. Undertakers are like squirrels with latex gloves. You never know when you're going to need a pair. "Run out there and grab a pair as well as that Sonic cup."

"What?"

"Moonie, what did the cruise line tell your guy Dwight not to do?"

A scowl crossed his face. After a moment, he lit up with the answer. "Don't drink the water."

"Right, and did he?" I already knew the answer, having just suffered through it, including gory autopsy details.

"Nope, but he did have a drink at a bar, and the water used to make the ice made him sick."

"Right. The ice."

"The ice?" Moonie was lost. Nikki was too.

"Badgers saved a sample of Blackwater."

"He did?" Nikki asked.

"In his freezer."

Chapter 34

Surprisingly, the mall was packed. The hardier people of Charleston, bored with sequestering themselves indoors, decided to brave a potential epidemic at the West Ashley shopping Mecca. Nikki had to make several passes through the lot before we found a spot in the back. We waited at the appointed entrance, and Hotapp arrived 30 minutes later and created her own spot. The perks of being a cop.

"You look like hell," she said by way of greeting.

"Funny, that's where I've been." I flashed back to the wooden door. Twenty-four hours ago, I had been clinging to a scrap of wood in the middle of the Atlantic. Hell isn't brimstone and fire like the funeral preachers promise.

"What?" She waved her hand. "Never mind. This better be good. I drove over here with my lights on."

I gestured to the cruiser. "Let's talk in here for a minute. I'll fill you in." People were streaming in and out of the mall like it was the holiday season, and I didn't want anyone overhearing. We ducked into her car. Cop cars usually don't have cup holders; they get stripped out to make room for the gear. Hers was no exception. I had to move a half drank bottle of tea to sit.

"You mind?" I asked, holding up the tea. It was diet green tea with honey and other horrendous stuff in it.

"You want it?"

"If you don't mind."

By the time she said "sure" and made a face I had polished off the tea. "Sorry," I said. "I can't seem to get enough to drink." The look on her face said it all, she thought I was unhinged. What with the secret meeting at the mall and the drinking of the tea. Quickly, I continued, "It all started," I did some mental math, "three days ago when I called for an Uber at the hospital—"

Hotapp didn't interrupt once while I gave her the quick and dirty version. When I finished she closed her eyes and crossed herself. Keying the mic, she said, "Dispatch, this is Hotapp. I need transport on a shoplifting case."

"Shoplifting?"

"I didn't request anything urgent in case his people are listening on scanners. You think he's in here?"

"I didn't get eyes on him, but at this point that's my best guess. He thinks he's tied up all the loose ends."

"Why not take off with the," she briefly searched her memory, "Blackwater?"

"I suspect he's not a foot soldier. Otherwise, why have someone like Badgers running around with it?"

Hotapp flashed a rare grin. "You ever consider being a detective?"

**

The food court was mostly deserted. The only food and water coming inside the cordon was on National Guard trucks and being distributed at specified areas. The pizza, pretzel, and ice cream joints started running low on supplies days ago. As they ran out of an item they'd tape a piece of cardboard over the item on their big, colorful backlit menus. Pickings were slim, but that didn't stop Moonie from eyeing up some potential snacks on the mostly darkened menus. He didn't dare stop. We were on a mission.

Bob was sitting on a wooden stool hunched over his phone at his cell phone accessory kiosk while the masses of shoppers swirled around him like water around a river rock. I held my hand out sideways and the rest of the trio stopped short. Today I had the element of surprise.

Sensing a presence, he looked up. I clenched my hands into fists and smiled. "Hi Bob."

The look on his face was priceless. Bob furrowed his brow, eyebrows almost touching from the effort, peering at me like a mall apparition. He would've been less surprised to look up and see Sasquatch comparing hand soaps at Bath & Body Works. Bob opened his mouth to say something, but no sound came out.

"Surprise asshole."

Shock was quickly replaced with fear. Fight or flight said his big brown eyes.

In the trailer court where I cut my teeth almost every difference was settled with fists. Despite the spit and professional polish I'd worked hard to cultivate over the years, every fiber of my being screamed *fight*.

Hotapp chose that moment to step forward. "Detective Hotapp. Hanahan PD." She flashed her badge. "Stand up. Turn around and place your hands behind your back. You're under arrest."

"You heard the detective." I gripped Bob's shoulder and hauled him to his feet.

The appearance of a badge and the weird energy produced by my little group of crime fighters, made the river of humanity stop and start to gawk. Despite the phones recording, I drove my knee into his groin. Bob's eyes rolled up into his head and he moaned, but I held him upright and whispered, "I still have the Blackwater. You didn't think Badgers wouldn't hide some did you?" For the benefit of the videographers—because I care about the quality of their film—I said loudly, "You heard the detective, hands behind your back." Bob grunted when I wrenched his arms behind his back. I could get used to this policing thing.

Hotapp snapped the cuffs on and guided him to the stool. He plopped down, breathing heavily and sweating. The phones continued to capture every minute of the mall drama. She unclipped her handheld and spoke into it, and then said to me, "We need to wait here until we can get someone to secure this stand. It'll need to be processed—" She stopped to snap at a heavyset balding man in sweatpants and a stained T-shirt reaching for Bob's cell phone, "Sir, don't touch that!"

The man withdrew his hand and stepped back into the crowd, a wounded look painted on his face. Several phone Zapruders aimed in the direction of Bob's phone, no doubt zooming in. It lay on the tiled floor where it landed after I ruined Bob's chance of procreation.

"You don't have a pair of gloves on you?" Hotapp asked out of the side of her mouth. She was clearly uncomfortable with the growing crowd.

"Nikki," I said. "Gloves?"

She rooted in her massive handbag and produced a single purple glove. "Will this do?"

Hotapp took the glove, retrieved the phone off the floor, and turned the glove inside out, so the phone was inside.

Two sheriff's deputies strode through the crowd. "Okay, folks show's over," the baby faced one said, motioning his arms. The crowd took a step back, and loosened up, but nobody wanted to miss any of the action.

"Let's get the star of the show out of here." Hotapp turned Bob to the deputies who marched him out, practically holding him upright. Poor Bobby's gut was still in knots.

The crowd quickly lost interest and started thinning out.

"I'm going to go and mosey on over to the food court and see what I can rustle up," Moonie announced.

To my surprise Nikki added, "I'll join you." Moonie's mustache did a little jig. They disappeared in the crush. I ambled over and sat on a bench leaving Hotapp standing with her arms folded, guarding the kiosk. The minutes ticked by and the uncomfortableness of the bench was no match for the exhaustion. I blacked out.

Hotapp shook my shoulder jolting me awake. "Clip, come on. It's time to go."

The people and lights were disorienting. Panic seized me, and I shot off the bench.

"Are you all right?" Hotapp asked.

Wiping a string of drool, I nodded. Two uniformed officers prowled around the kiosk while two women and a man in FBI windbreakers and latex gloves photographed and printed the kiosk.

"FBI?"

"Sheriff's evidence team got bumped." Hotapp started heading toward the food court.

I couldn't have been asleep long. Moonie was still sitting at one of the tables in the food court with wrappers from several eateries littering the table. His boots were up on the empty chair and a toothpick floated around his mouth.

"Where's Nikki?"

Moonie jerked his head into the bowels of the mall. "She went to look around some."

"Can you call her and tell her it's time to go?"

While Moonie did that, Hotapp said, "I'm going to need a formal statement from you, but by the looks of it you need to get some sleep. We can do it tomorrow."

"I appreciate that." I felt like I could go to sleep standing up.

We stared at each other for an awkward moment before Hotapp said, "Good collar." I nodded, and she disappeared toward the entrance, now choked with emergency vehicles.

I sank into the seat vacated by Moonie's boots and put my head in my hands. The nap left me feeling hungover. Everything was catching up. I just needed a long shower, a couple of sleeping pills and to sleep for a solid day.

"Want the rest of this?" Moonie held out a fountain soda. I didn't even bother to ask what it was. I accepted gratefully and slurped it down. It was cold and wet and sweet.

"Think they do refills?"

"The badge always gets—" Moonie adjusted his belt. "Shoot, I left my badge in the van."

Hotapp strolled up to our table.

"Forget something?"

"I hate to do this, Clip. Stand up and put your arms behind your back." Her words spilled out, clipped and terse.

I was still a little fuzzy from sleep. "Huh?"

She adopted a dominant pose, feet apart, arms at her side. "You're under arrest. Word came from above. I'd rather it be me than someone else."

Moonie shot up. "What are you doing?"

I stood and held out my hand. "It's okay. She's just doing her job." Last thing I needed were tensions running high between two people with guns in a crowded space. Moonie was loyal enough to go toe-to-toe with a cop.

"What's the charge?" Moonie asked, his voice loud.

"Moonie!" I said, sharply. It had to be one of the videos of me assaulting a suspect finding its way to the wrong person. I turned and placed my hands behind my back.

"Sorry about this," Hotapp muttered as she snapped the cuffs loosely around my wrists. Another crowd had formed. Phones were out and filming. "C'mon," she said, grabbing my shoulder and leading me in the direction of her cruiser.

"What's happening?" Nikki cried, rushing into the food court. She clutched bags from three different retailers in her hand.

I heard Moonie state the obvious, before Hotapp guided me through the door, "She arrested him."

The crowd followed us outside. Hotapp placed her hand on my head. "Watch your head."

Chapter 35

The interview room at the Charleston Sheriff's Department was nothing but a glorified closet. Two molded plastic chairs and a trapezoidal shaped table that reminded me of a high-school desk were the only furnishings, and the room was cramped. Bleached areas in the carpeting appeared to be the efforts of spot cleanup. Blood? A whiteboard without markers and an eraser was the only décor. The custodian hadn't done a very good job. The last crime scene was still visible in faint green, red, and blue ink.

At least three hours elapsed before the red light on the closed-circuit camera blinked off. Company would be arriving soon and not the good kind. The kind of company that doesn't want to be filmed. Ten seconds later the door opened and James Bailey made his grand entrance.

"You've royally fucked things up Clipper." Bailey took the unoccupied seat and folded his hands on the desk. Same cheap black suit. Same weak chin. Same predatory eyes.

I leaned back and laced my hands behind my head. Hotapp had taken her cuffs with her. I would've been a little put out had I been cuffed to the ring bolted to the trapezoidal table. "Hello to you too Jimmy."

His eyes stared daggers. "Do you have any idea what you've done?"

"I've been looking for you." Bailey's eyes reeled with confusion. He could try to come flex his federal muscle with his prison threats, but I was beyond caring. Getting locked in a casket and tossed off the side of a ship 50 miles offshore had seen to that. "I can help you."

"Oh?" Bailey fumbled. He wasn't expecting that response and was trying to change tact. "How?"

I leaned in and folded my hands. "Let's start with what I know. Your guy found dead at the reservoir, who I call Hansel." Bailey's eyes, again, looked confused. "He worked with you. The way I figure it, Hansel had Samuel Badgers under surveillance because he somehow figured out Sam was about to do something stupid. Presumably with our water, because of Badgers's background in hydrological engineering. But he didn't know exactly *what* which is why he was following him. Am I tracking here Jimmy?" Bailey continued to stare, his jaw clenching and unclenching.

"Something happens. And there's a confrontation. Badgers gets the drop on your guy, Hansel, and they kill each other. Crisis averted. Only not." I held up a finger. It had lots of little brown marks on it, splinters embedded under the skin from stabbing the shark. "Old Sam didn't have the entire potion. The bad guys panic and release what they have, thinking you all have the rest in your possession. Only you don't. The coroner's office has it logged in as a personal item. How am I doing?" I sat back and folded my arms over my chest and stared.

Bailey leaned forward and pointed to the faux wood grain on the table. "How are you *doing?*" He sounded like a man barely in control. "I just came from a meeting with a two star from the national guard, a two star from the army, the deputy director of the CDC, the assistant director of PAHO, deputy director of Biodefense, the FBI, and every goddamn state agency you can think of. This thing is spiraling out of control, and you just arrested the only known member of this cell!" He slammed his hand down on the table. "They use cutouts and wireless dead drops so we can't get a handle on them." Bailey was shouting. Screaming almost, a man coming unglued. "We can't get a handle on them, and don't have a fucking clue how far-reaching their operation is or how deeply embedded they are!"

Fear washed over me for a second, but I regained my composure. They knew no more than they did three days ago and sitting on their hands waiting for Bob to move hadn't given them a damn thing. I was their oracle of information and James Bailey knew it. I eased the chair up on two legs and reclined against the wall, arms folded on chest. "So, let me tell you what I know. I know what's poisoning the water." Bailey started to speak, but I interrupted him, "*And* I know how it works."

I had his full, and undivided attention. Holding up a finger, I said, "First, I want a tin of dip, a cup of coffee made with *bottled* water, and a few bottles of water." Bailey stood. "And," I said, stopping him, "you may want to get one of those fancy sciencey folks from your meeting in here, otherwise you're going to have to repeat everything." Bailey slammed the door.

Several minutes later my demands were arrayed on the table before me. The dip was an open tin of Grizzly Long Cut Wintergreen, obviously commandeered from one of the deputies. Under normal circumstances I'd complain but decided not to press my luck. Bailey resumed his position in the chair, and a severe looking woman with a leather file folder sat on a stool brought in for the occasion. Her credentials had been pitched to me as a consultant for the World Health Organization. No name was offered. I knew the code from my time in the military. "Consultant" means spook. The addition of the scientist spook made things cozy in the little room.

Bailey placed an MP3 recorder in the middle of the table. No names and details were given like the beginning of a standard police interview. This recording wouldn't ever surface in a court of law.

I downed two of the three waters, packed a lip, and took a sip of the coffee. The coffee would be safe even if it had been made with municipal water. The brewing process would get the water hot enough to kill *Shigella*. Not having caffeine for several days made me swoon. Bailey and the woman waited patiently. The woman tapped a pencil eraser against a leatherette portfolio.

When the head rush subsided, I said, "Who are they? You said 'they' and 'them'." Bailey and the woman stared. This was my only point of leverage. I had something they needed, and frankly, I desperately wanted to give it to them so they could patch up national security.

The second hand on the wall clock swept a full circuit before Bailey reached over and hit a button on the MP3 recorder. The machine blipped. "The organization is called Yah Allah in Arabic. There's no Farsi transliteration. The group is predominantly Persians. Iranian and Afghan nationals."

"Never heard of them." I knew of a lot of little-known militant assholes from my time overseas. Army of Islam. Abdulla Azzam Brigades. Mujahedin-e Khalq.

"They don't boast like ISIS, Al-Qaeda, or the other monsters. Yah Allah took a page out of the Soviet's Cold War playbook and planted deep cover jihadis right here in our towns, cities, and neighborhoods. They play the long game. The operatives get jobs in positions of power and trust and wait to be activated." Bailey suddenly looked very tired. "They're much smarter than the other groups, better trained, and much better funded." Bailey fell silent and I knew that was as much as I was going to get out of him.

"Yah Allah?"

"Hand of God."

I nodded, took another slug of coffee and nodded my head toward the recorder.

Bailey hit the button and it beeped.

"Blackwater."

"What?" It was a natural reaction. Bailey was expecting me to preface things.

"That's the name of the stuff that's killing people," I clarified. No Name and Bailey stared. "This group, Yah Allah, bought this bioweapon from some Russian gangsters. Apparently, the Soviets developed it in the '80s as part of their Bio prep program."

No Name paused her furious scribbling. "Biopreparat?"

"Yeah. That's it." Her scribbling resumed. "What is it?"

No Name paused and thought for a minute. "In a nutshell, the Soviets used these things called legends," No Name used air quotes, "which are basically cover stories. The Biopreparat legend was it was a civilian R&D program for defensive *against* bioweapons. The legend hid the fact that the military was developing and producing offensive biological weapons. It was an expansive program spanning decades and many research institutes. The West still doesn't know exactly what was going on."

"Sounds like a cheerful little initiative. Anyhow, the stuff Blackwater is *Shigella dysenteriae* that was weaponized to turn into Venezuelan equine encephalitis virus."

"What do you mean 'turn into'?" Bailey asked. He was out of his element and it annoyed him.

"As in a bacteria turning into a virus."

Bailey looked at No Name. "Is that even possible?"

No Name had stopped writing and had her head cocked, wearing a peculiar expression. "It appears it is. That explains a lot. We can identify the *Shigella*, but then the trail suddenly goes dark, and the patient has brain inflammation. The virus is coded with no antigens. Those are the things the antibodies—the body's immune system—recognize on the surface of the virus and attack," she said for the benefit of Bailey. "That's why we can't figure out..." She snapped herself out of her quasi-trance and jumped up. "I have to make a call."

"Should I continue?" Bailey held up his hand. I drank the rest of the coffee while we waited.

No Name returned after several minutes. "I've issued an alert. Every medical facility under the umbrella will have an update momentarily and have deployed the new protocols within 30 minutes so we can start treating for VEEV."

"Is there treatment?" I asked.

No Name looked pained. "No. Just supportive care."

After she sat, I continued, "So, here's how I came about this the information—" I started to tell them the story I'd already recounted to Moonie and Nikki. Unlike the previous version, this time I left nothing out. The most mundane detail could be vital to Bailey's pursuit. When I got to the part in the warehouse No Name tacitly took over.

"Did he give you any indication of the total volume they purchased?"

I shook my head. "No, but he made it seem like there were two bottles. The one in Badgers's backpack was a liter. So, my guess is two liters."

"He give you any idea how or why the conversion takes place?"

"No. I don't know what triggers the conversion, and I'm not sure the guy did either."

No Name frowned and scribbled in her notebook, and then made me recount several times how many people Baldie claimed the weapon could kill and the context of "the correct water system." She reminded me of a lawyer at a deposition, asking the same question but phrasing it differently. I answered and tried not to get irritated.

"Did he make mention of the word plasmid, RNA or DNA, or ID_{50}?" I shook my head. "Anything about mortality or morbidity?"

"No."

"Bonfire? Metol? Flute? Factor?" The questions came at me like machine gun fire.

I continued shaking my head. The questions grew more confusing.

"Did he mention Vector, SRCAM, Aralsk-7?"

"No, not that I can remember. I was drugged at the time, so I may have missed something."

No Name scribbled furiously, like she was making check marks or crossing something out. The questions kept coming, and for a time I wondered if she was still speaking the King's English. Nothing rang a bell, and I began to grow despondent that I wasn't helping at all, merely wasting their time. No Name abruptly shut up, and I continued. Both No Name and Bailey couldn't mask their astonishment at my adventures on the high seas, but neither interrupted. Bailey didn't cut in until the part where Moonie and I approached the cordon with the hard-ass lieutenant.

"He told you he got out how?" After I recounted it again, he put his forehead in his hand and shook it. "Christ." He continued shaking it as I detailed our reinsertion into Charleston. No Name looked on, largely uninterested because the conversation wasn't about atoms and molecules. "You're like a bad penny," he said when I finished. There was no malice in his comment, and perhaps a modicum of admiration.

"I figured, I'd be able make contact at Badgers's apartment. I didn't plan to ruin your investigation by fingering Bob."

Bailey stood and patted my shoulder. "His real name is Lal Darwish." A white business card landed in front of me. There was a single number printed on it. Nothing else. "Call that number if anything else comes to mind and keep your head down."

Bailey motioned for No Name. Interview over.

"Hey," I said to No Name as she snapped the folder shut and stood. "What's the mortality rate for VEEV?"

She frowned. "If memory serves, around one percent."

"Christ. This stuff is around 30."

"They engineered some nasty stuff and didn't lock it up tight enough."

Bailey opened the door. Just before the door closed, he said, "We'll get you out of here in no time."

It was another three hours before a deputy came and released me. In the interim, I'd had to pee so bad I filled two empty water bottles and finished the rest of the tobacco. My mouth tasted like a Christmas tree. I left the pee bottles sitting on the table and followed the deputy to the exit. The station was buzzing with more activity than seemed normal for this late in the evening. A wall clock read 10:13. Shift change?

Hotapp's cruiser was idling at the curb in front of the station. She buzzed her window down. "Need a ride?"

"Promise you won't arrest me?"

Hotapp held out a large Styrofoam cup with an unopened tin of Copenhagen on the lid. "How about a peace offering?"

"Accepted." I climbed into the car and popped the little mouth flap. The coffee was scalding.

Hotapp shifted into gear and blasted away from the curb. "Sorry about earlier. I was following orders."

"Think nothing of it. I understand following orders."

"That's why I'm here and not Philly. Orders. Not following them."

"Oh?"

"My lieutenant told me to ignore something. I couldn't. Found out after the fact he was dirty too." I looked at her, but she was focused on the road. "I couldn't stay after that. Even the clean cops resented me. So, here I am."

I sipped the coffee. "Not all orders are lawful."

Hotapp grunted. We continued in silence for a moment before she dropped a bomb on me. "I have some news. Your cellphone guy, Bob, killed himself."

I nearly spit coffee across her dash. "What? How?"

"We'll know more after the autopsy. Working theory is some sort of suicide pill."

"What, like in his tooth, like a bad spy novel?" I thought of those horsey chompers.

"Nope. Hidden in the frame of his glasses. The video feed of his cell shows him fiddling with them right before he started convulsing on the cell floor. Because of the circumstances he wasn't in gen pop, so we don't have any eye witnesses." She glanced over at me, her face alternately lit by the passing streetlamps. "Not that I'd believe them anyway."

I rested my head against the cool window pane. It felt good on the sunburn. Outside the car, the streets were mostly deserted. A city under siege, even if the attackers were measured in micrometers. "Why'd he do that?"

"I don't think he was headed for the criminal-justice system. Yeah, we booked him and tossed him in a cell, but he was about to be taken and he knew it."

"Taken?"

"Your guy had the body out of there minutes after it happened. And it was clean. Normally, there'd be a huge jurisdictional pissing match over something like that, but this body's gone like it was never there and the sheriff never said boo." She gestured to the now closed laptop between us. "I was checking as you were coming out. His booking record is gone too."

"As in, they sealed it?"

She shook her head. "As in vanished. It never existed."

I squeezed my eyes shut. It was over for me. I didn't have to worry about shit like this anymore. Let the people who get paid to worry about things like this worry about it.

When I opened them we were at the funeral home. "Go around the side," I directed. The candles burning in the windows of the old mansion was a sight I thought I'd never see again. The thought of Nikki making funeral arrangements with Maggie for a service with my body *in absentia* had crossed my mind more than once while clinging to the plank. I'd arranged a service like that before. It was for a roofer named Silas. Silas had been on his way to do a big commercial rubber torch-down roof when he got rear-ended. He hadn't been wearing his seatbelt and smashed his head into the windshield. When his truck caught fire he was out cold. The fire department didn't get there before the four propane tanks in his truck bed exploded. The fire marshal told the widow the blast was equivalent to a Tomahawk missile strike. I didn't think, in my professional opinion, it was the most tactful comparison to make to the widow. It didn't change the fact Silas was vaporized. Not a scrap of him was found. It's harder to grieve that way, when there's no body. The widow Silas would never get over it.

The familiar mix of botanicals filled my nose—sweet bay, gardenia, and magnolia—as I exited the cruiser. *Home.* Matey issued a caw of salutation from somewhere in the dark. Even the sound from the winged rat brought a smile to my face. Maggie. My work. Everything was here. And I was back. Safe and sound, and it was over. The thought of getting down on my knees and kissing the sidewalk crossed my mind. Hotapp stopped me.

"Clip, one more thing." I ducked my head back into her cruiser. "Bob hacked the phone system."

"What do you mean?" I really didn't care. I couldn't wait to run upstairs into the waiting arms of Maggie.

"After he made his allotted phone call to his lawyer, he was able to manipulate the switch hook to bypass our phone system, get an outside line and make a call."

"That's a thing?"

"Apparently. The brass and IA folks are going nuts that this happened and scrambling to figure out where the call was made."

"Think is concerns me?"

"Like I said, it's unknown where the call was made. Watch your back." Her eyes conveyed genuine concern.

"I appreciate it." I rapped my knuckles on the window sill. The jig was up for Bob, and my part was played out. My life could return to normal. I waved to Hotapp and turned to head inside. Everything got bright, brighter than staring into the sun.

The concussive wave tossed me across Hotapp's cruiser long before my ears registered the roar of the blast.

Chapter 36

Flaming debris rained on my crumpled form, the hot embers jerking me conscious. I clawed at them in jerky, painful fits. A loud ringing filled my head. *Maggie!* I dragged myself off the asphalt, palms digging into glass and ash. What was left of the funeral home was an inferno. Oily smoke billowed out of the brick husk.

"No!" I screamed, the words tearing my vocal cords in a sound I couldn't hear.

I sagged against the cruiser, only then realizing Hotapp was slumped over the steering wheel. Training took over. I pulled the door open and unbuckled her seatbelt. Grabbing her armpits, I dragged her from the car, across the street. A man ran up grabbed her ankles and helped me carry her to the corner and out of the blast radius if there was a secondary explosion.

The man's lips moved, frantic and urgent. I held up a hand and turned my attention to Hotapp. There weren't any visible injuries. Her pulse was strong and breathing was regular. The blast must've just knocked her unconscious. Pantomiming to the man for a pillow, he took off his sweatshirt. I balled it up and placed it under her head. Grabbing a large terra cotta planter, at the end of the neighbors walk, I emptied the flowers and soil and used it to elevate her legs.

"Watch her," I said to the man. Unsure, if he could understand me, I pointed to him, my eyes and then Hotapp. The man nodded.

I sprinted to the flaming house, making it as far as the lawn. The heat was too intense to go farther. The building was engulfed, flames stabbing the black sky. "Maggie!" I screamed, falling to my knees, tears streaming down my face. "Maggie!" The heat seared my body and the smoke choked my lungs, but I screamed at the blaze until a gloved hand grabbed my shoulder.

"Get off me," I shouted as another pair of hands grabbed my shirt and dragged me backwards. The firemen sat me on the running board of their truck and were in my face. Their faces were indistinguishable through my soot-stung eyes and tears, but I could see their mouths moving. I shook my head and pointed to my ears. After a while they gave up and left me alone. I continued to watch the blaze while the helmeted men scurried about.

At some point, hands placed a solar blanket around my shoulders.

***

"Clip?"

I opened my eyes. Blinding sunlight filled the room. I was momentarily disoriented until I saw Jackson clutching a steaming mug. It all came rushing back. *Maggie was dead.* A choking sensation rose in my throat.

"Mom said you could use some coffee." He looked unsure.

I clenched my jaw and struggled to control myself. A tear rolled down my cheek. Everything was gone. Everything.

"Clip?"

Dashing the tear, I groaned and struggled into a sitting position. The room smelled of char and the pillow was streaked black. My body hurt, but my hearing was returning. The EMT had conveyed to me my eardrums hadn't been blown, so my hearing should come back. Another waiver for medical care signed, though that had been a contentious issue. The lieutenant on the scene almost insisted on strapping me down and sending me to the hospital. Had it not been for Nikki arriving on scene things may have gotten ugly.

I swung my legs off the sofa and accepted the mug. It was a fancy ceramic job with tasteful flowers glazed on, the kind you'd buy at a kitchen store and only use for guests. It would be the kind of thing Maggie would buy. The choking sensation returned. I squeezed my eyes shut until the feeling subsided.

Jackson must've thought I was in physical pain. "Mom's in the shower, but she said to give you these." He opened his hand to reveal four aspirin and a red pill. Xanax.

I took the pills and washed them down with coffee. "Thanks."

Jackson stood there in his superhero pajamas, unsure what to do next. He reminded me of a puppy who didn't know how to use his new big, body yet. Not quite 12 he was already taller than his mother. He broke the awkward silence, "Want to play *Call of Duty?*" He looked longingly at the silent TV. My presence was cramping his morning's entertainment.

Jackson was fascinated with my military service, always asking me questions. I suspected it was from playing soldier-type video games but being a kid, he was better at video games than me and delighted in beating, "a real-life army man." My fiancée was dead. My business was in literal pieces. And I had a splitting headache. Actually, I couldn't think of anything I'd rather do than a little mindless violence. If I didn't do *something* I'd jump out of my skin. "Sure pal."

Jackson happily set about gathering the controllers while I gulped down the coffee. When Nikki poked her head into the living room Jackson and I were embroiled in intense combat. Her face was flushed from the heat of the shower. One towel was wrapped around her torso, another done up in her hair. Both were Pepto-Bismol pink.

"Jackson," she scolded. "I told you not to bother Mr. Clip."

"It's fine," I said. My momentary diversion allowed Jackson to shoot my character in the head. Blood splashed. Jackson celebrated.

"You sure?" Nikki asked, a worried look on her face.

"It's fine."

There was a knock on the door.

Nikki looked at the door, unsure. Southern manners dictated she answer the door. But they also dictated she answer it properly clothed. "I'll get it," I said. Nikki mouthed "thank-you" and disappeared. I struggled to my feet and hobbled unsteadily to the door. Though my hearing was returning, my equilibrium was a little off. Bailey was on the other side of the door. I didn't bother asking him how he knew my whereabouts but stepped aside.

Bailey eyed Jackson. "There somewhere we can talk?"

I shuffled into the kitchen, pulled out a chair and sat. Bailey did the same. "We caught—"

"You're going to have to speak up." I touched a finger to my ear.

Bailey looked unhappy, but continued, "We caught him last night." He produced a phone and pushed it across the table. On the screen was the photo of a familiar face, Baldie. He was wild-eyed, handcuffed, and bore a look of surprise like he wasn't expecting to be photographed. It was hard to tell where exactly the photo had been snapped, but it was outside and it was dark. "Recognize him?"

I nodded and handed the phone back. "He's the one that packaged me up."

"Nasir Tannous. Been in the country well over a decade. He manages a bank branch."

Bailey's words replayed in my mind, *they took a page out of the Soviet's Cold War playbook and planted deep cover jihadis...*

"We caught him kayaking up the Cooper River. There was a car waiting for him at Monks Corner we rolled up too. The bottle was sitting between his legs."

"Great," was about all I could muster.

"It was because of you. The roads and coast are sealed, but I put some drone support in the air after you traipsed through the cordon."

I don't care! I wanted to shout. Instead, I replied, "Glad to be of service."

"We'll need you to testify."

There it was. The ask. I was wondering why Bailey would track me down to *share* information. Bailey was a man who collected information. It all made sense now. Bailey shifted in his seat. "Want some coffee?"

His eyes flicked around the kitchen. "Sure."

I guessed Nikki kept her mugs above the coffee maker, and flipped the cabinet open, selecting a mug. "Tell me about the explosion," I said, placing the steaming mug before Bailey, and then refilled mine.

Bailey cleared his throat. "The official report the fire marshal will release will be a gas leak. Of course, you know that's not completely true." I nodded and he continued. "We think your gas line was tampered with, and the lower levels of the house probably filled with gas. The blast, however, was caused by RDX and oxygen bottles."

I closed my eyes. RDX is a military-grade explosive more powerful than TNT. "Maggie?"

"We've recovered some remains that are being tested." It was her. The tests would only confirm what I knew in my bones. Maggie hadn't been at the hospital. Nikki had the bright idea of calling last night from the scene, and for a few moments I was hopeful. But she hadn't been back to work since being discharged. Where else would she be in a city in lockdown? Home. Bailey cleared his throat. "I'll let you know as soon as I know. For now," he spread his hands on the table and studied them, "we're going to need to place you in WITSEC. We've heard your name in the chatter."

"Fuck them. I'm not scared." Bailey wasn't going to ship me out to some Podunk town in Iowa under an assumed name.

Bailey lowered his voice. "Ms. Adcock's name has been mentioned on the chatter too." The implication was clear. Nikki and Jackson were in danger.

"You serious? She wasn't involved in this." It sounded like an amateur interrogation ploy to get me to do what he wanted.

Bailey touched the screen on his phone and there was static and ringing. "Yeah?" a man's voice said when the line connected.

The familiar voice of Bob Darwish said, "The undertaker is alive. He has the Blackwater."

There was a pause. "Alive?"

"Yes. I would've called you from my cell but the battery is dead."

The line disconnected.

"That's a recording of the call placed by Darwish after he hacked the jail phone system. The last part is some sort of code alerting the recipient to the fact he's been apprehended or giving him the order to kill you. We're not sure which."

"Who'd he call?"

Bailey ignored the question. "Bottom line is, they seem to think you still have their toy. And they were able to mobilize mighty quickly. There was only about six hours between that recording," he pointed to his phone, "and the blast. We need to get you into protective custody."

"And if I decline?"

"You'll be subpoenaed to testify, but you won't make the trial."
He shrugged. "I could try to offer you some security, but this is a new
type of enemy. We don't know when he'll strike, what he looks like,
or how he'll strike. You'd be a goat staked out on the hillside waiting
for nightfall and the wolves."

Quite a poetic description. "Let them come at me. I don't care."
I tugged at my shirt. "Look at how successful they've been so far. I'm
still here. Get Nikki and her boy to safety."

Bailey cleared his throat. "It doesn't work that way. You're the
one with the testimony. She gets protection *with* you."

Strings. Always strings. Over Bailey's shoulder I called, "Nikki!"
She appeared wearing professional attire, rubbing her hair with a
towel. "Run that by her." While Bailey ran through his barnyard
animal metaphor again, I gulped down the rest of my coffee. When
he finished, I said to Nikki, "Get in touch with Risden. See what he
has to say about this. We'll make a decision once he weighs in. In the
meantime, Bailey and I have an errand to run."

Bailey raised his eyebrows. That was the extent of his surprise.

"I'm going to shower before we go."

"I'll be outside." Bailey stood, nodded to Nikki, and strode out
the door leaving his coffee untouched.

It was my first shower in days. I made sure to keep my lips
sealed. Despite scouring my skin with a pink loofah, I left two sooty
towels hanging over the shower rod. I mumbled something to Nikki
about replacing them and found a Suburban with tinted windows
idling on the street. Pulling open the rear door, I found Bailey sitting
in the back and the fat one driving. "Sure you don't have a van you'd
rather toss me in?" I asked, pulling the door shut.

"Where to?" the driver growled.

I directed him to the Country Gentleman, a men's store on King
Street, where he parked illegally. The usual scent of cologne and

leather greeted me, as well as Wayne, who appeared from the well-merchandised stacks of clothing wearing a grin.

The grin dissolved as he drew closer. "Lordy, what happened?"

Wayne is my go-to guy. I feel like I can trust his fashion advice because he's always immaculately pressed out, including the ever-present old-fashioned mourning armband. The armband is in remembrance of his partner I buried two years prior. Young guy. Forty-four. AIDS.

"There was an accident, and I need a suit." I motioned to my sooty clothing I'd been forced to put back on after the shower. "And I need it now."

Wayne frowned and tugged at his waxed Van Dyke. "A suit off the rack?" It clearly didn't sit well.

"I lost everything in a fire last night."

"No!" Wayne placed a hand on his breast, a look of dramatic horror painted on his face.

"I need this stuff like, yesterday."

"Certainly sir." Wayne offered a bow and began buzzing around the store pulling merchandise. "You're my first customer in three days," he said, while clipping tags off underwear, socks, oxford cloth shirt, silk necktie, and a blue merino wool suit. "But what I am going to do? Sit at home and fret? Might as well open the store and try to maintain some sense of normalcy." He held up the shirt and frowned. "Do you have a few minutes so I can steam a few items? I dread the thought of you walking about a wrinkled mess."

"We wouldn't want that."

"Certainly not!" Wayne said, the irony lost.

While Wayne steamed my purchases, I spied a marked car behind the Suburban and a uniform hassling the driver. I smiled.

"You're ready Mr. Clipper," Wayne said, gesturing to the fitting room where he had hung everything neatly. It appeared he had even taken the liberty to steam the underwear and socks. "Leave your old garments and I'll dispose of them." He almost pinched his nose.

I changed and gave a quick look in the floor to ceiling mirror. Despite being off the rack, the suit draped well in the right places.

"How about these?" Wayne held a small box with silver cuff links inset with blue stones.

A lump formed in my throat, thinking of the silver shovel cufflinks from Maggie. I blinked back tears and nodded.

"I'll just leave them here," Wayne said quickly, setting the box down and making himself busy elsewhere.

As I checked out, I grabbed a cologne tester off the counter and gave myself a spritz.

"Come back once things have settled down," Wayne called after me. He could barely mask his glee at the prospect of selling me an entire new wardrobe. The bell tinkled as I stepped onto King Street.

The driver eyed me as I walked several doors down to a trendy café that is usually bursting at the seams, but like most of the businesses in the shopping district, it was vacant. No tourists. No business. I bought two cinnamon buns and the largest coffee on the menu and returned to the Suburban, not bothering to apologize for not offering to get them something. These two had kidnapped me twice and the fat one had whipped my ass. Treating them to a three-dollar coffee was out of the question.

"Where to?" Bailey asked.

"Marriott in Summerville."

The truck rocketed forward. In no time we were at the roadblock on I-26. Whoever Bailey and his crew were they sure had suction. It just took a flashed badge and the National Guardsmen scrambled over themselves to get out of the way. Summerville was immediately north of the blockade. I hardly had time to finish the coffee before we pulled under the portico. I left the bag with the buns on the backseat, not having been able to force any down.

The interior of the hotel was modern and soothing. The lobby was bustling, no doubt people with loved ones trapped in Charleston who were waiting for the quarantine to be lifted. I approached the chipper receptionist. "Good morning sir! What can I do for you?"

Dialing it down a notch would be a great start. "Can I trouble you to call the room of Mr. and Mrs. Stryker and tell them Tripp Clipper is here?"

Chapter 37

In my line of work I personify death, but never have to be the bearer of the dreadful news. By the time I arrive, the announcement's been made by a doctor, nurse, police officer, family member, or some other poor schmuck. I've never once broken the news. I was terrified. There was an awful sense of dread in my gut as I stood frozen amongst the backdrop of gray woods and flashy fabric décor. Guests with their coffees and tablets linked up with free hotel Wi-Fi bustled around.

The elevators' doors pinged open, revealing Max and Liz Stryker standing hand-in-hand. I'd met them once briefly over the Fourth of July when they traveled to Charleston to visit Maggie. They looked like they were about to go enjoy a leisurely lunch at the country club in their attire, Max in a cashmere sweater and slacks and Liz wearing a floral capri pant getup with a knit sweater knotted around her neck.

Liz knew before she got to me. It must've been the look on my face. As she drew closer her face melted into grief. "The fire we saw on the news?"

I nodded dumbly, suddenly feeling ridiculous for putting a suit on. Honestly, I didn't know what else to do.

"No! My baby!" she wailed. Liz collapsed into her husband's arms, wailing. Max closed his eyes and stroked his wife's hair. The guests clutching their coffees and tablets gave us a wide berth.

"Why don't we step in here," I said, gesturing to a conference room. There was no sense doing all this in public, and I certainly didn't want to do it in their room. Max dragged Liz, who was having trouble staying upright. The room contained four people in business attire huddled around a large table. Their heads all jerked in up when I yanked the door open. "We need the room."

"I reserved it," a woman protested. Her hair was done up in a bun. She looked very officious.

"Now," I said rudely, and pointed.

The woman looked like she was going to put up a fight, but when she saw the look in my eye, coupled with a blubbering Mrs. Stryker, she quickly gathered up the papers spread on the table and fled. The others followed suit.

I poured two waters from a carafe on the sideboard and set them in front of the Strykers along with a box of tissues and sat opposite. Liz ripped out a half dozen tissues and buried her face in them. Max sat there looking shell-shocked. I waited. When Liz looked up, and slurped down the entire glass of water, I spoke. It felt like there were stones in my throat. "I'm so sorry...I loved your daughter...horrible accident—"

Max stopped my babbling. "What happened?"

I looked longingly at the water, wishing I'd poured myself a glass, instead clearing my throat several times. "It's too early to say for sure, but the fire marshal suspects a gas leak. I had just pulled into the driveway, and was walking into the house when," I paused and swallowed, "it happened. Hence all this." I pointed to my face. It was easier to blame all my curious bruises, burns and cuts on the blast then mete them out à la carte.

"Are we— Are we sure Margaret was in there?" Max asked.

Liz perked up, grabbing onto a scrap of hope.

"I got word this morning remains were recovered from the scene. The coroner's office will test them for positive confirmation, and then you'll be officially notified."

"So, she could be alive," Max said. It was a statement, not question.

I'd seen grieving folks cling to false hope before. It's not healthy, especially if the outcome is already known. "It's her." I cleared my throat. "We checked with the hospital last night. She wasn't working—"

"A worker of yours?" Max interjected.

"All my employees are accounted for." I watched the hope tumble like a landslide down Liz's face. She buried it back in the wad of tissues.

Max started to speak, but Liz snapped her head up and spoke for the first time since the lobby. "What caused it?"

"I don't know," I lied. The rage in my gut grew and blossomed. I knew exactly what: A couple bricks of RDX strapped to some oxygen cylinders. Darwish was lucky to be dead. Otherwise, I'd be on my way over to lockup this very minute to dismantle him. I kept my voice calm and repeated the cover story, "It may be weeks before there's an official report."

"Did she," Max closed his eyes, "suffer?"

"It was instantaneous." There was a long pause. I cleared my throat. "I don't know if Maggie told you, but," I cleared my throat again, "we were planning on getting married." I almost didn't get it out and took several ragged breaths to get my thudding heart under control.

A smile tugged at Liz's mouth. "Yes. We talked yesterday, and she told me. Margaret was so...excited." I squeezed my eyes shut and felt a tear roll down my cheek. That broke the emotional dam. We shared stories about Maggie for an hour. When we were emotionally spent, Liz said, "Will you pray with us?"

I reached across the table and took their trembling hands and bowed my head. It was the first time I'd voluntarily prayed outside of work or NA in, forever. It didn't feel bad. And it made one thing crystal clear. I knew who killed Maggie.

"Amen," Liz said.

"Amen." I raised my head and looked at the two ruined people before me. *I know who killed your daughter.* The power of prayer.

"Where to?" Bailey asked when I pulled myself back into the Suburban. He didn't bother asking what I was doing or who I was seeing in the hotel. He probably already knew.

"Back to where we started."

When we pulled up to the curb in front of Nikki's, Bailey grabbed my arm. "I'm putting a car on this place but do me a favor and let me know if you're going anywhere. I'll arrange for an escort."

I jerked my arm away. "Sure thing."

The Suburban pulled away and I went inside and picked up Nikki's landline and dialed the answering service and asked them to forward me to Nikki's cell. When she picked up I asked her, "When are the NA meetings at Calvary?"

"Sunday, Tuesday, and Fridays. Why?"

"I really need a meeting. When you come back, park on 10th Street a little ways back."

"Why?"

"I'll explain when you get here."

Chapter 38

Risden followed Nikki in the door, his massive shape filling the doorframe. Jackson trailed them drinking from a Muscle Bound cup. The contents of the cup were the color of swamp mud. "Why don't you play some games champ?" Risden suggested to the boy.

"Is your homework done?" Nikki asked sharply. She pulled off her heels and dumped them.

"Mom, I'm almost done." Jackson twisted his mouth up to the side in a half smile like he did when he was lying.

Nikki pointed. "Kitchen table. Now. You can play your games when it's done."

Jackson made a slurping sound with the straw as he vacuumed up the dregs of the cup. "Can't I start once Dad leaves?"

Nikki's finger didn't waver. The boy made a defeated sound and ambled into the kitchen.

"Let's talk in the back," Risden said, jerking his head. It was an awkward motion for someone with no neck.

Nikki's place wasn't big. "The back" was her bedroom. Like her appearance, her bedroom was neat and organized. Risden and I sat on the bed awkwardly, the mattress listing in his favor. Nikki shut the door and took the armchair. In private, Risden dropped his undercover affect and a bit of intelligence crept into his eyes. "Nik told me about what those animals did to you. Jesus, you're like a fucking cat Clipper." He shook his head in disbelief. "How far out to sea were you?"

"About 50 klicks."

Risden mouthed *wow*. "Listen man, I'm glad you're here." One of his meaty paws patted my knee. "Nik told me about WITSEC. I tried to do a little digging about Yah Allah, but I don't have the proper clearances. I know the FBI keeps tabs on about 50 local Islamic organizations that may have extremist ideals. Some of them are nothing, and others they watch closely. If the NSA is picking up chatter with your name in it, take the protection. They've come at you several times, and you've just been lucky. Even if I arrange for an around the clock detail I won't be able to protect you. They'll find a way to get you." He twisted his mouth up. "Don't want to risk using up that ninth life." Risden being humorous. Rare.

I didn't doubt his sincerity but I thought what he meant to say was, "I don't want anything to happen to my son." He knew the game; his family only got protection if I took it.

"How long will we be away?" Nikki asked.

"Forever," Risden said.

Nikki winced. "Seriously? This is our home. Won't things blow over?"

"Organizations have a memory. People that enter witness protection can't leave for their own safety. But don't worry, I think I'll be able to pull some strings and find out where you land. So, I can come visit Jackson," he added.

"Well, that's perfect if *you* can come visit us in Guam." Nikki sat back and folded her arms over her chest.

"It's for your own safety."

"I'm serious Risden, I don't want to end up at some crossroads in Oklahoma."

"You'll have to take that up with the Marshals. That's not my area." Risden swiveled his head on his shoulders like an owl to refocus on me. "The stuff you sent over with Moonie last week. I got it out of the city and sent it to Quantico." He pulled a slip of paper out of his pocket and unfolded it, squinting at it. "I never did well in science class. The sample contained something called *Shigella dysenteriae.*" Risden frowned after stumbling over the name. "Gram-negative, facultatively anaerobic bacteria." He frowned. "Whatever the hell that means. The guy in the Analytics Lab said it's a causative agent of dysentery because of the," he squinted at his note, "shiga toxin spread through contaminated food and water. Said it's kind of rare to see this species in the developed world."

"Yeah, this is what's causing the outbreak."

Risden nodded and frowned at the same time. "That was my first thought, but the guy at the lab said the mortality rate for a *Shigella* infection is low, especially in the developed world."

"This stuff is a weaponized version released by Yah Allah."

There was something in Risden's eyes, I'd never seen: fear. "Weaponized?"

I nodded "'Fraid so."

"I guess that explains the WITSEC. Also, explains the," he squinted at the paper, "interferon."

"Interferon?"

"Yeah. The guy at the lab said that was unusual."

"What's interferon?" Nikki asked.

"They're what the body releases in response to an infection."

"Wouldn't they kill the bacteria?"

"Good question." I'd wondered how a single liter of the weaponized water could infect so many people. The logical conclusion was the presence or absence of *something* would trigger replication. That something had to be the interferon. Without the interferon the bacteria would start multiplying. If my memory from medic training was correct, *Shigella* couldn't replicate outside of the gut. That meant the Soviets had tinkered with the genetic code. I made a mental note to cue Bailey in. Refocusing, Nikki and Risden were sniping again.

"—much safer in a safe house."

"Jackson's so much more comfortable here. We'll be *fine*."

"Bailey's people are watching," I assured Risden.

Risden shook his head. "Out of the question. A simple White Pages search online gives up your address. You're not safe here. These people are like roaches: if you see one, your walls are infested with them. I'm going to make some calls and send my people over to scoop you up just as soon as I can arrange for a place." Risden pointed at the closet. "I suggest you start packing."

Nikki didn't blink. "And if I refuse?"

"Don't try me on this. This is my son we're talking about." He pulled his phone out of his pocket, his federal phone, not the one he used for his undercover work, and left the room. The front door opened and closed.

"This is a nightmare." Nikki set her forehead in her hand. It was surreal for me too. Charleston had been my home for the past five years. After a life of being untethered, it felt like I was finally putting down roots somewhere. "Can you help me by packing Jackson's stuff? Just toss his clothes into one of the suitcases in his closet."

"Sure," I said. I had nothing to pack. The only things I owned were on my back. "Before I do that I have to do something."

"What?"

"I need to go to that meeting at Calvary."

"You serious?"

"Yes."

"Why?"

I told her. When I finished she said, "I'm coming with you."

"There's no need. It's a simple one-man job."

Nikki tapped her nails against her teeth. "One man?"

"One person. No sense opening both of us up if this thing goes sideways. Besides," I added attempting to be reasonable, "you stay here and get your stuff together." Just the makeup alone would take her hours to pack. I was intimately familiar with cosmetics. In fact, there's a whole course devoted to cosmetology in mortuary school, but the lotions, potions, powders, rouges, and creams on Nikki's makeup table would confound the most seasoned Avon saleswoman.

"You need me for cover," she insisted. "It'll be more natural. And I'm not worried about rushing out of here. Risden's lackies can wait until I'm good and ready to leave." She folded her arms, daring me to oppose her decree.

I played my trump card. "What about Jackson?"

"He's almost 12. He'll be fine for an hour. Besides, like you said, there are armed guards at the front door, and his knucklehead father is sending over more. How much safer could he be?" Checkmate.

"Okay, okay." When she got like this there was no sense arguing. "We're going to have to climb out the kitchen window so we aren't seen by Bailey's people."

"Then I best put on a pair of sensible heels." She flung open her closet and stared at the shelves upon shelves of heels.

Those are going to be a bitch to pack, I thought, leaving the room. I found Jackson diligently working on his homework. "Which one of these is your junk drawer?"

Jackson looked up and pointed. "That one."

I opened the drawer and nestled amongst the mis-matched brands of batteries, pencils, scissors, rubber bands, and Indian take-out menus was exactly what I was looking for. "Perfect."

"Glue? What are you going to use that for?"

"I'm building a time bomb, of sorts."

"Cool!" Jackson exclaimed, jumping out of his seat. "Can I help?"

"Sure. Do you have a funnel around here?"

Chapter 39

One of the addicts, a woman named Trina, had been at it for at least ten minutes. Her voice was like a speaker in a drive-through menu board: loud and unpredictable. I shifted in the metal folding chair. The room had gotten close after 90 minutes; the collar of my brand-new shirt was damp with sweat. I desperately wanted air but tried to remain attentive—or at least appear that way. Across the circle, Cam sat slouched, glaring and tapping a boot to an inaudible beat. She'd been discreetly glancing at me during the meeting; I could tell she was ready to end the meeting too if Trina ever finished.

After a long-winded and horrific story about addiction and all the supplementals—theft, prostitution, incarceration, disease, and desperation—Trina sat as everyone applauded politely. "Anyone else want to share?" Artin looked around the room. Every pair of eyes landed on me. With my bruised and burned face, they probably thought I was coming off the bender to end all benders. I stared back. Nobody else wanted to share. Artin distributed sobriety keychains, then we joined hands and Artin led the ending prayer, "God grant me the serenity—"

When the meeting adjourned Cam made a beeline for the door, and I made one in the opposite direction, towards the coffee.

Grounds were visible in the bottom of my cup when Artin broke away from a well-dressed young woman and headed my way. I plucked a water from the ice bucket and handed it to him.

"You read my mind," he said, cracking it and taking a big drink. "Listen, I've noticed you've never participated when we give out the keychains."

I shrugged.

Artin stepped close and lowered his voice. He was getting serious. "Look Clip, the program only works if you work the steps. How about you share next meeting?"

"Sure," I said, knowing it'd never happen. There wasn't going to be a next meeting.

Artin grinned and clapped me on the shoulder. "I look forward to it. It's a battle. I've been clean for seven years now, but every day is hard fought. Every. Single. Day. If you ever want to get together sometime over coffee, I know you love coffee," he pointed to my cup and grinned like we shared some sort of inside joke, "and just talk I'm here."

I envisioned collapsing his windpipe with my thumbs and watching the life slowly fade from his eyes. Instead, I smiled. "I'd like that. Cheers. To sobriety." I held up my cup. There were little red reindeer printed on the Styrofoam. Surplus from Christmas. Artin held up his water bottle and we clinked glasses. *Drink up you bastard,* I thought, watching him slug down the water.

Artin wiped his mouth with the back of his hand and patted me on the shoulder. "Good talk." He headed off to bullshit some other poor unfortunate. I picked up a powdered sugar doughnut and nibbled at it, tracking his progress.

By the time my doughnut and coffee were finished, most of the attendees had left. I began to fold up the chairs and stacked them on a metal trolley. Nikki broke down the refreshment table, carrying the unused paper goods to the kitchen. "Can you give me a hand? These things weigh a ton," she said, tugging on an urn.

I snapped together the remaining chairs, and humped the coffee urns to the kitchen sink, dumping gallons of steaming coffee. Nikki ran the tap and filled them with soapy water. "We'll leave these to soak."

I followed her out of the cramped kitchen, and Artin was in the process of turning off the lights. "Can you give me a hand carrying these to my car?" He pointed to the white doughnut boxes. "I take the extras over to One8o Place."

"What a nice thought." I scooped up the boxes. The only reason I said anything was because to say nothing would've been awkward.

"Careful you don't get anything on that fine-looking suit," Artin said, waiting for me to make my way across the room before turning out the final set of lights. I smiled and nodded and followed him upstairs. "Go ahead," he said at the exit door. Artin displayed a key ring. "I have to lock up."

I gave a quick scan through the small pane of glass but could only see an empty parking lot. Carefully planned landscaping created a private lot. Taking a deep breath, I stepped through the door. The only thing that greeted me were Artin's beat up Lincoln Town Car and Nikki's Escalade. Nothing moved, but something crawled up my spine. On alert, I stepped aside and let Nikki out. Artin brought up the rear, carefully locking the church door. Artin blipped the locks on his car, and I laid the three boxes carefully in the backseat.

"There you go." I rapped the top of the doorframe.

"Clip?" Nikki called. She stood on the driver's seat of her truck so she could look over the roof at me. "I think my battery's dead."

So, this is the way it's going to play. My pulse quickened and time slowed. I was acutely aware we were totally alone. Not a dog barked, nor was there the sound of children playing. There wasn't even the sound of cars passing on Meeting Street. "Do you have jumper cables?"

She shook her head. Of course not. There was a reason I had a pair in every funeral home vehicle—former funeral home vehicles. There's nothing more embarrassing than a dead hearse at a cemetery.

I turned to Artin. "Do you?"

Artin shook his head. "Hop in. I'll give you two a ride."

We were no more than four feet apart. I wasn't worried. His hands were in plain sight, and the only thing in them were keys. Nikki's pistol pressed against the small of my back. I eased my hand into a position where I could loosen it if he started reaching.

"At what point did you decide to radicalize Sam Badgers?"

Artin cocked his head slightly. "Excuse me?"

"You heard me."

He laughed. "Clip, what are you talking about?"

"Are you going to tell me next you don't remember Sam? That's pretty fucked up if you ask me, trolling—no, *mining*—addiction meetings for injured people."

The laughter ceased.

"Don't move," I warned. "My hand is resting on a .40 caliber that will splatter your brain all over that shiny Lincoln."

"How did—" he started, but quickly recovered. "Very good." He nodded. "You've proven to be quite the adversary. I must say I was surprised to see you today."

It took every ounce of self-control not to pull the gun and let it mow something the size of the Panama Canal through his skull. "I have something of yours I figured you'd want me to return to you."

"What?"

"I think you know what." Out of the corner of my eye, I saw Nikki's head sink below the roofline. Hopefully, she was on her phone. "Let's talk about where it *was*." I reached into my back pocket and retrieved a tin. Setting it on the roof, I popped the lid off one handed and took my time—I had a captive audience—scooping out a robin's egg sized wad. "Obviously, your protégé Badgers had some reservations or he wouldn't have saved some. I'm sure at some point your people tossed his place?" Artin remained expressionless, though I knew they had. "Well, you ought to firebomb the person that searched his place, unless it was you. Wait, it was you wasn't it?" I laughed, not because I thought it was funny, but to enrage Artin. It worked. His eyes burned. "Dummy." The name-calling was unnecessary, other than to infuriate. "Not as smart as you think you are. Badgers hid it in plain sight. He practically had a neon sign pointing to it. Didn't think to look in the ice cube trays, did you?" Artin's scowl said he didn't, and he was kicking himself for it. "Some cold isn't going to hurt your little army of creepy crawlies. In fact," I shrugged, "the feds tell me they're quite hardy." I spit a long rope of juice on his loafers. "Oops. Sorry."

"You think this will end?" His voice was even but filled with rage. "You arrest me, and everything is fixed. Poof." He snapped his fingers. "Like the end of a movie." He wagged his finger. "No, this is just the beginning."

Nikki appeared around her truck and walked toward us. "Risden is on his way."

"Stay there." I raised my arm to stop her, keeping my eyes on Artin. I clarified for his sake. "That means the cavalry is coming to Calvary."

Artin rudely ignored my witticism to continue his propaganda, "There are others that will continue—"

"You mean like your pal Nasir Tannous? He's been rolled up along with his getaway driver."

"You lie."

"Kayaking up the river to escape. That had to be your idea, what with your love of water sports."

Veins bulged in his neck and the bristles of his mustache quivered like a mouse's whiskers. "There are many soldiers to continue the fight."

The wail of a siren could be heard in the distance. "Tell me, how were you planning to do it?"

Artin relaxed and leaned against the car door. "When I excused myself during the meeting I was going to pop a tire, but your girlfriend left the car unlocked so I unlatched the hood and loosened one of the battery cables." He shrugged almost bashfully. "I was going to offer you a ride and take you someplace." He recited it calmly like it was a business transaction.

"Where?"

"Does it matter?"

"And kill us."

"Yes," he said very matter-of-factly. "As a soldier fighting a war, you understand the risks."

I decided not to argue the point that there wasn't currently a war going on American soil. "Nasir said I wasn't a soldier. In fact, he said some hurtful things." I was having fun. "He called me a mercenary and a mongrel."

Artin spit. He was smart enough not to land it on my shoes, but I got the point. "You got involved."

"I didn't want to get involved."

"All the same, you're in it. You understand the risks. Nothing personal."

"It's personal now." I stepped forward and jabbed him in the chest so hard he took a step back. "I could've crept up to whatever hidey-hole you live in and tossed a bomb in there and blown you to smithereens. But no."

Artin drew up to full height. "Why didn't you?"

"Too easy. Too painless. You deserve worse than that."

The siren was getting louder. Artin seemed unconcerned. "Perhaps. Only Allah knows."

"I don't know about that."

"Tell me Clip," Artin said, suddenly assuming his counselor-like NA affect, "did you wonder how we got you into that warehouse?"

I shrugged, non-committal. No sense giving him the pleasure even though it was something I'd wondered a million times while clinging to that scrap of wood.

"I have it on video. Want to see?" He held both hands up in front of himself and pointed to his pants pocket. "My phone's in there."

The siren was loud enough that I had to raise my voice. "Use your left hand. Slowly." I gripped the butt of the pistol, ready to whip it out at the first sign of trouble. Artin pulled his phone out, cupped it in his hand and swiped a couple of times.

He extended the phone. "Here."

I reached out to take it, realizing too late it wasn't a phone. Artin leaped forward and buried the fake phone into my neck. My legs turned to rubber and my body shook violently. There was lightning in my blood. The pavement rushed up. Artin rode me to the ground like a rodeo cowboy, running voltage the entire time. When my face connected with asphalt Artin stopped, and quickly snapped on a pair of handcuffs.

"Run!" I gasped.

Artin swept the pistol out of my waistband and pointed it at her back. "Stop!" Nikki obeyed and put her hands in the air. "Walk back to the sound of my voice."

The siren was on top of us. Artin twirled, pistol held in a combat grip, ready to open up into the windshield. I torqued onto my side, ready to kick him off balance. It was unnecessary. The marked car passed the church lot and continued down Meeting Street. The siren's wail quickly receded. The momentary distraction was all Nikki needed. She sprinted for her truck.

Artin spun, sighted, and squeezed off a shot.

Nikki collapsed in a heap.

Chapter 40

I struggled against the cuffs, but my muscles were knotty and unresponsive from the Taser. Artin stowed the pistol in his pocket and jogged to Nikki. She was writhing on the ground, holding her leg. Artin knelt and pried her hands off, briefly inspecting the wound, before jogging to me.

"You sonofabitch."

"It's a through and through," he said, pulling my belt off. "Nothing to worry about."

"Let me see." I struggled to my knees.

"Stay." He pulled out the Taser to prove he meant business.

Artin jogged back and used the belt to create a pressure dressing. He slung Nikki over his shoulder and carried her, groaning, and stowed her in the backseat of his Town Car. "Get in," he said to me.

I struggled to my feet and fell in alongside Nikki.

"Buckle him," Artin said.

Nikki wormed her arm across my chest and dragged the seatbelt back across. It took a couple of tries, but she managed to snap it in.

Artin grabbed the shoulder belt and yanked it, snugging it tight. Smart. There was no chance of me lunging forward. "No warnings. Don't fool with the seatbelt." He jogged over to Nikki's heels, gathered them up, and tossed them on the passenger seat before cranking the ignition. The old car turned over smoothly. The soft suspension hardly made a bump out of the parking lot. Artin pointed the car north.

"How're you doing?" I asked.

Nikki's face was white. She nodded and forced a smile. It came out a grimace. "I'll live. I'm not sure he's going to when I'm done with him."

"Put your leg up here and let me take a look at it."

"I don't think I can."

"You're going to have to. I can't help you." Nikki gritted her teeth used her hands to pull her leg up so it rested on my knee. "Undo the belt." She sucked in a breath and followed my instructions. It was a good sign not a lot of blood flowed out; hopefully no major vessels had been nicked. "Can you twist it so I can see the other side?" Nikki closed her eyes and nodded, twisting her leg, letting out a little cry in the process. Sure enough, on the other side of her calf was a little hole. Artin appeared to be correct. A through and through wound. I gave Nikki instructions on how to tear off my shirttail and dress the wound properly while Artin navigated through North Charleston.

"Where are you taking us?" I asked.

"You'll know when we get there."

"They'll hunt you, you know."

"They can hunt. I'll disappear. They've missed me hiding in plain sight for the past 20 years." Artin engaged his turn signal and changed lanes. His driving was careful and methodical, nothing that would attract unwanted attention.

"You're not that good. I didn't miss you." The light ahead turned yellow. Artin applied the brakes and coasted to a stop. A North Charleston cop pulled up next to us. The officer was hunched over his phone tapping out a text. Artin caught my eye in the rearview.

"Don't even think about it." He shifted in the seat. It was a subtle movement. "I have the gun pointed at you through the seat. You have to ask yourself, is your life worth mine?" Seeing my eyes, he added, "Is the cop's life worth mine?"

I glanced at the cop again. He looked no more than a year or two out of the academy, not enough mileage on him to even grow a decent beard. The light turned green and he sped through the intersection, still typing furiously. Artin let off the brake and accelerated smoothly.

"It should've been obvious from the get-go," I said, "but I was accepting facts as facts when they weren't. Quaid went on and on about your daily tests. And for the longest time, I wondered how this common bacteria was defeating your quality-control tests over and over. But it wasn't. You were simply altering the results. It was so obvious, it didn't even occur to me. You had access to the data coming in from the field. How long did you think you'd be able to keep that up before someone caught on?"

"Long enough for it to be effective."

"Nobody audited the results?"

"I expected Quaid would get suspicious, or the feds to start poking around in the mainframe, but everyone took my word that the data was good."

"I fell for it too."

Artin's eyes flicked up in the mirror. "How did you figure me?"

"Things didn't start clicking until the feds told me your guy, Nasir, was nabbed kayaking through the quarantine cordon, something you told me you like to do. Even then it didn't really compute. Prayer did it."

"You prayed to God to deliver me?"

"Basically. I was praying with the family of the woman you murdered and thought to myself, 'the last time I prayed was with Artin at NA.' And you know what?" I continued without waiting for an answer, "Then the thought popped into my head your name was Persian in origin..."

"What's that supposed to mean?" Nikki asked.

"His terrorist buddies are a group of Afghan Persians."

"Are you even an addict?" Nikki asked.

Artin glanced over his shoulder. "Does it matter?"

Nikki clenched her hands like claws. Her arms shook. "You bastard."

Artin sighed and turned off Rivers Avenue. We were north, up near the airport, in Hotapp's jurisdiction. "If it makes a difference to you, I am. As a boy I was conscripted to work the poppy fields and got addicted to opium."

"Everything you said in the meeting was bullshit?"

Artin turned at the library and I knew our destination. "Not fake, but I had to change the narrative." There wasn't a guard in the little guard shack on a Sunday evening, but Artin pulled up to the fence and badged a scanner. The LED light turned from red to green, beeped, and the gate lurched back.

"Where are we?" Nikki asked.

"The water plant," Artin replied.

Chapter 41

After the Town Car bumped over the metal threshold, the gate rolled back across the drive, effectively sealing us in. Artin seemed to relax and accelerated. We whizzed by a small stand of trees and a large employee parking lot, mostly empty except for a handful of cars.

"Just a couple engineers and technicians on the weekend," Artin said. "The whole operation is mostly computerized." He couldn't help but add, "My design. Programmable logic controllers keep everything running smoothly with minimal human oversight. We'll have the place to ourselves."

Artin cranked the wheel right onto a gravel access road. The car filled with the musky odor of rotting organics, similar to the marshy smell of a low tide. Despite the car's generous suspension, Nikki groaned with each bump. Her skin had turned the color of parchment. She was sweating profusely.

"How do you feel?"

She nodded, biting her bottom lip.

The road terminated at a bridge too narrow for vehicular traffic. Artin opened the rear door and wagged the gun. "Out."

I crabbed out of the backseat and was greeted with the sound of rushing water. The bridge spanned a massive man-made pond, easily several football fields in length. The sun was all but out of sight leaving just a red smear on the horizon, making the surface look black. Smaller pools, some circular, some square, fanned out past the big pond interspersed with brick buildings and large white domes that resembled a sci-fi Mars colony. Holding tanks?

"You too," Artin said to Nikki. She groaned but nonetheless slid across the seat. The cords in her forearms bulged as she pulled herself up using the doorframe, trying not to put weight on her leg. Her gaze was slightly unfocused. I'd seen that look before on many a soldier's face. She was going into shock.

"She needs to lie down," I said.

"Move." Artin jammed the pistol barrel in her ribs. Nikki winced and clung to the door.

"She can't," I said.

The barrel swung in my direction. "Help her."

"Can't you see she's about to pass out?"

"Move or I Taser her."

"Put your arm around my shoulder," I muttered, stepping in close and stooping. "I'll get you there." Nikki shuffled her hands across the door and around my neck. She smelled sour from the pain.

Gunmetal pressed into my spine. "Get going. We have 15 minutes before the lights kick on."

I lurched forward. Nikki grabbed my tie with one hand, practically strangling me as I dragged her across the gravel onto the bridge. The bridge was a concrete and metal structure. Not the pleasing Colonial metalwork and smooth municipal pours of downtown. No, this was an amalgam of big tack welds, galvanized beams, and spalling concrete of a heavy industrial structure. The only sounds were Nikki's labored breathing and the water running out of scores of tubes attached to the bridge. It sounded like a giant fountain.

"Stop," Artin commanded when we reached the halfway mark. "On your knees."

I bent over as far as I could. Nikki slithered down me and plopped on her rear. "Lie down," I suggested. "It'll help." She rolled on to her back and closed her eyes. I sank to my knees next to her, facing across the pond. In the middle the surface was calm. Like glass.

"What's the play?" I asked Artin. "Shoot us and toss us in the drink?" I forced a laugh. "The decomp gases will pop us to the surface in a day. Then there'll be questions." I was being fast and loose with the facts. There were lots of factors that determined how long a body would stay submerged—sometimes up to several weeks.

Artin stood to the side of me so I could see him out of the corner of my eye. "We had a bum get in here last spring. Somehow he fell into this sedimentation pond." He paused until I looked at him. "He wasn't discovered until his corpse jammed the sludge trough. Only when we reviewed the security tapes did we discover he'd been in there for almost a month."

"A bum? You mean someone like Sam Badgers? A homeless addict you wound up and set loose?"

"You mean someone who your society discarded like a piece of garbage? Did I feed him, clothe him, and shelter him?"

"He was sick. You took advantage of him."

"That's the problem with your society. He wasn't *sick*. Samuel lacked direction so he turned to sin. I showed him the path."

"Look where your 'path' led him. Lying in the mud missing half his head."

Artin made a face like I said something distasteful and waved his hand across the pond's arc. "The undercurrent is strong. Takes whatever it has right into the sludge bed. Like a lover's embrace. Could be a month or more before you clog the trough and they pick you out. Like that bum."

"When you pitch it like that, it almost sounds nice. You missed your calling in sales."

Artin looked momentarily confused. "Really?" he said reflexively.

I snorted and shook my head. "No asshole."

"Where's Blackwater?" Artin demanded, furious.

I grinned cheerfully. "Fuck yourself."

His face was a storm cloud. "Your girlfriend doesn't have to die."

"You already took care of that. Remember the explosion?"

Artin didn't take the bait. "You can save this one." He pointed with the pistol toward Nikki who wasn't moving. "She's loyal to you. Don't you think you owe it to her?" He paused. "And her son?"

"What about your bullshit NA prayer about accepting the things we can't change? I've accepted the situation. *Our* situation. If you were going to let her live you would've left her lying in that church parking lot."

"It could just be *your* situation. The girl isn't coming after me any time soon. By the time she makes it off this bridge I'll be long gone."

I looked at Nikki. Her eyes were closed and there was barely movement in her chest her breathing was so shallow. "*If* she makes it off this bridge. She's gone into shock."

Artin shrugged. "Best you're going to do."

I shook my head. "I don't buy it. She's seen your face. No way you let her live."

Artin shrugged. "Doesn't matter. It's time for me to move on." He said it casually, like the last line from a B movie, not like his mug was about to be plastered on the FBI's Most Wanted List. "So, what's it going to be?" He checked his watch. Clearly, he didn't want to be out in the open when the plant illuminated for the night.

"What's to stop me from lying to you?"

Artin squatted down so we were eye to eye. He was smarter than he looked. He stayed far enough way so I couldn't head-butt him. "You lie to me and I come back and kill your *jendeh*." He grinned. "Then I go kill her son. I'll behead him. And film it. And publish it. How about that?"

I smiled benignly and killed a couple more seconds. "Help me. My Arabic is a bit rusty, but I don't think you're talking nice."

Artin stood. "Enough!" He pointed the pistol at Nikki's head. "You have three seconds. One. Two—"

"Okay," I relented. "But promise me you'll leave her alone...and her son. They're civilians."

Artin nodded.

"Say it."

"Fine. I promise."

I nodded. "Reach into my right front pants pocket."

"You had it on you the whole time?" Artin's face was priceless. I could almost read his thoughts. He could've done us right in the church hall and been long gone by now.

"Something like that."

I saw stars as Artin kicked me in the head. I flopped onto the rough concrete. "Lie flat," he said unnecessarily. He put his knee on the back of my neck and fished in my pocket, pulling out a small plastic vial. "This is it?" He studied it like he'd found the Ark of the Covenant.

I pulled my knees to my chest and struggled into a squat. "Yup."

He squinted at the label in the darkness. "Aron Alpha?"

"Mortuary superglue."

He shook it trying to see the contents through the plastic in the dim light. "There's glue in here or Blackwater?"

"Glue."

"Is this some sort of trick?"

"It's the kind of the stuff that would reseal a plastic bottle enough to give it that *crack*." I waited for it to sink in. A look of horror slowly spread across Artin's face. "That's right, you drank Blackwater."

Artin's face morphed into something that approximated a sneer, and he took a step closer. I willed him to step closer. It would be so easy to spring up and smash his nose in like a ripe melon and then kick his body right into the pond. No hands needed for that. I leaned back, baiting him. He didn't take it. "You're a fool. Do you honestly think the people that created this wouldn't make something to protect themselves?"

I leaned back as far as I could, mentally willing him to close the gap. "Maybe there is. Maybe there isn't. But the question remains: if there's an antidote can you get to it before those little critters in your gut," I pointed my jaw at his belly causing him to look down, "do their job? I bet they're multiplying like crazy right now."

Artin snorted, but still looked a little green around the gills "There's no antidote, it's what *not* to take."

"That makes no sense."

"Think about it. Why are some dying and some aren't? The people that developed this counted on the fact it would be treated like any reasonable doctor would treat shigellosis, with Ampicillin. The cure is what triggers the promoter in the bacteria's DNA, morphing it in to a virulent strain of VEEV." I felt like I'd just been punched in the gut. It made so much sense why some were dying and some weren't. Maggie's allergy to penicillin had saved her. "Treat it with something other than Ampicillin, like a tetracycline or sulfonamide, and you're fine. Let your body's immune system fight off the infection and you just have a nasty case of diarrhea, nothing else."

I motioned to the swirling waters. "You're in the right place. You can shit right off the edge."

Atrin ignored the comment, his eyes shining with fervor. "It's a first-world weapon. Notice how there weren't many deaths out of the rural areas? Of course not, like everyone else in this mongrel land you sweep people like that and Sam Badgers aside. Did you know your government has stockpiles of medicines ready for emergencies? Now that they know we're attacking with this, they'll be ready for the next attack."

"It's gone. You drank it, and the feds have the rest."

Artin looked unconcerned. "The sinews of war are infinite money. Cicero said that 2,000 years ago. It's still true. If the price is right, I'm sure more Blackwater will come on the market."

"Either way, you're a dead man. Your people won't take your failure."

"Maybe." He shrugged, unconcerned. "But I live to fight another day."

Hot blood ran down my fingers as I struggled against the cuffs.

Artin saw me struggling. "Now, now," he said. "Accept your fate like a soldier." He grabbed Nikki's ankles. She hardly twitched despite the wound.

"What are you doing?"

"It won't matter in the end. She'll die of drowning or shock." He tugged her to the edge, dropping her legs off the side. Only the weight of her torso was keeping her from the swirling water.

"We had a deal!"

"And then you were foolish enough to poison me." Artin moved to push her shoulders.

It was now or never. Dying was a forgone conclusion, but Artin was coming with me. I popped to my feet and lowered my head like a battering ram.

Artin sensed movement and swung the pistol in my direction.

There was a loud click. Sodium halide lamps flooded the complex in intense light. The sudden, penetrating brightness caused Artin to blink. His eyelids closed in slow motion. The barrel of the pistol didn't waver. It looked like a train tunnel, black and yawning. Ten feet separated us. There was no way he could miss.

I charged.

The eyelids parted.

Artin's head exploded.

His body jerked several times like he was being electrocuted as a succession of rounds slammed into his head. He dropped, lifeless.

I couldn't stop my momentum and ran right over his body, tracking bloody footprints down the concrete.

"Stop! Back away!" a voice behind me commanded.

I spun around. Standing behind me holding a MP7 was a familiar figure with a purple streak in her hair. "A team is on the way." Cam brushed by me and grabbed Nikki's blouse and dragged her away from the spreading pool of blood.

"What's going on?" I eyed the futuristic looking weapon in her hand. It was fitted with an enormous suppressor and an extended magazine that protruded below the grip. MP7's are used almost exclusively by the special operations community. Last time I'd seen one was cradled in the arms of Shark, on a mission in Afghanistan.

Peering through her optic, Cam knelt and swept a 360 arc before standing. "Any more hostiles?"

I shook my head. "Not that I know of. Who are you?"

"Turn around." I complied. The cuffs released. "Step out of your shoes. Leave your socks on. Step around the blood." I complied again, shimming out of the new wingtips. "Take her. Go wait by the car." Cam pointed to the Town Car. I wasn't about to question someone with that kind of firepower. I knelt and gathered up Nikki. She fluttered her eyes when I slung her over my shoulder.

"Hang on. You're going to be okay," I murmured and stepped gingerly around the growing pool of blood near Artin.

Cam depressed the call button on her radio. "Copy that. Tango down."

I propped Nikki against a tire of the Town Car. Her pulse was thready, but she was breathing. For that I was thankful. The sky was completely black, and with it came a chill. Fall had arrived. I watched Cam talk on comms under the harsh glare of the floodlights with my hands buried in my pockets. The minutes ticked by slowly. It wasn't long before there was a loud crash. Seconds later two vans raced up the drive. They weren't the usual motor pool specials. These were Mercedes Sprinters with the extra room. The rear doors opened and figures clad in orange NBC suits swarmed out. A group of four headed for the bridge; the two-person team approached us.

"Come with me," one of the figures said. All I could see were eyes behind the glass in the mask, but based on the height, I guessed it was a woman. She motioned to a van. It wasn't a request.

I turned to retrieve Nikki. The woman grabbed my wrist. "We'll take care of her."

I shook off her hand and glared at the eyes behind the glass. They were bright, blue eyes. Intelligent. "Thanks, but I've got it." The eyes calculated, and the numbers came up in my favor, for she didn't make a move to stop me. I gathered Nikki up, and followed the two to their van. The inside was outfitted like an ambulance with cabinets of equipment and medications and a gurney in the middle. Based on the air-filtration unit bolted to the roof, it was a specialized ambulance. That was confirmed when the four of us clambered into the van and the bigger of the two people shut the door and spun a little dial, creating an air seal.

The two didn't waste any time hooking Nikki up to several monitoring systems. I felt the van going through the motions of a three-point turn. The woman looked up from the IV she was starting in Nikki's arm. "Relax. Everything is going to be fine."

I leaned back on the padded bench. "I know. Tell your CO to meet us where we're going. I know how to stop all this."

Chapter 42

Garret Maas waited at the corner of Broad and Logan ignoring the diesel rumblings behind him. A yellow bulldozer and excavator slowly crawled over the lot separating the skeleton of Granville & Sons into piles of charred scrap. He looked every bit the attorney, wearing a custom-tailored suit, French cuff broadcloth shirt with his initials embroidered on the cuffs, silk tie, and calfskin loafers. His meticulous coiffure was held in place by too much pomade. When the Suburban eased to a stop, he opened the rear door, slid his leather briefcase in and climbed in after it. The smell of expensive cologne and old smoke followed him in.

"Clip," he said, offering his hand. He nodded to Nikki and Jackson sitting in the third row. Balancing the briefcase on his knees, he popped the locks and pulled a pair of cheater glasses from one of the inside pockets and slipped them on before removing several sheaves of paper. The bundles were neatly bound with black foldover clips. "Here are the trust documents and the power of attorney. Sign for yellow, initial for orange." He handed me the stack and fished inside his jacket, producing a Mont Blanc fountain pen. I like a lawyer who's all business. They charge by the hour, and for what Garret charges, I wouldn't have minded if he had skipped the minor pleasantries.

I paged through the stack, scribbling and initialing next to the little colored stickies his paralegal had hidden while Garret talked. "I've set up an account with a re-mailing service in California. All your correspondence will be forwarded to my firm and we will mail it to California to the attention of," he frowned and glanced in his briefcase, "Henry Cattell." Cattell had embalmed President Lincoln. It was the first name that popped into my head when Garret and I spoke on the phone several days prior. "When you get to where you're going get in touch with the re-mailing service and give them your new address." He held out a card with the information of re-mailing service on it.

The Marshall in the driver's seat turned and held out her hand. "We'll take care of that."

Garret frowned, unsure. I plucked the card from his hand and stuck it in my shirt pocket. "Don't worry, I think I can handle it." It was the agent's turn to frown. The federal government is good at certain things. Managing a private citizen's life isn't one of those things.

Garret cleared his throat and continued, "I'll be the only one at the firm who will know who Henry Cattell is. As per your instructions, money from the trust will be deposited at the agreed upon intervals to a numbered account in Royal Cayman Bank and you'll be able to pull the funds from there."

I was at the last colored sticky and handed Garret the stack. He retrieved a stamp and seal from his briefcase and notarized a few places. From the backseat, Jackson whispered, none-too-subtly, in his mother's ear, "What's that stamp for?"

His mother shushed him.

"That it?" It was surprisingly easy to dismantle your life. Just a few phone calls to Garret and I was out of business and reduced to a slim file folder in his firm's archives. I felt like a tent revivalist preacher pulling up stakes after the town's pockets dried up.

Garret did his little throat clear thing again and dove back into his bag of tricks. "There is something else. Adam Dresser got in touch with me. He's an estate attorney—"

"I know Adam. I buried his wife the Christmas before last." Tragic death. Throat cancer. Weighed 83 pounds when she died. Never smoked a day in her life. In addition to Adam, she left behind two college-aged kids.

"Oh," Garret said. If he was even the least bit surprised he hid it. "Anyhow, Adam is handling Isabella Granville's estate. Aside from a couple of small bequests to some local charities, she left everything to you."

Nikki sucked in an audible breath.

"Pardon?"

"As you know they were both only children, and their only son was killed. Apparently, it was Lauren's wish that you get everything and continue their legacy." I looked at the remnants of their legacy through the tinted glass. The sight made my gut clench. "It's substantial," Garret continued, oblivious to my pain. "Given your current situation, would you like me to liquidate the estate and place it into the trust?"

"Yes." Aside from a few blackened beams, part of the massive brick chimney was the only part of the structure erect. "Wait, no." Garret looked up from his note taking and peered from over his cheaters. "Get a real estate company to rent their house out." They wouldn't want me to sell it, at least not on a whim. "I'm having the lot re-graded." Garret followed my finger pointing out the window. The heavy equipment operators must've knocked off for a break. Both machines stood still amongst the ruins of the funeral home. "We'll leave it that way, an empty lot. I plan on having cenotaphs for the Granvilles and Maggie erected there. Your firm can take care of making sure the taxes are kept up with."

"Absolutely." Garret nodded vigorously. More responsibility meant more billable hours he could levy against the now flush trust.

There was a loud knock at the Suburban's window.

"Are you expecting someone?" the Marshal asked. There was tension in her voice.

Risden placed his hand on the center console. "Easy. He's OK."

"We agreed to this meeting with your attorney only," the Marshal said, turning in her seat. Irate didn't adequately describe her expression. Before I could respond Moonie yanked the door open.

"You were right partner," he said without bothering to greet anyone. "The government car was easy to spot." Moonie practically climbed over Garret to get to the back row where he settled in between Nikki's casted leg and her son. The bullet had fractured the femur, necessitating an unwieldly cast. "I sure am going to miss you and your mama," he said to Jackson, pulling the bill of the boy's ball cap down. "But I'll keep an eye on things for you. He lingered long enough on "mama" to cause Risden to twitch.

I grinned in spite of myself.

"Where you been today that you're all gussied up?" Moonie ran his hand over my shoulder. It was another off-the-rack quickie from Wayne at the Country Gentleman, but it was passable.

"Had some business to attend to before we head out of town." Truth was, I was coming from Maggie's memorial service. I didn't want to tell Moonie and hurt his feelings that he wasn't invited. It was a private affair at the hospital. Bullying the Marshals into allowing me to attend had been a feat. It took me threatening to renege on my testimony to get some traction. I was spirited in and out through the kitchen like the president. But it had been worth the effort. I needed to say goodbye.

The tiny fourth floor chapel had been crammed with folks wearing scrubs. An eight by ten photo and vase of fresh cut flowers sat on the non-denominational altar. The photo was Maggie in her lab coat, mugging for the camera. Doing what she loved doing, doctoring. Max and Liz were taking an urn full of earth scooped at the blast site—ceremonial remains—back to Chicago to have a service with family and friends. The "remains" recovered at the blast were of no quantitative significance. After cremation there'd be nothing left but fly ash.

"You need anything else from me?" I asked Garret.

"I believe we're good." Garret offered a thin smile, slipped off his cheaters and snapped the briefcase shut. "I'll send any additional documentation to you."

I nodded and said to the Marshal and Risden in the front, "I need a word with Moonie privately."

The Marshal started to respond with an unsatisfactory answer, but Risden held up his hand. Not that it mattered. I was already following Garret into the bright sunshine. I released a stream of tobacco juice the length of the Nile onto what used to be the funeral home's lawn. A familiar avian dropped out of the sky and landed on excavator's flexed arm. Matey cawed twice, "Clip! Clip!"

Garret jerked his head toward the giant parrot who was busy under his wing itching. "Did that thing just—"

I nodded. "Yup." Matey's pelt, or whatever the hell parrots have, looked a little worse for wear. Singed and sooty. He must've been close to the blast. Frankly, I was surprised to see him. I figured he'd perished.

Garret tore his gaze from Matey who was shuffling around on the hydraulic joint, staring. "I didn't know you had—" Garret waved his hand. "Never mind."

"I didn't either. I inherited him."

"A day of inheritances, eh?" Garret grinned. Lawyer humor, I guess. He stuck out his hand. "Anyway, Godspeed."

"Wait a sec, Garret. One more thing. Moonie here is going to be taking care of some personal business for me." Moonie plopped his ten-gallon hat on his head, and adjusted his gun, and winked at Garret. The attorney did his best not to grimace. "You're to give him however much money he asks for. Understand?"

Garret looked at Moonie, then me. "That's irregular. No limit." The man liked contracts. Parameters. Things in black-and-white. No gray areas. Problem was, my life had been thrust into nothing but gray area.

"No limit. He has my complete trust." Moonie might be a bit simple, but if nothing else he wasn't a thief.

Garret frowned and nodded. "Understood. I'll send you the documents."

I'm sure you will. Attorneys and their beloved documents.

We shook. The attorney turned and headed for a big Mercedes parked in the direction of the cathedral.

"There's something I need for you to do for me." I put my arm around Moonie's shoulders and turned him so we were both staring at the ruins.

"Name it partner," he said, loving the attention.

I paused when a young couple strolled by. The guy was wearing a backpack. Students. The quarantine had been lifted. Folks were out and about again. They paused and the girl pulled out her phone and snapped a photo. "I heard there was ammunition stored in the basement," she said as they moved off.

"Seriously?" he boy replied.

"Yeah. Like, grenades and stuff."

"No—"

When they were out of earshot, I resumed, "You know what's buried under there."

Moonie pushed the brim of his hat up. Trick questions weren't his forte. "The cellar?"

"Yes, the cellar. I'm talking about *who's* in the cellar."

A look of recognition blossomed. "Ah, Mrs. Granville."

"Yeah. Truth be told, I body-snatched her from the incident morgue. DMORT thinks she went into the ocean." Moonie whistled. "At this point I don't need another headache, so I need you to get a few of your brothers and come out here tonight and dig that Ziegler Case out of the cellar before those workmen come across her and all hell breaks loose."

"I can get her out of there, but then what do I do?"

"Take her over to Palmer-Chase. Have Eddie handle it. He's all right, for an undertaker. Have them bury Isabella next to her husband in the St. Michael's churchyard. And Moonie?"

"Yeah partner?"

"Make sure they put her in something classy. Like a Mastercraft. Isabella was a woman of discriminating taste. The Fairchild Mahogany should do the trick." Moonie continued nodding. "I'll email you a burial permit in a few days when I get to where I'm going." I was going to have to login to the system and doctor an old case. Red flags would go up if Isabella's name appeared twice in the system. "Print it out and give it to Eddie. And tell him the truth, she was awaiting burial at the funeral home when the explosion happened."

His scar was a shade I'd never seen before—candy apple red. The pride color? "You can count on me. I'll be knockin' on ole' Eddie's door tonight."

"Hit Garret up to cover the expense and get whatever you and your brothers want for digging her out."

Moonie looked over my shoulder to make sure the truck's windows were closed but didn't bother to lower his voice to a whisper. "So, where'd they have you locked up?"

I lowered my voice. "A biocontainment room at the NIH in Bethesda. They wanted to make sure I hadn't contracted the Blackwater."

"Wait, I thought you told me it was curable."

"It is. They needed to make sure the cure," I used air quotes, "worked, and in the mean time I had been so close to the stuff they kept me locked up to make sure I didn't catch it and spread it."

"What's the deal with this Hydro-Engineering company I've been hearing about?"

"It's a dummy company set up by the government to take the fall, and lawsuits." A company named Hydro-Engineering was being named to the media as the company responsible for improperly installing the impeller that allowed for contamination.

"A dummy company?"

"Can you imagine the chaos if it got out you weren't safe from infection in your own home? The water you drink from or bathe with could get you sick? It would tear apart the very fabric of our country. Folks would always be waiting for the other shoe to drop."

Moonie removed his hat and scratched his head. "Will it drop? Are there more out there?"

I shrugged. "I sure as hell hope not, but who knows. Bailey seems to have a handle on things. His team is moving toward the source. Something about bio-signatures." There had been countless debriefs over the intercom and through the glass of my isolation room. There were still a lot of blanks. Bailey asked questions. Didn't answer them. He had answered one question by playing a video from the security camera feed at the fruit warehouse. It showed a regular box truck, pulling up, the driver dressed in a snowman suit.

The guards waved it through. At the loading dock, the snowman unloaded the only occupant, me, and the video cut several times following the snowman pushing the gurney to the casket staging area. I relived the conversation with Nasir Tannous mentally through the grainy black-and-white feed. After drugging me, I watched him remove the cinder blocks from the casket, and drag out the pouch already inside, before dumping my lifeless form inside. After stuffing the body bag on top of me, Tannous had to literally sit on the lid to latch it. The video then showed him tinkering with the strapping tensioner for a few minutes before giving up. His lack of mechanical aptitude saved my life. To fake it, Tannous simply took a roll of 100 mph tape—the military's version of duct tape—from the tool bench and taped the bands together. The color of the tape matched, so the sailors didn't notice. The impact with the water easily broke apart the taped bands.

I still wasn't clear on who or what exactly Cam was. Bailey didn't offer a nice little video on the other side of the hospital room glass to explain her role. In fact, he ignored me every time I asked. Risden said he'd heard the government was tinkering with asymmetric warfare, essentially fighting dirty. It made more sense that Bailey was running an off-the-grid, elite counterterrorism unit than being part of Homeland Security. His DHS credentials were what I suspected from the start, a cover. Hansel and Cam were part of Bailey's nameless unit. Possibly even Wesley Harris, the supposedly homeless Marine with the glass eye. It made sense. The alphabet soup organizations, especially the shadowy ones, recruit heavily from the military.

"Scary times," Moonie said, shaking his head.

I nodded. Indeed these were. The quarantine had been lifted, and the government was busy sweeping everything under the rug. "You gonna be all right?" I was glad he wasn't with the Charleston Coroner's Office anymore. Heads were going to roll there when the public discovered exactly what happened to the victims. Earl Blood would never be reelected, if he even made it that long.

"Hell yeah partner. Koziner is off my ass after clearing the John Does."

"He let you clear the spook?"

Moonie grinned, and hooked his thumbs in his belt. "I explained the situation to him." He made "situation" three separate words. "And ole' Koziner let me name him as Governmental Agent: Identity Confidential."

I held out my hand. "Good for you. I wish you the best."

"Aw hell, Clipper," Moonie said, and swept past my hand and wrapped me up in a giant bear hug. For a beanpole, he was surprisingly strong. "You take care of yourself. I'm gonna miss the hell outta you." He released me, pulled his aviator shades down and winked. "And you take care of Nikki too."

Something clawed at my guts. Sadness. As annoying as he was, we had become friends. I threw him a little salute. "I'll send you a Christmas card." A sudden impulse seized me and I raised my arm and whistled. Matey took flight. A couple of powerful flaps and he landed on my arm with the grace of a turkey. "Come on asshole, let's go."

"You're taking the bird? You only ever bad-talked him."

Matey squeezed my shoulder gently with his talons, or claws, or whatever the hell birds have. "Maggie would want it this way. Besides, he's like you, an acquired taste."

Acknowledgements

Like my character Moonie, I have a fondness for colloquialisms. And when writing a book it certainly takes a village. Many thanks to Dr. Douglas Stemke, a gifted mirco and molecular biologist. When I first approached him with my plot idea, he pointed me in the right direction, and continued to be an excellent resource. *The Soviet Biological Weapons Program: A History* by Milton Leitenberg and Raymond Zilinskas was an invaluable source and cast a light on a hidden, and very scary arms race.

Peter Muller and Paul Popiel helped shape the narrative in early drafts, as did my fellow scribblers in the Wilmington-Chadds Ford Writers Group during numerous critique sessions. Rick Harra, once again, lent his eagle eye to the final draft and vacuumed up all the remaining errors.

The following people lent me their professional expertise: Edward Babcock, a funeral director with mass fatality response experience; Coroner Lloyd Ward, of Barnwell County, South Carolina continues to answer questions about the coroner system; Captain Scott Harra helped with all things military and weapons; and Master Chief Petty Officer Jeff Clark (Retired) helped with all things naval, as did the many friends whom I called on with random questions.

Finally, thank you to Caren Johnson and her team, Brittany Brown and Ro Molina, of Johnson Books and Media, who carried this project across the finish line.

As a final note to the reader: please realize I tried to make this little adventure as authentic as possible, and any errors you find in the text aren't the fault of the experts. They're mine alone, and sometimes made purposely on the altar of plotting.

If you enjoyed *Patient Zero* take a moment out of your day to review it. Honest reviews not only drive book sales, but help readers find new authors.

You can visit www.toddharra.com for information on my other books or follow me on Facebook @toddharraauthor.